# WOLVES AT THE DOOR
## SHAPES OF AUTUMN, BOOK TWO

# VERONICA BLADE

PUBLISHING

Gardnerville, Nevada

Wolves at the Door

Crush Publishing, Inc
Gardnerville, NV 89460
www.CrushPublishing.com

Crush Publishing, Inc name and logo are trademarks of Crush Publishing, Inc and are used only with its permission.

The places, characters and events portrayed in this book are fictitious. Any similarity to real persons, living or dead, is coincidental and not intended by author.

ISBN 978-0-9853434-9-1

Cover design and layout by Rose Nomura

Printed in the United States of America

# FOR MEGAN & SHELBY

Don't ever leave me. Just don't.

# CHAPTER ONE

TREES WHIZZED BY me. I listened for Zack follow-ing behind, but couldn't hear him over the thump-thump of my paws striking the soft dirt. In my chee-tah form, I smoked his wolf ass.

*Okay, show off,* Zack said telepathically. *You win.*

I eased to a mellow lope and chuckled, which sounded like a cat hissing and coughing.

*Hair ball?* Zack asked from wherever he was. He might be slower as a wolf, but there was nothing wrong with his superhuman hearing.

The crisp air of the forest tickled my nose as I passed a giant birch tree. When I picked up a different scent, my knees locked into place. My eyes snapped into alert mode as I visually searched the dark woods, inhaling again. A new scent. Another freakin' were-wolf in town? Just great.

*Zack, stay where you are. Someone's here.*

*Who?*

*Not sure, but it's definitely wolf,* I answered. *We should get the hell out of here.*

*If you've sniffed him out, then he's definitely al-*

*ready on to you. Run, Autumn!*

My heart galloped. Run which way? How could I avoid the wolf if I didn't even know where he was? A twig snapped, crackling into the night air, and my gaze shot toward where we'd parked my car. Charcoal eyes glinted from just behind a low hanging branch.

The wolf growled and his lip curled up to expose long, white fangs. He stepped forward away from the tree and I got a good look at his dark brown, furry body. This guy was huge, every bit as big as Zack in his wolf form — double the size of an ordinary wolf.

Oh, crap. My chest tightened. Could he tell I was a shape-shifter? Of course he'd know. The wolf couldn't listen in on my silent conversation with Zack unless he was physically touching one of us, but he'd know that cheetahs weren't found in the forests of Southern California.

My heart slammed against my ribs as I inched backward and hissed. To warn Zack, I followed up with a feline growl that rivaled nails on a chalkboard. Then I spun, my claws ripping into the ground to give me purchase for flight.

If this wolf was ancient, he'd be stronger and obscenely fast. But maybe, just maybe, he couldn't catch the fastest animal on land. Except... knowing my overprotective boyfriend, he wouldn't let me deal with this werewolf alone.

*Zack, stay away from us. He can't know you're with me.*

*You're crazy if you think I'm going to stand by and —*

*I got this!*

*I'm not leaving you,* he growled into my head.

*Please, Zack. You're going to get yourself killed.* As I neared the narrow, winding road and heard a car in the distance, I realized I couldn't sense the werewolf behind me.

*Me get killed? What about you?* he asked.

I made a sharp turn, dirt spraying around me. *I think I lost him. He's not nearly as fast as me, but you don't have that advantage. If he comes after you —*

*I don't sense him anywhere,* Zack said. *No way he isn't following you though. I'm not going anywhere without you.*

*He's nowhere near me. Zack, just go!* Damn, why was he being so stubborn? *I'm way ahead of him. By the time he gets to this spot, I'll already have gone in so many circles, he'll never figure out which way I went. I'll be fine. I promise. Go to my house and I'll be there soon.*

† † †

I'd run through my neighborhood enough times to know who lived where, who had dogs and how big the yards were. I almost didn't even need the keen night vision that came along with being a shape-shifter, but the superhuman strength and speed sure were helpful when jumping the neighbors' fences.

At the edge of the forest, I morphed back into my human form, checked behind me one last time, then made my way toward my house. Three blocks from home, I spotted my silver convertible Mustang parked alongside the curb, which meant Zack had listened and made it safely to my house.

Hiding behind a bush, I slumped in relief and scanned the streets for signs of life. My next door neighbor, Ms. Morales, sat on her front porch. A few houses beyond her, a couple strolled along holding hands as they walked a small, white dog. The street certainly appeared safe enough.

*Are you sure you weren't followed?* I asked.

*Positive*, Zack answered. *He was too busy chasing you. You sure you're in the clear?*

*Definitely.* But just in case I wasn't, I wanted to avoid the front door where anyone could see me go in and know where I lived. *Unlock the back for me, would you?*

*I'm on it.*

I slipped through a neighbor's gate and jumped her fence to the next yard over, my body flying through the air as if pushed from a giant spring. Several backyards later, I reached my rear door. It opened and Zack folded me into his arms, squeezing me tight. He buried his face in my thick, dark hair and breathed me in.

"I'm glad you're okay. If anything had happened to you —"

"Likewise." I squeezed my eyes shut and inhaled the musky wolf scent I'd grown to love. Had it been only three weeks since I'd met him? Being with Zack was so easy now, it was as if I'd known him all my life.

He gradually loosened his hold on me. "How far did you run?"

"Couple miles. I zigzagged through the forest,

changed into a dog and cat here and there, even a squirrel, and then doubled back. Left lots of scents all over the place, but it stops a few blocks from here where I morphed to human again. He couldn't possibly track me." I cupped Zack's face and met his eyes. "How did it go with you?"

"I made all kinds of fake trails before morphing back." He brushed a finger along my cheek. "I only just got here."

"We'll have to allow extra time for our runs if this is how it's going to go." I relaxed again, resting my head on his shoulder.

Zack reached into his pocket and checked the time on his cell. "Speaking of time, Trevor and Maya will be here any second."

"We should cancel in case the werewolf finds us. We don't want to put them in danger. We'll see them at school tomorrow."

"That's assuming he's looking for us. If he is, being in your house doesn't make us any safer." Zack stroked my hair. "In your human form, no one can tell you're a shifter, so he'll never connect you with the cheetah he saw in the woods."

"What about you?" We had no business going out again.

"They won't connect me either," Zack said. "He was ahead of us where I hadn't left my scent. He couldn't know I was there. We're not going to get nailed for mixing species."

"Not tonight anyway." More accurately, mixing species would be having sex — which we weren't doing. We limited our contact to kissing. At night, we hung out at my house and slept for real. My parents were still out of town and since I'd recently turned eighteen, apparently they felt comfortable leaving me on my own. It gave Zack and me lots of time alone together, but I was still baffled by their one-eighty and lack of hovering. "Our luck's going to run out eventually."

"We knew that going in." He leaned away to study me. "Don't you want to go out?"

"What I want is to hang out with you and my friends, be normal." I groaned. Zack had officially been my boyfriend for less than three hours and our relationship was already proving impossible.

His brows rose. "Just a few hours ago, you lectured me on living life. I believe your exact words were 'You have to do what's right, even if you're afraid of the consequences. Otherwise, life isn't worth living.'"

I sighed, knowing he was right. "It's just unfair. Normal seniors get to date on Friday night without worrying about being captured... or worse."

Zack pressed a finger under my chin, forcing me to meet his gaze, and lowered his voice. "Let's enjoy the time we have together. Before I have to leave."

My heart ached at the thought. "All the more reason to stay home."

"Yeah, but being alone together opens the door to other things we can't risk doing."

Right. Sex. Legend had it that mixing species in that way would physically weaken us both — something Zack couldn't afford since he'd be running for his life soon. I didn't quite buy the theory though. I figured the werewolf king had made it all up to keep the weaker species — shape-shifters — at a disadvantage. By keeping us weak, he retained his power.

But just in case it wasn't a myth, we needed to be careful or we wouldn't be able to outrun things like dark brown, gray-eyed wolves.

Shape-shifters couldn't socialize with werewolves at all, except as slaves. Violating that particular law brought the death penalty. I didn't care though. Without Zack, I would probably waste away.

A horn honked outside, interrupting my thoughts, and an instant later, my cell chimed in my pocket. Maya and Trevor were waiting outside. Let's just hope the gray-eyed wolf wasn't.

† † †

My best friend Maya swiveled in the front passenger seat to face me in the back of Zack's Jeep. She flipped her long, blond tresses over her shoulder and grinned. "I'm reading this awesome new vampire book. I'll give it to you when I'm done."

"Sure." I flashed her a smile, though it was half-hearted. Now that I knew otherworldly creatures really existed, reading supposedly fictitious — and grossly inaccurate — stories about them had lost its appeal. Besides, I'd rather spend any extra time with Zack's lips on me. I snuggled closer against him and felt his arm tighten around my waist.

Trevor's gaze left the road for a moment to grimace at Maya. "Vampires?"

Her lip twitched. "Don't make me choose between you and them. I'm not sure you'd win."

"I could take a blood-sucker. Bring it on." His right hand left the steering wheel and laced through hers. "Read about vamps all you want, babe. I'll stick to aliens."

"Deal." Maya leaned over and her lips bussed his cheek, then she refocused on me. "You'll love this book, Autumn. My eyes were drooping last night at three in the morning and I still couldn't put it down. It's *that* good."

"I'm in the middle of a book right now about werewolves and shape-shifters." True statement. It was one of the books Zack's father had left for him before he died—the real deal, not fiction.

"Werewolves are hairy." Maya wrinkled her nose.

"Not when they're in human form." Thinking of Zack's thick, dark coat made me warm all over, but I knew Maya wouldn't appreciate that.

"Yeah, but they morph during the full moon or whatever and then it's hair-city. I'll bet they have fleas." Maya faced forward again. "I'll stick to vamps."

Barely suppressing a laugh, I glanced up at Zack.

Zack turned toward the window, rolling his eyes. *I don't get the attraction to vampires*, he said telepathically. *I can do everything they can do and more.*

*But they're such forbidden and tortured souls.* I suppressed a giggle. *Very hot.*

*Because being miserable is so sexy.* He snorted. *Be-*

*sides, their diet is so... limited.*

I held back a chuckle as Trevor rolled the Jeep to a stop in the parking lot of Bill's Bean and Brew. I cast a glance over my shoulder to the small, covered cement patio. It was nearly empty, like any normal Monday night. Good. The less people around, the less chance Zack and I had of being discovered.

Trevor vacated the driver's side and flipped his seat forward. Zack lithely climbed out, before turning and motioning for me to follow. As I ducked to clear the doorway, his hands circled my waist. I grabbed onto his shoulders for support and, an instant later, touched ground. His gaze met mine, as his mouth curved up at the corners.

I looked into his green eyes and the cars and everything else around me disappeared. As if they had a mind of their own, my arms slid up and wrapped around his neck, my fingers winding through his dark, silky hair.

He pressed against me and my back collided with the cold metal of the Jeep. When his mouth found mine, fire exploded in my veins.

"Hey, you guys can do that later," Trevor called out, pulling me out of my trance. "C'mon!"

Zack released me and glared at his cousin as if he'd disturbed us. Which he had.

The back of my neck tingled and my eyes darted around the parking lot. Empty. Had to be paranoia — not like that werewolf would spot me as a shape-shifter. Even when Zack had been within sniffing distance of me weeks ago, it had taken him a while to be certain. If his theory was right, when I reached my full shape-shifter potential, my scent would become heavier and my supernatural energy denser. And when that time came, I'd have to run from the werewolves or become their slave.

Zack would be running soon, too. Normally, the werewolf scouts claimed their recruits right after graduation and took them to the werewolf king, but his supervisor, Charles, had promised to let Zack stay a little longer to spend time with his mom since she was so ill. I had no idea how long Charles considered "a little while." For all I knew, he'd meant a few days and we had only the six weeks until graduation.

For now, I hoped to enjoy time with Zack and my friends — while I still could.

"We should go in." Zack sighed as he skimmed a thumb along my cheek, jerking his head toward Trevor and Maya who'd already disappeared inside.

I let Zack lead me through the parking lot. We passed through the patio of Bill's Bean and Brew's and the sprinkling of wrought iron tables and matching chairs. The scent of coffee hit me.

He opened the door for me and, as we crossed the threshold, I glanced over my shoulder. My gaze locked onto a man sitting alone in the far corner, sipping from a steaming mug and looking down as he scribbled on a napkin. My supernatural radar blipped and a tingle shimmied up my spine. Damn werewolves. At least this one wasn't snarling at me like the one earlier this evening.

To avoid drawing his attention, I hurried inside

after Zack. He took a place at the end of the line and spun to face me. His eyes darted toward the werewolf then back to me, lips pressed together as if to hint for me to keep my own zipped.

When we made it to the counter, Zack let go of my hand to dig out his wallet. "What would you like?" he asked.

I studied the menu behind the counter. "Um, hot mocha, I guess." Unease swirled in my stomach at the thought of sticking around and exposing myself to the strange new werewolf. I didn't think I'd be discovered, but why press my luck?

Thankfully, a wall separated us from the werewolf and he wouldn't be able to pick up on the energy created by silent communication. At least I could still talk to Zack that way. *I hope we're getting our coffee to go.*

Zack squeezed my hand and offered Trevor a bill. "Would you order that for Autumn and an Americana for me?"

My shoulders bunched up as Zack steered me to one of the inside tables and he sat on a stool. I stood beside him, unable to relax with a potentially dangerous werewolf just a few feet away outside. *Why are we still here?*

Zack nodded toward a stool. *We're gonna run into others now and then. We either deal with it or stay home. You decide.*

Double dating with friends was a luxury for us. One that would make a nice memory once Zack left in six weeks. Did I want to give that up for paranoia? I sighed.

*You're right. Not like he's going to attack us in public.*

I scooted onto the stool next to Zack. Through my curtain of dark brown hair, I snuck a peek past the wide window at the pale werewolf. He was tall for a guy, and looked like he could be in his early thirties. He wore faded jeans and a dock-striped blue and gray short-sleeved shirt. His clothes may have been considered casual-wear, but they screamed money. And his hair was just a bit shaggy, yet he looked like he'd just stepped out of a magazine.

He seemed familiar, yet I'd never seen him before.

I couldn't totally tell in the dim patio lighting, but something was up with his skin. The texture seemed off, like tiny little bumps puckering the surface. Scars maybe?

As he took a sip from his cup, he glanced my way and I recognized those gray eyes.

We should've left like I'd wanted to. On the upside, at least he was the same werewolf I'd just seen in the woods and not yet another new one. But that gave me little comfort since his mere presence made my muscles go rigid.

*You need to chill*, Zack told me silently. *Or you'll give yourself away.*

I tried to ease the tension in my shoulders to no avail. Instead, I eyed the man again on the sly without turning my head. *He was the one in the woods tonight.*

*Are you sure?* Zack frowned as Trevor and Maya approached.

*Same eyes. Positive.*

Zack shoved a stool toward Trevor.

"No way, dude. Maya wants to sit outside." Trevor headed toward the door right behind Maya.

Having no choice, we pushed off the stools and followed them out to the patio. Trevor landed at the farthest vacant table from the lone man. It was a small patio, though, which still put him only several yards away. Too close.

Dry leaves skittered across the cement past a couple huddled together near the door.

"Your mom seemed like she was feeling pretty good tonight, Zack," Maya said as she took the chair next to Trevor, oblivious to the tension filling the air.

Zack claimed a chair on Trevor's other side and motioned for me to sit. But I had no intention of getting comfortable near any werewolf except Zack — whose firm grasp on my hand prevented me from bolting. He tugged, forcing me to sit.

"Not so sure about that. She's probably just being extra perky so no one will fuss over her." Zack seemed thoughtful for a moment. "She's really pale and she's wheezing. Even the slightest movement winds her."

"You think maybe she overdid it earlier when she got up to referee our argument?" I hoped not. Without her help, I probably wouldn't have gotten Zack to finally admit he wanted me.

"No, she's been a little off for a few days now." Zack shook his head, his face strained with emotion. "I'm afraid it'll turn into pneumonia like it did last year. Her immune system can't handle that right now. I should take her to the doctor, but she keeps fighting me on it. Maybe I'll insist tomorrow."

"Don't you have to work after school?" Trevor asked. "You can't be two places at once."

"I'll take her," I offered. "Otherwise, I'll just stay home and worry." Maybe she'd let me pick her brain for child-hood stories about Zack, especially embarrassing ones.

"Thanks." He frowned, staring into his paper coffee cup. "But I'd rather do it. If she needs to go and Timo-thy needs me at the shop, I'll take her after my shift."

Trevor nodded, and Maya gave Zack a sympathetic smile.

The energy around us changed, like the air was denser, even slightly prickly. Zack met the man's gaze and I wondered if they were having a silent conversa-tion. If so, I wanted in on it. Resting my hand on Zack's thigh to make a physical connection, I listened in.

*Charles is your supervisor?* the man asked. *I don't know him. And what's your name?*

*Zack De Luca.*

Whatever emotion flickered in the man's eyes came and went so fast, I figured it had to be my imag-ination. I really hoped he wouldn't do what William had done and try to claim Zack as his own recruit.

Werewolf scouts only seemed to care about bring-ing new werewolves to the king and collecting their reward. Charles may be scum, but at least he'd said Zack could finish school, maybe even stay for his mom's last days or weeks.

*And you?* Zack asked.

*Renzo. See you around.* He stood and turned his

back to us, tossed his cup in the trash, and strolled in the opposite direction toward a midnight-blue Jaguar.

I released my breath in a whoosh, wishing I could feel more relieved that he'd left. But I couldn't. I suspected I'd be seeing him again soon.

Zack turned his attention to Maya. "Are you coming back to our house later?"

She smiled at Trevor. "Maybe."

We chatted about graduation as we finished our drinks and, after a while, Maya pushed her cup away. "I still need to study for that English test tomorrow."

On the way home, Zack and I sat in the back seat peering out the rear window religiously to make sure we weren't being followed. But I didn't see any midnight-blue Jaguars — or any other car — tailing us.

Several minutes later, Zack and I stood on the sidewalk in front of my house, waving good-bye to Maya and Trevor. Before going inside, we glanced around for any signs of werewolves.

*Nothing,* I said.

*We wouldn't sense him if he was a block away, though.* Zack shook his head. *He could be watching us from right around the corner, just waiting for you to open the door. He'd be here before we got inside.*

*If he's stalking us and he's a block away right now, he already knows where I live.* My stomach pinched as I fished inside my purse for my house key. I just wanted to get inside where we weren't so exposed and vulnerable.

*Yeah.* Zack ran a hand through his dark, thick hair.

*If not, he'd find out soon enough anyway.*

*Just great.* "You're coming in, right?" I asked. Maybe, finally, I'd get some time alone with him. Yes, my life could be in danger, but that didn't mean I no longer wanted Zack. Danger gave me all the more reason to take advantage of every moment with him.

"Sure." He looked preoccupied, his forehead creased.

I unlocked the door, entered and closed it behind us. Instead of following me to the kitchen table where I dumped my purse and sweater, Zack hung near the front door. His face still held a pensive expression.

My heart sank as I instantly gave up on any chance of us continuing where we'd left off on the couch earlier. "What's up?"

"I can't spend the night here anymore," he said, taking a step back. "It was safe before because we weren't together. Less chance of anything happening. But now..."

Before he could get away, I snaked my arms up around his neck. "Stay," I whispered.

"I want to." With the softest touch, he disentangled himself from me and stepped out of my embrace. "But how much willpower do you think I have?"

I dropped my arms in impatience. He'd asked me to be his girlfriend only a few hours ago and he was already pulling away. Memories of every time he'd turned me down these past few weeks clouded my vision, and rejection weighed heavy in my gut. "We can't even kiss anymore?"

"Not here. All alone, it's too easy to push boundaries and we can't risk it." Zack stepped closer and rested his hands on my hips, but held me at arm's length. "I'll be here in the morning and we can drive to school together."

I'd gotten used to him being with me every night and I hated the idea of being without him through the long stretch until morning. But was that really Zack's problem? Or was he having second thoughts about me? My stomach knotted.

He brushed his lips against mine. "I'll see you in the morning."

"Okay." I followed him out the front door and gave him a half wave from the top of the steps. What choice did I have, but to let him go? I certainly wasn't going to beg. Yet.

Watching Zack get smaller as he got farther away triggered a dull ache in my chest. I held my breath until I couldn't see him anymore, then went inside and hit the stairs to my room. The sooner I got ready for bed and fell asleep, the sooner I could wake up and see him again.

Once showered, I threw on some flannel shorts and a tank and crawled under my covers, but was still too wired to relax. Stupid mocha. Should've asked for decaf. Sleeping without Zack nearby wasn't helping either.

I fantasized about ripping his clothes off and getting myself some werewolf love. But what if it wasn't a myth and we became so weak that we couldn't defend ourselves when Renzo or Charles came for Zack? As if our youth didn't already put us at a physical disadvantage against the older and stronger werewolves.

After tossing and turning for what seemed an

eternity, I flung my covers off and switched on the bedside lamp.

Okay, so Zack and I couldn't spend the night alone. I couldn't sleep without him either. What were my options? Staring at the ceiling, I recalled our last conversation when he'd said it might be easier with people around. Zack lived with his mom and Trevor's family, so we wouldn't be alone. That was his objection, right?

I jumped out of bed, dashed down the stairs and snatched my keys on my way out of the back door. I leaped high over our fence, landing in the neighbor's backyard. It only took seconds before I'd traveled the few houses and arrived at Zack's bedroom window. It was open, of course. He tended to be warm at night.

After poking my head through the curtains, I saw him lying in bed. He faced away so I couldn't tell if he was sleeping. If he made any startled noises and woke everyone up, I'd have to bail.

What if his mom or aunt spotted me before I had a chance to get away? I flushed at the idea of getting busted creeping into his room. Especially by his uncle Mac. No freakin' way.

As quietly as I could, I squeezed past the window sill.

Zack was out of bed by the time I stepped onto the floor, his eyes darkening. Oops. Maybe this had been a bad idea.

# CHAPTER TWO

ZACK MOVED IN a blur and the next instant, his arms closed around me and his face was buried in my hair. "I couldn't sleep without you."

The tension eased out of me. "Same here."

Zack kissed my forehead, then hugged me tighter. "What are we gonna do now?"

"Nothing except go to *sleep*." I gently pushed him away, tiptoed to his bed and slid under the covers.

"Uh... we've never actually slept next to each other before." He hesitated at the foot of the bed.

I noticed then that he wore only boxers — at least I had on a tank, even if it was a little skimpy. The pale moonlight filtered through the curtain and shone on his smooth chest and rippled abs.

I gulped and resolved again not to let things get out of hand, especially not with his mom sleeping on the other side of the thin wall. But, oh, how good he looked. I wanted to run my fingers up his spine and watch him shiver. I wanted to feel his weight on me and —

No, *nothing* would happen tonight. Well, maybe some cuddling.

Slowly, he shuffled to the other side of the bed where he'd been lying before. But he didn't make a move to climb in beside me.

"It's either this or I have to go home and we both sleep crappy. How well will we be able to defend ourselves if we're exhausted?" At that, I turned away and waited for him to join me. "Come on. Spoon me."

He chuckled softly and slipped under the covers.

"We'll be good tonight. We have to be," I said.

"Easy for you to say."

Not really.

I squeezed my eyes shut and tried to ignore the feel of his warm skin and length of his thighs against the back of mine. The tip of his thumb pressed into my waist as his big, warm hand covered my hip and scooted me closer. Butterflies danced in my stomach and warm tingles spread over my chest.

I could resist temptation. I had to. Otherwise we'd have to sleep apart. I rearranged his arm so it lay at my ribs. Unfortunately, that was distracting in an entirely different way.

Zack brushed my hair off my shoulders and kissed the back of my neck. "I don't think I'll be able to sleep this way either," he whispered, sending goose bumps dancing along my skin. "But I'll be much happier while I'm wide-awake."

"Keep that up and I won't be responsible for my actions."

He groaned, snuggled up to my back, and stayed very still. After a while, his breathing settled to a steady rhythm. I knew rest wouldn't come as easy for me, but so long as I had Zack, I'd put up with a little sleep deprivation.

† † †

"Autumn, wake up." Zack shook me gently. "You need to slip out before it's light outside."

"Ten more minutes." My lids grated over my dry, tired eyes. The room was beginning to brighten.

"Shhhh! They'll hear you."

I was lying on my side facing him, our lips just inches away. His breath smelled sweet. Had he brushed already?

"Who are they?" I asked, speaking a little louder than was wise.

He kissed me, probably to shut me up. I cringed, afraid I'd offend him since I hadn't freshened up yet.

"Don't worry." Zack chuckled quietly. "Our bodies heal quickly, remember? We don't have the bacteria and all that stuff. You only need to brush if you eat spinach."

Seriously? Best news ever! I grabbed a handful of his hair and pulled him to me, my lips locking onto his. He slid over me as I turned onto my back. Zack's stomach pressed into me as our bare legs tangled under the sheets. Mmm. It was way too nice and I didn't want it to end.

But it had to. This time, I was the one to stop, pushing my palms against his chest as I got in one last lick on his bottom lip.

He rolled off me and ran his fingers through his hair. "You're even hotter when you're sleepy."

"Yeah, same to you." It was getting light outside and too risky to leave his room in my human form. Reluctantly, I rose from the bed, morphed into a squirrel and slipped through the open window.

† † †

Zack appeared at my door later that morning just before I had to leave for school, grinning and holding out a sprig of flowers. He wore a faded green shirt that read *Vampires are all talk. Werewolves are all action.* Lord, he was beautiful. And totally sweet. Warmth spread over my chest as I inhaled. Jasmine.

"Thank you." Opening the door, I gave him a quick kiss on the cheek and snagged the fragrant blooms.

As Zack passed me, his gaze drifted lower to my short skirt and bare legs. His mouth curved up. The look in his eyes made me want to drag him upstairs and skip school.

Shaking it off, I went in search of a vase and arranged the flowers.

We drove to school and my eyes instinctively scanned the perimeter as I exited the Mustang. Beyond the gate, cars lined the curb. Farther down the block, I could just see the front of a dark sports car. Midnight-blue.

Chills raced through me.

When I glanced back at Zack, his stony expression told me he'd seen it too.

*Probably not Renzo's car. Even if it is, he'd have to get through Charles.* Zack held my hand and walked me toward my homeroom class.

When we passed Gina — the skank who'd hooked up with my now ex — she glared at me. Her lips moved and even though she was yards away, I heard what she said. "Liar!"

The burning hatred in her eyes intensified as I neared her. Sure, I'd told her yesterday that Zack and I weren't together, but it was the truth at the time. Whatever. She wasn't worth stressing over.

At lunch, we sat with Maya and Trevor and every time I glanced at Gina, she was ignoring her table-mates and sending me a death glare. I sighed, mentally acknowledging the inevitable confrontation. I met her gaze, then jerked my head toward the exit and rose.

"Where are you going?" Zack asked.

"To deal with Gina." I quickly explained why.

He grinned. "Aw, you don't have to get into a cat-fight over me, babe."

I lightly slapped the top of his head, just enough to ruffle his hair, then left. Gina followed right behind me as I led the way to the bathroom where we'd have privacy.

Once inside, she scowled, fists planted on her hips.

I checked under the stalls to make sure we were alone, then raised my hand, hoping to prevent a ti-rade. "I didn't lie. It really was over between Zack and me yesterday, but we made up."

Gina sneered. "I'm supposed to buy that?"

I sighed. "It's the truth."

She dug out her eyeliner and began touching up her eyes in the mirror. "It's comforting to know that you, the Virgin Princess, haven't done the things with Zack that I have."

A knot formed in my stomach. "As if I'd believe anything you said. Besides, you guys barely knew each other."

"Not at first," she chirped, her words heavy with implication. While I digested that, she dropped her eyeliner into her purse and her mouth curled up. "What can I say? Daniel couldn't say no to me either."

Zack wasn't anything like Daniel and he'd easily resist Gina now. I was sure of it. But we weren't together two weeks ago. . . In fact, we hadn't even liked each other. Had he fooled around with her?

My stomach lurched, but I feigned boredom and folded my arms over my chest to mask the doubt creeping up on me. "It's not working, Gina."

Moving to stand directly in front of me, she got right up in my face. "Ask him."

Was this the rare moment Gina actually told the truth? If she was lying, she wouldn't be pushing me to talk to Zack about it, would she?

And just like that, my world turned a shade of gray.

I refused to let her see how much her words affected me. I pushed past her, trying to act more composed than I felt. "This is a waste of my time."

Storming through the corridor on my way back to the cafeteria, I couldn't get Gina's words out of my head. Should I ask Zack about it? Wait, if he had slept with Gina, did I really want to know? Did I really want images of them making out — and who knew what else — knocking around in my head?

Too late. They were already there.

I returned to our table and Zack reached for my hand, but it did little to ease my tension.

"What did she want?" Maya asked.

No way was I going to validate Gina's words by saying it out loud. "The usual. To irritate me."

"She's just jealous." Maya brushed it off with a wave.

She sounded so sure, and I wished I felt that confident. Still, for the duration of lunch and through the rest of the school day, I obsessed on how many things Gina might have done with Zack that I'd *never* be able to do with him.

I had to put it out of my mind or it would drive me crazy.

After my last class, I waited for Zack by the curb. Gina strolled toward me, then stopped, blocking my view of the wide double doors I'd been watching.

She smirked. "Did you ask him?"

"Zack's with me now and that's all I care about." I rolled my eyes.

Gina tapped her chin thoughtfully. "It's probably for the best that you don't bring it up. If he doesn't admit it, you'll always wonder if he told you the truth. Either way, you'll never be sure."

I stuck my hands in my back pocket to curb my temptation to slap her. "One thing I *am* sure about is that I'll never take your word over Zack's."

Her smile didn't waver, but her eye twitched. "Are you still saving yourself? Careful. Someone might come along and do your job for you. A man's got needs."

"Giving it up for some guy who doesn't care about you doesn't make you better than me." I started to turn toward my car, then paused. "It makes you a slut."

As I headed toward my car, I looked over my shoulder and saw Zack coming. Good. He'd keep me from pounding on Gina. A moment later, he fell into step with me.

"What was that about?" He glanced at her retreating back.

"She's just trying to get under my skin." Knowing Gina, though, annoying me wouldn't be enough. I didn't trust her. Not one bit.

# CHAPTER THREE

ONCE INSIDE MY house, I made sure all the doors and windows were locked. I'd grown paranoid after being stalked the last couple weeks by my psycho ex-boyfriend-turned-werewolf. Daniel might have been forced out of town, but that didn't mean he wouldn't come back. And then there were Charles and Renzo.

The threats were adding up, and I wasn't taking any chances.

While Zack finished his shift at the auto shop, I did all my homework, then finished his. It was strange how much easier school was since I'd begun maturing into a shape-shifter. I wondered if being healthier had somehow increased my intelligence.

I booted up my laptop and was just about to reply to an e-mail from my mom when I heard the front door creak open and footsteps patter into the living room. The skin on the back of my neck prickled. Who the hell was in my house?

I jumped up and moved stealthily to the top of the stairs before peeking down. Zack came into view and I raced down the stairs and leapt on him. He laughed, one hand at my lower back and the other on my leg, which was wrapped around his hip.

"Missed me, did you?" He grinned.

"Always." I planted my lips on his and gave him a long, searing kiss.

"You okay?" he asked, coming up for air.

"Sure. The door was locked and I thought some-one broke in. Forgot you had my keys."

He studied my face, his brows pulling down. "If it makes you feel any better, I saw Charles nearby. Ren-zo or anyone else will have to get through him first."

Knowing Charles was watching us didn't ease my mind one little bit. I rolled my eyes. "Awesome."

He chuckled, one hand sliding up my thigh. "We'd better go before we get too, uh, comfortable."

Didn't he miss me too? Why hadn't he said it back? Suddenly, I pictured him with Gina and took a deep breath. Damn Gina.

I forced a smile. "After dinner, we'll have the rest of the night to chill since I did all our homework."

"You're amazing." He kissed me again, but it was ob-vious he was holding back. "We should get to my house."

When I felt him begin to release his grip on me, I kept my legs wrapped around him, my fingers inter-locked behind his neck. "To pick up your mom?"

"No trip to the doctor today." He shook his head and sighed. "She insists she's fine."

"Maybe she is." I squeezed closer against his chest to discourage him from putting me down. "Zack?" Oh, crap I shouldn't ask. But I *had* to know. "Did you ever date Gina?"

"We hung out." He said it so casually, as if being with her in that way was no big deal. "You guys were best friends and she didn't tell you?"

I jumped off Zack and dodged him when he reached out for me. "Define 'hung out,'" I asked, incapable of hiding the disgust in my voice.

"Um..." He narrowed his eyes. "Autumn, you were still with Daniel. And you hated me then."

"So? That doesn't make it right. She's a skank."

He grunted. "Gina may have fooled around with your boyfriend, but Daniel tried to *kill* us. He's way worse and you dated him."

"He only got violent after he was turned into a werewolf." Although he had gotten kind of creepy and obsessive when I'd refused to sleep with him, then dumped him. "And anyway, at least he and I weren't hiding that we were together." I folded my arms over my chest and glared.

"Gina and I weren't hiding either and we weren't *together*. And you know what else? At the time, you liked her too. She was your best friend, so don't judge me." Zack caught me around my waist and dragged me against him. His mouth swooped down on mine, probably either trying to make me forget about Gina or to get me to stop talking. It wasn't going to work.

That said, Zack was a *really* great kisser.

Just as I melted into him, he withdrew. "That's why I was so pissed off at you for not telling me everything she'd done. If I'd known she was such a bitch, I wouldn't have hung out with her at all."

Yeah, but I still didn't know how far had they'd gone when they'd 'hung out' and I couldn't bring myself to ask.

† † †

After dinner at Zack's, I helped him with kitchen duty, then spent time with his mom while he talked to Trevor. I planted myself on the bed at her side. Her face was just as pale as the night before and her breathing just as labored.

"Isn't prom this weekend?" Favianne asked between breaths.

I smiled to try to lighten the mood. She looked in need of a distraction. "Yes. I didn't get to go to prom last year, because we moved a week before and I was too late for prom at my next school."

"They started you in a new school so close to the end of the year?" She frowned and sucked in another shallow breath. "I did it to Zack this year, but didn't think other parents were that cruel."

"You had to, because it wasn't practical to live on your own anymore. My dad, on the other hand, often relocates for work. He thinks it's easier to move us all together than leave us behind and commute. They were about to move me again, but I put up a fight."

"I'm not sure it's a good idea for you to live by yourself, but I'm glad you're still around." She patted my hand and yawned.

"I should let you rest." I moved to leave, then on impulse leaned over to drop a kiss on her forehead.

She smiled sleepily and raised a hand to rest against my cheek. "You're a nice girl. I'm so happy Zack found you."

She had to be the sweetest, most generous woman I'd ever met. I loved her more every day. "Me too. Good night."

I crept out and closed the door, running into Zack's muscular chest in the hallway.

"She looks better, doesn't she?" he asked, looking hopeful.

"I guess so." That wasn't the truth, but I didn't want him stressing. His brows furrowed as he entwined his fingers with mine. I rubbed his arm with my free hand. "So what's the plan for tonight?"

"We hang with my family until it's time for you to go, then I walk you home." A smile hinted on his lips. *Then we go for a run in the woods and later you'll sneak into my bedroom*, he finished silently.

"Excellent plan." I grinned. "It's cooling off outside. Let's go sit on the front porch."

Zack led the way. At the top of the steps, I brought my legs up and rested my chin on my knees. He sprawled out on the other end with his back against the railing, and faced me.

"I guess Gina got under your skin earlier, huh?" he asked.

I shrugged. "Maybe a little."

"You want me to talk to her?" Zack nudged my thigh with his sneaker. "Tell her to back off?"

And give Gina the opportunity to be alone with

him? "No, I can handle her. But thanks."

I heard footsteps and my head snapped around to look beyond the front yard. My whole body stiffened when I saw Zack's supervisor, but I took care not to let the tension show. In my peripheral vision, Zack straightened his spine and faced Charles.

"Good evening." He halted midstride and tipped his cowboy hat. "Nice night."

I forced a smile. "Yes, it is."

"How are you feeling? Any more fainting spells?"

As far as Charles knew, I was human. He had no clue that the chloroform Daniel had dosed me with the other day hadn't affected me or that I'd witnessed Daniel and Zack battling it out. Or that I'd seen Daniel's maker arrive, only to be run out of town by Charles. When the dust had settled, Charles had ordered Zack to convince me that I'd fainted so I wouldn't go to the police. Werewolves didn't like officials involved, because they didn't want to make their existence known to the mortals.

"Yeah, that was weird, huh? I've been one hundred percent fine since, but thanks for asking." I reminded myself that he *had* saved our lives the other day. I just wished he didn't have ulterior motives — like planning to take Zack to the werewolf king after graduation in only a month and a half or so.

Not that Zack intended to go with Charles. But whether Zack joined the king or escaped, I'd probably never see him again. Anyone who wanted to shorten my already limited time with him was most definitely my enemy.

"Glad to see all's well. Enjoy your evening." Charles

tipped his hat again and resumed his walk.

Out of the corner of my eye, I watched him cross the street and stroll to the end of the next block. He was far enough away now that he couldn't hear us, but I kept my voice low anyway.

"Having him around makes me nervous," I said.

"You may as well get used to it." His thumb made soothing strokes against the back of my hand. "Just because you don't see him doesn't mean he's not there. Charles is never far away. He's only obvious when he wants to remind me he's watching. But we're not in danger as long as I'm cooperating."

"I hope you're right." I'd have to tune in my supernatural radar to Charles.

"It's in his best interest to keep me alive. If he doesn't bring me to the king in good health, how can he justify the time he's spent here? Try not to let his appearances bother you."

"I'll try. But next time you're getting regular visits from a werewolf, you should clue me in instead of letting me find out days later." I raised one brow and eyed him. "Your habit of withholding information is getting a little annoying."

He held my hand tighter when I tried to jerk it away. "I didn't want you to worry."

"If I kept things from you, you wouldn't like it." Squeezing my eyes shut, I told myself to be patient. "I want full disclosure from now on."

"I promise." He raised a palm in surrender. "On another note, prom's on Saturday. Anything in particular you wanted to do before then?"

I scooted along the top step until we were hip to hip and he slung an arm around my waist. "Did you have something in mind?"

"Yeah." Zack cupped my face with his other hand and gazed into my eyes. "I thought we might go out. I want you all to myself. A *real* date. Plus, the last date didn't go well and I kind of want a do-over."

"Sure." My insides warmed and I beamed. "How about we go to my house now, just for a little while?"

Zack nodded. "Great idea. We need to arm wrestle and see how much stronger you've gotten."

Not exactly the kind of wrestling I had in mind, but I'd humor him.

Back at my house, he slapped his elbow on the dining room table and held out his hand. Sitting across from him, I gripped his palm.

"On three," he said. "One, two, three."

I gave it everything I had, but the back of my hand slowly drew closer to the table. I strained even harder, putting my weight into it. Except for the trembling that went all the way to my toes, our arms didn't move either direction, as if suspended in time.

As I struggled to overpower him, everything but Zack vanished from my vision. I strove against his force to raise my hand, but his arm wouldn't budge. After a long moment, my strength faded. I let go and my knuckles slammed into the table.

"Ow!" I stood, shaking out my hand. "That freakin' hurt."

He dumped his chair, stood and grabbed my hand to examine it. "Broke the skin. I'm sorry. Didn't mean to hurt you," he whispered, kissing my sore knuckles.

Butterflies in my stomach did twists and turns, sending tiny shivers through my limbs. "It's okay. The pain is already gone."

Zack leaned in to drop a kiss on the end of my nose. He closed his eyes, then inhaled and exhaled deeply, like he was trying to regain control. "We should go."

He was right; we couldn't get ourselves into trouble. Resigned to keeping my hands off him for the moment, I headed up the stairs. His voice stopped me halfway up.

"Hey, Autumn?"

"Yeah?"

"You're *really* strong."

I blinked. "You beat me, just like last time."

"No, this wasn't nearly as easy." He leaned an arm on top of the railing and looked up at me. "You'll be able to beat me soon."

I tilted my head. "I'll get stronger with time, but so will you."

He shook his head. "I've already finished with my initial power surge and won't change much. You have a few more weeks before you level out. Do the math."

"Maybe I've already leveled out."

"Our abilities increase along with our scent and your scent is still weak, which means all your powers have a ways to go."

"But you don't have any real life experience with

shape-shifters, other than me. Just the box of books your dad left for you. Maybe they're inaccurate." I shrugged, not knowing what else to say, then darted up to my room to get into my sweats.

† † †

Zack parked my Mustang in a deserted area under the cover of thick-trunked trees. We'd picked a different part of the forest to avoid Renzo and Charles, but switching playgrounds was no guarantee we'd be alone.

I rolled down my window to listen and breathed in the scent of pine and sage. There were no humans or werewolves close by that I could hear or smell.

"I think we're safe." Zack jerked his head toward the trees. "Before you morph, I'll patrol the area just to make sure."

"There's a more efficient way to find out." I couldn't wait to get out of the car and feel the night air rushing past me. But with Charles and the new werewolf in town, making sure we were alone had to come above all else.

I climbed out of the car, making a beeline for the cover of the woods. Once surrounded by brush and leaves, I scanned the area again, then stopped. I pictured myself as a hawk and felt the familiar vibration begin in my toes, then shimmy up my legs, stomach and arms. I glanced down. My hands had all but disappeared.

For the tiniest measurement of time, I was nothing and weightless. An instant later, I exploded into a physical presence again, long feathers lifting me off the ground and my wings cutting through the air until I soared above the treetops. Wind ruffled my feathers and tickled my skin.

Freedom.

From high above, I scanned the woods for movement. For Charles or Renzo in their human or wolf forms. Other than a couple deer, a coyote and a family of raccoons, there wasn't a soul in sight. *All clear. I'm going to change into a wolf while we're still alone.*

*Don't forget to go human first,* he reminded me, then he morphed.

*Yeah, like I need reminding.* Last time I'd tried to turn into something else without first going human, I got violently ill. I could become any animal I wanted, but my primary form was human so I needed my foundation between morphs. It grounded me.

As I drifted down toward the treetops, my eagle eyes spied a rat scurrying along a tree branch. The urge to swoop and snag my prey rose up and I stifled it. I could give in to the desires of whatever shape I held, but once I turned human, I knew my belly would regret eating a rat, especially a raw one.

I glided down toward the soft dirt near Zack. As soon as I touched ground, I mentally shed myself of my bird skin. The trembling began, and then the floating sensation. And, finally, nothing. For a split second, I was myself again before I shifted right into a wolf.

I took off after Zack, following his scent toward the heartbeat of the forest.

A rabbit scampered in my path. Instinct drove me to hunt it down and I almost veered off to follow. I made a mental note to have a snack before going out next time and morphing into a carnivore.

The forest echoed with paws pounding against the dirt floor. In the distance, leaves crunched and I wondered how far ahead Zack was. A moment later, I practically collided into him as he whooshed across my path. I skidded and turned to follow. As I trailed behind him, the scent of the rabbit invaded my nose.

*You're not going to eat that thing, are you?* I asked.

*I'm hungry*, he told me. In the near pitch-black night, all I could see was his bushy tail.

*Zack, really?* I asked. He slowed to a trot and I caught up, eyeing him. G*ross. Maybe you don't think so right now, but when you're human again, you might regret eating raw meat.* Not that I was one to talk since I'd almost snagged it for myself.

He spun to face me. *You're probably right.*

I moved alongside him, rubbing my fur against his.

Zack licked my ear and I nuzzled against him. Why did that feel so good? Made me wonder what else would feel different as a wolf...

If we were both in our wolf form, then technically we were the same species. At least for the moment. Would the mixing species thing still apply? I nudged him with my shoulder and he nipped the fur at my neck.

I turned into him, my tongue whipping out to lick his muzzle, then I rolled over onto my back. He stalked closer, his eyes dark as his throat rumbled. With a paw on my chest, he nuzzled my neck, his breath coming faster.

Zack froze, hovering over me. He waited a beat as if contemplating his next move, then he slowly backed away. *Fooling around like this is a terrible idea. When I almost ate that rabbit, didn't I just prove I couldn't be trusted in my wolf form?*

Yes, and obviously, so had I.

† † †

On the drive home, I didn't say much. I was too shocked at how close we'd come to having wild wolf sex. Zack was quiet too, which made me wonder if he was holding back again.

I swiveled in the passenger seat to face him. "Is there something you need to tell me?"

"Well..." He looked at me uncertainly.

Oh, geez, how bad was it? I inwardly groaned. "You promised no secrets."

His gaze left the road, long enough to eye me. "Time's running out. Only a few weeks until graduation. I need to start planning my escape. Charles would see it as a red flag if one day I suddenly left my house with luggage. He would see that. Renzo, too. I'd never get away."

My stomach pinched before I stared out the window, not wanting to have this conversation.

"I was thinking of bringing something over to your house every day, just one item I could hide in my pocket or under my shirt," Zack continued. "Eventually, I'd have a decent amount of stuff there. When it's time to go, I'll just pull my Jeep all the way into your driveway, so I'm right next to your bedroom window, then load up where they can't see and get to the freeway as fast as I can."

I wanted Zack to be safe, even if it meant him being

nowhere near me. But to *help* him leave? It was unbearable. "You can do that easier from your own house."

"Not really. My aunt and uncle park their cars in the driveway, so I'd have to carry my stuff to the curb. Charles could be watching two blocks away and I wouldn't sense him. He'd be all over me long before I made it to the car."

At least when we went to the woods, we could ensure we weren't being followed. At his house, we couldn't possibly know when Charles was around. "Maybe there's a cave in the woods or somewhere we could hide your stuff?"

"If my clothes give off a scent and they find my stash, then they'll know what I'm up to," Zack explained.

"Why not just hide things in your Jeep?" Anywhere but at my house. That would be a constant reminder. I gazed out the window, hoping the topic would die. At least for the next few weeks, I wanted to live in denial.

"I can put a few things in there," he said. "But if I fill up a duffle bag, Charles will ask questions. That's strictly for just a few emergency getaway items, in case I can't get to your house and have to leave with whatever I have on me."

A burning sensation started behind my eyes and a lump formed in my throat. The inevitable was coming, deep down I knew that, but talking about it....

Still, I needed him to be safe, even though I didn't want him to leave. "What if my parents really are shifters and not human? How will I explain the werewolf scent in my room when they pop in for one of their random visits?"

"Still think they're human. But in case I'm wrong, we'll

seal everything in bags and hide them really well," he said.

I was about to suggest sealing the bags for the woods, but we'd risk animals tearing into them and letting loose Zack's scent. "Good thinking."

I squeezed my eyes against the burning tears. Being involved in his plans made his leaving all too real.

# CHAPTER FOUR

ZACK, MAYA AND Trevor beat me to our usual spot at lunch the next day. After I slapped a sandwich onto my tray, along with an apple and a fizzy peach drink, I headed to our table.

When I glimpsed John waving me over, I detoured. As soon as I got close enough, he snatched the tray from my hands, grinning as he placed it in front of his own.

"Sit for a minute," John demanded.

I obliged, but glanced over my shoulder at Zack. *I just got hijacked. Be there soon.*

"What are you doing with your old car?" John asked.

"Selling it. Haven't got around to posting an ad. Why?" I bit into my apple.

"You could sell it to me." John grinned.

He was out of his mind to want my old, decrepit car. A full blown frown crimped my forehead as I chewed hurriedly and swallowed. "You should hold out for something better."

Zack's scent wafted into my nose and my tummy did a little flip as he rested his hands on my shoulders.

"No denying it's seen better days," Zack said from

behind me. "But I can attest it's been well maintained."

"How much are you selling it for?" John asked. Apparently, Zack's endorsement trumped my bashing.

Zack's thumbs gently dug into my shoulder muscles and my lids sagged in ecstasy. "My boss always says that any running car is worth a thousand minimum." The tips of his fingers traced my spine.

"Sold!" John slammed his palm onto the table.

"What?" I jolted, wondering if Zack had distracted me on purpose. I couldn't believe he'd just sold that piece of crap to a *friend*. "No, John, you don't want it. Trust me."

"If he doesn't want it, I'll take it," Ashley said.

Oh, just great. Having another potential buyer upped the car's market value. No chance of talking John out of it now. But I'd try. "I'll feel horrible if it breaks down on you. You guys should save up and get a real car."

"That *is* a real car." John's tone sounded a little desperate. "You know how hard it is to find something cheap that actually has an engine? Look, I'm working part time and taking the bus is sucking the life out of me. I need something now and yours is in my budget."

"See? You're doing John a favor by saving him from the horrors of public transit," Zack whispered at my temple.

"Fine." Obviously, I was outnumbered. "But don't say I didn't warn you."

As much as I hated burdening John with my old car, prom was fast approaching. I needed a few things for that night and now I had some extra money.

† † †

Instead of waiting for Zack by the curb after school, I dashed to my car to avoid Gina. She must have spotted me, though, because she made a beeline towards me. Damn.

"It's the Virgin Princess." She smirked. "Have that chat with Zack yet?"

"Actually, yes." I gave her a tight smile. "Sorry to break it to you, but we've never been better. Now you'll just have to go away and get a life of your own."

Her smile faltered, but she bounced back with a snicker. "It's not like he'll tell you how much fun we had together. Guys always lie about the girls who came before."

The possible truth of her words roared through my brain like a chain saw.

"I don't know what Zack told you," she went on with a sympathetic smile, "but if he said it was his idea to stop seeing me, he's not telling you everything. I'd already lost interest in Zack when Daniel dumped you and —"

"Daniel broke up with *me*?" I exhaled with a half snort. "Are you insane? Gee, that must've been your evil twin kissing Daniel in the bathroom just before I dumped his sorry ass."

Gina scoffed. "You're such a drama queen."

Zack draped an arm around my shoulder. I'd been so aggravated by Gina, I hadn't sensed him approaching.

"Hey, Gina, you're good friends with Natalie, right?" Zack asked her. "Jeff's her boyfriend, which

45

makes him perfect for you."

She glared at us and stomped off.

"She bugging you again, babe?" Zack asked, turning to face me.

"It's what she does best." It hadn't escaped me that Zack didn't deny anything Gina had said. Whatever. I didn't want to know.

As I was about to climb into the driver's seat, I spotted a dark blue sports car beyond the gate several cars down. I straightened. That was the second time I'd seen that car there. Had to be Renzo. Why would he be watching Zack at school?

"Blue sports car parked at eleven o'clock." I gave a slight jerk of my head toward the car. I hoped Charles would notice the new werewolf and still be protective of Zack. Maybe he'd even force Renzo out of town like he did my ex and the other werewolf.

"Yeah, I saw him when I was walking over."

I slid behind the wheel. "What took you so long, anyway?"

"Had to finish something up in my last class, then go to my locker." He checked the time on his cell phone. "It's only been five minutes. In a hurry?"

"No, but I don't enjoy my run-ins with Gina. I always feel so dirty after dealing with her." I reached for the driver's side handle. "Are you taking your mom to the doctor today?"

He shook his head. "I want to wait one more day."

"She shot you down, huh?"

Zack snorted. "Stubborn as hell. And bossy."

"Why don't I drop you off at work, then come get you later? I have some errands to run."

"What kinds of errands?" Zack's seatbelt clicked into place.

"Clothes shopping." I started the car. "I need more natural fibers." Zack may have been content with his synthetic fabrics not morphing with him, but I hated changing back totally nude and having to scrounge for my clothes. Incredibly inconvenient.

By the time I'd rolled the Mustang to the gate, the blue car had disappeared. I didn't see any sign of it on the way to the auto shop either. Maybe Renzo had taken off. If only he'd stay gone.

After I dropped Zack off at work, I stopped at the bank to withdraw some cash. The balance printed on the receipt had more digits than my checkbook register.

Everything had seemed normal when I'd talked to my parents. But why the large deposit? Maybe they planned to be gone a while longer and wanted to make sure I had plenty of emergency money.

It made me wonder if there was some other reason they hadn't come home. I missed them. But since it was my fault they'd left — I'd gotten tired of their hovering and blackmailed them into leaving — I had no right to complain. They could be cool, though. At this point, I'd gladly take them back, over-protectiveness and all.

† † †

After the mall, I stopped by the auto shop to get Zack, then took him home. I promised to meet up with him later and headed to my house to unload my loot. When I parked against the curb, I noticed an unfamiliar car in the driveway. Last time I'd come home to a strange car, it had been a rental when my parents had returned unexpectedly. What if it wasn't them this time?

I thought about calling my mom, but if the car out front didn't belong to her and she knew about the stranger at my house, then she and my dad would worry. I could find out who it was without involving them or putting myself in danger.

Staying in my car, I tapped the horn on my steering wheel and hoped my guests would show themselves. I waited a beat and the screen door opened. I abandoned my bags in the car and bolted across the lawn.

"Mom!" I leaped into her waiting arms, hugging her every bit as tightly as she hugged me. What felt like minutes later, I'd finally gotten my fill and released her.

"Still can't believe you picked a convertible." She nodded toward the Mustang. "Thought you didn't like the wind messing up your hair."

I didn't want her to think I'd shopped frivolously or that I'd changed drastically since she'd been gone. She'd only worry. "It has modifications, which according to the mechanic make it special. So I put up with it."

She chuckled. "You love it, don't you?"

"Yes." I grinned. "Why didn't you tell me you were coming?"

Her face grew solemn. "Let's go inside. I have something to discuss with you."

Once through the front door, my eyes scanned the living room. "Where's dad?"

"He couldn't get away." She sat and leaned back against the dining room chair. "Actually, we saw no point in him making the trip since you're flying back with me."

I blinked. "What?"

"We've decided our family's been apart long enough." She gave me her firm look. "We'll be in New Mexico for a while, which is what you wanted. To stay in one place for a long period."

Setting my purse on the table, I dropped into a chair thinking of all the lame things I could say when there was only one thing I wanted to know. "Mom, level with me. Why do you guys move around so much? Dad could work from just about anywhere and you guys would save so much money in travel expenses."

She studied me. "You've never complained before."

"Actually, I have. You just weren't listening." My tone lowered an octave. "Let me be clear. I don't want to move again."

She reached out to take my hand. "Once we're all settled in New Mexico, you won't have to worry about that for a while."

I pulled my hand away. "I'm not going anywhere."

"You can even keep the Mustang," she went on as if she could replace my friends, a high school diploma and the entire life I'd built in Southern California with a car. "We'll drive out tonight, once we're packed."

"Mom, we went through this a couple weeks ago. I told you how I felt about being uprooted." My blood began to boil. It was as if the conversation had never taken place. I sucked in a deep breath, then fixed my gaze on her and stretched my shoulders back. "Sorry. I'm staying right here."

She stared at me, like she still didn't quite believe me. "Alone?"

"Mom, I love you both and I really miss you guys, but I can't do the gypsy thing anymore. If you leave and sell the house, I'll understand. I can get a job and figure it out. I'd rather do everything on my own than move again."

"What's so important that you have to stay?" She narrowed her eyes. "Did you meet a boy?"

My mouth gaped. "You're still not listening. I want my diploma and I want to go to prom. I *hate* moving. And I don't think you and dad have been truthful to me." Oops. I hadn't meant for that last bit to slip out.

"What do you mean?" Her brows pulled together. "We've never lied to you."

No, but an omission amounted to the same thing. If my parents were shape-shifters, then they should've told me that I would be turning into one, too. If they were human, then that meant I was adopted. Again, they should've told me.

I was dying to just tell them I was a shifter and find out either way. But if they were human and I revealed my true nature to a mortal, I'd be breaking the most important law of the supernaturals. I could get killed for that. I was already breaking serious werewolf laws. I didn't want to press my luck breaking more. Besides, what did werewolves do with humans who knew their secret? I had no idea, but I couldn't take the chance that they were human and Charles or Renzo would kill them.

On the other hand, if they were shifters and I spilled the beans, I wouldn't be breaking any laws. But if they were shifters, wouldn't they have said something?

"Whatever." I wrapped my arms around my waist. "I'm staying and this conversation is over."

"You'll be on your own." Her voice softened. "How will you get through college and make enough money to get an apartment? You'll need to eat. Or do you plan to sacrifice your education and make minimum wage the rest of your life?"

"My education? Seriously? If you cared about that, you wouldn't be giving me an ultimatum. Come with me or cut me off? What kind of parenting is that? You guys make no sense at all." I exhaled loudly and lifted one shoulder. "I'll work it out, maybe stay at Maya's for a bit."

My mom was silent for a moment and I wondered whether she'd given up or was about to try a new angle. I caught a glimpse of the clock on the fireplace mantel, knowing Zack would be expecting me for dinner shortly.

"I'll be right back." I grabbed my purse and paused. "How long are you staying this time?"

"If you're not coming with me, I'm leaving right away."

"Meaning minutes, not hours?" I asked, unsuccessful at hiding my apathy.

She nodded.

"Why don't you guys just come back and *stay*?"

"Sweetheart, your father can't not work. We have rent to pay, your private school and —"

"Never mind." I'd heard it all before. I spun and hurried up the stairs to my room. After closing the door, I rooted through my purse for my phone and texted Zack with trembling fingers to tell him I'd been delayed.

Damn! Why had they forced me to make a choice? God, was I even making the right decision? Phone still in hand, I slapped it against my palm as I paced near the foot of my bed.

Staying and struggling to make ends meet scared the daylights out of me, but I loved my life here. Except Zack would be leaving in just a few weeks and then I'd lose him too. But I still had Maya and Trevor — until they went away to college, at least.

But that wasn't the point. I didn't want to move again. I was done starting over. Eventually, I'd be forced to leave when the wrong werewolf discovered me, but until then, I intended to live my life on *my* terms.

My parents would always love me. I knew that. And I could visit them. With that realization, my body began to calm and my breathing steadied. I quit pacing and ran downstairs, quickly locating my mom who held a phone to her ear. She eyed me, then said good-bye and hung up.

I hugged her. "I love you, Mom."

"Love you too. More than anything in the world." She held me close. "I'm so happy you changed your mind."

I squeezed one last time, then let her go. "I didn't. Moving isn't going to happen for me, no matter how many times you ask."

She tilted her head, her brows drawn. "But..."

"Do what you have to do, sell the house or whatever. I'll deal."

She turned away and seconds passed before she faced me again. She looked tired suddenly, defeated. But I reminded myself that it wasn't bad to stand up for myself.

She tapped her thigh with the tips of her fingers. "Okay. Stay here. We'll keep the house for now and make sure you have money for anything you need."

"Thank you." I threw myself at her. "You won't regret it."

She wrapped her arms around me again. "I hope you're right."

I loosened my grip so I could meet her gaze. "Please spend the night. We can hang out, stay up late and watch a movie or something. Dad will live without you one more day."

"Yes, I'm sure he'd survive. But I have to help him wrap up this job and prepare for the next one." Mom smiled, then glanced at her watch. "I should go. If I leave now, I can make the next flight."

It was absolutely baffling how my parents could do a one-eighty, from obsessively worrying to completely deserting me. Why couldn't the New Mexico job wait an extra day? But I already knew my questions would go nowhere. And I'd just had a huge victory with them supporting me while I stayed. I didn't want to press my luck.

Picking up a small bag, she touched my chin. "We'll be back soon, maybe in a few days. If I can make it on a weekend, we can spend the day together."

I forced my mouth into what I hoped resembled a genuine smile. "That would be great."

We walked to the rental car and said good-bye, then she drove away and waved out the window until her car disappeared around the corner.

# CHAPTER FIVE

AFTER JOHN SPUTTERED away in my old car later that evening, Zack and I hoofed it to his house to check on his mom.

With every intake of air, her lungs wheezed as they struggled to expand.

Zack sat on a chair at her bedside. "Mom, you need to go to the doctor."

"I said no. See how tonight goes. We'll revisit it tomorrow."

"But, Mom —"

"Go to the closet, *tesoro*, top shelf. Bring me the black metal box," she demanded.

Zack hesitated a moment, then did as he was told, setting the container on the bed next to her.

"The key is in my jewelry box on the dresser." She smiled sleepily at him.

Locating the small silver key, Zack unlocked the box and lifted the lid. I stood beside him, spying official looking items — credit cards, stacks of money and something that looked like a passport. His eyes darted to his mom. "Why are you showing me this?"

I backed away from the bed, not wanting to intrude on their private moment. "Um... I'll wait outside."

"Stay here. As long as you're with Zack, you're part of this family." Her eyes met his. "It's all in your name. Everything you need — account numbers, cash, my attorney's contact info. I've set up a trust so there won't be any inheritance taxes or anything else for you to worry about. If you spend it wisely, it'll last a while. You could go to college and study whatever you want."

"Mom." His voice broke and he cleared his throat. "It's not time for this yet. You're going to be fine."

She waved his words away with a sweep of her hand. "Tomorrow, I want you to withdraw everything from our joint account and deposit it into yours."

His eyes clouded and he shook his head. "No."

"Yes." Favianne's brows rose menacingly like only a mother could manage.

"Fine, I will. Under the condition that you'll let me take you to the hospital."

"Only if I'm not feeling better." She sighed. "I'll be fine. I'm just tired. You two have a nice night."

Dismissed.

Zack didn't budge. "Tomorrow you'll say you're feeling better and refuse to go. If you don't agree now, then this box goes back up on the shelf and you can't make me transfer that money. Doctor first. That's the deal." He stood straight and towered over her.

"Who raised you to be so stubborn?" Her mouth curved up and her eyes drifted shut. Suddenly they reopened and she grabbed my hand. "Let me have your *ragazza* for a moment, please. Alone."

*Ragazza*? Did she mean me? Why would she want me alone?

"I'll wait outside. 'Night, mom." He squeezed her other hand, gave me a quick kiss and disappeared into the hallway.

Favianne took my hand. "Promise me you'll take care of him when I'm gone."

"I think Zack's right. It's too soon to talk about this." My throat felt too tight to say much more.

"That might be true. But promise me anyway."

I nodded. "I'll take care of him as best I can, for as long as he'll let me."

"You've learned how stubborn that boy is, I see." She gave me a sleepy smile, then her lids slipped closed and a moment later, her breathing deepened.

"Good night," I whispered and tiptoed out. I found Zack waiting for me in the hallway. "Nice job getting her to agree."

"Only 'cause I resorted to blackmail." He shook his head.

Zack's aunt Cara appeared, crowding into the narrow passageway with us. "Autumn, can I see you for a minute?"

Zack shrugged. *I have no idea what she wants.*

Cara eyed her nephew. "Alone. Go say hi to Trevor."

"Everyone wants her alone. That makes three of us." Zack squeezed past us.

What did Cara have to say that needed to be said in private? I bit my lip.

"I want to show you something." She motioned for me to follow. At the end of the hallway, she opened a door and waved me in. Bookshelves lined the right side of the small room with boxes stacked in front of them. The left side boasted a small bed and at the foot were more boxes.

"It's nothing special, but it's a bed," she said.

I couldn't imagine why she'd offer me a room when she knew I had a perfectly good one at home. Unless she knew I hadn't been using it. My muscles bunched up. I really hoped she had no clue I'd been sleeping in Zack's room every night. "I don't understand..."

"Your parents are still out of town, right? It must be lonely in that house all by yourself."

I exhaled in relief. This confirmed she didn't know I'd been in Zack's bed every night.

She quirked a brow. "Not that you're sleeping there much. If you take this room, you won't have to sneak in and out after dark."

I cringed as heat rushed to my cheeks. "Uh, sorry." What else could I say? I'd been caught. Yikes. Wiping the sudden moisture over my brow, I blew out a breath and screwed up my courage. "How did you know?"

"Sometimes Mac has trouble sleeping. He happened to be looking out the window the last couple nights and saw you crawl through Zack's window."

A squeak escaped my throat.

"Normally, I'd remind Zack of house rules concerning girls in bedrooms. But I don't have the heart to take that from him right now. Not with his mom in her condition."

"You think his concerns are valid?"

Her chin trembled. "Unfortunately, yes. I worry just as much, but I was lucky enough to grow up with her and see her as a young, vibrant woman. For Zack, his mother being sick is almost all he's ever known. No young man should have that kind of burden."

I gave her a sympathetic nod as I unconsciously backed into the hallway, fervently hoping she'd forget all about the previous topic.

"Back to the sleeping arrangements." Cara touched my arm and I slumped in disappointment. "It's okay. I was young and in love once too. I know how it works. Besides, you're both over eighteen. I just hope you two are being safe."

She assumed Zack and I had already slept together. I inwardly cringed and I stared at my toes. "I don't know about Zack being *in love*. We haven't known each other that long."

"Just because my nephew is an *idioto* and hasn't told you so, doesn't mean it's not true."

I almost giggled but was still too freaked out over getting caught. "I'll believe it when I hear it from him. Oh, my gosh, this is so embarrassing." My voice broke on the last word and I took another deep breath. "Seems like it would be worse to stay in this room. What if Patrick or Brian caught me going into Zack's? Maybe I should stick with the window."

Oh, God, did I just admit out loud to sneaking around? Shoot me now.

She laughed and hugged me. "Whatever works for you, *tesora*. I haven't seen Zack this happy in a long time. I'm thinking it has something to do with you, which makes you a part of our family."

† † †

I lay in Zack's bed, cuddling with him. Thoughts floated through my mind like a buoy, refusing to sink into my subconscious. Like the newest werewolf, Renzo. Why was he there and would he try to hijack Zack from Charles? Or worse, did this Renzo guy have other plans, like maybe taking Zack before graduation?

Slimy as Charles was, at least he'd promised to let Zack stay and spend some time with his mom. The thought of losing Zack sooner and never seeing him again made me feel like I was suffocating. There had to be some other way to stop the werewolves. I just didn't know what.

Gina took up way too much space in my head, too. Whatever she was scheming would be something vile, for sure. And then there was Zack's mom. How much time did she have with her son? With her sister Cara?

I couldn't get my parents out of my head either. Were they shape-shifters? If so, why hadn't they told me I'd be hitting shape-shifter maturity right about now? Except Zack hadn't picked up their scent in the house or on their belongings, so they had to be human. Then again, my scent was nearly nonexistent and only detectable up close. Maybe it was the same with them.

On the other hand, if Zack was right and our scent increased with our powers, then my parents should smell like shape-shifters. But they didn't. Which brought me full circle. My head spun.

Maybe they hadn't adopted me but *stolen* me, which was why they were reluctant to tell me they weren't my real parents. I mentally shook my head. They weren't capable of that kind of cruelty. Or were they? Not like they'd been forthcoming about anything in the slightest.

"Go to sleep," Zack whispered.

"I'm trying, believe me, but my brain won't shut up." I gave him the condensed version of my thoughts.

"Hmm. Well, I still firmly believe your parents are human, but if the mystery is driving you to sleep deprivation, you need find out for yourself."

"That's not helpful. How am I supposed to do that?"

He rolled toward me. "They're gone and you have access to everything in the house. There has to be documentation somewhere. Time to snoop around."

"I'd have to poke through their things. It's a bit of an invasion of privacy, don't you think?"

"Absolutely. But they've kept things from you and there's no refuting that. If they'd been open with you, you wouldn't need to go behind their back. It's your right to know the truth. You can either live in ignorance or take action."

Damn. He had a good point. Tomorrow, I'd be at the hospital with Favianne, but first chance I got, my search would begin. No matter the truth I learned, I knew I wouldn't like it.

# CHAPTER SIX

AT LUNCH THE next day, Zack and I joined Trevor and Maya for lunch. Thinking about Favianne and all the doctor's possible diagnoses pretty much snuffed out my appetite, so I just picked at my food.

Zack nudged me with his elbow. "You should eat. Mr. Hagar's having a quiz next period and it'll be harder to concentrate if you're hungry."

"Can I tag along with you to the hospital?" I reluctantly took a bite from my sandwich. Zack was already stressing over his mom. He didn't need to worry about me too.

"I can hardly say no since I'm using *your* car." His mouth tipped into a lopsided grin.

"You seem to handle everything so well." I studied his carefree smile. "Why aren't you freaking out?"

"When you're stressed, it's contagious. My mom's had enough to deal with these last few years. I've always tried not to add to it." He shrugged. "It's habit now."

Trevor leaned toward us. "We're catching a movie tomorrow night. Wanna come?"

"Can't. Zack and I are going out on a real date," I

answered.

"You did that with us," Trevor countered.

"A real date doesn't include you two." I winked. "Besides, we were forced into it."

Trevor laughed. "You dressed for dinner and a movie. We picked you up and paid. It was a date."

"Yeah," Maya chimed in. "And aren't you glad? Look how well it worked out. Anyway, it's not like you guys need privacy. From what I hear, you're getting plenty of that already." She shared a smirk with Trevor.

I flinched, my eyes shooting to him. "Trevor?"

He snickered softly. "Everyone knows, Autumn. It's not that big of a house."

"Oh, God." I prayed there wouldn't be a repeat of yesterday's conversation with Cara.

"If you wanted to keep your late night visits secret, you should get Zack to fix that window so it's not so noisy." Trevor grinned.

Heat rushed into my face, strangling the words in my throat.

"Sorry." Zack squeezed my hand. "I didn't realize the walls were *that* thin."

"What's the difference?" Maya waved a hand. "Your house, his house. Who cares? Same thing going on, different place."

Knowing it was public knowledge that I'd been sneaking into Zack's bedroom made me feel cheap. Telling the truth, that we'd only snuggled and kissed, wouldn't be any more believable to them now than last week when I'd insisted we were just friends — which had been true at the time.

"So what about this weekend?" Maya continued. "We should do something together."

*They're going to bug us until they get their way. Besides, they're right — we still have every night together,* Zack said silently.

*And we have prom coming up*, I added. But why was he giving in so easily? The date do-over had been *his* idea.

"Okay," Zack said to Trevor, then resumed eating his lunch.

Trevor and Maya got lost in each other again, which left me nothing to do but think. Something was nagging at me. Gina. I could feel her eyes on me. My eyes snapped over my shoulder to confirm her scowling at me.

Sometimes I wished my perceptions weren't so sharp, because then I could be blissfully ignorant. Too bad I had a few more weeks before I was free of her. And I couldn't even look forward to it, because right around that same time, I'd lose Zack. I wanted time to stand still, even if it meant Gina would be there to annoy me.

Returning my attention to Zack, I noticed he'd stopped eating and was just staring down at his tray. "I don't get it. I thought you wanted a real date," I asked.

"I do." He took my hand and traced circles in my palm, sending little shivers up my arm. "But I can't imagine being much fun if my mom doesn't get better. With Trevor and Maya there, it takes the pressure off so I don't have to be entertaining."

"Who says you're off the hook?" I nudged his shoulder with my own.

Zack smiled halfheartedly. "Maybe you shouldn't go to the hospital. I can take the Jeep and you'd have your car. Or better yet, Aunt Cara is going there anyway. She could pick me up."

My brows drew together. "Why?"

"Well..." He rubbed his hand on his jeans and looked around the room. "The more attached you get to my mom, the harder it's going to be for you later."

"Yeah, better not get too attached." I chewed my lip. "But it's too late. I already love her."

"It's not just her, but my whole family. And me." He glanced at Trevor and Maya who were still busy talking, then he lowered his voice. "I think about what it's going to be like for you when I leave."

"What?" I stared at him. Why bring this up now?

"I'll never regret my time with you. Ever. But maybe you shouldn't *invest* so much in us."

My mouth hung open. Shouldn't he have thought this out before he allowed me to fall in love with him and his family? At the very least, before he asked me to be his girlfriend and invited me to prom. Bringing up his same objections at this point was just cruel.

"Excuse me." Eyes stinging from tears of fury, I steadied my hands and picked up my tray, then walked to the garbage can and stacked it with the others. As if he didn't exist, I exited the lunchroom and walked to my next class alone.

We still had six minutes before English Lit started.

Zack had that class with me. Damn. As I took my seat and faced the chalkboard, I could sense him close by. Sure enough, he strolled in and claimed the seat next to me. We sat there, just the two of us as the clock ticked.

Five minutes until start of class. Four.

I turned to face him. "Almost since we first met, you've been reminding me that you're leaving. Kind of hard to forget. And didn't anyone ever teach you how rude it is to return a gift?"

He looked puzzled.

"Love is something you give freely. The recipient can't get a refund or re-gift it."

Zack started to rise. "Wait —"

My palm shot out to stop him and he sat again. "I shouldn't invest so much, Zack? This isn't a business deal. You and your family aren't something I bought to make a profit. And anyway, friendship and loyalty aren't things you ration out."

"That's not what I meant. Maybe that was poor word choice." He fidgeted with his pencil, rolling it between his hands. "You're very... involved with my family and... the deeper you get, the harder it's going to be later."

I shot out of my chair to loom over him. "I knew the situation from the beginning. But if I get in too deep, it's on me, so you don't need to feel guilty."

My throat felt thick and swollen. It's not like I was under the delusion that Zack and his wonderful family were mine to keep, but I didn't want to be limited in how much I was allowed to love while I had them.

He stood, too. "I'm thinking of you. I don't want you to get hurt."

"You're really pissing me off, Zack." A fresh round of tears waited just behind my eyes to be set free. I backed away as someone entered the room and lowered my voice to a hiss. "If you've changed your mind and don't want to be with me, then just say so."

The sounds of the classroom filling up were drowned out by the roaring in my head. I plopped down in my chair next to Zack, turning away to avoid looking at him. But I could feel his gaze on me. How dare he pull that crap on me again? He'd been pushing me away since I'd first laid eyes on him. Last time I'd checked, our plan was to enjoy each other and deal with his leaving when we had to. Was he rethinking that or just losing interest in me?

I glanced over at Zack, searching for the answer in his face. His eyes had darkened and the planes of his face hardened. But I couldn't tell if it was anger, dislike or frustration.

The teacher cleared his throat and raised one brow. "Autumn, Zack. Would you prefer we leave the room so you can work things out? Or may I go ahead and get class started?"

My face heated and I squeezed my eyes shut, shaking my head.

"That's a relief," Mr. Hagar said dryly. "Please use a number two pencil. Anyone who doesn't have one, raise your hand."

Right! The quiz. Crap, I'd totally forgotten about

that. I whipped out my pencil and resigned myself to doing poorly on the test since I was an emotional mess and hadn't even studied.

As it turned out, my data absorption was tenfold since I'd hit shape-shifter maturity. I was pretty sure I'd answered all the questions correctly. At least there were benefits to being a shape-shifter, along with the drawbacks — like slavery or being killed.

Seconds before the end of class, I hesitated before rising. I wasn't sure if Zack would walk with me or flee from my wrath. When the bell rang and his eyes locked on mine, tranquil waters replaced the earlier stormy ones.

Without a word, he reached for my hand and escorted me to my next class where he pressed a kiss to my forehead. Was he going to treat me like a little sister now? Whatever. I spun and stalked into the classroom without speaking a word to him.

When school let out, Zack was waiting for me by the Mustang with a look on his face that warned me things weren't right. Was he ready to let me go now?

My stomach sank.

# CHAPTER SEVEN

AS I APPROACHED my car, Zack met me halfway. He stopped when we were a couple feet apart and I held my breath. Then his face softened and his arms opened for me. I dropped the backpack, stepped into his embrace and buried my face in his chest.

"I'm sorry." He kissed the top of my head. "I shouldn't have said those things. I want to save you from the pain but... looks like I'm making it worse and you're just as screwed as the rest of us. If you still want to come with me, I'd really like you there."

I raised my face to see him. "Okay, but please stop trying to save me."

He sighed and squeezed me closer.

The tension dissipated as I leaned into him to drink in his musky scent. "So you still want to double date tomorrow?" I asked when we broke contact.

"Your call. I just want to be with you." His fingertips caressed the nape of my neck.

Shivers danced on my skin. "We already told them we would."

"Then it's a double date." Taking a deep breath, he

released me. "But only if my mom is okay. Otherwise, I need to stay at the hospital."

I nodded. "Of course." I hoped for some miracle that she was feeling better. For her sake, as well as Zack's.

† † †

Years ago, a friend of mine from the neighborhood had been in a car accident and I'd talked my parents into letting me visit her in the hospital. I remembered the pungent smells of antiseptics and cleaning solvents, the nurses in their colorful scrubs and sensible shoes.

But my friend had been dealing with broken bones and abrasions in the emergency room. I hadn't been exposed to the diseases and illnesses of the terminal ward.

I could smell it now, the decay of life.

Zack wheeled Favianne through the double doors and over the worn linoleum to the waiting room. He relinquished the wheelchair to me when a nurse at the counter motioned him toward a stack of paperwork. I parked his mom near an empty chair, made sure she was comfortable, then sat next to her.

"How are you feeling?" My stomach sank at her pallid complexion. The only color on her face was in the dark circles under her eyes.

"I've been better." She readjusted herself in the chair.

I could hear her lungs wheezing and the slow thump of her heart straining. At least she'd finally agreed to get medical help. I glanced over at Zack, wondering what was taking so long.

"Relax, sweetheart," she rasped, like she was holding back a cough. "They'll take me in soon."

Zack turned around and headed our way, followed by a heavyset nurse. She grasped the handles of Favianne's chair and glided it toward another set of double doors. Zack and I followed.

"I thought I told you not to come back," the nurse chided.

Favianne laughed softly. "I couldn't pass up another opportunity to irritate you, Winnie."

"You didn't have to go to such extremes. A phone call would suffice."

Favianne laughed again. "You can blame it on Zack who coerced me into coming."

"You got yourself a good boy there. He's growing up just fine." Winnie continued through the doorway of a small room and stopped at a narrow bed.

Zack scooped up his mother from the chair and gingerly laid her on the mattress. I secured a spot in the corner, away from the machines and other equipment, and watched Winnie take her blood pressure. I just hoped they could help her. And fast.

After taking her temperature, Winnie occasionally asked Favianne questions, like how long which symptoms had been going on, then made notes in a file.

Zack joined me in the corner to get out of Winnie's way. He pressed his back against the far wall and held my hand while Winnie prepared a needle. Moments later, a vial began filling with blood.

"How ya feelin', honey? Breathing easier?" Winnie

asked as she removed the full vial.

Favianne nodded and smiled, but her droopy lids betrayed her exhaustion.

"The doctor will see you soon." Winnie deftly applied a bandage to Favianne's arm, patted her hand and shuffled out.

Zack and I crowded around the bed, being careful of the various contraptions. Although his face appeared calm, I could tell it was an act. His jaw was tight and a thin line kept appearing between his brows.

She squeezed his hand, then closed her eyes. "I'll be fine."

I stayed by Favianne's bed, trying to look like all the waiting wasn't driving me half crazy while Zack paced the small room, pausing now and then to peer out into the hallway.

After several laps, he stopped in the doorway and blew out a breath. "Dr. Preston, thank you for seeing her so quickly."

A man came into view wearing a white medical coat and a tight smile. After shaking Zack's hand, the doctor flipped open Favianne's chart. He positioned a stethoscope to her chest and a moment later shook his head, his lips thinning into a straight line.

"I'm ordering an x-ray stat," he said. "Meanwhile I'll put a rush on the lab work. The culture takes about seventy-two hours, but if it's pneumonia, which I suspect it is, we'll see enough evidence in the x-ray to start her on antibiotics right away."

Zack nodded.

"I'm not going to lie to you, son. I wish you'd brought her in sooner." The doctor sighed. "You can stay a couple more minutes, then you'll need to go to the waiting room while we do x-rays. I'll have a look at them and speak with you as soon as I can."

"Thank you, sir," Zack replied.

† † †

I sorted through the magazines in the waiting area, looking for anything that wasn't about parenting or health. Just as I gave up and abandoned the stack, I felt a familiar energy.

Werewolf.

Trying to avoid sudden moves that might draw the werewolf's attention, I slowly dragged my eyes across the gray-blue rug and the off-white walls to a girl sitting just several yards away at the other end of the room.

As if sensing my eyes on her, she looked up from her own magazine and gave me a friendly smile. I returned it, but on the inside I was freaking out. Yeah, Zack said my scent would be difficult to pick up, but at some point that would change and I didn't know when that would be.

She was the first female I'd come across and seemed far less intimidating than Charles or Renzo, but probably every bit as dangerous as them.

I grabbed a fitness magazine and let my dark hair fall forward to conceal my gaze. As I watched her on the sly, I quickly became fascinated by her flawless toffee-colored skin and tight curls that cascaded over her shoulders. Spaghetti straps curved over imposing yet feminine shoulders and held up a red, sweetheart neckline tank top. Black jeans sat below a tiny waist and molded to her lean hips. She couldn't have been much older than me.

"Don't stare. We don't want to call attention to ourselves," Zack said so quietly at my temple that I almost hadn't heard it.

A girl that pretty wouldn't give our stares a second thought. She had to be used to it. But I averted my gaze to avoid any further interaction with her. As my eyes scanned the thin pages of the magazine I'd grabbed, instead of seeing the text before me, in my mind I saw the image of the girl. Who was she? Why was she there?

I was dying to talk to Zack, see if he recognized the she-wolf. But we couldn't risk her sensing the energy that silent communication created. So I shifted in my chair, a ball of angst growing in the pit of my stomach.

Winnie approached and we rose from our chairs. "Dr. Preston is looking at your mother's x-rays now. He'll be ready for you shortly." She gave Zack a reassuring smile and turned, the crisp fabric of her uniform whispering to the rhythm of her stride. We sat again, resuming our vigil.

After what seemed an eternity, we were led into an office with maroon carpet and cream walls. Zack and I each took an overstuffed chair opposite the doctor who sat behind a wide, wooden desk.

"It's pneumonia, but it's more advanced than I'd thought," Dr. Preston began. My stomach tightened at his grave expression. "We've already started her on antibiotics, but with her compromised immune system, there's no telling how quickly she'll get better. *If* she gets better. She'll stay overnight for observation and, hopefully, we'll know more in the morning."

"Thank you." Zack's voice sounded strained.

"Go home. If there are any complications, Winnie will call you."

Zack shook his head. "No way. If there's a chance she won't make it through the night, I'm not going anywhere."

"It's not that bad. Yet. If the antibiotics don't kick in soon, tomorrow could be a different story. But that's tomorrow. Get a good night's rest. You can call us in the morning and we'll give you an update."

Zack frowned. "No, thanks. I'll stay."

I ran my hand lightly over his arm. "If she's really okay for tonight, you should get some sleep. What if she needs you tomorrow and you're too wasted to be any use to her?"

"Um... Yeah, I guess you're right." His brows lowered, like he was still struggling with the idea.

I laced my fingers with his. "You're not abandoning her. You're just taking care of yourself, so you can do the same for her."

He nodded and we rose together. Favianne didn't stir as we crept into her room, but we said our good-byes to her anyway and took off. On the way home, Zack gazed silently out the passenger window while I drove.

"Since everyone knows I'm sleeping at your house, I don't have to sneak in later, right?" I asked, stopping alongside the curb in front of his house. He nodded and reached for the door handle. "After my shower, I'll come back, okay? Unless... unless you'd prefer to be alone."

"No." He swept a thumb across my cheek and his gaze fell on my mouth. "I want you with me."

Well, if you ask like that...

Twenty minutes later, I returned wearing a soft, faded gray T-shirt and pink flannel lounge pants. Zack was camped out on the front steps. From the curb, vestiges of Aunt Cara's earlier dinner tickled my nose. Lasagna probably. I was sorry to have missed it.

I lowered to sit next to him. My ears picked up on sounds inside the house — machine guns blaring from a video game as Mac and Trevor playfully threatened to kill each other, and Cara warning her younger boys it was bedtime. My body told me it was much later, like the kids should've been in bed hours ago. For all the energy I lacked, I may as well have been a slug.

"I slipped out to the woods while you were gone, so that's done," he said, bumping shoulders with me.

Right. Werewolves needed to run and morph every night. Since I didn't have the same compulsion, it was easy to forget. I would've loved to go for a run and morph, whether I needed to or not, but I didn't love the idea of losing out on time with Zack. I leaned into him, resting my head on his shoulder.

The silence soothed me and the summer breeze warmed my skin. Angling my head to the right, I saw the full moon casting light through the dim streets. A couple blocks down, a dark figure slowly made its way toward us. By the gait and cowboy hat, I knew the man was Charles — the last person I wanted to intrude on my blissful moment with Zack. I silently warned him and he nodded, wrapping his hand around mine.

We waited as the werewolf strolled along the concrete in his own time.

"Howdy, neighbor," he said, pausing in front of the steps.

"Hello," Zack replied.

I smiled, but only enough not to appear rude.

"I was passing by earlier when you were carrying someone into the car. Your mother?"

"Yes, she had an appointment with her doctor."

Charles nodded and glanced toward the street as he continued silently. *Is she going to be all right?*

Zack ran a hand through his hair. *To be honest, I have no clue. Depends on how she responds to treatment, but she's been sick for a long time, so...*

"I see." Charles nodded once. "I hope she feels better soon."

"Thank you. Me too," Zack said.

"Well..." Charles tipped his hat, smiled again and continued walking. "Good night."

Zack sat rigid next to me and I couldn't blame

him. Charles reminded me of a vulture waiting for death so he could descend upon his prey. How would Favianne do during the night? It was too soon for her to go. Much too soon.

# CHAPTER EIGHT

MY EYES FLUTTERED open as the morning sunlight strayed between the curtain panels. My head was on Zack's chest, my arm slung over his ribs, and our legs were entwined. I snuggled closer against Zack.

If only I could stay this way forever. Alas, we had school. Ugh. I preferred the mall to studying any day. But on this particular Friday, clothes shopping and classes were the last things on my mind. I wondered how Favianne had fared through the night and what the doctor would tell us.

"Oh, good, you're awake." Zack rolled on top of me, pinning my arms over my head and nibbling on my neck. "Mmm. This has to last me through the rest of the day."

"Why?" Wouldn't we be together the next few hours?

"You're dropping me off at the hospital before you go to school, right?" His tongue flicked my earlobe, sending a tremor through me. "I won't see you until after last class."

Tingles spread all the way to my toes as he trailed kisses down my neck and to my shoulder. "You're not going to school? I thought maybe Cara would spend the day with your mom and you'd see her after."

"Autumn, my mom's in the hospital." His head popped up and he raised his brows as if waiting for it to sink in. He didn't have to wait long.

"Right." I blinked, trying to get with the program.

"Aunt Cara's been really worried, so she won't be able to stay away. But since she'll have other things to do, like pick up the boys, I want to make sure my mom is never alone."

With Zack on top of me, concentrating on anything but the feel of his hand at my waist was a herculean task. "Did you call and check on her already?"

"Yeah. They think the antibiotics are working." He rested his chin on my shoulder, his breath sending goose bumps over my skin.

"That's great news, Zack." I closed my eyes, wanting to stretch the minutes and keep him with me longer. "I wish I could miss school without them calling my parents."

"If they're shape-shifters, they're probably on the run. The last thing they need is for you to throw them off track by getting into trouble at school."

"So now you believe they're shape-shifters?" Just great. Because stressing over whether Favianne lived another day wasn't enough. Now I could worry if my parents would get captured by werewolves.

"I said *if.* I still think they're human, but I can't ignore how you barely smell like a shifter." His mouth slanted over mine and my lips parted for him. Just as our tongues brushed, he abruptly withdrew. "Maybe they're shifters and practically scentless like you. I have no idea. But if they *are* shape-shifters and school calls them, they'll ask why you weren't in school. You'll have to lie or you can tell them you were with me. If they already know I'm a werewolf, hanging out with me isn't going to sit well with them."

"And they'd worry even more." As the lies piled on, everything got more complicated. "All right. I'll drop you off before going to school." I arched my neck to give his lips better access. "Um... you don't seem in a huge hurry to get there."

"We have a couple minutes."

"Good." I freed my hands and rolled on top of him.

† † †

In theory, surviving a future without Zack in my life was totally possible — if you call plunging into a deep, dark depression surviving. Eventually, I might pull myself out of it and only skirt the edges of darkness now and again. Perhaps one day, I might find something that resembled happiness. Maybe even love another.

Yeah, right.

Being at peace without Zack would be a *very* long time from now and it disturbed me to realize how attached to him I'd become. How intensely I'd fallen for him. I had no intention of ever finding out what life would be like without him or seeing how devastated I'd be. Not going to happen. Ever.

That said, I had to get through this one day without him. Between worrying about Favianne and my own parents, school was the very last place I wanted to be. At least Zack had texted with two updates about Favianne. Both were encouraging. That was something.

Sixth period was Social Science. Not my favorite class since Natalie and Jeff were there. She'd been best friends with Gina before I came along and she'd never liked me. After Gina locked lips with my ex, I dumped her as a friend and Natalie no longer needed to disguise her loathing for me.

Except there were no glares today, no scowls. Instead, she looked smug. I knew something was up, but my mind was too wrapped up with Favianne to bother trying to figure out Natalie.

Mr. Collins handed out a quiz. I fidgeted through most of it, since it was almost too easy. Part of me wished it had been more challenging and maybe I wouldn't have been so anxious for the bell to ring. As soon as Mr. Collins dismissed us, I rushed out of the classroom like my ass was on fire, then sped to the hospital.

I slipped my car into the first parking space I saw and scrambled out. Taking a deep, calming breath, I walked at a human pace through the brightly lit corridors and waited like a good girl for the elevator. At last, I reached the correct floor. As soon as the doors opened, I bolted.

Cara and Mac came into view as I neared the waiting area and I pounced. "How is she?"

She smiled. "The antibiotics are working beautifully. Dr. Preston wants to keep her one more night though. If she continues to improve, she can come home tomorrow."

"Oh, thank God!" I hugged Cara. "Can I see her?"

"Zack's in there now. I don't think he'd mind if you cut in," Mac said, patting me on the back.

"Since you're here now, you can stay with Zack and we'll go home." Cara swept a soothing hand down my arm. "Favianne doesn't need every last one of us hovering over her."

"See you tonight." Mac nodded and steered his wife to the exit.

"'Bye," I called after them and made my way to Favianne's room. The door was ajar, but I tapped lightly to warn them of my arrival.

"Hey." Zack met me in the middle of the room and hugged me. "Mom was just asking about you."

"Yes, I was." Favianne smiled. The light had returned to her eyes, along with the color in her cheeks.

Releasing Zack, I moved to stand at her bedside. "I hear they might release you tomorrow?"

"That's what we're hoping," she answered. "In fact, it's not necessary for you two to stay."

"But Cara and Mac just left. We can't leave you alone." I wasn't anywhere near ready to be dismissed. "Besides, I just got here."

She raised a brow. "I will not allow you to waste a Friday night with me. I'll still be here tomorrow morning. You can visit me then — spend your whole day with me if you'd like. But tonight, you're going to enjoy being young and healthy."

"But —" Zack began.

"No buts. Spend the next couple hours with me, then go home and have dinner. Then get on with your evening." Her tone hardened. "Don't argue with me."

Zack blew out a breath. "Yes, ma'am."

"Tomorrow I'll come home and you two will go to prom as planned. I will not have your big day ruined by me. Understand?" She glanced from Zack to me.

"Yes, ma'am," we answered in unison.

"Good. Now, how was your day at school?" she asked me, her eyes lighting up as she flashed me a smile.

"It was okay. But I was worried about you."

She patted my hand. "Everything's going to be okay. Just as I promised. Do you play Rummy?"

"A little bit," I answered.

"Watch out for my mom." Zack rolled a stool my way, then claimed another one and scooted it closer to her bed. "She's a shark."

Favianne picked up a deck of cards from a nearby end table and began shuffling, one side of her mouth curving up.

Three games of Rummy later, two cups of coffee and a game of War, she kicked us out and sent us home. Although I didn't want to leave her, I didn't mind having Zack all to myself for a few minutes before we met up with Maya and Trevor.

"Do you need to go home first?" he asked as he braked for a stoplight.

"Only if you're coming with me," I replied.

"If your parents are shape-shifters, they'll catch my scent. Not a good idea for me to be in your house."

"But they're not home."

"True... but they have a habit of showing up without warning."

I wondered why my parents hadn't noticed Zack's scent when they'd come home before, so I rolled back the clock in my head. After school last week, I came home to compile my grocery list and had cleaned up a bit before I'd left for the market, especially on the couch where he'd slept the night before. If my parents were shifters, no way could they have detected werewolf with all the chemicals I'd used. Zack had barely been to my house since then, so when my mom came back a couple days ago, there hadn't been anything for her to sense.

"You sound like you're more and more convinced they're not human."

He shook his head. "No, I haven't changed my mind. But in case I'm wrong, we'd better not risk it."

We stopped at my house so I could change, but he waited for me in the car. Then we were off to Zack's for dinner, which was spectacular as usual — wine sauce over Italian sausage and angel hair pasta. I still skipped the meat though. Maybe with practice I'd learn to contain myself while eating that stuff, but with everything going on, I didn't think I could do it just yet. And acting like a cave woman in front of Zack or his family was at the very bottom of my To Do list.

While Zack and I cleaned up the kitchen, Trevor went to Maya's house and brought her back. We drove to Hollywood and Highland and saw a movie Maya chose. It seemed like a chick flick to me, but the guys liked it too.

Late that night, we went out for our run. We drove, because Zack wanted to explore an unfamiliar area on the outskirts of Angeles National Forest.

"Why don't we go to our usual place?" I asked when he parked in a spot partially obscured by trees.

"The more time we spend in one area, the stronger our scent becomes there. We should change it up." Zack's back went rigid. *This was a mistake.*

Before my mind absorbed his last word, I knew what Zack meant. From the passenger side, I glanced around in search of the werewolf.

*Whoever's out there would've heard us drive up. He already knows we're here,* he told me silently.

*Shouldn't we leave?* I asked.

*Why bother? A werewolf can run faster than a car. Let's get out and act normal.*

Normal? I wasn't sure what that was anymore. With wooden movements, I opened the car door and climbed out. Zack came around to my side, twirled me around and shoved me against the side of the car.

*Act like you like me.* One side of his mouth curled up. *We're just a couple of teenagers who came here for some privacy.*

I wrapped my arms around his waist and tilted my chin up. Pasting on a pleasant expression was difficult knowing someone was watching, waiting.

"It's kind of late for you kids to be out, don't you think? And alone in the woods. Isn't there a curfew you're violating?" Charles asked, slowly emerging from between the trees.

Zack turned around, still holding onto me. "We're over eighteen. And it's a great place to be alone." He grinned as if Charles, being a man, knew exactly what he meant.

I struggled through the fog, trying to remember how a human girl would act if she were caught making out with a boy and knew nothing of werewolf scouts or shape-shifters. "And what's your excuse for being here?"

Charles shrugged. "Just going for a drive. Decided to get out and take a look around. How's your mom doing?" he asked Zack.

"Much better. They'll probably let us take her home tomorrow."

"That's good news," Charles replied. Since I was still touching Zack, I was able to listen in when Charles switched to silent communication. *When I saw you last night, I'd already been to the hospital to check on her condition myself. I didn't think she'd make it, which is what I reported to my superior. Since I've already been here too long, they insisted I bring you in right away. They're expecting you right after graduation, whether your mom is alive or not.*

*But you said I could spend extra time with her,* Zack told him, his hands gripping my waist a little too tightly. *Tell them you messed up.*

Cold rage replaced Charles's amiable smile. *I will do no such thing. What's done is done. You'll work it out.* He turned to leave.

"You can't take him early!" I shouted. "It's not fair. You made the mistake. *You* fix it!"

Slowly, Charles pivoted, eyes spearing mine. "And how is it possible for a human to hear our conversation?"

My stomach knotted as terror gripped me. I'd just given myself away to a werewolf. Worse, we'd been making out and breaking a law that carried the death penalty.

Dead girl walking. And since Zack was consorting with a shape-shifter, he wouldn't fare any better.

Zack squeezed my hand. "She's human, but she reads minds."

"A witch?" The scout tilted his head, narrowing his eyes. "Or she's something else... like a shape-shifter. Maybe you were really coming here to morph." He took a step toward me, but I couldn't back up since I was already against the car.

Zack moved in front of me. "She's human."

Charles smiled. "If that's the case, allow me to confirm it."

"Suit yourself." Zack moved aside and waved a hand toward me. He appeared unruffled, but I sensed an undercurrent. I could also hear his heart pounding wildly. I'd bet anything that Charles could hear it too. He'd know Zack was scared... and lying.

"Thank you. I will." Charles reached out and brushed my hair away, exposing my neck. He leaned in and inched toward me. As he inhaled deeply, the amusement faded from his eyes and they darkened.

Busted.

*Zack doesn't know*, I told Charles silently, hoping if he thought I was to blame, it would keep Zack safe and give him time to run. Two fledglings could never take down a mature werewolf who was possibly hundreds of years older. *He hasn't learned about shape-shifters or their scent. He thinks I'm human which is perfectly legal. Punish me, not him.*

Charles returned his attention to his recruit. "Your girlfriend just informed me that you're ignorant of the fact that she's a shape-shifter. And that *she* is the one who should be punished, not you."

Zack's eyes grew wide as he stared at me. *What the hell are you doing?*

I opened my mouth to keep him from spilling the truth to Charles. Either way, I was toast. At least this way, one of us might live.

Charles shot us both a crooked smile. "It's unfortunate both of you will need to be eliminated."

"Why? Zack didn't know about me until you told him!" I hissed.

"If he's too weak and stupid to detect a shifter, he has no value to the king. No point in keeping him alive."

I didn't think. All I knew was that Zack's life was in danger. Adrenaline roared through my body like water through a fire hose and an instant later, I exploded into a grizzly bear. The force of my morph spiraled Charles backward and he crashed into the thick tree trunk. Before he had a chance to reorient himself, I was on top of him, my paws on his chest and my teeth at his throat.

He morphed into a brown wolf and his ancient-strong jaws slashed my flank and side. Despite catching him by surprise, I was no match for him. Pain burned through my middle and my power waned.

# CHAPTER NINE

JUST AS MY eyes started to lose focus, Zack appeared at my side, his fangs at Charles's throat, paws holding Charles down. I pushed my full weight into the brown wolf, mashing him into the soft topsoil as I swatted him with my massive paws until his teeth rattled.

Zack had once said that in our animal form, some things became unimportant — like baths and blood. We wouldn't kill an animal or hunt humans just for the hell of it, but the act of killing when it needed to be done wasn't abhorrent to us.

He wasn't kidding. On instinct, I went wild — my jaws snapping and tearing at Charles's flesh. His blood splashed into my mouth and I reveled in the kill. I opened wider and fit his skull in my mouth, then bore down, jerking my head side to side. Blood drained from Charles's flaccid body and pooled onto the uneven ground. Hot delicious blood.

*Autumn! Enough! He's dead*, Zack shouted into my head, still in his wolf form.

The words, human words, coursed through my mind bringing my thoughts into focus. Slowly, I released Charles's head, a new burst of energy flowing through my veins. I glanced down at my side where his teeth had sliced into me. The bleeding had stopped and the wound was nearly closed.

*Don't turn human yet until we clean up. Otherwise, when your clothes morph back with you, they'll be ruined. We won't be able to explain all the blood to the mortals.*

I shook my fur like a dog after a bath — not to remove the blood but to pull myself out of the frenzied rage I'd plunged into. I shook again and blood droplets exploded into the air. Charles's blood.

Rearing up on my hind legs, I extended my snout high into the air. *I smell water to the left.* I glanced over at the scout. *Are you sure he's dead?*

*You ripped out his intestines and crushed his skull. He looks pretty dead to me.*

I glanced down at what remained of Charles. If I'd ripped out his insides, where did they go?

Zack looked at me, his eyes cautious. *So how does werewolf taste? Anything like chicken?*

Looking at the wolf's carcass, I realized more than his guts were missing — a foot, a chunk out of his arm and shoulder. Possibly more, but he was so mangled it was difficult to tell. And those body parts were all weighing in my happy stomach. Maybe I'd feel some sort of revulsion later when I became human again, but right now, I felt well-fed and smug.

I stretched my furry muzzle into what I hoped resembled a smile. *Pretty tasty, actually.*

Zack made a strange noise, like a cross between

a gag and a cough. I hoped he was amused, but the grimace said slightly horrified.

*Since he died in wolf form, he'll stay that way. Anyone will just assume a bear killed him. Which is exactly what happened. We'll leave everything exactly as it is. Let's go.*

† † †

After we'd cleaned up, Zack drove. I trembled as I snuggled against him, resting my head on his shoulder. I couldn't think about the fact that I'd just killed a man and werewolves were bound to come looking for him. I needed to concentrate on Zack and that he was safe.

Just as the tremors in my limbs subsided, Zack sighed heavily. Now what?

"You promised you wouldn't do that."

I lifted my head off his shoulder to look at him. "Do what?"

He glanced down at me, frowning, then returned his eyes to the road. "Make deals with a werewolf to save my life."

Crap. I'd forgotten what a fit Zack had thrown the last time I'd tried to save him by negotiating with my psycho ex-boyfriend Daniel.

"Your life was at stake, Zack. I had to do something."

"But your life in exchange for mine isn't something you can decide for me." He reached for my hand and laced his fingers through mine.

"I wasn't *exchanging* my life for yours. He was going to kill me either way. But I hoped that maybe I could save *you*." I absentmindedly skimmed my fingernails down his arm and smiled when he shivered.

The image of Charles dead body assaulted me again and I wished I could morph and stay that way, so the act of murder wouldn't bother me.

"Hey. We're safe now." Zack's thumb brushed my finger.

"I know he'll stay a wolf now that he's dead, but what if another werewolf recognizes him and they do DNA testing and figure out it was me? I could get arrested."

He slowed for a red light. "You're overreacting. Even if —"

"I ended someone's life, Zack. He's dead. It's impossible to overreact to something like that."

"I was there, too. I helped you kill him and I'm freaked out too." He growled, casting a quick glance my way before making a turn. "I'm really trying not to think about it. And we're not going to get caught. Even if someone realizes he's a werewolf, they'd never match grizzly DNA to you."

But I'd still know I did it. Charles was never coming back and that was because of me.

I shuddered.

"Autumn, he was going to kill us both. You did what you had to do."

Yeah, I did. And I'd do it again. Most likely, it would come to that sooner or later. God, I really needed to think about something else. "Your family is pretty tolerant about me sleeping in your room, considering what they think we're doing."

He laughed softly. "We're both over eighteen and they know they can't stop us. And they still remember what it was like to be our age. My mom and Aunt Cara can try to sway me in my choices, but in the end, that's all they can do — try. I guess they figure so long as we make our mistakes under their roof, they'll be there to help us fix it."

"So you could have a beer or do some shots of —"

Zack scoffed. "Nothing illegal. That's where I'm sure they'd draw the line."

He pulled the car against the curb in front of his house and, suddenly, my limbs were too drained to move another inch.

"Let's get you into a bath and to bed. You've had a big night." He brushed his lips against my temple. "You were magnificent."

Yes, I was. And now, Charles would never bother us again. The part about me partially consuming him still hadn't sunk in. Maybe it never would.

† † †

Following the smell of coffee, I crept out of Zack's room, still a bit loopy from lack of sleep. Momentarily blinded by the bright light in the hallway, I jolted as Trevor's youngest brother slammed into me. He must have been moving at warp speed because his head felt like a bowling ball crashing into my ribs. My hands shot out to his shoulders to steady him and I quickly scanned him for injuries. He looked totally fine.

"Oh. Hi Autumn," he said, as if it were any other day.

"Good morning, Patrick." I glanced away, hoping he wouldn't wonder why I was at their house so early — in my pajamas.

"You slept in Zack's room?" he asked, startling me out of what remained of my daze. His light brown hair stuck out in every direction.

"Hey." Zack snaked around me and ruffled the boy's hair. It looked exactly the same afterward. "We were out late last night so instead of driving home when she was tired, we had a sleepover."

Zack could've explained that Cara had invited me to stay in the small room, but he'd obviously forgotten about that. Watching him dance around it was more entertaining anyway. I held back a nervous giggle.

"Like a slumber party? Is Maya here too?"

"No. It was just the two of us," Zack said with a straight face.

"After we visit Auntie, we're going to Legoland," Patrick said and I breathed a sigh of relief for children's short attention span. "Are you coming too?"

"Nah." Zack mussed Patrick's hair again. "We have things to do, hopefully bringing your Auntie home."

"Okay." Patrick disappeared around the corner.

"Finally, someone who sees it as innocent as it really is." I beamed at Zack, thankful Patrick didn't know I only lived a block away or he might have seen through Zack's thin excuse. Apparently, I'd worried for nothing about being a bad influence on the boy.

"That's because he's only six. But Brian might be a different story. He's ten."

"Oh." A little more time to bask in my triumph would've been nice.

"I want to get to the hospital early." Zack jerked his head toward his bedroom door and I followed him in. "I'll be ready in just a minute."

Sitting at the foot of his bed as he stripped off his sweats, I pretended I wasn't staring. Boxers weren't all that different than shorts though. I sagged in disappointment. At least I got to gawk at his washboard abs once he'd peeled off his T-shirt.

Zack stepped into a pair of jeans, then shuffled to the closet where he chose a white button-down shirt. I sighed as he covered up that beautiful, flat, firm stomach. Such a shame. Grabbing a pair of socks and his sneakers, he sat on the bed next to me and put them on.

I scanned his face, noting a trace of stubble around his chin and over his lip. My stomach dipped. He looked sexy as hell. I hoped he didn't plan on shaving.

"You ready to go?" he asked, running his fingers through his hair.

Go. Right. I reined in the lust. "Yeah." I followed him to my car, Zack fully dressed and me in my PJs. A minute later we arrived at my house.

"We should arm wrestle again," Zack said once we went inside. "While we're here."

I paused halfway up the stairs. "We just did that yesterday. You think I'd change in twenty-four hours? Or do you just enjoy whipping me?"

He shrugged. "Humor me."

I tromped down the few steps, flopped into a kitchen chair and slapped my elbow on the table. His hands wrapped around mine and our gazes locked.

"One...," he said, "Two... three."

As our forces clashed, our hands trembled and our elbows pressed into the hard surface of the table. Heat flooded my body and I struggled against Zack. As the moments stretched on, our arms frozen, he growled. "I don't know if I can take you."

We may have been equally strong, but I didn't have his werewolf stamina. My muscles slowly turned to jelly and my knuckles gently hit the table. "You won again."

"Barely. Impressive strength increase for just one day." Zack's eyes thinned to slits. "I wonder why."

"No idea." I lifted a shoulder, then let it fall. Zack couldn't be right about shifters being weaker or when I'd plateau. Since I was already this strong, I must have already peaked. "I'd better get dressed."

I didn't bother closing the door to my bedroom since Zack was still downstairs. I stripped off my pajama bottoms and walked to my closet, wearing only my panties and pajama top.

Hospitals were cold, so even though it was supposed to reach nearly ninety degrees today, I chose a faded black T-shirt instead of a tank top. Still in only my panties, I draped the T-shirt over my arm and shifted to face the pile of folded pants on the shelf.

A tingle danced up my spine and I spun to find Zack sitting at the foot of my bed, watching me. Just like I'd watched him when he'd dressed in his room earlier. "I thought you were downstairs."

"I'm glad I'm not." He grinned.

"Um..." Grabbing a pair of jeans, I pulled them on as quickly as I could manage, nearly tripping myself in the process. "Wouldn't you be more comfortable in the living room?"

"Nope."

"Are you sure?" I bit my lip.

"Positive. You watched me dress. Now it's my turn. And don't be sneaking into the bathroom to finish."

"Fine." In my rush, I stumbled to the top drawer of my dresser. Selecting a lacy pink bra that matched my underwear, I snatched it and held it to my stomach, hoping he wouldn't see.

"Nice choice."

Damn.

Ignoring him, I darted back into the closet and angled my body so he could only see my back. Shrugging off my pajama top, I put my hands through the arm holes of my bra and reached behind to hook it.

"I'll get that for you."

Zack's warm breath on my bare shoulders had my every nerve at attention. I held absolutely still as he found both ends of the strap. The back of his hand was warm against my skin, but I couldn't see what he was doing. Or *not* doing. It became harder to breathe as I waited for him to either finish or...

"Are you going to hook me up?" I asked, my voice unsteady.

"I'm thinking about it."

What did that mean? He couldn't be considering discarding the bra altogether. Though I secretly hoped he would.

As he and I had gotten to know each other over the past weeks, he'd held back every step of the way, afraid that the legend of mixing species was true. Even if it was, that wouldn't stop me from being with Zack. We just had to be careful. But with Charles dead now, I only had Renzo to worry about. For all I knew, he'd only been passing through and was long gone now. If we did get weaker, maybe no one would be around to know and we'd have time to recover. *If* werewolves and shifters recovered from that kind of thing...

Whatever. I couldn't think about any of that. Didn't want to. All I wanted was for us to be together, however we could manage it, and damn the consequences.

A second later, I felt a slight tug on one side of my bra strap, then the other, as Zack connected the ends. Disappointment mingled with relief and I told myself it was for the best.

With him fully clothed and me in only a bra and jeans, I felt underdressed. I'd never been without a top in front of him — or any guy, for that matter. Except in a swimsuit, but this felt totally different. A wave of shyness washed over me.

His hands slid around my waist to my stomach and he pulled me against him. I leaned back and let my head loll to the side. He kissed my shoulder, then my neck as his hands traveled back to my hips and up my sides. A delicious shiver coursed through me. Then he gently turned me around to face him.

"God, you're amazing," he whispered into my ear.

Hope renewed, my heart pounded in anticipation as I unbuttoned his shirt and slid it past his shoulders, then tossed it across the room. He growled, scooped me up and laid me on the bed. The mattress dipped as Zack moved over me, his gaze wandering to the swells above the lace of my bra. When his warm, soft lips covered mine and our tongues tangled, electric fingers of pleasure spread from my stomach and out to my toes.

I arched toward him, my body straining to get closer as my fingers dipped past his waistband, my thumb brushing his zipper.

Zack sucked in a breath.

I bolted upright, planted my hands on his hips and gently pushed him back against the mattress. When I straddled him, his face was unreadable, eyes dark. Had I gone too far?

And then I was flat on my back again and he was on top of me, his mouth devouring me. Just when I didn't think I could hold back another second, he blazed a trail of kisses down my neck then settled on the exposed flesh around my bra, the stubble on his chin sending little goose bumps over my skin. Sliding a thumb underneath the bra strap, he dragged it over my shoulder.

I wanted Zack and had no doubts about my feelings for him. We'd never said those three words before, but they were hovering on the tip of my tongue now, begging to be set free. But did he love me back or was that just wishful thinking on my part? Did I really want to find out too late that he didn't feel the same way about me?

Zack whispered another kiss at the hollow of my throat. But now that my brain was working again — for the moment — I couldn't push those questions out of my head.

He didn't seem inclined to put on the brakes. In fact, he'd gone further than ever before. If neither of us stopped, how much further would we go and how weak would we become? How long before we regained our strength? Just a moment ago, I'd been willing to risk it all, but would a morning of bliss with Zack be worth risking our lives?

I wouldn't have him at all if we were both dead. But even if we lived, I couldn't predict the future and had no idea how long Zack was going to stick around. Not only that, he'd never even admitted he liked me. It was obvious he *lusted* me, but one L word was not exchangeable for the other. I knew he cared, but if he couldn't say it out loud, he wasn't ready to take the next step.

The room spun and I desperately wanted to stay on the ride. But we couldn't. I knew we shouldn't. "Zack…"

"What?" His eyes had a faraway look. "Did I do something wrong? Tell me what you like."

I laughed nervously as I extricated myself from him. "Oh, I like all of it," I said in a trembling voice. "A lot."

He blinked. "Then what's wrong?"

I couldn't believe he had to ask. Why wasn't he being the sensible one like usual? I pointedly put my palms on his face, lifting his chin and bringing his gaze above my neck. "Zack. We can't do this, right?"

"What?"

"We'll get weaker, remember? What if that guy at the coffee shop comes after us? Or werewolves come looking for Charles? We have to be able to protect ourselves."

Zack leaped off me and flattened himself against the far wall. Putting his head down, he squeezed his eyes shut and took a deep breath. "Oh, God, you're right. I'll wait for you in the car." He grabbed his shirt off the floor and disappeared.

"Uh, okay." Yeah, I was trying to be practical but he didn't have to run from me like I had the plague.

I hurriedly finished getting ready, locked up the house and got in the passenger side of my car. After putting on my seatbelt, I glanced his way when he still hadn't started the car. "Are you upset with me?"

His jaw tightened. "No, of course not. I'm the one who let it go too far. God, I can't believe that I have so little control that I almost put us in a vulnerable position."

"Zack, it wasn't *all* your fault. I was there too, you know."

"But I started it. Autumn, we can never be alone in your house again."

Damn, we had zero privacy anywhere else. "You're missing the point, though. We *did* resist and we're okay. Everything's fine."

"Next time might end differently though." He started the car, shaking his head. "Never again."

I flinched at his tone, then turned to stare out the window. It was a ten minute drive to the hospital and we spent half of that time in silence before he pulled over and pivoted in his seat. Looking down, he absently scratched on the fabric of the car seat with his index finger.

"I want you, Autumn. Like *really* want you — as you could tell. So this isn't me trying to push you away. But it's just plain stupid to risk our lives this way. I can't put you in danger like that."

Fresh from my bedroom victory — I mean, what girl wouldn't want that kind of a reaction from a guy? — I shouldn't have been so sensitive to what sounded like a prelude to dumping me. Again.

I stiffened.

# CHAPTER TEN

"WHERE ARE YOU going with this, Zack?" I wasn't sure I really wanted the answer.

"We're in too deep. We have to stop."

Not even a week had passed since he'd agreed not to push me away again. "Zack, you promised!"

"That was before we killed a scout," he said. "When Charles doesn't check in, others will come looking for me. I'll plead ignorance and point out how much weaker I am, that I couldn't have killed him. They'll buy that. But with more werewolves around, your chance of being discovered increases dramatically."

I held up a hand and glared at him. "I'm sorry, but I'm still stuck at the part where you broke your promise."

He turned away and leaned against the headrest, sighing. "That's not it at all. I'm still here, and I still want to be with you. I just think we need to do things differently from now on."

"And how's that?" I tilted my head, narrowing my eyes.

"For one thing, we shouldn't go running together anymore. Telling Charles we were there to make out worked with him, but it might not work on the next guy. I'll run alone from now on."

"Okay." I didn't love the idea, but if only one of us could go, it needed to be Zack. I didn't know how long I could stay in my human form, but I had a feeling it was a while. "What else?"

"People can't know we're together."

My brows scrunched in the middle and I twisted in my seat to face him. I really didn't like where this was going. "Because of Charles? He's dead. We don't have to worry about him anymore."

"No, but there will always be other werewolves. Renzo is proof of that." He bumped my knee with his knuckle and softened his voice. "All Charles had to do was get close enough to you and he figured it out."

"So we can't hang around together? Ever?" My chest tightened. Maybe Zack was about to break up with me after all. "Is that what you're saying?"

Zack shook his head. "Not exactly. They're more lenient with new recruits and you're my cousin's girlfriend's best friend. We can't help but get thrown together now and then. But we can't be a couple in public. It's too risky. And it's just smarter if everyone thinks we're only friends, even our friends and family. Otherwise, it could get messy."

But being apart could get messy too. "Because we'd have to explain to Trevor or Maya why we're pretending to break up."

"Exactly. Too complicated and too easy to slip up."

I pursed my lips and cast him a sideways look. "It feels like you're dumping me."

In one swift movement, he cupped the back of my neck and dragged me against him. Holding tight around my waist with his other arm, his mouth ravished mine until I was dizzy. My entire body tingled and I was pretty sure my eyes were glassy as he withdrew and breathed against my cheek, "You're still my girlfriend."

That was just the reassurance I needed to hear. I melted and rested my forehead on his shoulder.

Wait a minute... I covered my mouth to stifle a giggle.

"What's so funny?"

"Before, we pretended to date, but we weren't even friends. Now we're actually together, but we'll be acting like we're not."

Zack smiled for the first time since the bedroom incident.

"So far your plan doesn't seem too bad, I guess. What else?" I asked.

"You need to get better at sneaking in and out of my bedroom window. If my family knows you're doing it, so will a werewolf."

At least he still wanted me to do that.

"And it might be a good idea to have lunch away from each other now and then."

"Okay." I'd have to go all day without kissing him and some days sit at another table? Ugh. "Anything else?"

"Yes." He turned the key in the ignition and resumed driving. "Sometime over the next couple days, we need to have a big fight and break up in front of everyone. Like... tonight during prom."

So soon? "No, I don't want to ruin our prom. Let's

wait until Monday. Do it in the cafeteria or something."

"Autumn," he began, shooting me a quick glance before making a turn. "This is serious. The sooner we break up, the safer you'll be. For all we know, someone could be looking for Charles now. Who knows how often he checks in? What if they've already noticed he's missing? Someone could show up tomorrow."

Everything was happening way too fast and my already limited time with Zack was getting even shorter. I groaned. "If we do it too fast, they're not gonna buy it."

"You're probably right. Maybe we should have a little fight tonight at prom, then hang out with Maya and Trevor Sunday and have another one," he suggested. "That way it won't be such a surprise. I don't want them too freaked out."

"Brilliant." At least he was thinking things through and I could relax and enjoy my prom. Except for a small fight. "Which reminds me, I can't stay long at the hospital. Maya's meeting me at my house later. You know, we have to do our nails and hair and stuff for tonight."

† † †

I eyed the Scrabble tiles staring back and me, which spelled V-O-R-T-E-X. I found the perfect place to play it too — on a triple word square with the R set at the end of D-A-N-C-E, which made a new word and gave me even more points.

I'd won our last game by eighteen points and led this game with Favianne by a few less. With my current letters and us being near the end, she might not catch up. It didn't feel right to slaughter her two games in a row.

"I have crappy letters," I said. "Maybe I'll just skip my turn."

The smell of fresh brewed coffee tickled my nose, signaling Zack's return.

"Nice word," he said from over my shoulder. "Mom, you're going to get stomped on."

Her eyebrows flew up. "How interesting. Autumn was just complaining about her hand and threatened to pass."

Heat roared into my cheeks.

Zack laughed. "What were you thinking? My mom is ruthless when it comes to games. You would've regretted it."

"Do it," she ordered. "Take your turn. Zack, make sure she plays that word."

I laid the tiles one at a time and counted up my points. When I finished, she made a seven letter word, getting bonus points for using them all. Zack was right — crime wouldn't have paid.

He set the cardboard tray of lattes on a chair. "I'm going to see what's taking so long with the release papers. Be right back."

Too intent on my letters, I waved good-bye without looking. This time, my tiles really did stink. After searching the board for a place to play, I finally made a word.

"That's the best you can do?" she asked, smothering a smile.

I sighed. "Yes, all my letters are one-pointers. I

promise."

She nodded and studied her own letters.

"I was wondering..." I hesitated and reached for my coffee, taking a big gulp. "I'm not sure if it'll bother you to talk about this but..."

She abandoned her task and looked up. "You won't know unless you ask."

"How did Zack's father die?" Immediately, I regretted the question and making her relive it. "If it's upsetting to talk about it, though, you don't have to tell me."

"I can talk about it. With you." She inhaled and looked out the window. "We were camping one night, just a few miles from here. Lucio went searching for firewood while I stayed in the tent. He was gone for over a half hour, so as soon as I heard the growls, I knew something wasn't right. I ran to him as fast as I could, but it was too late." She shivered.

"He was already gone?" I asked.

"Not yet, but the bear still had him and was gnawing on his neck. There was so much blood everywhere. Even if I'd somehow gotten rid of the bear, Lucio wouldn't have made it. No one could have survived that." Favianne's eyes clouded with tears. "The bear dragged him away and I never saw him again."

That was the last image she had of Zack's father, the man she loved. My heart ached for her. "They never recovered his body?"

"No. Not a trace. I called the police right away. They said scavengers probably got the rest of him." Her eyes shone with tears and she blinked them away.

Had he been eaten, like how I ate Charles last night? He may have been a wolf at the time, but he was also part human. I'd eaten parts of someone who was also human. I hadn't thought about that aspect of it until now. *Human.*

"I'm so sorry." My stomach churned.

Yep, it had finally sunk in. A torrent of revulsion rose up in me and I knew I was going to hurl. "Be right back."

Forgetting there was a bathroom in her room, I scrambled out the door and booked it down the corridor. I found another restroom, grateful for single occupancy. I locked the door, dashed to the toilet and puked up my breakfast and all the coffee I'd just drank, until I was heaving up yellow goo.

Standing, I wiped my mouth with tissue and breathed deeply. If I ever found myself in that situation again, I'd be very sure not to eat my opponent. At that thought, I felt sick again and bent over.

Finally, I stopped convulsing. After rinsing my mouth and splashing my face, I finally left the bathroom. Zack was waiting for me in the hallway.

"Are you okay?" He felt my forehead and scanned my body, then finished the examination by sniffing me. "Sick?"

I nodded.

He narrowed his eyes. "But that doesn't happen to us. Ever," he said quietly. "What's going on?"

"When I was a bear, I didn't care. But now..." I shivered, grimacing. "I ate Charles."

Zack folded me into his arms. "It was him or us."

I crumpled against him. "Why can't we just be normal? Worry about what to wear to prom instead of wondering when a scout will turn up to kill us."

"Sorry, baby." His arms tightened around me a moment before he stepped back and skimmed his fingers down my arm. "Go finish your game and I'll follow up on the release papers. We're just waiting for the doctor to sign off. It should only be a few more minutes."

I nodded and returned to my chair in Favianne's room.

"I didn't mean to upset you." She shot me a worried look.

"No. It wasn't that," I lied. "Just something I ate. No big deal. Did you take your turn yet?" Getting off the subject would probably be a good thing.

"No, I was too concerned about you."

"I'm fine." I was absolutely certain my smile was convincing.

She returned to her letters and picked up a tile, then she put it back. "It's still hard to believe my Lucio is gone. A few years ago, I imagined seeing him in a crowd. He looked straight at me. I blinked and when I focused again, no one was there. Just wishful dreaming I guess."

"Does Zack know you saw him?" My intense curiosity would probably seem odd to her so I fiddled with one of the tiles to appear casual.

She shook her head. "It wasn't my Lucio — just my imagination. He's dead. I *saw* him die."

I nodded. "You never told Zack?"

Favianne smiled. "About my wild imagination? Heavens, no. Zack was devastated when he lost his father. We rarely talk about him."

"Does Zack know how he died?"

"No and I'd appreciate you not telling him either. I don't want that image in his head. You didn't even know his father and look how you reacted."

"It was just something I ate. Really." It was true, except in this case, it was the *memory* of something I'd eaten. I shuddered as my stomach turned again. "So how does Zack *think* he died?"

"A very bad car accident."

I was surprised Zack had bought that story. I couldn't imagine a werewolf being easy to kill that way, unless it was a really grisly accident. Regardless, Lucio was dead. Because, surely if he were alive, he would have made his presence known, at least to his son. Either way, Zack didn't need false hope.

"So... you're feeling better?" she asked me.

"Yes, I'm fine. I felt nauseous, but it passed."

She studied my face a beat, then spoke hesitantly. "It's not... morning sickness, is it?"

"What?" I prayed to God she didn't mean what I thought she meant.

"Is it possible you might be, uh, pregnant?"

My eyes widened and my jaw dropped to my chest.

She shrugged. "I have to ask, sweetheart and you're in the right place to find out. A blood test will tell us, even if you're not very far along."

"You're sprung, Mom." Zack entered the room, proudly brandishing several pieces of paper. "A nurse will be here in a minute to wheel you out."

"Zack," I said. "Your mother thinks I was throwing up from morning sickness."

He frowned. "Morning sickness?"

Favianne raised her eyebrows at Zack.

His face went white. "Mom, it's impossible. Trust me."

She didn't look convinced. "We've talked about protection and you know how important it is but, accidents happen. You can talk to me."

Zack shook his head. "Mom, please. Just drop it. We haven't progressed that far in our relationship. I swear. And that's all I'm going to say about it."

Her smile faded and I thought she looked disappointed. I wondered what it must be like for her to know she wouldn't live to see any grandchildren born. Zack and I were too young for that, though, and we had way too much going on. And, of course, we'd only known each other a few weeks.

But did I want to have children with Zack some day? Absolutely.

I squelched the feelings rising up. Weird emotions — like wanting to have a baby with him right away, just to watch the joy on Favianne's face.

I pushed that thought from my mind.

# CHAPTER ELEVEN

"WOW, MAYA." HER dress was to die for. The exquisite beaded halter top dipped low in the front with a long, pleated pink chiffon skirt. "Trevor's going to faint when he sees you in this."

Maya laughed. "I hope so. Right about when Zack keels over at the sight of you in that lacy cream number you'll be wearing."

"Oh, I traded that in a few days ago. Forgot to tell you."

She gave me a startled look. "Why'd you get rid of it?"

"Because I bought it to wear to prom with Daniel. I don't want to think of him while I'm with Zack. Ew."

"I don't blame you." She jumped onto my bed and grinned. "Let's see the new one."

I disappeared into my closet and reappeared a moment later. After unzipping the bag, I pulled out the dress and held it in front of me.

"I liked that cream dress, but blue will go much better against your olive skin." Maya fingered the shimmering fabric. "Love that it's strapless. *Super* sexy."

"My thoughts exactly." I smiled.

"Try it on," Maya demanded. "Maybe it will give me

some inspiration for what to do with your hair."

Humoring her, I let the robe drop to floor. I stepped into the dress and faced the mirror while Maya zipped me up. No bows, ruffles, layers or folds. Just elegant simplicity that gently molded to my waist and thighs before draping luxuriously around my ankles. Faint slashes of silver covered the length of the gown like silver rays of sunshine and a sprinkling of darker blue sequins made the fabric come alive.

"Totally classy," she said when I twirled for her. "And really shows off your smokin' bod. Zack won't even be able to stutter like when you wore that purple dress on our double date. He'll go straight into a heart attack."

I giggled. "It has matching gloves that go to my elbows."

"Zack's a dead man."

† † †

I'd been saving pictures of hair and makeup for the last few months, just waiting for the day when we would put those ideas to use. Other girls paid professionals to pamper them before prom, but Maya and I enjoyed doing our own hair and makeup. As particular as we were, we'd probably backseat drive the professional and drive her crazy anyway.

After setting Maya's hair in hot rollers and finger brushing it out — which was a laborious task considering all that thick, blond hair — I gathered a section from her crown and temple, then pinned it up. Soft, wavy locks cascaded strategically over her shoulders and down her back.

I grabbed the makeup box and chose a smoky blue eye shadow for her eyes, going a little heavier on her lids than I normally would. Some mascara, just a little bronzer, then a soft pink lipstick that matched her dress.

She grinned at her reflection. "Wow."

"I'm going to dump Zack and go to the prom with *you*," I said.

"No offense, but I prefer Trevor for that sort of thing. Okay, your turn. Sit." Maya spent a moment running her fingers through my hair as she studied it. "Definitely an updo... maybe let it go a little messy. If it's up and out of Zack's way, he has easy access to all that incredible skin. What's up with it anyway? You have this glow about you."

I shrugged.

Her eyes popped. "Are you... oh, my God, are you pregnant?"

Heat crept into my cheeks and my mouth fell open. The most embarrassing assumption ever, twice in one day. I hated having to convince everyone that Zack and I did little more than cuddle. And that when we *slept* together, we really were sleeping. "No, I'm absolutely positive that I'm not. I swear."

"Pregnancy tests aren't one hundred percent accurate, you know." She gave me a doubtful look.

Sure, I was about to waste my breath, but I couldn't tell her that as a shape-shifter my body always strived for its optimum state and the glow stemmed from being so healthy. "Maya, Zack and I haven't gone that far."

She gathered my hair and studied my reflection in the mirror. "Maybe it's from being in love."

Zack and I were in love? Yeah, right. And that's why we were about to have a fight later tonight at prom. This was a perfect opportunity to plant the seed, so they would buy our breakup later. My stomach tightened at the thought. I knew it wasn't real, but still...

"Too bad he doesn't return my feelings."

"You're blind. That boy is crazy for you." She scoffed and let my hair drop. "Maybe most of your hair should be down with just enough held back to show off your shoulders and all that glorious skin in between. The bangs should be straight and parted at the side and the long sections in the back wavy."

She got busy creating her masterpiece. When she finished nearly forty-five minutes later, I looked in the mirror. "I don't know what to say, Maya. You really outdid yourself."

"I know." She beamed. "Zack can thank me later. And now for your makeup. We want soft yet sophisticated." She tapped her chin, then plucked a charcoal shadow with a hint of silver from the box, highlighted my brow bones with a lighter shade and defined my brows. "Just a smidge of bronzer then lip gloss. No color on those lips."

I nodded.

She rolled it on then handed it to me. "Put this in your purse. I have a feeling it's not going to last long once Zack sees you." Maya chuckled. "I can't wait to see his reaction. Don't forget, we have to stop at my house so my mom can take pictures."

A cloud of loneliness for my parents wafted over me and I wondered if my mom felt like she was missing out on this big day. My parents had chilled a lot these past weeks but not seeing me off to prom? I was sure they would be here if they had a choice — which only made me more certain that something was definitely up. Tomorrow, I would begin the search for clues into their past.

"Geez, what planet did you fly off to?" Maya asked, jolting me.

"Just missing my mom," I answered with a sad smile.

She rested a hand on my arm. "We'll take lots of pictures for her. C'mon, let's get into our dresses. The guys will be here soon."

We helped each other into our gowns and, right on time, the doorbell rang. I slipped on my gloves and we grabbed our purses. Maya and I answered the door together, not knowing which date would be there at the door.

Both. And they stood locked in place with their mouths open.

"Maya, will you marry me?" Trevor blurted out.

She laughed. "Let's see if you feel the same later when I'm no longer wearing this dress."

"If I got you out of that dress, I'd be even more positive that I want to marry you."

"That's not what I meant." Maya giggled, thumping his chest playfully.

I watched Zack and waited for a response, wondering if he had any other reaction than catching flies. I reached out and applied a gentle pressure under his chin, coaxing him to close his mouth.

"Let them go." Zack's eyes smoldered. "You and I can stay here all night."

"In my house? Alone?" Obviously, he wasn't in his right head.

Zack stepped up onto the threshold, put his hands at my hips, and steered me away from the front door. "Good-bye Maya, Trevor." Without taking his eyes off me, his foot shot out and kicked the door. Just before it closed on Maya's face, she jumped back with wide eyes.

"Zack, what's going on?"

"I just want to be alone with you." He growled low in his throat. "Let's find out if it's true or just a myth."

I took a step back, my brows flying up. "Whatever you're thinking, stop. What about staying strong to survive?"

"Don't care anymore," he rasped, stalking toward me.

"We can't risk losing our powers."

His eyes devoured the length of me as he reached for my waist and dragged me against his chest.

Oh, my God, he hadn't heard a word I'd said. Or he really didn't care. As our mouths fused together and heat shot through my veins, I wasn't sure I cared either.

No wonder Hannah and Eli were willing to die as humans.

According to werewolf legend, Hannah was a werewolf betrothed to the king. She'd fallen in love with Eli, a shape-shifter, and ran away with him. Despite being the most hunted werewolf and shape-shifter in history, they were never found or heard from again. The entire werewolf community believed they'd grown so weak from mixing species that they eventually became human and died of old age.

It sounded tempting to grow old with Zack. But first we had to worry about the next few weeks.

I pushed against his chest and when I'd gained a few inches, I raised my voice. "Zack, we can't."

He blinked and a moment later, grabbed my hand and tugged me toward the door. "We have to get out of here."

"Exactly." I breathed a huge sigh of relief. As much as I wanted him, now was not the time.

Thankfully, Trevor and Maya hadn't left yet and we climbed into the limo with them.

*I don't know what I was thinking*, he told me silently. Then he said aloud, "You can't blame me for losing it. You're the most beautiful girl I've ever seen in my life."

It wasn't as good as saying he loved me, but his words made me quiver inside. I leaned toward Zack and kissed him on the cheek. "Then we're perfect for each other, aren't we?"

† † †

Getting pictures taken at Maya's turned out to be a pretty big production. Her mother flitted around her daughter with watery eyes, cooing phrases like, "My baby's all grown up," and "I can't believe how beautiful you look!"

By the time we made it to the front door, I couldn't handle another second of her gushing. It reminded me how much my own parents used to hover over me. But as we made our way to Trevor's for another round of pictures, I wished my own parents were around to gush. My chest tightened every time I thought of them.

At Zack's, Aunt Cara and Mac double-teamed us — one camera getting shots for Zack's mom and the other camera for them. Favianne had ventured out of her room for the occasion, resting on the living room sofa and choreographing our poses.

"Make sure to get some pictures of only Autumn," Favianne told her sister.

Zack left my side to stand beside Cara. Before to-night, I'd only seen him in casual clothes and I'd been so sure it couldn't get any better.

I'd been dead wrong.

As my gaze lingered on Zack in his classic black tux and bow tie, he grinned and my heart fluttered. It wasn't his movie star looks or his musky scent that made me quiver. It was the way he looked at me, like I was the only one in the room.

At that moment, I knew with utter certainty that I'd never love anyone else the way I loved him. If he could return even a fraction of my feelings for him... well, it would be epic. My heart soared at the thought. An instant later, it plummeted to a crash landing when I remembered he wasn't mine to keep. Soon, Zack would be gone forever.

# CHAPTER TWELVE

NOT EVERYONE GAWKED at us as we passed through the doorway of the school gymnasium — a few of the guests had their backs to us. Since Zack and I had a squabble planned, an attentive audience was convenient. But a ball of dread formed in the pit of my stomach just thinking of what we were about to do.

The gym was decorated in an Egyptian theme. Giant palm trees lined the entryway and gold lamé strips of fabric draped the tops of the walls along the ceiling. Busts of Pharaohs stood in the corners interspersed with mummies and fake sarcophaguses. A sphinx sat by a table covered in linens decorated with hieroglyphics.

The center of the huge room was packed with people thumping and gyrating to the beats of a rap song. It boomed through the speakers and vibrated into my toes. So much for anyone overhearing our fight. We claimed a table in the corner where we could watch the action. Just as I settled into my seat, the DJ switched to a slow song.

Zack offered me his hand. "Will you dance with me?"

I slipped my hand into his. "Absolutely."

Leaving Maya and Trevor to hold our place, I let him lead me to the dance floor. Thinking he'd go slow like everyone else, I slid my arms around his neck. With one hand flattened against my lower back, he held out his other hand for mine. I frowned, wondering what he was doing. Before I knew it, we'd slid effortlessly across the room. With his thumb at my waist, he coaxed me away and raised his arm, compelling me to twirl. Then suddenly, I was pressed against him.

I laughed. "You've got some good moves, Zack De Luca."

"My mom made me take lessons with her," he explained, gliding us past other couples. "I hated it at the time, but now I'm grateful."

"I'll have to thank her for that later." I wasn't sure if my heart was beating faster from the exertion or from dancing with the guy I loved. His breath tickled my temple and I became aware of his hand resting dangerously low on my back, his thigh brushing mine. I closed my eyes and rested my cheek on his shoulder as emotion flooded me.

"Mmm..."

"What?" I squeaked and cleared my throat.

"You smell really great," he whispered.

"Oh." A million butterflies in my stomach flapped their wings in unison. I was in way too deep with Zack and couldn't imagine not being with him. What if they came for us tomorrow and this was our last moment together?

"You're trembling."

I grimaced, not wanting to spoil our night with a dose of reality. But if I avoided the question, he'd just be more persistent in finding out what was bothering me. "Just wondering if we'll make it to graduation before more werewolves show up."

"Shh. Don't think about any of that. Let's just enjoy ourselves tonight and forget they exist." He lightly stroked my spine. "You look beautiful, as always."

"Thanks." Zack was right. Worrying wouldn't change anything. Except maybe suck the fun out of my time with him. I smiled, determined to stop stressing. "You clean up well."

Something vaguely familiar in my peripheral vision drew my gaze to the gymnasium door — the black girl we'd seen when we'd taken Zack's mom to the doctor. I went rigid in Zack's arms. "That's the girl from the hospital."

The she-wolf was just as lovely as when I'd first seen her. She wore a slinky black floor-length dress that clung to her slim curves — but not too much. Her tight black curls had been straightened and fell past her shoulders. She turned to face the guy next to her, giving us a view of the back of her dress — or lack thereof — revealing her back and shoulders.

"What's she doing here? She doesn't go to our school," he mumbled as he twirled me again.

I snuck another quick glance at her. Greg, our senior class quarterback, slung a beefy arm around the she-wolf's shoulders. "I wonder what she sees in that scum."

My very first day at Verdugo Hills Academy, I'd had to return to my car after the bell rang. The parking lot was deserted except for Greg who'd been standing by an old faded sedan. He gingerly untied a plastic bag and dumped the contents through the open window into the back seat. I only got a glimpse of the brown blob, but that was enough to know I didn't want my nose anywhere near that car after the sun had baked it into the upholstery. From that day on, I always kept my car windows shut tight.

"What are the chances that her being here at our prom is just a coincidence?" I couldn't see her anymore without craning my neck and I didn't want to be obvious. But I could see Zack and he was still staring.

"Slim, I'd say," he answered, eyes narrowed.

When the song ended and the tempo picked up, Zack escorted me back to our table. Maya and Trevor huddled together, lost in their own little world. I scanned the room for the werewolf girl, wanting to keep tabs on her.

Instead, my eyes found Gina. Her auburn hair had been pulled tight against her scalp and knotted at the nape of her neck. Long beads of clear crystal hung from her ears with a matching necklace and bracelet. Her hooker-red gown was open at her waist with thin strips of fabric connecting the rest of the dress parts and revealing an awful lot of skin. With each step, her legs peeked through a slit that ran all the way to the top of her thigh.

Scanning the faces of the other students, I saw a lot

of guys ogling her. "Gina looks pretty," I said to Zack.

He squeezed my hand. "You're worth a hundred of her," he whispered in my ear. "And it isn't just how you look, but... just everything about you."

I flashed him a smile, but concentrating was difficult with a strange werewolf nearby.

"Let's get something to snack on. You two want anything?" he asked Trevor and Maya.

They shook their heads. "We'll get something later," Trevor said.

A dozen people stood in line for food, so I wanted to be sure it was worth the wait. I took a moment to check out the spread — even though my stomach was probably too nervous to do anything with it.

"Hi."

I turned around, startled to see Greg's wolf-date.

"I saw you two in the hospital waiting room a couple days ago, didn't I?" she asked with a friendly smile.

I nodded, afraid she'd keep talking. As nice as she seemed, she was still a werewolf. Zack didn't say anything either.

"I'm Alura. Nice to meet you." She held out her hand, her smile widening when I took it. Then she shook hands with Zack.

"How'd you hook up with that douche bag?" He nodded toward Greg as he released her hand.

A giggle escaped her. "Barely know him. I saw him a couple times at a coffee place near our hotel. He mentioned going to prom and I told him I'd never been to one so he invited me."

"Probably best if you kept it that way. You know, the barely knowing him part," I said, melting into a little imaginary circle with her. I found myself liking her despite my reluctance. She was so warm and open and hard to resist.

"I believe you," she grinned. "Especially since he's already hinted twice about a hotel reservation and he only picked me up a half hour ago. As if I'd go there with *him*." She made a gagging noise and her eyes darted to Zack — as they frequently had the last couple minutes. I sensed something. I hoped it was just an innocent camaraderie, a recognition of their mutual werewolfness.

Zack's fingertips made contact with my arm as though he wanted me to hear what she said silently.

*My uncle said he met a young werewolf and three of his human friends at a coffee shop the other day. Was that you?* Alura moved ahead in line, leaning over and taking a paper plate as though she weren't carrying on a telepathic conversation with another werewolf.

*That would make Renzo your uncle*, Zack replied, breaking contact with me, mimicking her actions and handing me a plate. I took it and reconnected with him again by resting my other hand on his arm.

*Who's your supervisor?*

*Charles.*

*I didn't sense any other werewolves at the hospital or near here. Did he go out of town or something?* Alura loaded her plate with crackers and cheese.

Great, that's all we needed — someone asking

questions about someone I'd killed.

*Not that I know of. He's around somewhere.* Zack set two cookies on his plate then one on mine. *What brings you here? Haven't you been assigned?*

*Yes, but since we haven't married yet, I've been granted special permission to accompany my uncle on vacation.*

*That's cool.* Zack poured some punch into a plastic cup, briefly glancing my way. He handed me the cup and fixed another. *How long is your vacation?*

*A few weeks, I think, depending on when I'm needed back.*

"These desserts look great." She plopped a chocolate number on her plate, then stepped away from the table. "Well, I'd better get back to the douche. Maybe I'll see you guys around. I'm at the coffee shop a lot. If you see me, say hello."

"We will," I said. "Nice meeting you."

She waved and swished gracefully away.

Zack surreptitiously watched her leave. "She's absolutely perfect," he whispered for my ears only.

"What do you mean?" Perfect for what? Although I wasn't sure I wanted to know.

"To break us up."

I stared at him, rooted to the floor. "I hope you're kidding."

He headed toward our table. When he noticed a moment later I wasn't behind him, he doubled back. Up close, he lowered his voice. "Not for real. You can *pretend* to be jealous. You know, accuse me of cheating on you."

"Oh." It was slightly alarming to be so relieved. And disconcerting to discover how precarious our relationship truly was. Realizing those things did not give me a good feeling at all. Sure, I was still one of the most popular girls in school. But popularity was a façade, an illusion. It was all about who was the better actor and who was more convincing, not who was the better person. Greg was proof of that. Me? I was the same insecure girl who just last week so easily believed that the boy I loved didn't like me back.

What was I doing with Zack anyway? Trying to keep a werewolf who could never truly be mine. And through all our kissing, playing and cuddling, he couldn't even verbally express his feelings for me. What if they weren't strong enough? What if the only thing that carried our relationship forward was physical attraction? Something that shallow could only be temporary. I needed more.

"Autumn, what's wrong?" Zack asked.

"Just not looking forward to our breakup, I guess." I smiled even though I didn't feel it.

"Don't worry. We'll make it fun. You could slap me and make a scene." He grinned then, noting my expression, lifted my chin to look into my eyes. "It'll be okay. We'll just have to get through each day, then we'll be together again at night."

Right. We'd still have our nights. He wouldn't say something like that if he didn't really care about me, right?

Gina tapped Zack on the shoulder. "How about a

dance?"

I couldn't believe she had the balls to ask knowing Zack would say no. Her only purpose had to be to piss me off. It worked.

He seemed to consider her offer then turned to me, a questioning look in his eye. *She could break us up too*, Zack told me silently.

I realized Gina was perfect — just as perfect as Alura. *Gina would enjoy it, that's for sure. It's your call.* I left them standing there, returning to Maya and Trevor.

"Sure," I heard him answer to Gina. The contents of my stomach churned.

# CHAPTER THIRTEEN

I GLANCED OVER my shoulder and watched Zack lead Gina to the dance floor. Seeing them together was like being buried six feet under and slowly running out of air.

Maya's eyes narrowed. "Why is Zack dancing with that whore?"

"He likes to dance. Besides, they have a science project they're doing together." I shrugged, making an effort to get the words through my constricted throat. I wasn't sure if what I'd said was still true, but it was the best I could come up with.

Maya glanced at me, then Zack. Trevor did the same. She rose unexpectedly, marched to them and cut in on their dance. Gina could've made a scene but, thankfully, she had enough sense to see that fighting with Maya over someone else's boyfriend would've made her the talk of the school for days. Gina held her head high, smiled and casually walked away. I laughed and looked at Trevor.

"Maya's amazing, isn't she?" He grinned.

"Yes, she is."

Trevor and Maya went inside for the after-prom party, but Zack and I lingered in the limo. He dragged me onto his lap, then pushed a button and the divider rolled up to block the driver's view.

"This is our last weekend in public as a couple."

"Yeah...," I said. "And I'd like to enjoy this time together, so can we not talk about the end, even if it's only pretend?"

"We don't have to talk at all." With his hands at my waist, he gently pressed his thumbs against my hips to coax me backward, until I lay horizontally along the seat. His eyes roamed my face, slowly, like we had all the time in the world. "It's like... you're too perfect to touch."

I made an extra effort to force my lungs to work. Breathe. "But you'd better touch me or I'm going to be super pissed off."

Zack laughed softly, scooting to the edge of the seat at my side. "The first time I saw you..." He moved a lock of dark hair off my shoulder and trailed a fingertip along my collarbone to my shoulder. "I thought you were super pretty. But I also thought you were totally stuck up. You can't imagine my annoyance when I couldn't stop staring at you. It was frustrating being drawn to someone I didn't like."

That's why he had always seemed to be scowling at me.

"A couple times, I picked up your scent and followed

you, just out of curiosity." He held each side of my waist and took a long slow breath. "I didn't think you could get any prettier but, I swear, you *have* since you've started maturing into a shape-shifter." His voice quieted. "Everything about you makes me want you more."

It was difficult to determine which would lead to trouble faster — his words or his touch or the way he was looking at me. A hum worked its way through me, building. If he didn't kiss me soon...

Lowering his lips to mine, his inquisitive tongue brought the hum to a purr. He kissed me deeper. Caught up in Zack, I hadn't realized he'd shifted his full weight onto me.

"Maybe we should have the driver drop us off at your house," he said between kisses on my neck.

Zack had made it clear multiple times that my place was the riskiest place for us to be. Apparently he no longer possessed clarity of thinking. It was up to me now to keep us strong.

Reluctantly, I pushed my palms against his chest. "We should go inside, don't you think?"

"No." He stared at me a moment longer, then nodded. "Yes."

I chuckled as I straightened his tie and checked his suit. After making sure my dress wasn't askew, I let him usher me out of the limo.

John and a few of his friends had saved up all semester for an after-prom party, knowing they would *never* be invited anywhere by the popular crowd. One of their dads owned a packaging plant and agreed to let them use it, providing they paid for a cleaning crew. The most important requirement, though, was that they not allow any alcohol on the premises. They happily agreed and handed over their meager savings. The boys had spent their Saturday moving things around and preparing. John deejayed and Janine took turns with the other party masterminds, making sure no rules were broken.

The place was jammed with people. And it was louder than the gymnasium, if that was possible.

As Zack and I entered the huge warehouse, my eyes found Gina right away in her bright red gown. What was she doing there? Shouldn't she be at an A-lister party? Searching the crowd, I found Alura too. I tried telling myself it was a good thing; it would give Zack and I more fuel for our imminent public quarrel. Still, it bothered me to have them there. Gina for obvious reasons and Alura because she was exactly the kind of girl he needed — beautiful, sweet and the same species as him. Unlike me.

"Zack, I'd better not catch you dancing with anyone but Autumn," Maya warned, appearing at our sides and giving him the evil eye. "Do you hear me? I still haven't forgiven you for dancing with that slut earlier."

"Yes, ma'am," he answered solemnly, a smile teasing the corner of his mouth. "I'll get started on that right away."

As he led me to the dance floor, I caught Gina staring at us. She looked way too smug. Whatever her scheme of revenge against me, it was already in motion. It had to be. And it wouldn't be long before I knew all about it. Once Zack and I "broke up," she'd be even smugger. Just great. I reminded myself again that our fight wouldn't be real and he'd still be mine.

Thinking about the impending doom wasn't helping my mood. I needed a distraction. After a quick check around the room and seeing that Alura was too far away to sense the energy from our silent exchange, I asked Zack, *What did you mean earlier tonight when you asked Alura if she'd been assigned yet?*

He raised my arm over my head and twirled me. *Every newly matured female werewolf gets assigned to a pack and a mate, once they finish orientation.*

*So if she's been a werewolf for any length of time, she's engaged or married?* I glanced over my shoulder to make sure Alura was still at the other end of the room.

*Yeah. If she were married, she wouldn't be allowed to leave her husband or the pack for more than a few days at a time.* He held me a little closer and pressed his lips to my forehead.

A fast song kicked up so we took a break from the dance floor to get refreshments. I spied Alura heading our way.

"Great party, huh?" She smiled.

As much as I didn't want to like her, I couldn't help it. There was something so genuinely nice about her. Exactly the opposite of Gina.

"Yeah, John really pulled it off," I said.

Zack slung an arm around my waist. "What brings

you here? I thought maybe you'd go to one of the cooler parties."

She grinned. "I thought *this* was the cool party. You guys are here, right?"

"You should sit with us." As soon as the words were out of my mouth, I regretted them. What was I thinking? I glanced at Maya who was looking at me like I'd lost my mind for bringing in a fifth wheel — and a hot one at that. But I already knew hanging out with another werewolf was the worst idea ever.

Alura accepted, choosing a seat on the other side of Zack. Maya quickly warmed up to her, asking where she was from and how long she planned to stick around. Soon, we were all talking like old friends, but I hadn't forgotten that Alura might be the catalyst to end my ideal life with Zack.

I wondered how our new relationship would weather the outside interferences once we were "single." Would Alura view him as a prospect? I knew she was engaged, but she seemed too casual about being away from her fiancé who had been assigned to her. Maybe she didn't love him. How easy would it be for her to fall for someone else?

"You ready for another dance?" I asked Zack.

"Absolutely." He grinned. As soon as we got to the center of the room, the tempo changed and everyone slowed. "Perfect timing." He flattened me against him and buried his face in my hair.

I concentrated on the feel of his arms flexing around me, the warmth of his body, his musky scent, and the way he held me close on the dance floor with his cheek against mine. Everyone else fell away and it was just Zack and me. Peace settled over me and for the first time since we'd left Zack's house earlier that evening, I forgot about shape-shifters, werewolves or ex-friends plotting revenge. I was just a girl, dancing at prom with the boy I loved.

† † †

In the early hours of morning, long after prom ended, we dropped Maya off, then me. I said good night to Trevor, gave Zack a quick kiss, and climbed out of the limo. I intended to go to their house shortly, but I had to dress down first. Sneaking into Zack's room later would give me practice using his bedroom window so I wouldn't get caught doing it after we "broke up."

After changing into some sleep shorts and a tank, I sprinted over to Zack's. Under the cover of a bush close to his room, I watched Mac and Cara's window. Likely, they were asleep, but that's what I'd thought before and been spotted. No shadows moved beyond the curtain, no whispers, and I could hear their steady breathing.

Even if one of them woke, it didn't matter. I had no intention of anyone knowing I was there. After shifting into a raccoon, I crept the several feet to the window. I waited on the ledge, my tiny paw scratching on the glass.

Zack lifted the window and I squeezed through the opening, shifting as soon as I hit the floor. I stepped into his arms and laid my head on his shoulder. Running his hand over my hair, he rubbed his chin against my cheek. *You always take too long to get here.*

The way he touched me made me feel so... loved. I had a powerful urge to tell him I loved him. But I restrained myself.

*I was thinking...* Zack said, leading me to the bed. *Maybe you should start eating meat again. If you're satisfied, it might be easier to kill a werewolf without eating him.*

I crawled under the covers. *So... you think if I weren't denying myself, I'd have more control?*

*Maybe.* He scooted onto the bed and snuggled up against me. *It's something to consider.*

*The meat thing is intense. I don't want to deal with that craziness every single day.* I turned on my side to face him. *Using your logic, though, maybe we need to make out more so you have better control. You've been slipping lately, not that I'm complaining.* I rolled over on top of him and snickered.

*You're not very helpful.* He suppressed a laugh and pushed me off.

I giggled quietly, taking my usual position with my head on his chest. *So what's with the werewolves arranging marriages? Kinda behind the times, aren't they?*

*Yeah. They're technologically advanced, but King Mortimer has been ruling forever and hasn't changed much over the centuries. Neither have his subjects. Women are still property with almost no rights and they're told who to marry.*

*A thousand years of that crap. I don't understand why the women don't rise up against the system.* I turned over and faced the other way, taking his arm with me and slinging it over my waist.

*The majority of werewolves have been around for centuries,* Zack replied. *The newly turned ones are outnumbered and much weaker. They don't stand a chance. And the rare born werewolf like Alura would be raised to think just like them and wouldn't know any different.*

*Why do you think Alura was born and not turned?*

*Because she mentioned Renzo being her uncle. I guess that doesn't necessarily guarantee anything though.* Zack scooted closer against my back, making me grateful to the guy who invented spooning. He deserved a medal. *If you think about it, werewolves aren't that different than humans. People had slavery less than a hundred and fifty years ago and women only got the right to vote in the last century, right?*

*There goes any hope I had of shape-shifters being seen as equal any time soon,* I said.

*I'm glad I wasn't exposed to their way of thinking. Although it'd be a lot easier if I was more like them. Both of us would be safer.* He softened the sting of the words with a kiss at the nape of my neck.

*It's fascinating how you talk about werewolves as* they *and* them, *like you're not one of them.*

*I'll never be one of them.*

*No, you won't. Maybe one day when the women are free, shape-shifters will be too.* My lids closed against my will.

*Thank you for tonight, Autumn. I had a great time.*

† † †

Feather-light kisses rained down, caressing my cheek, my forehead and lips. I squeezed closer to the warmth, wrapping it around me along with the comforter.

*Autumn, time to wake up.*

I tried to quiet the voice in my head, but it wouldn't obey.

*Autumn!*

Opening my eyes, I saw Zack. "Good morning," I whispered.

*Time to go. The sun will come up any minute.* He yanked at my covers.

Blanket thievery. Brutal. I blinked and sat up, nodding.

*We'll meet later, okay? It's our last official day as a couple*, he said. *I definitely want some time alone with you before the big fight.*

*See you soon.* I planted a quick kiss on his nose and hopped out of bed to make tracks for home.

My entire house needed a good scrubbing and I was desperate to do laundry. As I gathered my dirty clothes, my thoughts drifted to Gina. She'd tried to hook up with Zack before the dance, and he'd made it clear he wasn't interested. By now, she had to accept nothing would happen between them. But maybe she wasn't trying to snag him. Maybe she just wanted to cause enough friction so we'd eventually break up.

When the public breakup happens and she realizes her wish has come true, will she still hold a grudge against me? And how hard would she pursue him now that he was supposedly single? She didn't stand a chance of winning him over, but I'd want to smack Gina as she tried.

Zack's reactions to me yesterday proved his control wasn't always perfect. I wondered again how far he'd gone with Gina when they'd dated weeks ago. Could she have tempted him to go as far as she'd hinted? I couldn't think about the answer without wanting to pluck out my own eyeballs.

*Autumn?*

*Zack, where are you?*

*We can hear each other a block away. Cool.*

I smiled to myself. *Yeah, pretty handy. What's up?*

*We need to arm wrestle, but it has to be in private. Your house is perfect.*

Lip wrestling sounded like so much more fun. *Sure. When?*

*I'm running some errands for my mom, then I'll stop by. Do me a favor and have some real clothes on when I get there?*

I chuckled. *See you soon.*

# CHAPTER FOURTEEN

OUR PALMS LOCKED against each other, elbows braced on the table as we mentally prepared ourselves for battle.

"One...," Zack said. "Two... three."

I drove my hand toward his. As if frozen in time, neither arm moved. He put more force behind his push, nudging my arm backward and I matched it.

"Are you going to cry uncle?" he asked, after several moments of a standstill.

"Ha! You're just trying to distract me so you can avoid a beating."

Zack chuckled, which opened the door for me to gain on him. My arm budged an inch in my favor. "It was nice seeing Alura last night," he said. "And Gina."

I lost my inch of momentum and ended up at our starting point. "You're a shark, just like your mom."

"Yep." His muscles strained against my arm. "I don't think either of us will win this one."

Though my energy waned, more power simmered just below the surface. Maybe he'd give up before I did. Or not. "Shall we call it a draw?"

Zack nodded and released his grip. "The older we get, the stronger we are."

"Yeah. So?" I tilted my head, wondering where he was going with it.

"I wonder if we inherit our parents' strength. You know, if the parents were ancient, would you be stronger than a shape-shifter with younger, weaker parents?"

That made sense. Food for thought anyway. "You never read anything about that in your books?"

He shook his head. "No."

I mashed my lips together as I contemplated this new theory. Abruptly, he stood and tugged on my hand, one side of his mouth curving up mischievously. He slowly brought my arm up to drape over his shoulder then clamped onto my hips and yanked me against him.

Uh-oh.

He bent toward me but instead of kissing me, he nuzzled my neck. A web of tingles swept over my skin and I shivered. I dragged his mouth to mine and opened. His hand slipped under my shirt and his hot fingers on my bare skin woke me up from my Zack-induced haze. Obviously, Zack's will power had completely deserted him. If he went any further, I wasn't sure I could stop either.

I flattened my palms against his rock hard stomach. "As tempting as this is... no. We need to go." I backed away, turned and snatched up my purse before darting outside.

He joined me on the front porch, grinning. "Once again, you saved me from myself."

I groaned. "Yes, well, it's not easy. What are we doing today?"

"I was thinking of a museum. There's an arboretum just a few minutes from here, if you'd prefer that."

"The arboretum sounds good." I beamed.

† † †

We held hands, ambling through the narrow paths past the exotic plants and the scents of fragrant blooms wafting up to invade my senses.

"What exactly does your mom have?" I asked.

"Autoimmune disorder." He glanced at me, then faced ahead again, veering around a boulder. "Her body attacks itself. She takes suppressants to calm her immune system, but they leave her open to getting sick easily."

"That's why she's weak and stays in bed?"

"She's weak because over the years, the various illnesses have damaged her heart and lungs."

"I feel so bad for her." I stared at the sidewalk as the cracks in the concrete passed under my feet.

"Me, too." He stopped, interlocking his fingers with mine and bringing the back of my hand to his lips. "She's doing better, even up and around, since the antibiotics."

"That's great. So much improvement in just a couple days."

"The last few weeks have been rough, but she's not usually in bed all the time. It'll be a while before I lose her."

"Which means you'll stay here as long as she's alive." I gazed into his deep green eyes and wrapped my arms around his neck. When a couple and two children squeezed by us, I was vaguely aware we were blocking the trail.

Zack averted his eyes. "Charles talked to the king's people, which means it's too late. I'm already on their radar. They'll send someone else for me, Autumn. I'll still have to leave when school is over."

"Yeah." I dropped my arms and turned.

He followed my lead, continuing our walk through the rows of plants. "I wish I had better news, but we need to be realistic."

"Let's get something to eat," I said, changing the subject.

† † †

When we'd seen everything at the arboretum, we walked the nearby streets of the quaint little town of Montrose, occasionally poking our heads into gift shops. Zack asked me about the places I'd visited and I regaled him with the stories of all the states I'd lived in — all but Hawaii, Alaska, and a handful of others.

"It's strange how much your parents move around. Almost as if they're running from something," he said.

"Avoiding werewolves maybe?" I raised a brow.

He shrugged. "You'll never know until you find out. After today, we won't be spending as much time together. You'll have a chance to snoop around."

"Yeah... I guess we won't be hanging out together

if we're broken up." I stopped and stared unseeing through the window of a novelty item store. It wasn't just about pretending we were only friends — we'd actually have to stay away from each other in public.

"I can still hang out with my cousin and you'd hang out with Maya. So at school, for instance, we can sit at the same table. If our break-up fight isn't too ugly, no one would think it was strange, right? If anyone asks, we could say we get along better as friends."

My chest pinched and I forced a smile. "It's a great plan."

"It's a terrible plan," he said. "But we don't have a choice."

"Yes, we do. Let's just skip the breakup and take our chances."

"And if we get caught by Alura and her uncle, then what?" he asked, his voice low. "You think we'd be as lucky next time? At least this way, we still have our nights. That's better than death."

"Yeah, a lesser of two evils," I whispered, a dull ache taking up residency in my chest.

We sensed a presence at the same time and looked discreetly toward the end of the block. Alura headed our way with her uncle Renzo. As usual, she looked stunning, the skirt of her white sundress swishing around her thighs. He didn't exactly look like a hobo either in his snug T-shirt and black jeans.

Zack nodded toward the door of the store. I smiled and waved to Alura, then went inside. Moments later, the door creaked open, then shut. They'd followed us.

Knowing Renzo would talk telepathically to Zack, I looped one arm through his and picked up a purple glass paperweight with my free hand.

*You seem to be missing a supervisor*, Renzo said silently.

Zack pretended to examine a picture frame. *What makes you think Charles is missing?*

*He hasn't checked in with his supervisor for a couple days. Scouts don't leave their recruit, especially without informing anyone. Something's up.*

*Charles and I spoke on Friday, but not since.* Zack set the frame down and meandered down the aisle. I stuck close, wanting in on every silent word.

*Let's assume the worst, that he's dead*, Renzo said. *His absence would be noticed and there would be an inquiry into his death. And he'd be replaced by at least one more.*

*That's up to King Mortimer. I'll just do whatever I'm supposed to*, Zack said.

*And that's what you want?* Renzo asked. I would've loved to see his expression. But since I wasn't supposed to be aware of their conversation, I let my gaze wander the shelves and pretended to be oblivious.

*Of course. My life is about joining a pack. Why wouldn't I want that, to be with my own kind?* Zack paused to pick up a figurine. "See anything you like?" he asked me.

"Not so far," I answered.

"Me neither. Let's check out the next shop."

We left and Renzo stayed behind with Alura.

*Do you think Renzo's an ally or setting a trap?* I asked as soon as we we'd passed a couple buildings.

*I'm not sure, but dropping my guard would be too risky,* Zack said.

*Let's get out of here,* I said. *He makes me nervous.*

*Hopefully, we'll see them tonight at Bill's Bean and Brew though, so they can witness our breakup.* He steered me to my car.

† † †

That evening, as Zack and I cruised through the driveway of Bill's Bean and Brew, I caught a glimpse of Renzo and Alura already seated at one of the wrought-iron tables. After parking, we picked a table where we'd be easily seen. Zack didn't want the werewolves to miss the show. Moments later, Maya and Trevor arrived.

"Hey, Alura." Maya flashed her a smile. "Did you have a good time last night?"

"Sure, after I dumped my date." Alura grinned, then took a sip of the steaming liquid from the paper cup. "It was a nice crowd."

"Did you find anything you liked in any of the shops today?" I asked, trying to keep a slight distance so she couldn't catch my scent as easily. With my increase in strength, in theory my scent should follow.

"No," Alura answered. "It's a great little street though. I'd love to come back around Christmas. You all know my uncle Renzo?"

"Nice to meet you," Maya said. "I'm Maya."

"Hey." Trevor gave him a man nod. "Trevor."

"A pleasure to meet you. Thanks for taking such good care of Alura last night." He took a sip of his coffee and switched to silent communication. *Any sign of Charles?*

*No*, Zack answered.

Renzo observed us while Zack pretended not to notice. Maya made small talk with Alura while I eyed Zack from under my lashes. He met my gaze, lifted one brow a fraction of an inch, and I remembered why we were there. I dreaded Maya's disappointment to our breakup. Worse, I wasn't looking forward to the werewolves witnessing my humiliation. Most of all, I knew I was losing Zack in some small way.

*Remember, anything I say means nothing.* He rested a hand on my thigh and squeezed. *Do it.*

"I know she's pretty, Zack," I raised my voice slightly. "But you think you can stop staring for just a few minutes?"

Zack glanced at me. "What do you mean?"

"First you dance with Gina, then you stare at the new girl." My voice grew louder. "I'm not enough for you?"

We had Maya and Trevor's attention, the werewolves riveted.

"I don't know what you're talking about." Zack narrowed his eyes.

"Zack, of all the things you could have done, dancing and flirting with Gina was the worst. And if you could take your eyes off Alura for just a minute, you'd see what a jerk you are! I mean, did you think I wouldn't notice? Or did you think I'd be totally fine with it?"

"Autumn, you're paranoid. I'm not interested in either of them." Zack slammed his cup down and caramel liquid sloshed over the rim.

"Yeah." I stood, reaching for my purse. "That's what Daniel used to say. At least if you admitted you were staring, maybe I could get over it. But the fact that you're denying it only makes me lose faith in everything else you say."

Zack rose too, grabbing my wrists. "Autumn, don't do this. Sit down and we'll talk about it."

"I can't be with a guy I don't trust." I shook my head. "I'm not mad, Zack. I just think maybe this was a mistake and we're better off as friends." I switched to Trevor. "You'll drive him home?"

Trevor nodded, stunned into silence. Maya stared at me, eyes wide and mouth slightly parted.

"I'll see you guys at school tomorrow." Spinning away, I bolted toward my car without looking back at Zack, my friends or the werewolves. I hit the clicker before I passed through the parking lot. When I reached for the door handle, Alura had moved in front of the door, blocking me from getting inside.

"Autumn, I —"

"You're really pretty and he's a guy. Can't blame him, right?" I forced a smile, waiting for her to step aside so I could get in my car.

"There's nothing going on between us. I swear. I'm engaged and even if I wasn't, Zack doesn't interest me in that way. Besides, I could never crush on a guy who has a girlfriend." She rested a hand on my arm, her eyes pleading.

"That's no longer an issue." I sighed, shaking my head as tears burned the back of my throat. It felt like we'd broken up for real. "It doesn't matter. I like him a lot, but things were easier when we were just friends. This isn't your fault. Really." As if the whole thing wasn't traumatic enough, now I had to console the girl who'd broken us up.

"Okay. But it's a shame, that's all," she said. "He obviously cares about you."

"The real shame is starting something we shouldn't have. I need to go." I nodded pointedly toward my car door.

"Oh, sorry." She moved aside. "Well, I guess I'll see you around."

"Yeah. 'Bye." I flung the car door open, scrambled in and peeled out of the parking lot.

When my car hugged the curb outside my house, my fingers still trembled on the steering wheel. As if in a trance, I let myself in through the front door, hung up my coat and keys, then sat on the couch and stared at the wall.

Should I wait for him to call or should I just show up in his room?

*Are you okay?* Zack asked me from wherever he was.

*Not really. You?*

*Trevor and Maya are taking it hard. Trevor thinks you're being hormonal. Says you'll calm down if I give you some space. But Maya isn't speaking to me anymore.*

*Right this second, she's demanding that Trevor spend the rest of the evening talking some sense into me.*

It didn't slip my notice that he hadn't answered my question. I'd asked about *him*, not Trevor or Maya. Wasn't he freaked out at all? *I hope they don't start having problems because of us.*

*Me too. I really don't like lying to them this way.*

Was that all that bothered Zack? He wasn't the one who had to do the dirty work and upset his friends by acting like a jealous psycho. *It's good practice for lying to your mom and Cara.*

*Yeah, but we don't have to deal with that tonight. Man, I'm not looking forward to tomorrow.*

What about tonight? Was he looking forward to me sneaking into his room or did he not care anymore? *Me neither.*

*It'll be interesting to see what happens when all the guys at school realize you're on the market again,* Zack said. *And when I say interesting, what I really mean is annoying. Are you coming over?*

I wanted to let him stew in it since the whole unpleasant thing had been his idea. But I couldn't. I needed to see him. *When do you want me?* Seconds later, his answer still hadn't come. *Zack?*

My head swam with pain and a hint of nausea crept up my throat at how real our fake breakup felt. To distract myself, I darted upstairs to take a shower.

It wasn't just Zack that upset me, but Maya too. She'd interrogate me tomorrow and once the news spread through school, everyone would be whispering. Gina would gloat, of course.

*Sorry*, Zack said, while I was scrubbing with suds in my hair. *Maya was saying good-bye to Trevor, but she had to scold me first. We're heading home now. Let me know when you're on your way.*

*I will.* I closed my eyes and the warm water rolled over my face, rushing past the threatening tears.

Breakups sucked.

# CHAPTER FIFTEEN

THE NEXT MORNING, I woke to Zack's lips nuzzling my neck. My eyes fluttered open and I met his gaze with a sleepy smile.

*Today, everyone finds out about the breakup,* he said. *And then we'll meet here tonight, right?*

My smile faded. It would be more than twelve hours from now before I could be alone with him again.

*Just remember it's not real.* Zack's fingertips caressed my skin as he swept up a lock of my hair and gently moved it away from my face. *We'll be fine.*

The bed creaked as he rolled over on me, hooking a hand under my thigh. My greedy fingers hungrily sought his bare skin and raced up his back, pulling him closer. Our lips touched and he released a shaky breath, then he growled and rolled off me. *You'd better go before we're too weak to move.*

And that was a bad thing? Oh, right. Of course it was. I shook my head and the Zack-induced lust-trance began to fade. Not all the way though. Forcing myself out of his bed, I muttered a quick good-bye, morphed into a tabby cat and scurried out his window.

Once I found a parking spot at school, I dialed Maya's number. After my fake spat with Zack at the café, she had to be dying for the scoop. Maybe even crazy-worried about me. I'd been too wrapped up reminding myself the fight wasn't real that I'd completely neglected calling my best friend. I should've let her know I was okay. Some BFF I was.

She picked up after one ring. "Hey, Autumn! Where've you been?"

"Home. I needed to be alone. I'm sorry for not calling you." The lie stung but I knew I had no choice. "Just got to school."

"We can talk in a minute. Zack's about to pull in now."

Of course. Now that he wasn't driving around with me in my Mustang, he had to repossess his Jeep that he'd let Trevor use. Maya and Trevor got to drive with Zack, but I couldn't. A pang of sadness just about swallowed me whole. Only a few hours and I'd be with him again. I could do this. *Zack, what did you tell Maya?*

*I told her you were fine and she didn't need to worry. That we talked on the phone last night and agreed to be friends.*

*And she bought that?* Just then, I spotted the old, red Jeep rounding a row of cars.

*She will when you confirm it.* Zack turned away from his passengers to shoot me a smile as he slid the Jeep between a car and the chain link fence.

I gave him a half smile, feeling a little awkward and uncertain. How were people supposed to act as only friends after being so intimate just that morning?

Maya strode ahead of Trevor and Zack and ushered me into the ladies' room without giving me a chance to say a word to Zack. She ducked to check under the stalls for feet, before grasping my arms. "I called you a million times yesterday. What happened? How are you?"

I dug into my purse for my cell and scanned the missed calls. The last four were from her last night. "Oh. I forgot my phone in the car, then stuck it in my purse this morning without looking at it."

"Seriously?" Maya gave my arms a gentle shake. "You broke up with Zack. I've been worried out of my mind."

"I'm sorry." It seemed backwards to be apologizing to her when I was the one who'd just lost my boyfriend.

"Thought you really liked him." She exhaled noisily. "Why don't you look upset?"

"Numb, I guess." I shrugged and checked my face in the mirror, even though I knew it didn't need anything. "Him dancing with Gina was too much. Then Alura last night. I can't do that again, be with a guy who isn't totally into me. You know?"

"Yeah, but he *was* totally into you." Maya tilted her head. "I was so sure of it."

"Maybe things were getting too serious and he got scared. Whatever. I'm actually relieved." I gave her a smile, which was a million times brighter than my mood. I really hated lying to my best friend.

Maya rolled her eyes. "So long as he doesn't start dating Gina, I'll deal."

I shrugged. "He's not my problem anymore. Let's get to class," I said before I gave in and spilled the whole scheme to Maya.

† † †

John snuck peeks at me during fourth period like he knew something was up, but when the bell rang, he said good-bye and rushed off to meet Janine for lunch. Thankfully, he wouldn't be interrogating me about Zack.

At the entrance to the cafeteria, I quickly located Maya sitting with Zack and Trevor. I wanted to sit with them, but anyone else who knew we'd broken up would get confused if I sat at his table. I compromised and sat on the other side of Maya where I had only a partial view of my "ex."

I was about to say hello to him, but lost my chance when Maya asked me about my after-school plans. Maybe she'd noticed how uncomfortable I looked and was trying to distract me. A couple minutes later, though, Trevor captured her attention and I was back to feeling the awkward silence.

*How's it going?* Zack asked the second Maya turned to her boyfriend.

I took a bite of my sandwich since we could easily talk telepathically with our mouths full. *Okay. And you?*

*Just fine. You did a good job with Maya, huh? You were pretty convincing.*

Of course he would've been listening to Maya and me in the bathroom earlier. But why did he seem irritated with me? I did exactly what he'd asked me to do. It was the *right* thing to do to keep us safe — what *he* wanted. I glanced at him and he looked up from his sloppy joe, zero emotion on his face except... was it just my imagination or was there a hint of the old Zack who had thought so little of me when we'd first met?

*Isn't that what you wanted?* I asked.

*Yes, but...*

*What?*

*It's a little scary, that's all. You're very good at lying.* He took a sip of his juice, then set it back down as if he didn't have a care in the world.

Zack was right. I'd been very persuasive in getting Maya to believe me, but demonstrating Zack's unworthiness hadn't been difficult since he *had* danced with Gina and he *had* been looking at drop-dead gorgeous Alura.

*Our lives are at stake, Zack. Would you have been happier if I'd done a crappy job?*

*Never mind. I'm sorry I brought it up.* He stared at the food in his hands.

Sorry because he regretted ever getting involved with me? Or sorry he was being such a jerk? Acting like I was upset with Zack wouldn't be so hard after all.

I had no business sitting with him, which only made it all so much more uncomfortable. I gripped my food tray. *Maybe I'll sit with John and Janine.*

He'd already taken another bite of his sloppy joe without looking at me. *It'd be more convincing, wouldn't it?*

Ouch.

"I'll see you later, Maya," I told her and walked away.

When I sat my tray next to John, across from Janine, all eyes at the table were fixed on me.

"Hi." John stared at me cautiously, like he was bursting with curiosity, but didn't want to upset me.

"Hi." I gave him a weak smile — it was all I could muster.

"What's up?" Ashley asked.

"Zack and I broke up. We agreed to be friends, but it felt a little weird over there."

Trying not to notice their shocked faces, I took another bite of my sandwich. After a long silence, I set my food down and looked at John, then Janine and Ashley. "What's the big deal? People break up all the time."

"Well, yeah," Ashley said, setting down her fork too carefully. "But we weren't expecting it from you and Zack. You seemed so happy."

I sighed, not wanting to go through all the details. I mean, geez, I wouldn't want to upset Zack by lying too well, did I? "We were, until he danced with Gina at prom. Didn't any of you see that?"

"He danced with Gina? Are you kidding?" Janine scowled. "What a creep."

"And last night, we went out for coffee and there was this girl there." I looked at each of them. "You know that girl who was sitting at our table on prom night?"

Janine gasped. "Oh, no. Did he hook up with her behind your back?"

"No, I don't think so." I shook my head. "But he couldn't take his eyes off her. It reminded me too much of Daniel, so I got mad and broke up with him."

Ashley patted my hand. "I'm sorry."

"Me too." I felt dirty for lying to my friends and that yucky feeling permeated my skin, seeping into my bones. Worse, Zack had to be listening and I wasn't totally sure anymore where he and I stood. I wanted to go home and bury my head under my pillows.

I ate the last bite of my sandwich and checked my watch. "I want to get to my next class early. See you guys later."

Stopping in the bathroom, I rooted through my purse for my makeup bag, finding it just as Gina walked in.

"Hi, Autumn." She stood beside me and smirked at my reflection in the mirror. "Heard Zack dumped you. Too bad."

Ah, she'd come to gloat over the news that traveled very fast. "You're welcome to him if he'll have anything to do with you."

"Poor Autumn." She gave me a sympathetic look, which quickly turned smug. "When I asked him about our science project this morning, he suggested we get together tomorrow night. In private."

I'd known Zack and Gina had Lab together, with a project due soon. It's not like he could blow it off and get an F. He had no choice but to spend time with her, which would likely involve working on it outside of school hours. But Gina made it sound like a date. I knew it wasn't but... Zack had seemed awfully irritated with me during lunch. Maybe the strain of keeping up pretenses was already getting to him and he realized our relationship wasn't worth the trouble.

Gina gave me a smug grin, spun and sauntered out. My temples throbbed and I worried I might puke. Checking the other stalls to confirm they were empty, I squeezed my eyes shut, leaned over and gripped the sides of the sink. Breathe in. Breathe out.

My limbs felt strange, like that moment just before I morph when I'm not quite comfortable in my own skin. I took a few more deep breaths, willing the tiny tremors in my body to subside.

My next class was English Lit with Zack. I didn't want to see him again so soon, especially after he'd made plans with Gina. Mr. Hagar had a test last week so there was a good chance I wouldn't miss much today. Leaving the bathroom, I headed straight to the nurse's office. Since I'd never been sick at school, I'd never met the nurse. She turned out to be an Asian woman and I towered over her tiny frame.

"I'm not feeling so good," I told her.

"Autumn Rossi, right?" she asked. I nodded, wondering how the staff learned the names of every single student, even those they'd never met. "What are your symptoms?"

"A little sick to my stomach. Can I just lie down

for a while and see how I feel next period? Maybe I won't have to go home."

Giving her the impression I didn't want to miss out on school was apparently the exact thing she needed to hear. She showed me to a cot right away, then found a thermometer and inserted it under my tongue. After a few seconds, she pulled out the thermometer and examined it.

"It's normal."

"Maybe it was something I ate and I'll feel better in time for my next class."

She patted my shoulder. "Lie down. I'll check on you in a bit and we'll see."

I smiled but kept it subdued, since I was supposed to be sick. She wandered off, leaving me alone with my thoughts. Damn.

Zack had made arrangements with Gina earlier in the day which allowed plenty of opportunity to tell me during lunch. But it was typical of Zack to withhold information, wasn't it?

*Why aren't you in class?* Zack asked me. *Where are you?*

Oh, crap. The long distance talking started off cool, but now I had no escape. *After a lovely talk with Gina at lunchtime about your date with her, I didn't feel like going.*

*So you're playing hooky?*

He wasn't going to comment on his date with Gina? Zack really knew how to drive me crazy. The nurse bustled past me and I closed my eyes. *Technically, no.*

*I'm in the nurse's office, but I plan to go to sixth period.*

*I'll meet you at your car after school, okay?* he asked.

*After going to school, then the auto shop and doing your homework, then having Gina over tomorrow, are you sure you can squeeze me in?*

*Autumn,* he growled into my head. *Would you just wait for me at your car?*

I hesitated, too annoyed to willingly commit to more aggravation. Still, I wanted to see him.

*Autumn?*

*Fine. I'll see you then.*

Why were we meeting at my car if we were broken up? Did Zack want to break up with me for real? Apologize? I wished he'd just left me alone during fourth period. Now I'd spend the rest of this class and my last one dwelling on what he might say. Plus, I'd mentioned Gina twice and he hadn't commented or denied anything either time.

Now I really did feel sick to my stomach.

I spent the next half hour agonizing over Zack, the same thoughts rolling over and over through my head. The bell went off and it was time to go to last class. I got up and found the nurse. "I think I'm okay to go to my next class."

She smiled and handed me a letter addressed to my parents. "I'm glad you're feeling better."

I took the envelope and left for Social Science, claiming my usual seat. Natalie perched on her desk at the other end of the half-full room. Usually, she arrived at the last second. Why was she early? As my eyes passed over her, I caught a sly smile. What was up with her?

The teacher cleared his throat, sitting behind his wide desk. "Autumn, would you come here please?"

Leaving my books on my desk, I approached the front of the class.

"Your test from Friday." He handed me a sheet of paper with a giant red F scrawled across the top.

How was that possible? I'd aced that sucker. No doubt in my mind. "I don't get it."

The teacher lifted his chin and put his shoulders back, giving me a stern look. "After class, I'd like to speak with you about this. Don't leave, okay?"

"All right." I frowned and backed up.

Every time I'd walked into Mr. Collins class, I was always left with the impression that every part of his life was a business arrangement. No exceptions. Of all the classes to have something go screwy with a test, this would've been my last choice.

By the time I made it to my seat, the room was packed, but the only presence I felt was Natalie. I glanced over at her again. Her smile wasn't sly — it was openly smug.

She'd set me up on the test. But how? This had to be the surprise that witch Gina had been brewing up for me.

When the bell rang, I stayed in my seat. Natalie weaved toward me through the tables and chairs. "Good luck," she whispered conspiratorially. "You're going to need it."

So she *had* framed me. Fury rose up and consumed me at her confirmation.

"Autumn, come here, please," Mr. Collins demanded.

I obeyed, seeing Natalie's smirk before she disappeared beyond the doorway. My hands balled into fists.

Mr. Collins leaned back in his chair and watched me, brows raised as he pointed at my test sheet. "Care to explain this?"

"Oh. I was hoping you would do the explaining. I don't understand why I'd get an F."

He sighed, shaking his head. "Because all your answers are exactly the same as Peter's."

Peter always sat to my left. That made sense, I supposed. "But if he copied my answers, shouldn't *he* be the one getting an F?"

The teacher gave a quick laugh. "He didn't copy yours. You copied *his*."

"I did?"

"Friday, you were distracted. You wanted to be anywhere but here and when the bell rang, you took off like a rocket. You didn't do the test at all. Instead, because you couldn't be bothered, you copied Peter's answers."

Friday? Oh, yeah, Favianne was in the hospital and I'd been worried about her. True, I'd been fidgety, but I still took the test. And they should've been all correct. "Can I see that answer sheet?"

He pushed it toward me. "Be my guest."

I scanned the page, but it showed only the answers. I couldn't remember the questions that went with them.

"And these are the same exact answers as Peter's?"

"Yes, they match exactly." His lips thinned.

I squinted at the page. "How do you know he didn't copy from me?"

He inclined his head. "I worked with Peter the other day after school. The exact questions he missed on the test are same things he had trouble with before. These are *his* answers."

I wiped my palms on my jeans and sucked in a breath. "Mr. Collins, if I'm sitting in class and I know the answers — which I did — why wouldn't I just mark them? No matter what, I still had to stay there and I knew that. Why would I take a chance on messing up my grade point average by copying answers from someone else who might not get them right? It doesn't make any sense. Mr. Collins, don't you see? Someone set me up."

"Autumn, you know how long I've been teaching?" He continued when I shook my head. "Twenty-nine years. And in that time, do you know how many kids I've caught cheating?"

"I have no idea." My voice went flat. This wasn't looking good for me.

"Unfortunately, a lot." He smiled, but it wasn't pleasant. It was the condescending face you give your opponent just before you take your turn and end the game, slaughtering him. "No one *ever* admits to cheating. They claim they're innocent, accuse me of favoritism, racism, threaten to get me fired and the list goes on. But the most common defense is that they've been set up."

I heard a slam as that last nail hammered into my coffin.

"We'll have to call your parents," he said.

If my mom and dad had to come back to deal with this, they'd be annoyed. And disappointed. They'd also be very insistent that I leave with them. I wouldn't go and they couldn't make me, but it would be very unpleasant while they tried. No way could I allow the school to call them. "Mr. Collins, how about I redo the test? Give it orally right now and you'll see I know all the answers."

He groaned. "Autumn, getting an A won't prove to me you didn't cheat. I already know you could do better — if you *wanted* to. This is about copying answers from someone else because you didn't feel like making the effort that day."

He rose as if done with me.

"But... you can't call them. They're out of town."

"No problem. We have their cell phone numbers on file." He locked a desk drawer and closed a cabinet, then picked up a briefcase.

"Wait. What can I do? What if I can *prove* to you I was set up? Please don't call my parents. Please give me a week. Please. Please."

He stared at me as if he couldn't believe I was begging, couldn't believe a cheater would have such nerve.

"Since I came to this school, my conduct record is perfect in academics." Panic was setting in and breathing became a chore. "If I really didn't cheat, which I did *not*, I deserve the chance to set things right. It's just a week. It won't hurt you, but it could mean everything to me. Please!"

He nodded. "You've been an ideal student on all counts, it's true. Fine. You have one week to gather evidence and make your case."

I almost wept in relief. He motioned me out and I left, stopping at my locker to get my homework.

One week. How would I prove my innocence if I had no idea how Gina and Natalie nailed me? I had to find out. But how?

Lugging my backpack on one arm, I stopped in my tracks and stared straight ahead, unseeing. Would cheating go on my permanent record? Either way, word would spread to the other teachers, maybe even the rest of the school. For the remainder of my senior year, I'd be known as a cheater.

After graduation, I may never see any of them ever again, but that wasn't the point — I was innocent and refused to go on record as being a cheater. And ignoring what had happened wouldn't stop Gina from sabotaging me again — or someone else less capable of defending herself.

Damn Gina! No wonder she'd seemed overconfident. It wasn't about stealing a boyfriend or starting a vicious rumor. Nothing so frivolous. She was out to make me miserable.

# CHAPTER SIXTEEN

"AUTUMN. WHY ARE you just standing there?"

I looked up at Zack, my mind blank.

"You were supposed to meet me at your car."

Should I spill it and burden him with my problems? Between his job, werewolf scouts and a dying mother, he had enough to worry about without piling my crap on his plate. Besides, I wasn't even sure if we were still together.

"Um... Mr. Collins wanted to go over last Friday's test with me. No big deal."

He scrutinized my face. "Not sure if I believe that's all there is to it, but okay. C'mon."

Zack walked me in silence down the corridor, through the double doors of the school building and along the path to my car, stopping at the driver's side. "So..."

"Yeah?"

"Did you break up with me?" he asked.

"Well... that's the story we've been telling everyone," I answered.

"No." He leaned on the side of my car. "I meant did you break up with me for real?"

"Uh..." I stared at him, unsure how to answer. I hadn't broken up with him, of course, but if I said no, would he be relieved or disappointed? "Is that what you want?"

"You're not answering my question." He studied me, eyes narrowed.

"I... thought maybe *you* broke up with *me*."

His brows drew together. "Why would you think that?"

"You were annoyed earlier."

He rolled his eyes. "You were... weird. Distant. And it kinda freaked me out how good you are at lying. It still does, actually."

"So you *do* want to break up with me?" I asked, hoping and praying his answer was no. After my awful day, being dumped might start me bawling like a baby.

"No." He ran his fingers through his hair. "Are you coming over tonight?"

Much to my horrification, my eyes blurred with tears. "I'm sorry. It's been a very stressful day."

He growled deep in his throat. "I can't touch you right now. Someone might see."

I nodded and wiped my eyes.

He inched toward me, but kept his arms at his sides. "This morning, I told my mom about our break-up."

"Oh." I wished to God I could come up with a more intelligent response, but I was too wasted from my day to manage it.

"She was pretty upset. When I told her we were still friends, she insisted you come over for dinner. Are you up for it?"

"I guess so."

"So... meet you at my house at 5:30?"

"Um, okay."

"And maybe later, after Gina's gone, you can go to the coffee house and we can accidentally run into each other." He smiled.

I laughed, but it came out embarrassingly like a sob. "That sounds good."

"Autumn?"

"Yeah?"

"Today was hard for me too," he said softly.

I nodded, afraid to speak.

"You know what else?"

I shook my head. "What?"

"Trevor took Maya home in my Jeep." He grinned. "I need a ride to work."

I gave a watery chuckle. "Get in."

† † †

After dropping Zack off at work, I stopped at the grocery store so I wouldn't starve during the week. I did my homework in record time, finished my laundry from the day before, then headed to Zack's house for dinner.

Cara answered the door and smiled, swinging it open. "Trevor's not back yet from picking up Zack, but they should be here any minute. Come on in."

When I went inside, I found Favianne sitting on the couch playing a video game with Patrick. The boy scowled, but she looked like she was having a blast. She was probably slaughtering him.

She saw me and held out her arms. I went to her, reaching out to take her hands. She swatted mine away, stood and drew me into a hug. "Let's go talk in private."

For a split second, I mentally flinched. I'd easily handled everyone at school, but Zack's mom? He'd complained I could be very convincing, but would she see through the lies?

I followed Favianne to her room and got comfortable in the chair. She sat on her bed, bringing up her legs and leaning on her pillows against the wall. Her lungs wheezed and her heart rate went up, but not nearly as bad as before. She sounded great considering her activity the last couple minutes. Her skin looked good too. More color.

"You look great. I guess you're feeling better?" I asked.

"Yes." She smiled. "But we're not here to talk about me."

"The weather?" I teased.

She chuckled. "Nope. What happened with you and Zack?"

Knowing she'd corner me at some point, I'd already given my answer some thought. I'd treat her the same way as I had my over-protective parents — give her selective truths. "Zack and I... we like each other and we get along, but we're so different." I rolled my eyes for effect. "We're practically different species."

She nodded and folded her arms over her chest. "So far, you haven't told me a thing."

Fortunately, I'd prepared for that reaction too — I needed to lead her away and throw in a half-truth or two. If that didn't work, I'd flat-out lie, which I *really* didn't want to do.

"We want different things. Sometimes enjoying each other isn't enough, you know?" I shrugged and glanced at Favianne, feeling suddenly thirsty. I licked my lips with what little moisture my mouth had left. What else had I been about to tell her? Oh yeah. "We realized we got along better when we were just friends."

Favianne took a deep breath, staring at me.

Sweat tickled the palms of my hands. I was in big hairy trouble.

"Although I appreciate the effort, I'm not buying it."

Uh-oh. "Why not?"

"You're trying too hard, for one thing." She lifted one brow. "I want the truth. Now. And don't try to feed me anymore *merda*. It's not on my diet."

"We didn't really break up." The words rushed out of my mouth. But, hell, how could I explain why we were pretending to break up without telling her about our werewolf problems? If she knew our lives were in danger, she'd worry and stress. She could get sick again.

"My ex-best friend has been pretty awful. She's holding a grudge against me because Daniel and Zack both rejected her for me. Rather than dealing with all that drama, we figured if we broke up, it'd be less likely she'd be weird and stalkerish like Daniel was. There's only a few more weeks of school, then we probably won't see her again."

Whew! I gave her the truth... just not all of it.

The door opened and my guilty eyes flew to Zack.

"What's going on here?" His eyes narrowed. "Autumn?"

"She was just filling me in on the status of your relationship." Favianne's mouth tightened.

"Really?" His eyes returned to me, cautious as he approached us. "What did she say?"

"That we staged the breakup, so Gina won't get any worse. I'm sorry, Zack, but it's your fault for not getting here in time to rescue me." I suppressed a giggle, happy that I wouldn't have to lie to Favianne. "Don't you think you should've warned me that your mom uses guerrilla tactics?"

Favianne motioned him over, took his hand and held it between hers. "I'm so happy you two are still together. But don't you dare lie to me ever again."

"Sorry, Mom." Zack gave her hands a squeeze, then walked around the bed and stood behind me, dropping a kiss on the top of my head. "It seemed easier to give the same story to everyone."

"Dinner's ready," Cara called out from somewhere beyond Favianne's room.

"Mom, please don't tell anyone," he whispered. "The more people that know, the more confusing it'll get. Trevor and Maya could give it away at school or at the coffee house or whatever. I don't want them in the line of fire. Gina can get pretty nasty. It's just until the last day of school."

"Okay." She nodded. "You two be careful."

*I can't believe you got us out of that.* Zack said silently. *You're brilliant.*

*Yes, I am.* I grinned. *It comes from lots of practice with my parents.*

† † †

Feeling antsy all alone in my house, I left for Bill's Bean and Brew early. I entered through the side door, got my coffee, then carried it through the front door and onto the patio where we always sat. Just as the door closed behind me, my legs locked into place.

Werewolf. Damn.

Anxious to *accidentally* run into Zack, I'd forgotten that Renzo and Alura came here, too.

"Hey, Autumn." Alura beamed up at me. "Are you alone?"

"Yes." I returned her smile and waved to Renzo.

"Come join us." She glanced at him and he shrugged.

"Sure." After making her feel bad for breaking up Zack and me, I couldn't refuse. But sitting next to her uncle was the last thing I wanted to do. On the other hand, avoiding eye contact with him seemed like a pretty good idea. I grabbed the nearest chair to his and plopped down. I leaned back in my seat, though, which put distance between us. I didn't want him to catch my scent and figure out I was a shape-shifter.

"Did you and Zack make up yet? I feel terrible about what happened."

"None of that was your fault. I'm sorry if I made you feel that way." I gave her an apologetic smile. "And anyway, now that Zack and I are back to being friends, we get along great."

"How long have you known him?" Renzo asked.

Instinct told me he was fishing for information. I'd have to be careful. I didn't think I could handle any more stressful situations today. "Just a few weeks and we weren't dating all that time. It was never that serious."

"Zack!" Alura's pretty face broke into a huge smile.

Crap. If they invited him to join us, things could get even more awkward.

"When you get your coffee, come back and sit with us," she said.

I glanced over my shoulder and smiled at Zack. That's what a friend might do, right? "Yeah, Zack, you should sit with us." Oh, hell. He disappeared inside the café and I spun to face Alura. "So have you guys done anything touristy since you've been here? Disneyland?"

"Not as much as I'd like." She wrinkled her nose. "Uncle Renzo claims to be on vacation, but he spends most of the day taking work calls. I spend mine at the mall."

"The perfect vacation." I grinned.

"Yep." Alura giggled, her gaze moving behind me.

But I had already sensed Zack.

"Autumn, what are you doing here?" He sat between Alura and me, sipping from his cup.

"I got bored home alone. You?"

"Same." He lifted the paper cup to his mouth again.

My eyes darted to Renzo who discreetly watched Zack at every possible opportunity. Just then, his gaze captured mine and I squirmed in my seat. "So what do you do?"

"I run a few businesses," Renzo replied.

"My uncle is modest. He owns them and it's more than a few."

My extreme discomfort at sitting with two werewolves pretty much killed any interest I had in his business affairs. I tried to look impressed anyway, maintaining eye contact with him. Once again, I was struck with how familiar Renzo seemed. He didn't look like anyone I knew but there was something about him... what was it?

*Seen Charles yet?* he asked Zack, glancing toward the parking lot as though he wasn't carrying on a silent conversation.

I hadn't realized Zack's knee was touching mine under the table.

*Not since Friday,* Zack answered.

"Alura, where are you guys from?" I asked.

She smiled. "San Diego."

"I've passed through there. Beautiful," I said.

"Um, I didn't plan on staying." Zack stood. "Was just stopping for coffee on my way home. Nice seeing you again, Renzo. Alura. See you tomorrow in English Lit, Autumn."

"See you later." Alura waved to Zack, then turned to me. "Do you have to go, too?"

That would look suspicious, wouldn't it? My only regret was that Zack had thought to leave before I had. He was free and I wasn't. "I have a few more minutes."

And that's all the time I could afford. My gut told me that any more would only give Renzo more opportunity to figure out what Zack and I were hiding.

# CHAPTER SEVENTEEN

IN TRUTH, I had nothing pressing going on, nothing I needed to get home to. Homework was done and I'd answered my mom's e-mail from my phone earlier. I could stay at Bill's Bean and Brew a couple more hours and still get to Zack's before he fell asleep later.

But the longer I hung with Renzo and Alura, the riskier it became. I needed to go. Now. Which meant I needed to make up some excuse to get the hell out of there. In my head, though, nothing sounded right or natural.

Faking it with my parents and everyone else had become second nature, but with Renzo, I was just too nervous and the lies twisted up on my tongue.

When Alura asked me questions about my parents and what they did for a living, my plans for college and where I hoped to be in five years, I stuck to the truth. *That* I could handle. Lies, not so much.

I told her how graphic design and websites intrigued me, but that I thought I might have to wait until next year, maybe go to trade school. More than likely, none of that would ever happen. I'd probably be on the run for the rest of my life — I kept that part to myself.

When the conversation lulled, I opened my mouth to tell them I had to get back home. I paused when Renzo dropped a straw wrapper and leaned over to pick it up before the breeze carried it away. His knee brushed against me and I strained to keep from flinching.

*She's lying, Alura. Zack's scent is all over her. You don't get that much werewolf on you if you're just friends. Any idea why they're hiding it?*

At least he didn't sniff me out. That was something. Still, my heart slammed against my ribs, my adrenaline spiking.

My hair caught a light breeze and he abruptly sat upright again, his eyes trained on me.

Oh, crap, had he smelled me? I shot them each a casual smile. "I really should get going. Still have homework to do." I moved to stand, laying my palm on the table.

Renzo pressed his hand over mine. "No. You don't have to go," he said in a low voice only Alura and I would hear.

"I don't?" I said, slowly returning to the chair.

"No." He watched me, eyes narrowed. "Does Zack know about you?"

"What do you mean?" I forced a small laugh.

"You know *exactly* what I mean," he growled, his eyes darkening.

My gaze darted to Alura.

*Autumn knows she's been caught.* His hand still covered mine, so I could hear him. His words were obviously directed at Alura, but he didn't take his eyes off me. *She can hear me and she knows I know.*

"Uncle Renzo, you're scaring her. Autumn, he's not going to hurt you." She scowled at him.

"Are you?" I asked him.

"I'm on vacation." Renzo enunciated the last word slowly, leaning closer. "You didn't answer my question. Does Zack know you're a shape-shifter?"

Alura gasped. Clearly, she hadn't figured it out yet.

That's it. I was going to die. There was no point in denying I was a shape-shifter, but that didn't mean Zack had to go down with me. "N-No one knows, not even my parents. H-How did *you* know?"

"When I spoke telepathically to Alura, your expression changed. Your eyes shifted, your heart rate accelerated, then you immediately tried to bolt."

"Are you going to kill me?" I wiped my sweaty palms on my jeans as my eyes darted from her to him and back again. "For socializing with a werewolf?"

Renzo reached over and gently grasped my wrist. "Listen to me carefully. We're on va-ca-tion."

I squeezed my eyes shut. "Vacation?"

A smile teased his mouth. "Yes. Vacation."

"Autumn," Alura said. "It's okay. You're safe with us."

My breathing became easier and my pulse slowed. "And Zack? What about him?"

Alura shook her head. "We're not watchers or scouts."

"Where's Charles?" Renzo asked, his eyes turning to slits again.

This unfortunate turn of events with Renzo and Alura was just one more in a string of awful incidents today. My eyes stung and, to my horror, my bottom lip trembled. "I don't know. Can I go home now?"

Alura reached across the table and squeezed my hand. "Of course. We'll drive you home."

I mentally wrestled with the idea of getting into a car with one of them. Alura and Renzo had each insisted they meant no harm, but were they telling the truth or setting me up? "I have my car."

"I know," Alura said softly. "But seeing how distraught you are, I'd feel better if I saw you arrive safely."

If I refused the escort and they meant to kill me, wouldn't they be waiting for me at my house anyway? A weak and solitary fledgling shape-shifter stood zero chance against two older werewolves and I had no intention of involving Zack. Even with his help, we'd be dead meat. If I were doomed, maybe I could buy myself some time by playing along.

"Okay, sure. A ride would be appreciated." I started to get up again, but halted at Renzo's voice.

"Did you and Zack kill Charles?" His eyes bored into me.

"No! And I told you, Zack doesn't know about me." I shook my head, terror gripping me. "He's going to be so pissed at me for not telling him."

"Let's go." He rose, taking my elbow. "Alura will drive your car and I'll meet her there."

"Please don't say anything to Zack," I pleaded as he guided me off the patio toward the parking lot. "I put him in danger and I'm sorry. Don't know what I was thinking."

Renzo gave me a small nod in acknowledgement. "I'll keep it to myself, for now. Meanwhile, keep your relationship under wraps. Mixing species will get you killed faster than just about anything and you never know when you'll meet up with a werewolf who isn't on vacation."

Or when Renzo would decide his vacation was over. Would that be two hours from now or two days?

My heart pounded in my throat.

Just as we hit the asphalt, he yanked my arm to a stop. "Why'd you tell everyone you broke up when you hadn't?"

"Th-there's this girl at school harassing me." It's what we'd told Zack's mom and all I could think of. "We thought we'd lie low and see if she lets up."

I felt a driving need to get away from Renzo before I tripped myself up in my lies. I moved just a hair and he clamped a hand around my wrist. "Why is your scent so light?"

"I haven't finished maturing, I guess. I don't know." I prayed they wouldn't ask who mentored me during my change into shape-shifter and my first morph.

"I still should've been able to sense you right away," Renzo said. "Why couldn't I?"

My pulse quickened. "I told you. I don't know."

Alura rested a hand on his shoulder, a low hiss emitting from her throat. "Uncle Renzo, can we take a break and resume the Spanish Inquisition another time?"

He sighed and loosened his grip on my wrist. "Fine."

"I'll see you there," she told him, cutting across his arm and forcing him to release me the rest of the way.

I got in the passenger side of my car and she started it up and pulled onto the road.

"I live off Foothill Blvd. Make a right about three lights down."

Alura looked directly at me, her eyes steady. "I know where you live."

She did? What else did they know? A tingle raced up my spine.

Minutes later, she pulled into my driveway. "Are you okay to go inside by yourself? You want me to come in with you? I can have my uncle wait in the car. I'm annoyed with him right now anyway." A mischievous smile curved her lips.

Alura seemed so sweet and I wanted to take her up on her offer. But could she really be that nice or were they setting me up? What did they want? "Thank you, but I'm fine."

"You should run a hot bath. Relax."

"I might." I eyed the ignition. "Can I have my keys back?"

"Sorry." She climbed out and handed me my keys as the midnight-blue Jaguar glided to the curb behind us.

After mumbling a good-bye, I hurried inside, locked the door behind me and collapsed on the sofa.

Worst day ever.

Since it wasn't quite ten o'clock, I took Alura's advice and dragged myself upstairs. I could turn myself into a teabag and steep in a hot bath for twenty minutes and still be at Zack's around eleven.

Oh, God. He needed to be told that Renzo knew about me and the fake breakup.

Except Zack would probably do something stupid like break up with me for real, just to keep me safe. Or he'd leave town. I'd probably never see him again and he'd lose precious time with his mom.

Or worse, he might play hero and get us both killed. And I couldn't take the chance that Zack might accidentally give himself away and Renzo would realize Zack had known all along what I was. Renzo may be on "vacation" and probably not a threat right this second, but I doubted even he would let Zack get away with knowingly being involved with a shifter and breaking the law.

No, Zack couldn't know about this latest development — for his own safety.

# CHAPTER EIGHTEEN

THE CLOCK ON Zack's nightstand told me it was just past four in the ungodly morning. There was no point in going back to sleep when I'd need to wake up again in less than an hour. At which time, I'd have to go through the painful eye-opening process all over again.

Zack was still sleeping. I lay there a long minute, cuddling with him and trying to commit everything to memory — his musky scent, his long deep breaths, the feel of his arm around me. Perfect.

I scooted closer to reach his lips, knowing this one, quick moment would have to last me the rest of the day. Abruptly, Zack rolled over and trapped me beneath him, his warm musky scent ravaging my senses.

I could think of worse ways to kill time.

"Hope you weren't planning on leaving so soon," he whispered into my hair.

Trapping his hair in my fists, I dragged his lips to mine. Would I always want him with the same fervor and intensity? Part of me hoped not. It drove me crazy, the madness of wanting. I craved that release, the satisfaction.

But was it worth dying for?

My pajama top had ridden up and I could feel his warm skin against mine. His thumb found that sensitive spot on my lower stomach near my hip.

Yes, definitely worth dying for.

I imagined us succumbing to our desires. I didn't think it would be difficult eliciting Zack's cooperation — he didn't need seducing. But how much would my friends and family be hurt if anything happened to us? Plus, dying would give me less time with Zack.

Sighing, I closed my eyes, nudging his chest and disengaging his lips from the hollow of my throat. Lord, stopping him was the last thing I wanted to do. *I should go.*

He rolled off me and ran his fingers through his hair. *Yeah.*

*Remember when we decided to collect some of your things at my house for a quick getaway? I can wear some of your clothes to my house right now.*

*Good idea.* Zack left the bed to rummage through his drawers for a pair of jeans and a T-shirt, and handed them to me.

They were huge. I threw them on over my pajamas.

He gave me a quick kiss, then stepped away. *I'll see you at school.*

I waved just before morphing into a cat and jumped out the window.

† † †

I had plenty of time before I had to be at school, so I checked my e-mails. Two from my mom. She raved about how beautiful I looked and gushed on and on about my dress. Then she asked the dreaded question: Who took me to prom and could she see the pictures of us? I told her the truth — a cousin of Maya's boyfriend escorted me. I didn't even consider sending them, because anyone could tell by looking at the photos that Zack and I weren't just friends. That would only give her more to worry about.

A few weeks ago, she'd dropped me off at school and Zack had been standing in front of the entrance. My mom had asked if I knew him, then she'd rushed off. If my mom was a shape-shifter, she would've known he wasn't human and she and my dad would do everything in their power to stop be from dating him. No, I definitely couldn't tell them about Zack.

Totally avoiding her request for pictures of my date, I threw in some questions about Dad and how they liked Montana. Then I clicked the send button.

Since they'd left, my mom texted me twice but that was weeks ago and she'd only contacted me because she wanted me to check my e-mail. They'd never once called to actually speak to me. For two people who'd been so protective of me all my life, it seemed odd they'd let me go so easily and be satisfied with e-mails.

Normal parents would call once in a while. Why the complete one-eighty?

Maybe once they were gone, they enjoyed the vacation I'd blackmailed them into. Maybe they had an epiphany and realized my life wouldn't fall apart if they weren't around every second of every day. Possible.

Or they'd been spotted and were being chased by werewolves. Maybe they *couldn't* use their cell phones. Maybe they were so busy running that they could only manage an e-mail now and then. Was that why they showed up without warning and left so quickly? The idea of them being hunted was terrifying.

Zack was right — I needed to find out who my parents really were.

With a little time before school, I ventured into their bedroom and poked around. I checked all their drawers, taking them out and looking inside the dresser itself. Nothing. I slid my hands between the mattress and box spring, peered under the bed and even checked the pockets of their clothing hanging in the closet. Still nothing.

Empty handed, I vacated their room and made a beeline for my dad's office. Beyond the open door, papers cluttered his desk and file cabinets guarded either side. The kind of thing I needed would never be left out in the open and I'd done their filing for years. I needed to look where I'd never been. But that would have to wait since I was out of time.

Sighing in defeat, I turned away from his office and got ready for school.

† † †

My deadline to figure out how Gina had framed me was fast approaching. The only way that I could think of getting information out of her was to make friends with her. Ick. I hoped she wouldn't make me grovel.

Since meeting Gina months ago, I'd learned a thing or two about the school food chain. There were two kinds of popular kids: the ones who ruled by intimidation and the ones who got to the top by treating others fairly. I was the latter.

Because Gina bullied and manipulated to get her way, she needed someone like me around to make her appear more likable. If I forgave her flaws, then others might too. Not that she needed anyone's forgiveness to inflict terror, but being friends with me gave her the benefit of the doubt in other's eyes, which gave her more power for her dirty work. That was my theory anyway.

The girl honestly didn't know the first thing about real relationships or how to earn respect.

I parked in the far corner of the school lot where my car wouldn't be obvious. Grabbing my books, I hurried through the double doors. Instead of continuing, I waited inside, just beyond the entrance against the wall where I'd be easily missed. As students arrived, I eyed each as they passed. At last, I saw Gina and fell in step beside her.

"So, how's it going?" I asked as if there had never been a rift between us.

Gina flinched and stopped in the middle of the corridor to stare at me. "What do you want?"

"Well... Neither of us have boyfriends anymore. It's just us again." I shrugged, staring down at my feet, then drew my eyes back to her puzzled face. I sidestepped as someone nudged by me. "Never mind. I don't know what I was thinking."

I took off, not looking back, hoping I'd appeared sincere and praying like hell that my plan would work.

Gina had been a complete bitch these past few weeks, but our relationship hadn't always been that way. We'd hung out since my first day at Verdugo Hills Academy, I'd eaten dinner with her family and watched her interact with them. We'd been through bad times and good. I knew the real girl under the provocative clothes and platinum highlights. She may have been selfish and spoiled, but behind the snide remarks lay a lonely and very insecure girl. Just like me.

Except I solved my problems differently. For one thing, if I liked a guy, I'd never resort to hijacking him, especially from my best friend.

I'd planted a seed with Gina and if my gamble paid off, I wouldn't have to wait long for it to take root. Until then I needed to give Maya the heads up.

I arrived outside just in time to see Maya get out of Zack's Jeep.

*Hello, beautiful.* On the outside, Zack barely acknowledged me, his face void of any emotion for onlookers' benefit.

I tried not smiling, but failed. I did, however, successfully restrain myself from showering too much sunshine in his direction before sharing it with Maya and Trevor.

"Hey, Autumn," Trevor said.

"Hey." I switched to Maya. "Can I talk to you?"

She looked inquiringly at Trevor before tipping her face up to receive his kiss.

He smiled, his lips meeting hers. "See you at lunch."

I flinched, wishing I was doing that with Zack. But I couldn't. The single life at school was already wearing on me. Waving to the boys, I led my friend away. Once in the bathroom, I checked the stalls to see if we had company. Empty. I couldn't believe my luck.

"Is this about Zack? Are you regretting breaking up with him?" she asked.

"No." I shook my head. "I don't need a boyfriend like that. Anyway, listen. I need to talk to you alone, but I don't want Zack knowing about this. You know how he is, coming to my rescue all the time. He'll feel obligated to help me and I don't want him getting dragged into this mess." I took a deep breath and exhaled. "I got caught cheating in Mr. Collins's class and —"

Maya gasped. "You cheated?"

"No." I shot her an irritated look. "Why would I need to do that? The point is that Mr. Collins *thinks* I did. He was going to call my parents. That's all I need, right?"

"They'd be back to hover over you." She grimaced. "I don't think I could go through that again. It was painful to watch."

"Exactly. Anyway, I talked him into giving me a week to prove my innocence. Natalie's in that class with me. I'm pretty sure Gina put her up to... whatever Natalie did."

She scowled. "Those bitches. Do you have a plan? I'd love to nail Gina. How can I help?"

I leaned against the sink, listening for anyone who might be about join us. "I don't know yet. But I think it might be a good idea to patch things up with her."

Maya's jaw went slack and she took a step toward me. "You can't make nice with Gina. Not after what she did."

Laying my hand on her arm, I nodded. "It's just pretend. Maybe she'll let down her guard, slip up and give me a clue to how she did it."

Maya visibly relaxed and grinned. "That's brilliant. *If* she'll make up with you. That's a pretty big *if*."

"I'm still popular, even though she's trying to ruin me, and she can't stand it. If anything, she'll want to pretend to be my friend so she can take me down."

"Be careful." She bit her lip.

The door swung open, ending our chat.

† † †

I purposely lingered around the food, hesitating by the yogurts in hopes that Gina would seize the opportunity to reconcile with me. I chose raspberry and placed it on my tray, keeping my head down while surreptitiously scanning the cafeteria for her.

An arm snaked around my waist, a nose poking the back of my neck. Greg, the jock douche. I wiggled out of his reach.

"Autumn. Damn, you look hot in those jeans." He gave me a lopsided grin, his breath smelling of smoke.

I'd become too familiar with cigarette smell from

my parents. This wasn't from that kind of smoking. Greg was high. Maybe he thought I might be more receptive to him hitting on me while he was in that condition. Because, yeah, guys were so much more attractive with a lower IQ.

Not.

"Hi, Greg." I didn't smile, moving away to pick out a drink.

"So... dumped the loser, huh?"

"Ancient history, Greg. Daniel and I broke up weeks ago." I pretended to study the selection of sodas, annoyed with him for wasting my time when I could be working Gina over.

His brows flew up and he giggled, making a piggy noise, which made him laugh harder.

I rolled my eyes and turned my back to him, making my way to the tables.

He appeared at my side again, walking with me. "I meant your latest boy toy, Zack."

Stopping to face him, I put my innocent face on. "Zack and I are still friends. And, if they were both in a loser contest, Daniel would win."

"So if he wins in a loser contest, he's the winner and biggest loser too?" He laughed, sounding a little like a hyena. "That's funny, Autumn. I always liked your sense of humor. So when are we gonna go out? You know, hook up?"

"Hook up?" My stomach lurched at the thought, but at this point, I didn't want to alienate him. That would get back to Gina and I needed to convince her of my eagerness to be in her crowd again, which wouldn't happen if I was rude to her friends.

"Yeah." He grinned, stroking under my chin with his finger.

"Um..." I swiveled and continued walking, then stopped to scan the lunchroom again. I'd unconsciously walked to Zack's table when I hadn't intended to.

Zack's gaze burned through me. *Tell him no.*

I turned around to face Greg. "The thing is... it's too soon for me to date again. I went from Daniel to Zack and right now, I just need some space. I'm not looking for another relationship just yet."

"Who said anything about a relationship, babe?" Greg oozed, giving me his sleaziest grin. "Let me know when you're ready for a real man. No strings attached."

Nodding, I commanded my face not to scowl. "I'll do that." I didn't give him a chance to reply, pivoting and taking a seat next to Maya. I risked a peek at Zack, but his expression gave away nothing as he chowed down his burger.

I ate in silence, listening to Maya and Trevor carry on about what a jerk Greg was and the nerve he had for hitting on me with Zack just a few feet away. Zack barely looked at me during lunch, much less spoke to me. I sighed, loathing school and stupid jocks. Mostly, I hated the lies that had piled up and were working hard to tear Zack and me apart.

*Zack. Everything okay? You're awfully quiet.*

*Yeah. Everything's just fine,* he said, but he didn't even glance my way.

Why was he being weird? It wasn't as if I'd invited Greg to hit on me.

I wasn't hungry anymore. Leaving the table, I went to put my tray away. I dumped the trash in the bin and jolted as something brushed my arm.

"Hey, Autumn."

It was Cameron. He was a jock too, but nothing like Greg or Daniel. He was actually nice, even a little shy. I'd had a crush on him the first few days when I'd started school, but Gina had carefully explained school hierarchy and why he wasn't good enough for girls like us.

Cameron had never made a move anyway. Daniel had swept in and I'd barely thought of Cameron since. Then Zack came along and now, no guy could compare to him.

"You gonna be around after school?" he asked.

"I guess so." I really hoped he wasn't going to ask me out. It was kind of expected from a jerk like Greg, but I hoped Cameron had more sense than to hit on *any* girl so soon after a break up. It'd been less than two days.

"Ashley's having some people over after school today. You going?"

I stifled a surprised laugh, my brows raised. "You mean her parents are allowing *any*one to come over since that fiasco? It was what, less than two weeks ago?" Daniel had spiked the drinks and the partiers seized the moment. Chaos ensued. I was sure Ashley would be forbidden to have anyone over for a very long time.

He shrugged. "She can have people over, so long as it's not too many. And everyone has to be gone by dark. Bring your bathing suit. It should be fun."

He'd asked me if I was going, which was totally different than asking me out. Definitely not a date. And being with other people would take my mind off Zack while he was at work. "I'll be there."

"Cool. See you then."

I smiled and waved as he turned and left. On my way back to our table, Zack got up and walked toward the back exit leading to a hallway and outside.

*Where are you going?* I asked.

He didn't turn around. *Just getting some air.*

Was he mad at me? If so, why? If I was fake-single, I couldn't be expected to never talk to another guy. If I avoided interaction with other guys, it would look odd, especially when I sat at Zack's table so often. I had to do something to show we weren't still together, right?

Besides, it's not as if I'd flirted with Greg. The way Cameron informed me about the pool party was as harmless as an invite could get. And if Cameron was interested in me, he would've acted on it months ago.

I held myself in check so I wouldn't chase after Zack, my eyes glued to his back as he eventually disappeared beyond the doorway. I could reason away why Zack had no right to be mad, but my gut told me he was furious anyway.

# CHAPTER NINETEEN

EVERY MUSCLE IN my body screamed to chase after Zack, but that would undo all our hard work. Instead, I sat next to Maya until lunch was over, making small talk and twiddling my thumbs until the bell rang.

Maya's next class was close to mine, so we walked to fifth period together.

"I saw the way you were looking at Zack when he left. You're totally stuck on him."

Damn. I'd have to be more careful.

I laughed once. "No, I'm not."

She stopped and turned to me, searching my face. "Yep. You still like him."

I looked away for an instant while I gathered my wits, then I focused on her. "Of course I still like him. He and I are friends, remember? Friends usually like each other. I was just trying to figure out why he left so suddenly. It's strange for him."

She lifted one brow. "I think Zack wants you back."

He wanted me back? My heart soared. Then I remembered that he'd never lost me in the first place. "What makes you think that?"

"You should've seen his face when that jerk was perving on you."

"Oh?"

"Yeah," Maya answered. "He didn't take his eyes off you guys for an instant. He looked... dangerous. Trevor was all tense and everything in case he needed to pull Zack off the guy. Are you *sure* you don't want to get back together with him?"

"Positive." I nodded toward the stretch of hallway ahead of us. "We should get to class."

"What did Cameron want?"

"Ashley's having a few people over for a swim after school today."

"And you're going?"

"I thought I might. It'd give me something to do" — I'd almost said *while Zack was at work* — "since my parents aren't around."

She seemed to buy that and we went our separate ways. As I neared my English Lit class, Zack talked to Gina just beyond the doorway.

"So we're still on for tonight?" she asked.

Zack nodded. "Yeah, around seven?"

"See you then." She gave him a flirtatious smile, then spun around and walked past me.

By the time I switched to Zack, he was already seated. I stopped right in front of him. "Hey."

"Hi," he said, then changed to silent communication. *What did Cameron want?*

I took my seat and pretended to organize my materials, wondering why Zack was asking about Cameron when he'd heard every word of our conversation. *Ashley's having a mini pool party and wanted me to go.*

He eyed me intently. *Ashley wanted you to go?*

*Yeah.*

*But Cameron was the one who invited you.*

*He didn't exactly invite me.* I risked a quick look at him. *He informed me about it and asked if I was going.*

*That's just semantics.* As the classroom slowly became more crowded, Zack sighed. *In Cameron's mind, it's a date, Autumn. And you agreed to it.*

*That is not a date!* The bell couldn't ring soon enough for me. *It's a few people swimming at her house.*

He made a funny little grunting noise. *Whatever.*

*Using your logic, the little get-together with Gina tonight is a date, too.*

*That's different.*

*How so?* I couldn't wait to hear how he justified it.

*We'll be studying, Autumn.* He tapped on the surface of his desk, then flipped the cover of his book open. *Besides, you knew about it yesterday and you didn't say anything about it then.*

I cleared my throat, keeping my head down. *You mean if I made plans to do something with Cameron tomorrow and you knew about it today, then it's not a date?*

The bell rang and he growled. *Just forget it.*

At the end of class, I gathered my materials, then turned around to grab my sweater off the back of the chair. By the time I turned around, Zack was gone.

The school drama was getting old. Since my next class was with Mr. Collins and Natalie, it would likely get a little older.

Science finally let out and I looked around for Gina who was nowhere in sight. How was I supposed to cozy up to her if she kept disappearing? After a couple minutes of searching, I gave up and headed to my car, hoping to spy Zack along the way. I immediately located his Jeep in the parking lot and waved to Trevor and Maya. Where was Zack?

Intending to stow my books in my car until he appeared, I walked to the Mustang. And there was Zack, leaning against the hood of my car, surrounded by three giggling girls. He smiled charmingly, inviting each of them into his personal circle.

Flirting with girls right at my car? Zack spotted me and each of the girls shifted to follow his gaze. Two of them scowled like I'd just vomited on their new shoes. The third girl seemed surprised. I glared at the two less friendly girls and they backed away a smidgen. Though they were a nuisance, I reminded myself it wasn't their fault. Zack probably didn't put up a fight when they attached themselves to him.

I fantasized about being alone with him for a weekend, just me and him. No girls chasing him, no vicious girls setting me up for cheating and no jerks like Greg hitting on me when they're stoned. Even if Zack liked the idea, could we get away without anyone knowing we'd left town together?

"Hey, I need to speak to Autumn. I'll talk to you

guys later, huh?"

"I thought you two broke up." The little brunette pouted.

"We did. But I left a couple things at her house and I need to get them back. It'll only take a minute if you want to wait."

"We'll wait," the blonde said huskily. "C'mon Emily." She gave him one last seductive smile before sweeping her friends away to huddle a few cars down.

"So are you coming over tonight?" Zack asked, keeping his voice low.

"Are you sure you'll have the energy after satisfying those girls, then doing your shift at work and seeing Gina?"

He closed his eyes a moment as he inhaled and exhaled. "It's all for show and you know it. Are you coming over or not?"

"Yes," I hissed.

"Fine." His jaw tightened just before he stalked off to reunite with the three girls.

I got in my car and left, pretending I had blinders on so I couldn't look at Zack laughing with them. What I really wanted to do was stomp over to the girls, stake my claim on Zack, then order them to stay the hell away from my boyfriend.

But Renzo had told me to keep our relationship under wraps, that we never knew when we'd meet up with a werewolf who wasn't on vacation. Even if no other werewolves showed up, Renzo was the last person I wanted to cross. Just thinking about being cornered by him again, made me tremor from my toes all the way up to my spine.

† † †

I slipped a pair of shorts over my bathing suit, so I wouldn't have to worry about changing once I got to Ashley's. Grabbing a towel, I dashed out of my house, looking forward to a few hours of stress-free swimming with friends.

Ashley lived only a few blocks away on the outskirts of the forest. Driving down the rural road reminded me of Charles and I wondered what had happened to his remains. I didn't watch much TV, nor did I normally pay attention to the news alerts that popped up on my browser. I didn't need to because my parents usually clued me in on anything noteworthy. If they missed something, I'd hear about it at school or from Mrs. Morales next door who'd bring a basket of muffins and chat about everything she could think of until we were properly informed.

Yet I'd heard nothing at all from anyone.

Wouldn't finding an over-sized, mutilated wolf carcass hit the local news? Especially since wolves weren't common in our area? It's not as if we'd hidden the body — we'd left it right on the ground close to where we'd parked the car.

I detoured and turned up the road that would take me to that spot. About a mile along I pulled over and climbed out of the car. Where was it? The forest looked completely different during the day.

As I trekked along the dirt road, I inhaled, trying to pick up the scent of wolf. I hiked a few yards farther, then the stench of old blood filled my nostrils. I recognized the raised tree root, a broken branch and big rocks scattered about. It was definitely the spot.

I didn't see a body, though. Even if the animals had scavenged him, wouldn't there be something leftover, like a skull or a tuft of hair?

But no such traces existed. I waved my nose in the air, trying to find a scent trail, a direction the carcass may have been dragged off to. Or walked... Could Charles have survived with his insides ripped out? According to the movies, the only way to kill a werewolf was a silver bullet. How much truth did that theory hold?

After a few more minutes searching the immediate vicinity, I walked back to my car. I was about to open the driver's side door when a ranger truck parked next to me.

"Excuse me, sir?" I asked as he got out of his truck.

He swiveled around in his short-sleeved, crisp uniform. "Not sure it's a good idea for you to be out here alone, Miss."

"Extenuating circumstances. I needed to check something out. Saturday morning, we were hiking around here and saw a dead wolf right over there." I pointed to where we'd left Charles.

"We don't have wolves in this area, Miss. Must've been a coyote."

"It was definitely a wolf."

He gave a sigh, which said it all — someone so

young had no business telling him about his job. He'd never buy the wolf theory. If I pushed it, he'd think I was stupid and he'd be less likely to take me seriously.

"Okay, it was definitely dog-like." I shrugged. "Did you see it or maybe someone called it in?"

He folded his muscular arms over his chest, shaking his head decisively. "No. Probably got eaten by local scavengers. Why so much interest in it?"

"Felt bad when I saw it." I softened my voice. "I assumed he was dead, but then I got to thinking maybe he was wounded and needed help."

That was all I needed to say. The ranger was obviously an animal lover. "We patrol the area frequently. If there was a wounded animal, I assure you, we would've seen it and taken care of it."

Then why was there no trace of the body? Scavengers would've left bones and fur, right?

"Thank you. That's comforting to know," I said, really laying on the innocent act. I got in my car and resumed the short drive to Ashley's.

When I arrived, John and Janine greeted me at the door and ushered me to the backyard.

"Hey, Autumn, glad you could make it." Ashley hugged me and handed me a soda from the cooler by the table.

I took it and hugged her back, happy to see her and thankful for the company.

"Um." She frowned. "I invited Zack this morning, thinking it would be fine since you guys still hang out. But when I saw him at lunch, he looked pissed off. You guys still okay?"

"Yeah, I think he was mad about something else. He and I are good." I smiled and waved my hand, unsure how I felt about Zack showing up. A part of me was anxious to see him, but the other part loathed the thought of continuing the charade. I just wanted to take it easy for a little while and not have to pretend, not have to lie to anyone.

"I guess he has to work, so he's not coming until later anyway. If you feel weird about it, you can always slip out before he gets here. But I'd like you to stay... if you want," she added uncertainly.

"Thanks. I'll have to go home to eat at some point anyway, so I'll play it by ear."

"My parents are springing for pizza."

There went that excuse, but I liked her idea of dinner much better than what I'd find at home. "Pizza sounds awesome."

"Hey, Autumn," Cameron called out from the pool. "Water's great. Come on in."

If Zack was right and Cameron thought it was a date, I should keep my distance, so he wouldn't be led on. Since he was the only one in the pool, I figured I'd wait until he got out before I got in. "Yeah, maybe in a bit."

Wait a minute. If Ashley invited Zack, wouldn't that be a date, according to him?

*So... following your philosophy, since Ashley invited you over to her house, that means it's a date. And you're seeing Gina later for another date. You should be careful—you don't want to overlap your women.* I wondered if the hypocrite could hear me three miles away at the auto shop.

*It's not a date, Autumn. Ashley is the host. She in-*

*vited several people, not just me. I have to work now, okay? I'll see you at Ashley's in a little while.*

I didn't answer, realizing that now he expected me to be there when he arrived. I was locked in, pizza or not.

Cameron got out of the pool. Seeing the perfect opportunity to avoid him, I stripped off my shorts and tank top, feeling many pairs of eyes on me. I became aware of the skimpiness of my bathing suit and wished I'd brought my one-piece instead. Not that this one was any more revealing than any other bikini at Ashley's today, but the straps were thin and the bottom was cut so that it rode up, exposing a smidgen of my rear. Between the bright green and the ruffles around the top, I may as well have been a beacon showing everyone the way.

I dove in. Instead of being soothed by the warm water carelessly lapping against the sides of the pool, I stressed over the possibility of Cameron joining me and making it awkward. Plus, my nerves were jumbled in anticipation of Zack's arrival.

Just as I'd feared, Cameron jumped in a couple minutes later. Thankfully, Ashley did too, along with a few others who provided the perfect diversion. Cameron didn't try to talk to me again and after a few minutes, I began to have fun.

Then Zack arrived.

He said hello, then promptly ignored me. As far as they knew, I wasn't his girlfriend anymore so it wasn't as if he could give me special attention. I understood that, but it still stung like rejection.

When the pizza arrived, the pool emptied. Cameron handed me a piece of pizza and I gave him a smile while observing Zack out of the corner of my eye. He was talking to some pretty blond girl I didn't recognize. She smiled at him a lot and every time she shifted her weight to another side, she somehow inched closer.

I couldn't watch anymore, so I pivoted until they were out of my line of vision.

Cameron asked me about my classes and if I planned on going to college. At the first opportunity, I turned the questions around on him. When he looked like he was about to switch subjects and tie me with him longer, I clutched at the chance of escape.

"Thanks for inviting me Cameron, but I should go. I still have stuff to do tonight." Leaving some crust on my plate, I set it down.

"Yeah, I have to go soon too. Guess I'll see you at school tomorrow, huh?"

He looked hopeful. Crap. Zack had been right. Cameron considered it a date.

"Unless you've switched schools." I grinned as I stepped into my shorts and grabbed the towel. "'Bye John, Janine." I waved at everyone and hurried out, nearly bumping into Ashley.

"You're leaving?"

"I have homework and some other stuff to do. I'll see you tomorrow. Thanks so much for inviting me — I had fun." Just beyond Ashley, I spotted her parents. "Thanks for having us over and feeding us."

They nodded and smiled and I got the hell out of

there — without looking back at Zack.

Starting up the Mustang, I leaned back in my seat and sighed. If I could get through the next few weeks of school, then Zack and I would have fewer people to pretend in front of. Except by then Zack might not be around at all.

My heart hurt just thinking about that. The next few weeks, miserable or not, might be all I'd have with Zack.

Gunning the engine, I took off in a huff. I had to figure out a way for Zack and me to get some quality time together. I passed the road that led to where we'd left Charles and realized I'd forgotten to tell Zack about the recent developments.

*Zack, I took a detour on the way to Ashley's earlier and went to the spot where we'd left Charles. He wasn't there.*

*Maybe he got eaten by wild animals.*

*Even the bones and fur?* I asked. *There wasn't a hint of him anywhere. I talked to a park ranger who said no one's seen any wolves, dead or alive.*

*Let's not get worked up over this. It's not like he could get up and walk off without his guts, right? There has to be another explanation.*

*I guess so.* But it still nagged at me. Something wasn't right.

† † †

Homework was almost too easy. Once I wrapped that up, I paced the floor and wondered what do to next. I really wanted to read some of the books on shape-shifters and werewolves that Zack's dad had left for him. But I was too antsy to focus on that kind of stuff.

Passing the hallway, I stopped. My parents had to keep their paperwork somewhere, right? I seriously doubted they always traveled with all their important documents.

I surveyed my dad's office again. File cabinets. Desk. Chair. Closet... I opened each drawer of his desk and removed them, looking inside through the rectangular hole they slid into. I found nothing but empty space. Back to the closet, I examined a box of envelopes and various supplies.

My eyes caught on the paper cutter that sat on a black cloth. But it wasn't either of those things that stole my attention. What was that square metal box under the cloth? I lifted the corner to reveal smooth silver.

Ah, the safe. I'd forgotten it was there since I'd never had a reason to think about it.

I tucked the cloth under the weight of the paper cutter and eyed the large knob covered with small numbers. Damn. How was I supposed to get past a combination lock without the combo?

A few months ago, I'd watched a movie about a thief. He'd filed his fingertips to make them sensitive enough to the feel the clicks on the lock. Another old flick had the burglar use a gadget to amplify the sound and listen for the little clicks.

I wondered if I could do either of those things. My superhuman hearing should be more than adequate.

Kneeling, I shook out my hands and did my best to relax. I put my ear to the cold metal of the safe and turned the lock ever so slowly.

After hearing a faint click, I turned the knob in the other direction. Another click signaled I'd found the second number, so I reversed the direction. I heard a different kind of sound, like a soft thump, and pulled the handle to open it. The door gave way with no resistance.

I'd cracked the safe!

Peering inside, my fingers instinctively reached for what looked like a checkbook. I automatically began searching for the last entry. The balance column had too many digits. That couldn't be right.

If my parents were rich, why were we always moving and using the excuse that my dad needed to work? And why did we live in a three bedroom house when we could afford a mansion? And why let me drive around in a vintage Taurus for two years?

To make sure it wasn't an error, I looked earlier, but couldn't find anything amiss. Each entry gave a large balance that increased with every page.

I set the check register aside and pulled out everything else, not paying any attention to where the items came from. Should I worry that my parents would notice that their stuff had been rearranged?

Nope. After how they'd deceived me, I didn't really care what they thought.

I flipped through papers until I hit on what looked like a birth certificate. Everything else fell to my lap as I brought the paper closer. According to the document, Autumn Nicholson was born in April on the same day as me, to parents Richard and Patricia Nicholson. What the hell? Obviously, the child was me. But who were Patricia and Richard?

This discovery was huge.

Not to mention upsetting.

I squeezed my eyes shut and took in a deep breath before zooming to the scanner to make a copy of the certificate. It didn't tell me whether my parents had adopted me from these people or if they were, in fact, Richard and Patricia and had changed their name. But it told me something was up, that's for sure.

The scanner spit out a piece of paper. I snatched it from the tray and stared at it as though it would tell me all its secrets. My parents' secrets. After a few seconds, I returned to the safe.

I was about to shove everything back inside when I noticed a small, square tray. I grabbed the card on top which turned out to be an ID. It had a picture of my mom on it — with blond hair. As long as I could remember, she'd only ever worn her hair dark. So why did she need an ID with different hair? Strange.

I eyed the box again, reaching for the next card in the stack. It was a credit card in my mom's name. Thinking I might have a use for the ID and credit card, I held onto them and put everything else back, shutting the door and spinning the knob.

For what seemed an eon, I stood in my dad's office, unmoving, alternately staring at the copy of the birth certificate and the ID.

Maybe Zack was right all along and I'd been adopted. But that didn't explain why I looked so much like my mom who had raised me. Of course, she could've gotten lucky with a genetic similarity. Or maybe they were my real parents, but had changed their name. But why would they need to do that?

In a daze, I walked the few feet to my room and opened my laptop. A search under Patricia Nicholson brought over a million results, more for Richard Nicholson.

I tried again, adding my birth city, but with such a common name, nothing usable popped up. Giving up on that, I clicked on the map. The hospital was located in a small town near Yosemite, about six hours by car from Los Angeles.

Assuming that Richard and Patricia were my biological parents, and not the people I knew now as my parents, did Richard and Patricia know what I was? Maybe Zack was right and my real mom was a human who didn't know my father was a shape-shifter. Like Zack's mom who had no idea her husband was a werewolf. Maybe my dad had died, leaving my mom single, and she couldn't keep me.

I released my breath, squeezing my eyes shut. As the seconds ticked by, I knew I couldn't ignore this new information and I had to find Richard and Patricia Nicholson. But without any other clues, where would I begin? With no home address on the birth certificate, how would I find them?

Plopping back against my pillow, I stared at the ceiling.

*Autumn?*

*Hey, Zack.*

*You still coming over?*

*Do you want me to?*

There was a pause. Geez. Did he have to think about it so long?

*Around ten?* he asked.

*I'll see you then.*

Zack had seemed annoyed. Maybe he planned to break up with me for real before booting me out of his room.

# CHAPTER TWENTY

AS USUAL, I morphed into a common house cat and scratched on Zack's window. My foot had just touched the floor in my human form and Zack was there, holding my face in his hands and dropping kisses on my mouth.

*I don't want to talk about it, okay?*

Whatever *it* was, I was pretty sure I didn't want to talk about it either. Probably my conversation with Greg or my *date* with Cameron. *Talk about what?*

*Anything. And I don't want to argue.* He buried his face in my hair and his arms wrapped all the way around me.

I closed my eyes, my cheek pressed against his neck. I had no interest in hashing out any of that either. Besides, if we got to talking, I might spill the beans on the birth certificate and that I planned to go out of town this weekend to get information on my birth parents. I might even tell him I'd been accused of cheating on a test. God forbid I should let it slip that Renzo and Alura knew about me.

I didn't want to think about any of that right then, much less discuss it. *If you don't want to talk, what do you want to do? It's still early.*

Zack had already guided me to the bed where he gingerly coaxed me lower until I was horizontal. *I just want to be with you.*

*Okay.* No kissing?

He nudged my shoulder to turn me until I could no longer see him, then he pressed his body against my back, his face swallowed up in my hair. Draping his arm around my waist, he squeezed me even closer and his legs tangled with mine. I didn't feel or hear him breathing. He made no noise except the steady beat of his heart and no movement but the light strokes of his hand on my wrist.

I melted into him. It was almost better than kissing.

† † †

It was still dark. I was on my side with my back to the clock so I had no idea what time it was. It didn't matter — my body said it was time to wake up.

Zack's hand moved on my hip. *You awake?*

I turned over to face him, our lips inches apart. *Yes.*

He stayed perfectly still, watching me. Tentatively, I brought my hand up to rest on his cheek. Sighing, he removed my hand and turned his lips into my palm. The softest of kisses trailed up my wrist then he placed it on his waist and scooted closer to me, his thighs melding to mine.

Zack pushed against me, rolling me back. Lightly brushing my lips with his, he moved closer, crowding me, and the nerves in my limbs sprang to life. His mouth touched mine again, teasing, his tongue tasting my bottom lip.

It was killing me.

Kissing Zack was the most exciting thing I'd ever done but this time was even better — the perfect balance of anticipation and bliss. All too soon, he drew back and looked over his shoulder at the clock.

I got a glimpse of the time. It was later than I'd thought.

*It'll be light soon. You should go.* He left the bed and handed me a pair of jeans and a T-shirt. *Take these with you.*

I nodded, wondering how he could turn it off so easily while I stood there trembling. Even though he hadn't wanted to talk, perhaps he was still angry with me from yesterday. Zack wasn't exactly big on sharing his feelings and I refused to ask him. Vowing not to dwell on it, I stepped into his jeans and shrugged on the shirt.

But he needed to know I was leaving this Friday — that was only two days from now. *Um...*

He closed the distance and held me by my shoulders, studying me. *What's up?*

*Remember when you suggested I snoop around, look for something on my parents?* My gaze wandered to his chest.

*Uh-oh. What did you find?*

*I came across a birth certificate with totally random people listed as my birth parents. I'm going to drive out to the hospital where I was born and see if I can dig up anything on them. Canvass the neighborhood maybe.*

*Drive out where?* he asked.

*Small town near Yosemite.*

*That's several hours away. You're not driving out there alone. Hell no.*

*It's not like you can come with me*, I said. *How would it look if we went out of town together when we're supposed to be broken up?*

*Let me see what I can come up with. We'll figure something out. But you're not going alone, that's for sure.*

I gave him a quick kiss on the cheek, then I headed out the window. I booked it home, going straight to the back door of my house.

Finding my key, I raised it to the lock and froze. Renzo's scent wafted up my nose and my heart thumped wildly against my ribs.

"Autumn."

Spinning around to face him, I looked into his eyes and saw tornados wreaking destruction. Why was he angry? Had he changed his mind and decided he was finished vacationing? Did Charles come back to life and tell Renzo what we'd done?

"Where. Is. Charles?" he growled.

Whew. He didn't know and I needed to keep it that way. I wanted to bolt, but with him directly in front of me, there was no escape. That would only make me look guilty anyway.

I backed up against the door and inhaled deeply to steady my pulse. "I told you I don't know."

"You're lying and that's why you're frightened right now."

"I'm not lying," I said. "I'm afraid because you're in my backyard, uninvited, and you're a very scary dude."

"But Alura isn't scary?" He raised one brow.

I shook my head. "No. She doesn't sneak around my house and block me so I can't move."

"Meet me at the coffee house later. I'll make sure Alura is there too."

Why would I meet with Renzo *on purpose*? "What if I say no?"

He laughed softly, which was even more terrifying than the storm in his eyes. "Then I'll find you."

"Fine. I'll meet you guys tonight," I said quickly, then got distracted by his skin. Despite the fear inside me, I found myself leaning forward almost imperceptibly to get a closer look.

"Problem?" he growled, eyes narrowing.

I'd never seen him up close during the day. "You have fine little scars all over your face. I thought werewolves and shifters both healed completely."

"We do. But some wounds are so deep, they take longer."

"How long ago was it?" I asked.

"None of your business, little one." His tone told me I'd asked enough questions.

"What happened to you?" I pressed unthinkingly, too curious to resist.

"Maybe, like you, I asked too many questions." He didn't say good-bye, disappearing as if he'd never been there.

I shivered at his veiled threat, glad he was gone. Wait... Was Zack supposed to come with me to the coffee house? Renzo hadn't specifically requested him. I'd go without Zack. No point in putting his head on the chopping block, too.

I scurried through the door then locked it, my mind drifting back to Charles and how his wolf body had vanished. After scrambling up the stairs, I checked my computer for recent local news, even though I suspected it was a wasted effort. Twenty minutes later, my suspicions were confirmed. Not even a whisper about an oversized dead wolf.

He had to have healed somehow. There was no other explanation.

If he was alive, he'd come after us, and this time, he'd kill us for sure. Fingers of terror clawed at my heart.

† † †

With only three more school days to prove my innocence to Mr. Collins, I still had no idea how to squeeze the data from Gina. She seemed to believe I wanted to be her friend, but she hadn't let anything useful slip yet.

When I arrived at school Wednesday morning, I backed into the parking spot so I faced the lot, easily seeing any new arrivals. I slunk down in my seat, until Gina drove up in her black convertible Mercedes. I got out of my car, just as she exited hers — followed by Natalie. Damn. Natalie was a lost cause. My odds were better with Gina, but with Natalie there, forget it. I retreated to my car to wait for Maya.

*We have a couple ways we can approach this Yosemite trip*, Zack's words invaded my mind.

*And how is that?*

*First, you're not going alone. That's out of the question.*

I had difficulty arguing with him since I was dying to get him all to myself anyway. *Okay. What else?*

*My mom knows the truth about us so we could enlist her help. Maybe if we bring it up over dinner, she can order me to go with you.*

*Brilliant*, I said, glancing around. The parking lot was filling quickly.

*Or*, he continued, *we make up in public*—

*And throw away all our hard work?* I loved the idea, but felt like I'd sacrificed a lot. Besides, Renzo had told me to keep our relationship under wraps. He wasn't someone I wanted to cross. And I didn't want to scrap our progress only to have to start all over again when the next new werewolf showed up.

*If Charles is alive, we'll need to go back to spending every moment together again anyway. Safety in numbers.*

*So you think he's alive?* I asked.

*Not really. But I think we should be prepared either way.*

Zack, always practical. *Are you almost here?*

*Yes. Think about our options and we'll talk later.*

The red Jeep slid into a parking space and Maya and Trevor climbed out. I was there before Zack locked up.

"You have no makeup on," Zack commented.

"Didn't have time."

"Really? What were you doing all morning?"

Trevor and Maya eyed Zack curiously.

"Do I look bad or something?" I asked him.

"Not at all. You look... wholesome," he answered.

"Wholesome," I repeated, grimacing.

He chuckled. "It's not necessarily bad. It's just different. Sometimes change is good."

"I thought you liked the slutty look. I figured you'd have to, otherwise you wouldn't have dated Gina."

Maya punched Zack in the shoulder, scowling. "Eeww! You dated Gina?"

*Sorry*, I told him silently, biting my lip.

"Hey!" Zack flinched, rubbing his shoulder. "It was ages ago, before I knew you guys."

"Whatever." She switched targets, zeroing in on Trevor. "Did you know about this?"

The boys needed saving, so I stepped in. "It was before he knew she'd slept with Daniel. It's not their fault."

Maya sighed. "I'm sorry for hitting you, Zack. I guess I'm just mad at you for not fighting for Autumn and being such a wuss about everything."

"C'mon. Let's get to class," I said, hoping to save Zack from having to respond.

*Thank you,* he told me silently.

† † †

I waited for Gina after my last class, but she was glued to Natalie. It made sense that Gina would drive Natalie home since she drove Natalie to school, but it still sucked. Trying to get Gina's attention during lunch had been pointless since she sat with Jeff, Natalie and Greg. Another day wasted.

Disappointment wedged itself in my throat like a ball of fire. How was I going to clear my name if I couldn't get close to Gina?

My only other idea was to force her to fix it. Blackmail? But with what?

I dragged my gaze from Gina's glossy, black convertible, but ended up eye-to-eye with Cameron. He turned away from me as he arrived at his truck. Crap. He'd been staring at me. I hoped that didn't mean what I thought it did.

"What's up?" Zack studied me a beat, then glanced around. Thankfully, Cameron had already disappeared inside his truck.

My shoulders slumped. "Gina and Natalie set me up in Mr. Collins class and now he thinks I cheated on a test. If I can't prove my innocence by Monday, he's calling my parents."

Zack's jaw set in a hard line. "Are you sure it was Gina?"

"Pretty sure." I nodded. "I was going to try to suck up to her, hoping she'd slip. Epic fail so far."

Zack grinned. "Sounds like you need a pinch-hitter."

Huh? "Is that some kind of football term?"

He laughed. "I mean, what if I'm the one sucking up?"

"You're my hero!" I squealed.

"Why is Zack your hero?" Trevor asked.

"Yeah, why?" Maya echoed.

"He's going to suck up to Gina, try to get her to confess to setting me up."

"But Gina won't open up so long as you keep hanging around Autumn," Trevor pointed out. "People already think your relationship is strange. I know I do."

Just when I thought the school situation with him couldn't get any worse. If he had to work on Gina, I'd spend even less time with him.

"What's so weird about us? It's not like no one's ever broken up and stayed friends," I said, hand on my hip.

"Trevor's right though. If I'm your friend, she won't let me in," Zack said.

On the sly, I looked over at Gina and Natalie who were still hanging around Gina's Mercedes. They weren't facing us dead on, but if anything happened in our circle, they'd see. It was a perfect opportunity.

"Well, I'm sorry in advance." I slapped Zack's face hard, the sound echoing off the pavement as I powered up my vocal cords. "Staring at other girls right in front of me? I was trying to stay friends with you, but forget it! Stay the hell away from me!"

I stomped off toward my car, which allowed me to observe Gina and Natalie who stood rooted in place, their mouths wide open. They looked convinced. Good. Now I just had to wait for Zack to work his magic on them. If he was still talking to me after this. It was the first real hope I'd had since Mr. Collins had accused me of cheating.

Getting in my car, I started up the car and peeled

out. *I'm so sorry. It didn't hurt too much, did it?*

It was so strange to hear him laughing in my head. *You were perfect. Remind me never to get you mad for real. By the way, I'm seeing Gina tonight to wrap up our project.*

*I don't want her anywhere near you. Just get what I need so you don't have to see her again.* I loathed being the voice of reason right then.

*Working on it. Coming over later?*

*Of course.*

My cell phone rang and I pulled over to rummage through my purse. It was Maya. "Hey."

"I can't believe you did that." She snickered. "What a beautiful performance. You should have seen Gina's face. Wait. That *was* an act, right? You weren't really mad at him, were you?"

"No. Zack and I are still friends."

"Okay, whew." She exhaled audibly. "What are you doing the rest of the day?"

"Homework, chores." Meeting with a terrifying werewolf who knows I'm a shape-shifter and hooked up with a werewolf. Hoping I won't die. "I have to check in with my parents and some other stuff." But if Maya and Trevor went out for coffee and saw me with the werewolves, they'd catch me lying. "Oh, and Alura invited me for coffee. I said I'd pop in."

"Maybe we'll stop by too," Maya said.

"That sounds great." Having friends there would make a meeting with Renzo seem less like standing in front of a firing squad. Or maybe not.

# CHAPTER TWENTY-ONE

AFTER FINISHING MY homework, I grabbed the shape-shifter book I'd been reading and dropped onto the living room couch, unsure when Renzo and Alura expected me. I'd been too fear-stricken when Renzo had summoned me that I hadn't even thought to ask what time he wanted me there.

As the evening drew closer, I set the book aside and checked my e-mail, but became too antsy to concentrate on anything. What if Renzo got mad at me for being late? Getting to the coffee shop before them wasn't an option either. The waiting would drive me crazy. What did he want anyway? To continue the interrogation, probably.

Thankfully, Alura would be there to diffuse the worst of it. That is, if she were still acting like she was on my side.

I wondered if I could talk to Alura or Renzo telepathically like I did with Zack. Concentrating on Alura and visualizing her in my head, I said, *Hey, it's Autumn.*

*Hi, Autumn!* Alura sang in her calming voice. *I'm quite impressed you're able to talk to me this way.*

I almost lied and blurted out that I'd learned about it from the SWAAST website, rather than involve Zack. Then it occurred to me the Shape-shifter Werewolf Alliance Against Slavery and Tyranny were the most hunted supernaturals ever. Having information on werewolf or shape-shifter rebels would give Renzo one more reason to eliminate me.

I'd have to find new sites with the same information. And fast.

*What time are you guys going for coffee? I asked.*

*Around seven.*

*Thanks. I'll see you then.* I shut her out, suddenly panicked that she'd suspect I'd been lying about everything. I'd told them my parents were human and that Zack didn't know about me. There weren't any other shape-shifters around to mentor me and I hadn't known I was a shape-shifter long. So how could I explain why I knew so much about our world?

Contacting her that way had been a stupid move. I needed to be smarter. Refocusing on my laptop, I opened the browser to look for alternative websites to tell them about.

Wait... Renzo had talked to me telepathically at the coffee shop the other day so they already knew I could hear them. I exhaled in relief, the heaviness in my shoulders dissipating as I forced my body to calm, limb by limb.

But I knew the stress would return soon enough.

I felt a little like those drivers you see on the news, barreling down the highway with cops chasing them and helicopters overhead. The driver knows he's going to get caught, but so long as he has hope for freedom, he keeps driving.

This weekend would be different though. I had some real hope for a break. Zack and I would get away, just the two of us with nothing to do but look for information on my birth parents. Once we figured out a way to leave without anyone following us, we'd have over forty-eight hours of freedom.

Suddenly, I missed my mom and dad terribly. Finding my phone, I scrolled to my mom's cell phone number, but then stopped. A live conversation wouldn't do. I loved them just as much as ever, but no way could I keep the bitterness out of my voice after they'd lied to me. I couldn't talk to them just yet and I hoped they wouldn't show up out of the blue. Because I'd surely lose my temper.

I settled for shooting off a quick text reminding them I loved them.

Focusing on my computer screen again, I willed myself to concentrate and find some sites with usable information on shifters. The thought of arriving unprepared for my meeting with Renzo made my pulse quicken.

† † †

Hearing a knock at the door, I tore my eyes from the computer monitor and rubbed them. I hoped it wasn't Renzo... or worse, Charles. I crept toward the peephole.

"Autumn, are you in there?" Zack called from the other side.

I swung the door open, a big smile waiting for him. "Hey!"

He wasn't smiling back. "I'm glad you're okay. Where have you been? You were supposed to have dinner at my house, remember? I've already briefed my mom."

Right. I planned to talk about the trip so she would order Zack to go with me. "Sorry, I got caught up in something."

"Caught up in what? Everything all right?"

"Alura wants to meet for coffee later."

"Alura?" His eyes snapped to mine. "What about Renzo?"

"Him too, I guess. It seems like they're always together." I felt sleazy coloring the truth, but at least I'd told him about the birth certificate and getting caught cheating. Only one lie left. And it would stay that way so Zack wouldn't take matters into his own hands and leave town. Or worse, get himself killed to protect me.

In any case, it would be too dangerous having to keep track of Zack knowing that Renzo knew about me, but that Renzo didn't know that Zack knew that he knew, and on and on. My head reeled with that garbage.

I figured it wouldn't be too difficult to handle Zack if he caught me in a lie, since he'd been guilty of it so many times himself, but I could barely handle Renzo as it was.

Plus, I couldn't allow Zack to be distracted by Renzo and the fact that I'd been discovered. I needed him focused on helping me expose Gina's frame job.

"Autumn, you need to stay away from them."

I didn't want to have this conversation with him.

The more I talked about it, the more chance I'd slip up. "After we've already hung out with her?" I asked. "I couldn't think of a way out of it. And if I were really human, I'd probably accept her invitation. I didn't want to raise suspicion."

Zack studied me a moment, then glanced over my shoulder into the living room. "Are you alone?"

"No, I have the entire cast of The Vampire Diaries inside." That was a strange question. "Of course I'm alone. Who else would be here?"

"You tell me." Zack folded his arms across his chest.

Was he jealous and thought I might have Cameron over? Way to trust your girlfriend, dude. Not that I could blame him since I wasn't being totally honest with him about other things. I opened the door the rest of the way and motioned for him to come in. "See for yourself."

"Not a good idea." He shook his head and stayed put. "After Yosemite, hopefully we'll know more about your parents. If they're human, it'll be safe to come inside because they won't smell me."

Folding my arms over my chest, I eyed him. "If I remember correctly, that wasn't the only reason you didn't want to be here alone with me. Lost interest in me already, have you?"

I eyed Zack and the strange look on his face, trying to figure out what was up. The next instant, he'd passed through the doorway and was pressing me against the wall. His mouth explored mine, his palms on either side of my hips so I couldn't get away.

Exactly what I needed after a long day of stress. Zack all over me. Mmm.

His lips left my mouth in search of the hollow below my jaw. "Does it seem like I've lost interest?"

"I suppose not. We should go," I said, as his hands splayed at my ribs, thumbs at the edge of my bra. "Or not..."

He chuckled as his lips found my mouth again.

As good as his kisses were, we couldn't stay. Laying my hands on either side of his face, I forced him to look at me. "As much as it pains me, we really have to stop." Grabbing my purse and phone, I led the way.

Zack blinked, then ran a hand through his hair and followed me outside.

We strolled along the sidewalk and his little yellow house and wide red porch came into view. I breathed a sigh of relief. "Why does she want to meet with you?" Zack asked.

"Maybe I'm likable." I glanced over at him.

He shook his head. "No, that's not it."

"I'm not likable?" I teased.

Grabbing my arm, he pulled me to a halt. "I think she wants something. Be careful. They'll fish for information. Try to give them as little as possible."

Like I hadn't already been there and done that. And failed epically.

"You're meeting in a public place so they won't act. After I finish up with Gina, I'll come by," he said. "To make sure everything's all right."

"Okay."

He didn't seem inclined to continue to his house. At this rate, we'd be very late for dinner, we'd look very suspicious and Cara would be annoyed.

"You're hiding something." His eyes turned to slits as he studied my face.

My brain worked overtime to come up with a response which was the truth, but not *the* truth. "I just didn't want to complain. This whole thing sucks. We have a short time before you're forced to leave and this is how we spend it. Strangers by day and stealing time together at night."

"I'm sorry. It's not easy for me either, but I don't have another solution just yet. C'mon. Let's get to dinner before Aunt Cara disowns me." He turned and resumed walking.

"Zack, tell me again why you think my parents are human."

"I can't detect any shape-shifter scent on them."

"But no one has detected any on me either. The only reason you do is because your nose gets literally against my skin. You haven't been that close to my parents. You haven't even met them."

"But if they were shape-shifters, Autumn," he said, "don't you think they'd clue you in on what you are? By not telling you, they're throwing you to the wolves. Literally. I have a hard time believing they'd be so irresponsible."

He had a good point. We sprinted up the steps to his house and he opened the door for me. Everyone was already seated at the dinner table, including Maya. Good. She was the most important person to convince.

"Finally," Cara said, one brow raised.

"Sorry. I got immersed in homework and lost track of time. Hi, everyone." I smiled, my eyes searching out each person at the table.

"*Tesora*, sit next to me. I don't see you as often since you dumped my poor son." Favianne was really working it.

I tried not to giggle. "Dinner looks great. Thanks so much for having me."

We all passed dishes around and served ourselves, making small talk along the way.

"So how are you doing all alone at your house? Things working out?" Favianne asked.

*Now's your chance to tell them about your trip*, Zack said.

"Actually, things have been... interesting." I glanced at Maya. "I was poking around the house and came across a birth certificate. It was strange and... well, I'll show you." I got up to fetch my purse and dug out the folded copy of the document. I handed it to Maya and returned to my seat. "See how it has a different last name for me and completely different parents? The birthday matches mine exactly though."

"So..." Maya looked at me, obviously trying to wrap her head around it. "What does this mean? You were adopted or something?"

"I don't know yet." I shrugged.

Maya blinked, then closed her mouth as Trevor

slipped the certificate from her fingers. "Who woulda thought, huh?" she asked. "You look so much like your mom."

"Yeah," I agreed. "But maybe they just changed their identity. I didn't get anywhere searching those names on the Internet, so I thought this weekend I'd drive up to the hospital where I was born to see what I can find out. If I do have different birth parents, they might still live there and someone might know them. It's a small town, not like a big city where it's easier to disappear, right?"

"Sorry, I'm still in shock." Maya made the time out sign. "It's hard to believe Mr. Rossi might not be your real dad."

Tears burned behind my eyes and I fought them away. "I'm going to find out more before I jump to conclusions."

"I've never heard of Oakhurst, California. Where is it?" Trevor asked, glancing up at me from the certificate.

"It's a few minutes' drive from Yosemite," I answered.

Favianne raised a brow. "Who's going with you?"

I shrugged. "I figured I'd go alone."

"No. Zack will drive you." Favianne stared him down. "Right, Zack?"

He frowned. "Um... Mom, we broke up. Autumn doesn't want to be stuck with me on a road trip."

"Friends can do road trips together." Favianne switched to me. "You can't go alone. I'll worry about you the whole time."

"I don't really mind going alone but —"

"We should all go." Maya's eyes were huge with excitement. "All four of us. Wouldn't that be fun?"

Oh, damn. I hadn't planned on that possibility. There went my weekend alone with Zack where we didn't have to pretend. It had been my one chance...

"Yeah," Trevor chimed in. "If we were with you, *we* wouldn't worry either. Let us do this for you, Autumn."

I looked at Zack for confirmation, hoping he'd come up with something to stop them.

"Fine. We'll all go." Zack held up his hands in surrender, then shoveled in another bite of pasta, impressing me with how convincing he could be. I reminded myself that, like me, he'd had practice. For the last couple years, he'd been persuading his family and everyone else to believe he was human.

"Wonderful. I'll feel so much better knowing Zack is looking out for you." Favianne returned to her meal, looking puzzled that our scheme had backfired.

"I was planning on leaving right after school." Less chance of being followed. "That way I could arrive in Oakhurst early enough to talk to people and do some digging. Diners will still be open, the hospital, maybe even some stores."

"Yeah, but why waste a Friday night on the road when we can leave Saturday morning?" Trevor asked.

"Because I want to make sure there's plenty of time to find out everything I possibly can. It's too far away to make the trip twice."

Maya looked from me to Trevor. "We have plans

for Friday night — a concert and we already have the tickets. You sure it can't wait until Saturday?"

I raised a brow. "If you were me and found a birth certificate like that, would you want to wait?"

"No," she conceded. "We'll give away our tickets."

Zack groaned. "Guys, forget it. I'll go with her. It'll be... nice to get away, I guess. And if Autumn's running around all over the place, it's going to be *work*. You guys will probably get bored anyway. It's not like you'll have your own car. If you do, it defeats the whole purpose of driving together."

"True," Maya said.

Zack, saving me again.

† † †

I helped Zack clean up the dinner dishes. After a chat with Cara, then Maya and Favianne, it was almost time for my meeting with Renzo. My stomach felt queasy but I'd feel worse if he came after me.

It was seven on the nose when I walked through the side door of the coffee house. After getting my drink, I made my way to the front patio. The werewolves were already there. Waiting to pounce.

I took the seat next to Alura. Zack could sit next to scary Renzo this time, if he stopped by.

"Good evening." Renzo nodded at me, unnerving me with his steady gaze.

"Hi." I took a sip of my coffee. "Zack will be here later, maybe our other friends, too. So if you're going to grill me, you should get it out of the way now." I hoped Renzo bought my attempt at being nonchalant. In reality, my nerves were frayed from angst and my fingers trembled. I was a wreck.

"Uncle, you're making her nervous. Please stop."

"If she weren't afraid of getting caught in a lie, she'd be more relaxed." He brought his coffee cup to his lips, his eyes steady on mine.

"I'm sure it has nothing to do with the fact that our species have been at war for centuries. Or that you could probably kill me with one strike." I shot him a scowl, then sucked in a lungful and released it. "Plus, I'm not used to being forced into meetings with werewolves."

Renzo leaned forward. "Then tell me what happened to Charles."

"You keep asking me that, but I can't magically know something simply because you want me to."

"You're lying." His deep dark eyes bore through mine. "I saw you in the woods yesterday."

My body froze.

I was so dead.

# CHAPTER TWENTY-TWO

I CLEARED MY throat, stalling for extra seconds, but it was impossible to think with his heated gaze bearing down on me. "All right. I'll tell you the truth."

He sent Alura a smirk. Her frown deepened.

Taking a breath, I said, "I went running Friday night and came across a dead wolf. It was a bloody mess. You kept asking about Charles and yesterday I put two and two together. Thought I'd check it out."

"You killed him," he accused.

"Me?" I laughed. "Attack and kill a werewolf much older and more powerful than me? You give me too much credit."

"Uncle Renzo, another werewolf could've done it. Sorry, but I just don't see Autumn capable of over-powering him."

"Exactly," I said.

Renzo didn't look convinced. He leaned back in his chair and eyed me. "Why do you barely smell like a shape-shifter?"

"How should I know? I thought it was because I was still maturing and the scent would become stronger with time."

"It'll get stronger, yes, but I should've been able to spot you immediately."

"Really? Then why couldn't you?"

His eye twitched. "That's what I'm asking *you*."

"Look, anything I know was learned on the Internet and they didn't cover that in Shape-shifter 101." I blew out a breath. "*You* should be the one telling *me*."

"Do your parents know you're maturing?"

"I told you, they're human. I don't plan to inform them."

Renzo picked up a stir stick and impatiently tapped it on the table. "If they're human, you couldn't be a shape-shifter." A corner of his mouth lifted, but not in a friendly way.

"I must've been adopted. Or maybe my real dad was a shape-shifter and my mom never knew what he was. Maybe when she found out she was pregnant, he wasn't around. For all I know, he could've been taken as a slave or something."

"So when you began to mature, you had no one to help you?"

"No one." I called upon my years of practice at faking calm for my parents' benefit, then met him eye to eye. "My first morph was shocking, to say the least. I remember looking down at my paws and freaking out. When I came home, I did a bunch of research on the net. A lot of the info was myth, but I weeded out the garbage by trial and error. As my senses got stronger, I realized Zack was a werewolf. I was afraid if he knew what I was, he wouldn't want me. So I kept my mouth shut."

"Wow," Alura said. "I couldn't imagine going through that all alone. You must have been scared."

"Yeah, I had my moments. But the rest of the time..." I grinned. "It was like finding out I was a superhero. Isn't that everyone's dream growing up?" Thinking of Charles, I reminded myself to speak of him in present tense since I was supposed to believe he was alive and well. "I had no reason to be freaked out until Charles came into the picture. But it hasn't been a problem since he thinks I'm human."

"You know, of course, it's illegal to mix species?" Renzo said, his voice quiet.

I kept my expression neutral as I made an extra effort to breathe. Denying it would be stupid since our last coffee date he'd smelled Zack on me and knew I was lying about being broken up with him. Plus, I'd freaked and asked if he was going to kill me. He'd have to know I was fully aware of the laws. "Yes. Which is why I've made sure Zack doesn't know about me."

"You must be very careful. It isn't just about legalities, but safety too."

"Um..." Was Renzo talking about sex? Ugh. I stared into my coffee cup, praying that my admission of guilt wasn't like signing my death warrant. But he'd already known this and hadn't killed me. "Mixing species causes some weird chemical imbalance and makes both weaker, right?"

"Yes, you would be putting Zack in danger. Promise me you'll *never* do that," Renzo insisted.

My arms prickled in fear. "I would never put Zack in danger."

"You've not seen Charles since Saturday, you said?"

Another attempt at tripping me up. I wasn't falling for Renzo's trick, now or ever. "No, Friday night. Are you going to tell me how you got those scars?" I knew he wouldn't cough it up, but I hoped turning the questions on him would make him feel like he'd had enough of me and maybe he'd leave.

"Be careful, little one. The next werewolf to arrive at your doorstep might not be as forgiving as me." He rose from his chair and glanced at his niece. "Alura?"

Still reeling from his threat, I swallowed. "You're leaving?"

"Yes," he answered.

Alura gave him a tight smile. "I'll stay a little while and visit with Autumn."

"As you wish." He nodded once and walked away, stopping at the blue Jaguar.

"I apologize for my uncle's behavior." She rolled her eyes.

It was hard to gauge if they were playing good cop bad cop or if Alura was being sincere. She sure seemed genuine and I needed answers.

"Your uncle's a werewolf. You guys don't like my kind, right?" I asked.

"Not necessarily." Alura gave a delicate shrug. "Depends on the werewolf and how he or she was raised. I'm neutral."

She seemed responsive and I had so many questions. God, where would I begin? Looking around to make sure nobody was close to our table and could hear us, I still lowered my voice. "Are you a born werewolf or were you bitten? That's how you make a werewolf, right?"

Her brows rose. "Just dive right in. Yes, it only takes one bite."

"Is it a saliva thing? Or is there something with the fangs? How does it work?" I took a sip of my coffee.

"The bite creates a path into the body and the saliva carries the virus. I'm a born werewolf, so I didn't go through that, thank goodness."

"Born werewolves are rare though, right?" I'd been wishing for Zack's early arrival, but now that Renzo was gone and I could pump Alura for information, he could take his time. "Because females can't carry a child to term."

"Right. We're incapable of having children because our urge to morph is too strong and the baby dies when we change form. My mother was human when she had me, as was Zack's." Her lips curved up. "Being on your own with no one to talk to about this, you must have saved up a bunch of questions."

"Yes. I have tons. I—"

"Hi, Zack," Alura called out. "Would you like to join us?"

Glancing over my shoulder, I saw Zack heading toward us from the Jeep.

"Hey," he said, once his feet touched the concrete of the patio. "Let me get a coffee and I'll join you guys."

"Is Maya coming too?" I asked him.

"Yeah, she and Trevor are in the car. They'll be out in a minute." Zack passed through the front door of the coffee house.

I made sure he was gone, then whispered as quietly as I could. "Remember, he doesn't know I'm a shape-shifter or that you know we're still together."

"Gotcha covered." Alura smiled. "And there they are."

I glanced over my shoulder and beamed at Maya. Thankfully, werewolves had rules against hurting mortals or involving them in anything that would flag the police and expose us. At least I didn't have to worry about my friends' safety. "Hey, get your drinks and sit with us."

She grinned. "We'll be right back."

Wait... what if Maya or Trevor mentioned our road trip in front of Alura? Not only that, but what if someone from school saw Zack and me hanging out? If Gina heard we were friendly, then his attempt to gain her trust and trap her would be a waste of time. That would ruin everything. Unless Zack had made progress with Gina tonight, but I hadn't heard from him yet.

My stomach constricted as I battled to keep the pleasant smile on my face. I had to get out of there.

"You know, I don't think I'll stay after all. I'm tired and still have homework to do. I'll let Maya know. Want a ride to your hotel?" I stood, the chair scraping on the cement.

"Sure. It'll save my uncle a trip." She flashed me perfect, white teeth.

I went inside to say good-bye and reminded Maya and Trevor that Zack couldn't hang out with me. I told Zack telepathically that I'd see him later and exited the front just as Alura was throwing away her coffee cup.

My moment of solitude couldn't come quickly enough. I was exhausted from the intense stress and fear of being caught in any of my vast number of lies.

"Where's your hotel?" I asked.

"We're staying at the Cavalli in La Crescenta."

Now that I knew I'd be home soon, the stress of the day — especially my time with Renzo — hit me hard. I sat up straighter in my seat to perk up. "I'm exhausted."

She chuckled. "Yes, my uncle has that effect on people. I'm sorry about the interrogation. I'd tell you it's all out of his system, but it probably isn't. He doesn't trust people easily. So prepare yourself for more."

"Well, thanks for the heads up." I sighed, pulling out onto the street. "If you and Renzo aren't scouts or watchers, what do you do for the king?"

"We do... other things."

"You're not going to tell me, are you?"

"Maybe another time."

It was just as well. I shouldn't be talking to Alura at all. My brain was fried and it would be too easy to slip up in this condition. I melted into the driver's seat and concentrated on the road.

"Make a right into the second driveway after the light," Alura said after a few minutes.

Biting my lip, I crossed the intersection and turned the steering wheel. "Alura? Can I ask you a question?"

She swiveled toward me. "Sure."

There was no easy way to ask, so... "If Renzo knows of my crimes, then why doesn't he kill me? Or report me to the king?"

She paused as if mulling over her answer. "We're not scouts."

"Then what are you?"

Alura laughed softly. "That will have to wait for another time. But you can trust Renzo. He can't help, though, if you don't tell him the truth."

Were they setting me up? Whatever. No way would I call Renzo helpful since he hadn't done anything other than follow me, threaten me, and force me to meet with him. All he'd accomplished so far was to scare the hell out of me.

Alura was guilty by association — not that I'd trust a werewolf to begin with. Why would they want to help us anyway? What was in it for them?

Stopping in front of the double swinging doors of the Cavalli hotel, I put the car in park. "I'd be more likely to trust Renzo if you told me what you did for the king."

She gave me a regretful smile. "Thanks for the ride, Autumn."

As she walked toward the hotel doors, I shook my head. She didn't trust me enough to confide in me, but she wanted me to trust her? No way.

From now on, I needed to stay away from both of them. I couldn't know when Renzo might suddenly no longer be on vacation and Alura was sure to side with him. I had a feeling, though, that avoiding them wouldn't be easy.

# CHAPTER TWENTY-THREE

BY THE TIME I got home from meeting with Renzo and Alura, I collapsed on the sofa. After the torturous day of pretending Zack and I were broken up, watching lamely while girls flirted with him, keeping track of all my lies, and enduring Renzo's cross-examination, lethargy ruled me like a despot.

For a moment, I considered blowing off Zack and sleeping in my own bed, simply because I didn't have the energy to sprint the block to his house. But I wouldn't be able to get near him all day tomorrow at school since we were supposedly no longer on speaking terms. I didn't want to go that long without being with him.

Gotta get up.

While I set out school clothes for the next day and washed my hair in the shower, I thought of our trip. How would we escape without any werewolves following us? Charles wasn't around — I hoped — but what if another scout had arrived and was lying low?

Zack was great at figuring that stuff out. He was probably working on it now.

*I'm here at your house, waiting for you out back,* Zack said, just as I finished getting dressed. My heart skipped and I bounded down the stairs with renewed energy. When I opened the back door, he pulled out a plastic bag from under his shirt and shoved it at me. *For our Yosemite trip. Hide it with the other stuff.*

Zack stayed by the back door so he wouldn't leave a trail of his scent through my house, while I darted upstairs to stow the plastic bag in my room. Moments later, I returned to the back door. "Done."

"Good." His gaze drifted to my midriff-baring tank top and my stomach flipped. "We need a plan to get out of town without the werewolves knowing."

"You still have the spare key to my car. After school you can sneak into the Mustang." I wrapped my arms around his waist and laid my head against his shoulder. "If they're watching, they won't follow me, because they're interested in you, right?"

"Good idea." His arms closed around me.

Didn't matter how tired I was or how badly I wanted to remain ignorant of Zack's date with Gina. I still need-ed to know what happened. "How did it go tonight?"

He rubbed his chin on the top of my head. "To-day was all about earning her trust. We worked on the project and I steered clear of hot topics."

Wise move, but that meant Zack would have to meet with her again. Unfortunately, now that they'd built trust, she might be a lot more friendly with him next time.

† † †

I slipped out of Zack's room as tendrils of light peeked out from the horizon — just after he'd pressed me into the mattress and kissed me until my IQ began to drop. He hadn't seemed inclined to stop.

Since he no longer exhibited signs of control when we were alone, maybe it wasn't such a bad thing I'd cut our make-out short and had taken off so early.

Being good felt like a bad thing, though.

Tomorrow we'd start our road trip together and my entire being tingled in anticipation. Since Renzo hadn't made any openly aggressive moves — other than scare the hell out of me — it was too easy to think we'd get away with it.

But we weren't fooling anyone, as my conversations with Renzo had proved. He could turn on us at any moment. And what if Charles was indeed alive? If he was off somewhere healing, how long before his return?

It didn't matter how much I was looking forward to being alone with Zack in a hotel room, I couldn't allow myself to forget how much more dangerous his life was now — especially with me in it.

In my room, I grabbed my laptop I'd left on my bed the night before and checked my e-mail. A new one from my mom gave me a blow by blow of the beauty of Montana from the rocky mountains to the vast lakes. They'd gone horseback riding, hiking and visited scenic tourist places from Yellowstone to Glacier National Park. She asked how things were going and if I'd changed my mind yet about coming out there. I replied, asking her to send pictures and assuring her I wanted to stay.

After spending the rest of the morning on the Internet, I rushed to school, hoping to get a few minutes with Gina before first period. Just because Zack had a plan didn't mean I should abandon my own. What if his failed?

I waited in front of the double doors of the school and pretended to rummage through my backpack in search of something, keeping half an eye out for my wayward ex-friend.

"Autumn." Cameron smiled uncertainly as he sidled up next to me.

"Hi." If he did like me, I didn't want to lead him on, but the least I could do was make eye contact. I didn't want to be rude. Just then, I caught a glimpse of Gina as she passed me. I'd missed my chance. Damn! "How's it going?" I asked, giving up on Gina for the moment.

"Good. I hear Ashley's having some friends over this Saturday. Are you going?"

"No." Oh, why hadn't I prepared for this? "My... parents... I'm doing something parent-related. It's an all weekend thing."

"Oh." Cameron's face fell. "I heard your parents were out of town."

"They've been back a couple times. And when they're here, I want to spend time with them."

"But all weekend?" he asked.

I rolled my eyes. "They're my parents. They get on my nerves, because that's what parents do. But I kinda like them, you know? And I haven't seen much of them the last few weeks."

"Well, maybe next weekend," he said, his eyes dull.

I forced a little enthusiasm into my face. "If Ashley's doing something next weekend, I'll probably go."

Cameron brightened up. "Cool. I'll see you at lunch."

"See you then," I returned.

*You just made two dates with Cameron.* Zack's tone was more of a statement than a question.

I scanned the vicinity and found him talking with Gina by the double doors. Actually, she was doing the talking, but he clearly wasn't paying attention if he was eavesdropping on me.

*I did no such thing.*

*You just agreed to meet him at Ashley's next weekend. Then you agreed to see him at lunch today.*

My nostrils flared. *Zack, I didn't say yes.*

*But you didn't say no either.*

*I'm trying not to hurt his feelings.*

*It's worse if you lead him on. I'm just sayin'...*

*Noted.* I turned to go inside.

"Autumn!"

I hadn't noticed Maya standing next to Trevor about a yard from Zack.

"Hey." I felt better already.

"I was wondering..." She waved to Trevor, motioned me inside the building and lowered her voice to a whisper. "If by some miracle you and Gina talk today, would you mind if I made a scene? You know, have a rant about how you can't be friends with someone like her. If I rage against your friendship with her, that will make her want to be friends with you all the more. What do you think?"

I grinned. "Looking forward to it."

† † †

Weeding my way through students in the corridor on my way to the cafeteria, I kept an eye out for Gina. In the food line, she found me while I picked out a drink.

"Hey." She didn't smile, her lips in a pout as she held her tray of food.

"Hi. What's up?" I was far more generous with my mouth, doing my best to curl it up at the corners. Setting a soda on my tray, I stayed still, uncertain where I'd be settling now that Gina and I were speaking.

"I was thinking about what you said, you know, about neither of us having boyfriends now. It was dumb to let a guy come between us. Such a silly thing to fight over."

Because sleeping with someone else's boyfriend was inconsequential. And she'd do it again in a heartbeat with Zack. One day, I'd tell her how I really felt, but not now. "Exactly."

"We're sitting over there if you'd like to join us." Gina pointed across the room to a table occupied by Natalie and Greg — two of the most unpleasant people in school. No way.

But I didn't want to say anything bad about Natalie. Yet. "Um… things have been intense lately. First breaking up with Zack and now we're not even friends. I just want to enjoy my lunch and Greg's too obnoxious."

"Of course." She nodded sympathetically. "A guy like Zack, well, he's gorgeous. It must be hard for you."

You wish. "Not at all. I don't need a boyfriend who scams on other girls."

"We can sit there for a minute." She pointed to a table close to the trash cans. It was an unsavory spot, but at least we'd be alone, allowing me a chance to work her over.

I walked toward the table, the smell of rotting food assaulting my nostrils. "You and Zack are working on your science project together, right?" She nodded and I went on. "Just a heads-up, I don't think he's looking for a relationship."

"Maybe I'm not either."

"You might change your mind." I shrugged, unable to believe how little hesitation Gina showed over dating a friend's ex-boyfriend. You just didn't do that. "The longer you hold out, the longer you get to keep him."

*Geez, Autumn, you're making me sound like a dog who's only out for one thing,* Zack pushed into my mind.

*Are you really worried about your rep as far as Gina's concerned? Please. Now stop eavesdropping and go away. You're distracting me,* I told him, then I refocused on Gina who looked like she was mulling over her options.

"It doesn't matter," Gina said. "We have a science project together. Once it's over, so are we. I'm not sure if I'm interested in him anyway."

Liar, liar, pants on fire. I rolled my eyes. "Whatever." Yeah, I wanted to gain her trust which would involve a little bit of sucking up, but some things I couldn't let pass me by.

She ignored my comment and picked up her sandwich. "So you guys hate each other now, huh?"

"I don't feel anything at all, one way or the other."

She swallowed her food and eyed me under her lashes. "So you wouldn't care if I dated him."

The girl lacked decency and consideration of others. But if I objected, she'd think I liked him. If I acted too anxious to please, she'd suspect something. I raised a brow. "Since when do you care how I feel about you hooking up with my boyfriend or ex-boyfriend?"

"From what I hear, you're no longer the Virgin Princess." Gina was smooth, but not smooth enough to fool me. She was changing the subject — and fishing while she was at it.

"Just be careful," I warned.

"How could you be friends with her again?" Maya asked so loud that a hush fell over the cafeteria. "She slept with your boyfriend, Autumn, while you were still with him! There's not much lower for her to go, yet you're still speaking to her. Have you gone insane?"

I hadn't expected her to make *that* much of a scene. But it might work in my favor if Gina sees me defend her honor. "Maya," I hissed. "I think Gina has learned from her mistake. Forgive and forget."

"That is exactly what I thought when she slept with *my* boyfriend last year!" Maya said even louder.

"Maya!" I didn't have to pretend to be shocked — I truly was. We'd arranged for her to come over but she hadn't said anything about involving the entire student body.

"It's not my fault he preferred me over you." Gina skillfully combined a smirk with an eye roll. "Really, you're to blame for being so boring."

"Whore." Maya glared at her. "You work so hard to get these guys and you can't keep them."

"Why would I want to?" Gina shook her head, picked up her tray and rose. "It stinks at this table. I'm going to sit with Natalie."

Thankfully, Gina didn't try to lure me along. I'd had as much of her as I could take anyway.

Maya grinned, sitting down with her back to Gina's retreating figure. "That was so awesome."

I suppressed a laugh while I struggled to keep a straight face. "It was beautiful," I whispered. "I wasn't expecting that."

"Gina's right though. It stinks at this table. You should come with me. If you sit far enough away from Zack, you can still pretend to be enemies."

"It's fine. Go eat with your boyfriend. I can find someone else to sit with," I said.

"See you after school then." She gave me a wink and left.

Making my way to John and Janine's table, I heard someone call my name. My eyes whipped around to see Cameron waving me over to his table crowded with jocks and cheerleaders. I headed their way, tray in hand.

"Hey, what's up?" I asked.

"Sit down." Cameron waved a hand at a tiny space across from him.

A couple of the girls scooted over, making room for me — which gave me a perfect view of Zack several tables away.

"I'm in love with Maya now," Cameron said. "Too bad she's got a boyfriend."

*Don't forget* you *have a boyfriend*, Zack slipped into my head.

"She's our new idol," the girl next to me said. "Anyone who'd nail Gina on her bull like that is worship-worthy."

Cameron and his friends exchanged horror stories about Gina while I finished my lunch.

*If you're not careful, I'll think you're jealous*, I told Zack.

"He seems like an okay guy," Cameron said, jerking his head toward Zack.

"I guess so." I lifted one shoulder, my eyes compulsively darting to Zack who was busy chatting it up with Gina. Wasn't she the social butterfly flitting from table to table? "I never minded except he doesn't bother discouraging other girls. Just like Daniel."

Cameron looked over at Zack again. "*I'd* discourage them for someone like you." He watched me as if gauging my reaction.

Uh-oh. Cameron was no longer being subtle. This could get awkward.

I glanced at our table mates who weren't paying any attention to us. No one to rescue me. "Um..." I gulped the last sip of my drink as the bell rang.

"Better get to class." He smiled and grabbed his tray.

"Yeah, see you later," I said, returning his smile.

As I walked to fifth period, Zack kept his pace a couple yards ahead of me.

*Did you make another date with him? Firm up your plans for the weekend maybe?* he asked. Of course he'd sense I was close behind him.

I ignored Zack's stupid comment, which seemed even stupider considering I had plans with *him* this entire weekend. Shadowing him into our next class, I took my seat by him.

*Well?*

*No. But you have a date tonight with Gina.* I pretended to flip through papers looking for my completed homework.

*That's different and you know it.*

*Zack, can you please try to be mature about this? Your weirdness over Cameron is exhausting. He isn't a vulture like Gina. If anyone should be jealous, it's me.*

*But you're not jealous,* he said. *Which is exactly my point. Cameron isn't anything like Gina. He's a decent guy.*

Is that what bothered Zack? That I hadn't put up much resistance with Gina? Zack and I both knew he wouldn't stoop that low. But Cameron... he was super cute, sweet and confident. He wasn't fake or manipulative. And he clearly liked me...

*Zack. I'm not interested in him that way. Okay?*

The bell rang, saving me. Zack didn't try talking

to me again and when the bell went off at the end of class, I wondered if he was angry. I hated this roller coaster ride.

Zack spoke the truth when he said it would be easier if we weren't together. Unfortunately, that didn't make me love him less. I didn't want *easier* if it meant being without him.

My next class was with Mr. Collins and time was running out. What if Zack couldn't get the information tonight? Our last chance would be tomorrow before we left town, but what if we failed then too?

When the bell rang at the end of last period, the room emptied. As I approached the teacher's desk, he raised his brows.

"I don't have anything yet, but I do have a lead."

He sighed, shaking his head. "A lead isn't proof."

"Well, neither is a goofed up test. I could've gotten all those questions right and you know it. Being distracted that day is not a motive to throw in the towel and risk everything I've worked so hard for. Besides, aren't I innocent until proven guilty?" I watched the scowl slowly disappear as he mulled over my words. "Please, Mr. Collins, would you extend it until Wednesday? Just two extra days. And I swear I won't ask again. Please?"

He threw his hands up in the air. "Fine. Wednesday."

"Thank you." I smiled and departed before he could change his mind. Passing through the double doors of the building, I saw Zack climbing into the Jeep with Maya and Trevor. She spotted me and waved.

"Autumn," Cameron said from behind me.

I spun around. "Oh, hey."

*This guy's getting annoying. Are you going to dump him or not?* Zack asked, his car slipping through the parking lot gate.

*I can't dump him if he was never mine in the first place*, I answered.

"A bunch of us are going to Bill's right now. Want to meet us there?"

Doing my homework wouldn't take long then I'd have nothing to do but stew over Zack and Gina's impending date. An idle mind could be a dangerous thing. I glanced up to see the Jeep long gone. Too far away now to hear my reply. "Sure. See you in a bit."

† † †

I sipped my coffee, my thoughts wandering. I had a bad feeling about tonight. Gina would do everything possible to hook up with Zack. Images of her plastered all over him haunted my mind. How would Zack handle her if she jumped him?

Cameron and his friends were okay, but it didn't feel right hanging out with them when they didn't have my full attention. I was too distracted to enjoy myself anyway.

"This was fun, but I'd better head out now," I told Cameron, standing up. "I don't want my parents to come home to a dirty house. They'll be annoyed and think I need a babysitter."

He stood too. "I'll walk you to your car."

"'Bye," I said generically to everyone at the table.

Just before we got to my car, I hit the clicker so I wouldn't be delayed getting inside it once we got there. The less time Cameron had to corner me, the better. But when I reached for the handle, he leaned his hip into the driver's side door, effectively blocking my escape. Damn.

"So you can't hang out all weekend, huh?" He smiled — the kind of smile a guy gives a girl when he walks her to the door at the end of a date — just before he kisses her good night.

I backed up just a hair. "Not at all. But I'll be back at school on Monday."

He reached a hand to my shoulder. I watched him take a lock of my hair and rub it between his fingers. When I raised my chin to look at him again, his lips ambushed mine. Stunned, I didn't react or make any move to stop him. He took that as willingness on my part and his mouth opened, compelling me to give way. His tongue met mine as he pressed the palm of his hand to the back of my neck, drawing me closer.

Finding myself squeezed between his hard body and my car door, I raised my hands to push him away. But he'd already pulled back.

"I'm... really..." My mind was mush from shock. I wasn't sure if I was more surprised that he'd had the guts to kiss me or that my body had reacted so quickly. A little tingle was still circulating through my veins. Cameron knew how to kiss.

"Beautiful," he finished my sentence.

"Cameron, I... I can't do this."

"Why not?" He dropped his arms and stepped back, his mouth turned down, eyes wide like a lost puppy.

"Emotionally, I'm just... not available."

"Oh." His brows furrowed and his lips formed a thin line. "Still stuck on Zack, huh?"

"No. But, well, I dated Daniel and then him, back to back. You're really nice, but I can't go there again yet. It hasn't even been a week and I'm still raw."

The light came back into his eyes, but I wasn't sure that was such a good thing. "I understand. Then I'll wait."

That wouldn't do at all. Cameron couldn't hang around — in the end, he'd be even more hurt. How could I get out of this? If he thought I was stuck on Zack, would Cameron give up on me? Except, I really didn't want people to think I still liked Zack. How humiliating. Since I couldn't think of another way out of it, I had no choice.

"Look, I really liked Zack. A lot. I'm not, like, all gooey over him and wanting him back or anything, but it's hard to get over how perfect I thought he was for me. I'm not instantly going to get over something like that and magically stop missing what we had."

"But if he was cheating on you, then what you had was a lie," he said. "He's not who you thought he was."

"It doesn't matter. I still miss it — I miss it with *Zack*." Cameron looked like he was about to object so I rushed on. "Do you really want to get with a girl who's on the rebound? You don't want to win by default, do you? You deserve better than that."

"Yeah, but I like *you*." He looked down, seeming to study the asphalt. "I guess I'll see you at school tomorrow."

"Thanks for the coffee." I made sure he left before I jumped in my car, not wanting to appear too anxious. I'd already put him off — no point in making it obvious how eager I was to get away.

On the way home, I couldn't stop thinking about him. Had Cameron liked me all year, but been too shy to do anything about it? If he'd gotten to me before Daniel and Zack, would we still be together now?

# CHAPTER TWENTY-FOUR

ONCE I'D FINISHED my homework, I made myself something to eat and tried not to think about Zack and Gina. They would be meeting shortly.

At Zack's house.

Probably in his bedroom.

I'd encouraged my boyfriend to be alone with a piranha. How stupid could a girl get? But I still had no leads to save me from the cheating fiasco and Zack was my only hope.

Would getting proof that I didn't cheat — if he was able to do it — be worth risking my relationship with Zack?

*Hey, just got off work. What are you doing?* he asked.

*Nothing. Just killing time. We're still getting together later tonight, right? After your meeting with Gina?*

*Yeah, when that's done, I'll come over and get you.*

*Great.*

After cleaning up the kitchen and straightening up a little around the house, I couldn't take it anymore. If I went to Zack's house to spy, would he sense my presence? If I hid far enough away... probably not. It's not as though I didn't have perfect vision at almost any distance. So long as his drapes weren't closed, I could keep an eye on them. I'd probably be able to hear every word.

I checked my watch. Gina was due to arrive in ten minutes. Snatching my house key, I slipped out the back and zipped over to Zack's. I snuck into their yard, being careful not to get too close to the house. In the far corner, I crouched next to some hedges, my eyes quickly locating Zack's room.

Not only were the curtains open, but his window was all the way up. Perfect.

God, what was I doing? Spying felt dishonest. But my being there had zero to do with doubting Zack. Gina was the one I didn't trust. And if she confessed to any part of framing me, I wanted to hear for myself.

A few minutes later, I heard a car pull up, then a car door open and close from just beyond the house. Moments later, a knock sounded on the front door and Cara answered it.

"Hello, Gina." I could almost hear the frost in Cara's voice. I wanted to hug her.

"Hi." Gina actually sounded genuine, which was shocking. "Is Zack here?"

I heard Patrick and Brian bickering, but tuned them out just in time for footsteps on the wood floors, then Zack's voice. "Hey Gina. Let's go to my room. Everything's already set up."

Careful to make sure I was concealed by the

bushes, I stepped back until my shoulders touched the fence and I stretched taller to get a peek at Gina. Great. I was a Peeping Tom.

But I reminded myself that if she hadn't set me up, I wouldn't be there at all.

My mouth dropped open when I got a good look at Gina's clothes. She wore a barely-there tank top and tight, low-slung jeans. Her face was all made up and her platinum-streaked hair immaculate. Yep, she was totally ready to hook up with Zack. *My* Zack.

Clenching my jaw, I resisted the urge to climb through his window and tell her to get the hell out.

Zack appeared to be all business, though, and she seemed to go along with it. I hated that I was grateful they were keeping it to business, but at the same time, I needed Zack to get friendly so she'd let her guard down.

As the minutes passed, Gina moved closer to him. I understood why Zack didn't inch away, but their proximity grated on my nerves anyway. I couldn't wait until tonight was over. I knew I should go home, but couldn't make myself just yet. Besides, no matter what I busied myself with at home, I'd worry and wonder what Zack and Gina were doing.

Yep, I should add stalker to my resume, too.

I lowered to the ground and leaned against the fence. Rolling my shoulders to relieve the tension, I listened to them as I gazed up at the stars.

It was eight thirty when I checked the time on my cell. By then, I lay on the grass with my hands behind my head.

"So what's the deal with you and Autumn?" Gina asked. "She had some nasty things to say about you."

I bolted upright.

Zack grunted. "Doesn't surprise me. She's not who I thought she was."

"My thoughts exactly."

"Did you see her slap me yesterday?" Zack sounded genuinely pissed off about it and I wondered if it had bothered him more than he'd let on.

"Yeah," Gina replied, sympathy in her voice. "That's so messed up. What was that all about?"

"I still have no idea. Guys aren't mind readers, but apparently I'm supposed to be the exception to that." Zack scoffed. "Whatever."

"In a lot of ways we're alike, Zack. I took Autumn on as a friend since she was new at school and I've been putting up with her attitude since that first day. You have no idea what a chore that's been."

"You hung out with her today at lunch," he pointed out, making me want to cheer at his logic.

"I did it for the same reason we were friends. I'm a nice person and I felt sorry for her. She lost Daniel and me, then you."

"I don't feel sorry for her. She's the one who alienated us, right? Sorry I gave you such a hard time a couple weeks ago. If I'd known the real Autumn back then, I wouldn't have believed everything she said."

"No apologies necessary. How could you know? She had me fooled for months."

Gina was lucky I wasn't actually the horrible person

she created in her head. Because if I was, with my supernatural abilities, I'd crush her into a red paste. For a moment, I let my mind wander and imagined her no longer around to bother me. Just sticky pulp under my feet.

But it was only a fantasy and I'd never do anything to bring it to reality.

Wait. Why were they so quiet? I made sure the bushes still concealed me and peered into his room.

They were sitting at the foot of his bed, her torso twisting around to face him, arms circling his neck. His arms were wrapped all the way around her, a hand reaching up behind her to cradle her head. Their lips moved against each other and my stomach churned, my throat swelling in rage.

I'd told him to flirt, not do this. How could he kiss that bitch? I wanted to scream silently into his head, but then he'd know I was spying.

Zack stood up, distancing himself and I exhaled in relief even as my eyes burned.

"Something wrong?" she asked, her eyes narrowing.

"We don't have much privacy."

She made a show of looking around the room. "Nobody's here, Zack. Just you and me."

"The walls are paper thin, as Autumn and I discovered when she'd spend the night. Trevor can hear everything. And I mean *everything*."

Gina smiled sweetly and whispered, "I can be very quiet." She didn't wait for a reply, standing up and fastening her lips to his.

He gently nudged her away. "I'm not looking for a

relationship, Gina. I've had my fill of that crap."

"Neither am I, so there's nothing to stop us from taking what we want."

"There's always a price to pay for a hookup." Zack laughed softly. "I've had that itch scratched recently anyway."

Her brows rose. "With Autumn?"

"Who else?"

Did he just tell her we'd slept together? It didn't matter, since everyone thought we'd already done that anyway. But still...

"C'mon." She slithered against him. "You've been broken up a few days. You're young and healthy. And I know you think I'm pretty."

"You realize that Trevor is probably listening to everything you just said?"

"Then let's take a drive," Gina whispered into his ear. "Go somewhere that we can be alone."

His hands rested noncommittally at her waist.

"Oh, I get it." She drew back. "You're not playing hard to get. You still like her."

Zack growled, picking Gina up and tossing her on the bed. "I was just trying to be a gentleman. But you make it impossible."

I couldn't take my eyes off of them, my nails cutting into my palms as I clenched my fists. The whole thing was like a car wreck, the kind where the car is on fire and you know someone is inside. You should look away so the image isn't seared into your brain. But you can't.

He continued to kiss her, slowly pushing her back until he was on top of her. Gina wrestled his shirt off and ran her hands up his bare back. I pressed my fist against my chest to stop the pain deep inside me. I wiped at my eyes, trying to plug the leak, but it wouldn't stop. Was it really necessary to be almost naked with his tongue down her throat in order to convince Gina properly?

I didn't think so.

Zack eased off her, propping himself up on his elbow and drawing little circles on her skin. His shoulders began to shake.

"What's so funny?" she asked.

"Did you hear Autumn got caught cheating?"

"Yeah." She grinned. "Couldn't have happened to a nicer person."

"That's what I thought," Zack said. "It's strange though. She used to do my homework when I was at work and I always got A's. She doesn't need to cheat."

"Some rich people don't need to steal, but they do it anyway."

"True." Zack looked pensive as he sat up and scooted away a few inches. "It's out of character though. You think Natalie set her up? She's in that class with Autumn. I'd love to know how Natalie managed it. Pretty impressive."

Gina smiled. "Why don't you ask Natalie? I wasn't there." She sat up again and tried to resume the tongue bath.

He held her by the shoulders, halting her. "My

family's going to think I'm a player."

"You're a guy. What else would they expect?"

He gave a quick laugh. "They like Autumn a lot."

She groaned. "It's your life, not theirs."

"But I have to live with them. And, strange as it may seem, I want them to think well of me."

"That's why we should go." She gave him a sultry smile.

"They'll still know. Besides, I need to spend some time with my mom."

"What are you saying?"

"You should go." He yanked her against him. "I'll see you Monday at school. Maybe we can do something together after."

"Sure." She angled her face toward him until their lips were a breath away.

Zack gave a quick laugh and slammed his mouth down on hers.

I muffled a sob. It may have been an act, but Zack was way too convincing.

Finally, after what seemed like years of groping, they came up for air. Zack put his shirt back on and they left the room. I sat on the grass, staring unseeing into his dark empty room.

If he really didn't want to make out with her, he would've found a way out of it. I could only assume that kissing and touching her wasn't exactly a hardship. Maybe he was comfortable visiting familiar territory or something. Maybe he was a cheater like Daniel.

Or perhaps he'd just grown tired of me and all the stress of the last few days. Who could blame him?

Using the bottom of my shirt, I wiped the tears off my cheek. Where was Zack? Why hadn't he come back into his room? Had he gone off with Gina for a drive after all?

My throat constricted and tears pricked my eyes again.

*Autumn? Where are you?*

Crap. I couldn't tell him I was at his house stalking him. *Go away, Zack.*

*What? Why? Are you okay?*

*Just fine. But I don't want to see you tonight.*

I rose, waiting for him to reply, to fight for us, but only silence met me.

*Autumn?*

*What?*

*Were you at my house tonight? Maybe watching through the window?* he asked.

*Of course not.*

*Are you still there?*

*Where?* My eyes darted around the yard to make sure no one was around. I booked it home.

*Are you at my house? Because I'm at yours.*

It took only seconds to travel the block through the back yards. He turned around, sensing my presence, just as I arrived at my back door.

"Let's talk inside," Zack said.

"It was your idea not to come inside. I think we should stick to that." I refused to look at him as I dug in my jeans for my house key.

"We'll have to make an exception. Don't you think we need to talk about this? Not like we can really do it out here."

"I don't want you in my house." I folded my arms over my chest, glaring at him. I didn't want to imagine what I looked like after crying. Hopefully, the moonlight would look on me favorably, and Zack wouldn't notice.

He sighed. "I'm not going anywhere. And last time we arm wrestled, you didn't beat me. So have fun trying to get rid of me."

"Fine. Come in. We'll talk, then you'll leave," I said, an edge to my voice. I pushed through the back door. As soon as the door closed behind him, I rounded on him. "Say what you have to say and get out."

"You're being unreasonable, Autumn. You saw for yourself how relentless she was and suspicious of every excuse I gave her. How was I going to lure her to my side if I rejected her?"

"We would've found another way." I wrapped my arms around my waist, averting his eyes. "You don't kiss other girls when you have a girlfriend. That's called cheating."

"I didn't want to kiss her. But she kissed me. And I know how important it is for you to be vindicated with Mr. Collins. You didn't expect something like this was going to happen? Autumn, you *know* Gina."

"Oh, please. Don't blame all of it on her." I gave a watery laugh as I glared at him accusingly. "*You* threw her on the bed."

"Autumn," he growled. "I had no choice. You told me to do this, remember?"

"I didn't say by any means possible! I mean, when Cameron kissed me, he didn't get another chance. I made sure of it. Because that's what you do when you're already with someone."

"Wait a minute." He shook his head as if he'd misheard me. "Cameron kissed you?"

Oh, hell, did I just say that out loud? "Yeah, but he ambushed me."

"Today?" Zack stalked toward me, his eyes dark.

I nodded. "When he walked me to my car."

"At school?" His eyes had turned to slits.

"No. At Bill's Bean and Brew." I took a step back.

"You went *out* with him?" His teeth ground against each other.

"In a *group*. There were other people there." I gulped. "It was a friend thing and I needed a distraction so I wouldn't think about you and Gina. I didn't expect him to kiss me."

"You didn't?" he asked softly.

I shook my head. "Of course not."

"Tongue or no tongue?" He inched closer.

My breath froze in my lungs when I saw the faraway battle in his eyes. I didn't want to lie, but I absolutely did not want to tell the truth either. Turned out, I didn't need to answer at all. He already knew.

He hit the wall and drywall crumbled. "Damn it, Autumn! I can't believe you put yourself in a position where he'd kiss you. And you *let* him."

"Look who's talking!" My voice trembled and the words tumbled out. "He faked me out, okay? I looked away, then turned to him and he was already swooping."

"And you couldn't get him to back off? No, you had to give him time for a little tongue action first?" Zack loomed over me with a murderous scowl.

"At least there wasn't a bed involved and our clothes stayed on. Unlike with you Gina. Cameron kissed me once. You were *on top of her.*" My voice rose. "You have no right to make *me* out to be the bad guy here."

"Of course not," he growled. His breathing became unsteady and his voice dangerously low. "I wouldn't dream of it. Good-bye, Autumn."

And just like that, he was gone.

# CHAPTER TWENTY-FIVE

THIS TIME LAST year seemed like a lifetime ago. I was in another state with a different set of friends. My best friend Jenny had a longtime crush on this guy in her math class. One day, he asked her out and she said yes. After their date, Jason dominated our conversations. She was on cloud nine and I was happy for her.

A couple weeks later, he completely blew her off with no explanation. Jenny was devastated. She'd created this fantasy and built her whole world around him. Her entire identity and happiness revolved around him and what he might do. Would he be nice to her that day? Bless her with his smile?

When he'd dumped her, it was as if he'd taken a piece of her soul. At the time, I didn't understand why Jenny couldn't still be Jenny without him. People made their own happiness, right? If *they* didn't make their life better, no one was going to do it for them. And Jason wasn't worth her tears.

She'd seen him as this perfect guy, but his perfection existed only in her imagination. I tried to tell her that, but she wouldn't hear me.

After witnessing what happened to Jenny, I vowed never to allow a guy to become so important that I lost a part of myself.

But Zack had seemed nothing like Jenny's creepy object of obsession, nor was he anything like Daniel. Zack had been there for me when my car broke down, when Daniel tried to hurt me, and when I didn't know I was a shape-shifter. He'd *never* deserted me. Zack wasn't just my boyfriend, he was my *friend*.

But he wasn't coming back tonight and he wouldn't invite me over — I knew that as sure as I knew I was a shape-shifter. We wouldn't see each other again until tomorrow at school.

I didn't throw things. I didn't run upstairs and bury my head in my pillow.

I didn't do anything at all.

With my back against the wall near the door, I slowly slid down until my bottom touched the floor. I crossed my legs, my arms hanging limply at my sides while I stared at nothing.

I didn't cry. I was too numb for that.

† † †

Rolling over in bed, I watched the sun come up. The thought of getting out of bed was too much to possibly consider. My limbs were heavy with a fog of gloom smothering me.

I wanted to be understanding and try to see Zack's perspective, but budging on the Gina incident wasn't going to happen. Making out with her had not been part of the plan.

If we fought about it again, he'd say he did it for me, to help me out of my predicament. He'd expect me to apologize for kissing Cameron, but I couldn't. I wasn't to blame for the kiss.

Perhaps I should've been smarter and dodged Cameron more skillfully. I was superhuman, after all. Still, kissing Cameron had been an accident. But Zack had knowingly put moves on Gina.

No, I wouldn't give in or beg forgiveness. I had no intention of forgiving him either — not that he'd ask for forgiveness. And he probably wouldn't want to go to Yosemite with me.

The idea of making the long drive by myself was daunting. I could pull over and get a hotel room any time, since I had access to the money my parents had wired into my account. Plus, the credit card I'd lifted from the safe. But I'd rather have Zack with me.

Whether he came with me or not, I needed to pack. I had to be ready to leave straight away after school. I forced my legs to move and eventually made it out of bed. As I gathered items for my trip, I came across Zack's things.

I paused, unzipping the little black bag he'd given me the other night. Inside was a toothbrush, toothpaste, razor, and various other grooming tools. Should I bring his stuff in case Zack went through with our plans?

Before we'd started dating, he'd spent time helping me when he didn't want to. Because he couldn't stand by and do nothing while anyone suffered. If Zack stayed true to his nature, he'd insist on coming along, just to make sure I was safe. His mom would probably insist, too.

Although I hated myself for it, part of me wanted him to be waiting in my car after school like we'd arranged. Even if we didn't speak the whole way to Yosemite, having him with me when I discovered the truth about my parents would mean everything to me.

I packed his things with mine.

Mapping my route, I printed it out, along with information on nearby hotels and restaurants, just in case I had a spell with no cell service. I didn't want to make a hotel reservation yet in case I got everything I needed the first night. If we didn't need to stay, Zack might want to return home immediately.

Now I just had to load the stuff in my car without anyone seeing. If any of the werewolves thought I was getting ready for a trip, they'd watch me closer. I darted downstairs with my duffle bag, then backed my Mustang farther up the driveway. Once I'd positioned my car to block the view of the side yard from the street, I went inside again and shoved my bag through the window. Back outside, I tossed it into the trunk.

Finally, I was ready for my trip and headed to school. I was dying to skip it and stay home, but cutting class wouldn't make me appear any more innocent to Mr. Collins. Not only that, I really didn't need my parents to get a phone call. They might come home and I wouldn't be there.

As I drove to school, my throat constricted at the thought of Zack. Did he think we'd broken up? Was he even thinking about me at all?

I glided my car into a space by the gate, far from the school building, and sat in my car until the warning bell rang. I didn't want to see or talk to anyone just yet. Especially Zack.

Crawling out of my car, I put my head down and made a mad dash for my first class.

"Autumn!"

Oh, damn, Maya would know how screwed up I was and I didn't want to talk about it. I mean, how would I explain the betrayal I felt at watching Zack make out with Gina when he wasn't even supposed to be my boyfriend? Worse, she'd think I was twisted for spying in the first place.

I met her at the double doors.

"I don't have to guess what you were up to last night." She lifted one brow, her mouth thinned into a straight line.

Oh, God, how did she find out I'd been spying on Zack?

"This is probably all over school by now." She flashed her phone screen.

I gasped. It was a picture of Cameron and me kissing. And if it was already all over school, like Maya said, then Zack had probably seen it too. Or he soon would. Right then, I couldn't imagine forgiving Zack and making up, but I'd already discovered firsthand how much it sucked to watch someone you loved kissing someone else.

Not that Zack loved me. He couldn't have done those things with Gina if he had.

A groan escaped me. "I don't know who took that picture, but I wasn't a willing participant in… that." I pointed at the phone. "Cameron took me by surprise, I swear."

"Fill me in later." Maya sighed. "We'd better get to first period."

My classes before lunch were spent in a daze. I had no clue if Zack still wanted me and, if he did, whether or not I could forgive him. All I knew was that my heart felt like it had been ripped open and I missed Zack something fierce.

I just needed to get through the day. Once on the road later, I would work on being happy again. I could do it. I had to. And looking for my birth parents would give me something to do, give me a sense of purpose. I needed that.

At lunchtime, Maya found me in the food line. She leaned toward me, lowering her voice. "Autumn, are you okay? I saw you after second period and shouted your name. You just walked off like you were hypnotized or something."

I groaned inwardly. She always sat with Zack and Trevor. No way could I join her. But if I didn't give her some kind of explanation, she'd push and push until I told her what happened. How could I tell her how Zack had crushed me when she and everyone else thought we were already over?

"I feel gross today. I should've stayed home." I peeked at Zack out of the corner of my eye to see him smiling at Gina. My hand shot to my stomach which was now queasy at the idea of eating.

"Oh." Her brows drew together. "Maybe you should go to the nurse."

Out of the question. I didn't think Zack would really be waiting for me in my car after school, but if the nurse sent me home, it would be impossible for him to get to my car. "I've only got two more classes. I'll tough it out."

Maya rubbed my arm soothingly. "Okay, but if you need anything, just ask. Gosh, I hope you're okay for the trip."

My smile felt completely foreign to my face. "I'll be fine. Probably just something I ate."

"You could take your mind off your stomach by telling me how Cameron's lips ended up on yours." She shot me a disapproving look. "What was up with that?"

We were at the front of the line now and I scanned the selection of sandwiches. "He ambushed me and I brushed him off." I sighed. "Cameron's nice, but it's too soon after my breakup with Zack."

If she asked the right questions, she might figure out how truly horrible last night had gone and I wouldn't be able to explain any of it. As much as I loved Maya, hanging out with her right then probably wasn't such a good idea. I needed to sit by John, Janine and Ashley, who wouldn't pry too much. Besides, I didn't want my rotten mood rubbing off on her. She was in a healthy relationship and I wanted her to enjoy it.

When we'd finished loading our trays, Maya glanced over at Trevor. I followed her gaze and noticed Zack huddled with Gina at the next table over. I bristled. "Go. I'm fine. I promise." I smiled again, my face protesting the movement.

"I'll look for you after school." She patted my shoulder and returned to her boyfriend. "Text me later and let me know how you're feeling, okay?"

"I will." Tray in hand as I turned away from Maya, I tried to give the impression everything was right in the world. I'd been successful at hiding my emotions from my parents for years. It shouldn't be too difficult to do it with my schoolmates.

As I made my way toward John's table, I wondered what Zack was thinking. Was he relieved to have an excuse to dump me, happy that he'd dodged a bullet? Or was he as miserable as me? Ashley made room for me next to her, across from John. As soon as Zack was out of my line of vision, my breathing became easier and the pressure lifted from my chest.

"Hey." I peeled the foil off my yogurt and stirred it, wondering what Zack was thinking at this moment. Did he miss me? Did he want me back? Was he sorry? Zack was always difficult to read. The only way to pick his brain was to ask him and I refused to talk to him. No way.

I kept telling myself I'd eventually get over Zack, that I'd been through worse things. But the pain in my chest was so fierce and raw, I knew it would never pass. My superhuman powers were useless to me in love.

"Autumn, I was wondering if you'd give me your thoughts on something," John said.

I blinked, remembering where I was. Setting the spoon on the table, I realized I'd been absently stirring the yogurt.

John needed my input on something? I was grateful for the distraction and wanted to throw my arms around him. "Sure."

He looked around and leaned forward. I glanced around too, certain no one was listening.

"Let's just say that I needed help, but I wouldn't ask for it. And I wouldn't volunteer anything about what was going on either. And let's just say that you had no idea why and no clue how to help me, but you were absolutely positive I was all screwed up."

John checked again for eavesdroppers, before leaning closer. "Would you let me stay in that dark place or would you try to pull me out? Would you wait for me to ask for your help or would you throw me a rope? As a true friend, what would you do?"

Now this was something I could help him with and having something else to think about was a godsend. "That's easy. Just because a friend doesn't ask for a rope, doesn't mean they don't need it. Sometimes, people don't realize they need help. Even if they do, they might not know how to go about getting it. I'd definitely throw you a rope."

"Okay." He nodded, eyeing me for a moment. "I'm throwing you a rope."

"What?"

"Autumn, do you want to talk about it? Tell me how to make it better for you."

"I didn't see that coming." I grabbed my soda and chugged, the carbonation burning my throat. John was an amazing friend and it meant a lot that he cared that much about me. But I couldn't confide in him or give him any semblance of the truth. I didn't want to lie either. I'd had enough of lies. The only other option was to stay silent.

"What's going on?" he asked.

I sighed. "I can't talk about it just yet. Maybe never. Normally, I would, but this is just one of those things that..." I shook my head, letting my words trail off.

"Are you ..." His eyes darted around again and he lowered his voice to a whisper. "Are you pregnant or something?"

I groaned. Why did everyone keep thinking I might be pregnant? "No, John. I swear that isn't it. It's not life threatening either, but I'm not at liberty to discuss it. I'm sorry."

"I get it. But if you change your mind, I'm here, okay?"

"Thanks." I gave him a weak smile. "That means a lot, really."

It didn't ease the hot poker stuck in my chest, but it was sweet of him to try. I stood, gathered my things and headed toward the garbage can to dump my tray.

Cameron came up beside me. "Everything okay? You look sad."

The worse I felt, the harder it was to hide. My eyes darted to Zack for the millionth time, but he wasn't looking at me. I knew he could hear our conversation, but I doubted that he cared to listen in.

Cameron followed my gaze, his eyes landing on Zack a moment, then returning to me. "He looks dark and broody today. Something put him in a sour mood. You sure it's over between you two?"

"Very over. I heard from a reliable source that he and Gina hooked up last night. She can have him. I don't care."

"That's obvious," he said as if he didn't believe a word I'd said. His eyes narrowed. "Did you tell him we kissed?"

I stared at Cameron's shoes. "Yes," I blurted without thinking. "But not on purpose."

He eyed Zack again and shook his head. "You said he scammed on other girls, but I've never noticed him looking at anyone the way he looks at you. I don't know what's going on with him and Gina now, but he doesn't act like someone who's over you. Maybe you're both too stuck on yourselves to give the other a break?"

I gave a quick laugh that made me sound like I was choking. "What are you talking about?"

He moved closer and lowered his voice. "Don't be dumb. If you want Zack back, tell him. Don't wait until it's too late. I can tell you from personal experience it sucks to chicken out and then miss your chance."

Guilt oozed through me since he was obviously referring to me.

"Decide what you want and go for it. Then maybe you'll have one less regret to live with." Cameron squeezed my shoulder and returned to his table.

It was a great pep talk and I appreciated it, but the only way to fix things with Zack was to make peace with what he'd done with Gina. That wasn't going to happen. And apologizing for kissing Cameron, when it hadn't been my idea, was every kind of wrong.

Out of my peripheral, I spied an empty seat where Zack had been sitting. I took comfort in knowing he couldn't have heard Cameron's low voice over the din of the cafeteria. Zack didn't need to know how he affected me.

A purse was shoved into my hand and fingers gently grasped my arm as John steered me toward the door. "Geez, Autumn, you're standing there like a zombie. I understand if you don't want to talk about it, but can you please try not to scare your friends?"

It was horrifying to think I'd been standing there with a vacant look on my face. I really needed to get a grip.

"I'll walk you to class to make sure you survive."

"Um." What else was there to say?

John dropped me off and dashed to his own class. The seat next to mine in English Lit was empty. I took my seat, expecting Zack to arrive any second, but the bell rang and he still hadn't shown up. Did he hate me so much that he couldn't bear to sit next to me? If that was the case, then a road trip with him was definitely out of the question.

After English Lit ended, I shuffled to my last class. Nausea swirled in my stomach and a haze followed wherever I went. Where was Zack?

Mr. Collins droned on and I suffered through it, using body language like little nods and occasional eye contact to appear as though I was paying attention. But I barely heard him. In just minutes, I'd be on the road. Alone.

Zack would stay here, maybe go on a date with Gina. Now he was free to have fun with her without a pathetic girlfriend watching through the window. Where was Gina today anyway? Aside from lunch, I hadn't noticed her all day. Then again, I hadn't noticed much else either.

When the bell rang, I walked to my locker like a corpse, my heavy body dragging along the linoleum.

Maya leaned against my locker, her arms folded across her chest. "Okay, spill it, Autumn. What the hell is going on?"

I glanced from her to my locker, realizing she was blocking it. There was no way to avoid her questioning. I'd have to cough up something to pass as truth... actually, I *could* give her the truth. "Zack and I aren't friends anymore. But for real this time."

Her eyes softened and she squeezed my hand. "What happened?"

"He was with Gina last night. Like *really* with her."

"No way." Maya's mouth dropped open.

"It's true. He admitted it."

"Gross." She gave a mock shiver. "But if you're just friends, why can't he date anyone else?"

I blinked. "Gina is a skank."

"That does explain why she looked so happy today. She kept making goo-goo eyes at him during lunch and anytime I saw her between classes. Made me want to vomit."

So Gina *had* been at school for more than just lunch. And I hadn't noticed her other times for the same reason I hadn't noticed myself standing like a zombie in the lunch room. I acted as though I was on another planet, but I was still on Earth.

Except that it was extremely hot. Yep, I was in hell.

Maya snapped her fingers in front of my face. "Autumn! Where did you go? Come back to us. Hello?"

"Yeah. I gotta go. It's a long way to Yosemite."

"Zack's not going with you?" she asked.

I held up my hands, palms up and lifted my shoulders. "Why would he come with me when he could be hooking up with Gina?"

"Trevor and I will come then. You're not going alone. We can go to the concert another time."

"No. Please don't do that. I'd rather go alone than screw up your plans. And you don't want to be stuck with me in a car right now. Trust me. I'll just make you guys miserable. Seriously."

"I'll get Trevor and be at your car in five minutes. I mean it, Autumn. Don't you dare drive away alone."

I was the last person in the world they should hang out with —I wasn't fit to be with humans and ruining their weekend was unthinkable.

Maya disappeared down the hallway and I stuffed my books in my locker, then bolted to my car, in a hurry to make my getaway.

Scanning the grounds, I didn't see Maya or Trevor anywhere. Or Zack. As I approached my car, despair thickened in my throat and I slowed, not wanting to face an empty car.

Not wanting to face my future without Zack.

# CHAPTER TWENTY-SIX

TRYING TO EASE the feeling of being suffocated, I took a deep breath and trudged toward the Mustang with my head down. As I drew closer, my skin tingled, and a woodsy sent wafted up my nose.

Zack.

I couldn't see him, but knew with every shape-shifter cell in my body that he was inside my car. But why would he be there after our fight? Oh, right. I was a damsel in distress — his specialty. I texted Maya with an update, then started up the engine and backed out.

*I'm surprised you're here*, I told him silently, just in case anyone was watching.

Zack didn't answer and was still silent at the freeway onramp. In my rearview mirror, I could see the back of his head as he craned his neck to see behind us. With so many cars on the road, it wasn't easy to tell if we were being followed.

I bit my lip, unable to believe that he'd actually come, and equally unable to believe that I'd let him. But I didn't hate that he was here and that made me nervous. He'd already hurt me enough.

Checking the mirror, I frowned. "Are you going to ride in the back the whole way?"

"Maybe. Did you bring my things?" he asked.

"They're in the trunk. Why weren't you in class?"

"Because I needed to get inside your car without being seen. So after lunch I faked being sick, went to the nurse and she sent me home. Instead, I used your spare key and waited in here."

"For *two* hours? It's freaking roasting in here."

"No kidding. Hand me your phone and I'll navigate."

He would've had a much more comfortable afternoon if he'd bailed on me. I was still mad at Zack for the Gina incident, but baking in my car for two hours, just so I'd have someone to drive with, went a long way to calm my fury.

I grabbed my phone and stretched my arm behind my head. Zack relieved me of it and for the next few minutes all I heard was the backseat creaking.

"Nobody's following us. I'm coming up." He snaked between the two front seats and strapped himself in. "We'll stay on the five north for a while, then we can choose between taking the forty-one all the way up to Oakhurst or the ninety-nine to the forty-one. We can decide once we get there."

"Okay." I glanced sideways at him. "Or let the map decide for us."

Zack turned and faced the window, making me feel awkward about saying anything else. Being with him didn't feel the same and I hated it. I hated Gina. I hated him for what he'd done with her and for ruining what we had.

I sighed. This was going to be a long ride. Turning on the music, I let myself slide into the lyrics as I imagined accomplishing everything I wanted from this trip. Then I could confront my parents on which lie they told, whatever that was, and move on from Zack.

About an hour later, Zack pointed to a fast food sign. "Take this next exit. I'm hungry. And I'll drive, if you don't mind."

"No problem." I did as he asked. "Drive-thru or do you want to go in?"

"Drive-thru. The sooner we get there, the sooner we might learn more about your parents."

And the sooner he'd be back home and free of me.

Zack made no attempt at more conversation and I couldn't stand the quiet — that was when I did most of my thinking and I didn't want to go down any crazy mental paths. I had to break the silence, but I needed to do it right.

"So... did you want to break up with me? Is that why you did that with Gina?" Clearly, I should've given this more thought, but then again why beat around the bush?

"Make a right here. I want a cheeseburger," he said at the end of the off ramp.

"Sure. I'll just get a veggie burger or something." I seethed over my unanswered question as I pulled up to the drive-thru window and put in our order.

He tapped the dashboard, waiting for his food. "Is that why you did it?"

"Did what?" The car ahead of me moved forward

and I took his spot.

Zack avoided my gaze. "Why you kissed Cameron. Was it because *you* wanted to break up?"

I gaped at him, my stupor preventing me from coming up with an intelligible response. The car behind me honked and I moved my car forward again.

"I get the appeal. Cameron's a good guy. And he's human," Zack continued. "No laws to break, no scouts to avoid. You could do worse."

Was Zack trying to pawn me off on someone else? The drive-thru window opened and I gave some cash to the pale-faced girl wearing a headset. She handed me our food, then I passed it to Zack and eased the car back onto the street.

"Let's fill up the gas tank so we won't have to stop again." His hand disappeared into the food bag then reappeared a second later with a french fry.

I nodded, still unable to speak as I rolled the car along the row of gas pumps. How could I reply to his comments about Cameron? Should I agree with him or tell him the truth — that Cameron could never replace him? That even after what he'd done I still loved him?

Zack climbed out of the Mustang and began working the pump.

I rolled down the window so he could hear me. "We could say the same about Alura. She's really pretty and your life would be a lot easier being with her."

He glanced at me for a second, then focused on the pump. "She's engaged."

Otherwise she'd be an option for him? I ground

my teeth. "You didn't answer my question. Did you hook up with Gina to break up with me?"

"No. I did it because you *asked* me to." He turned back to the digital readout on the pump. "Do you want to be with Cameron?"

"No."

"Okay then," he said, as if those two words settled everything. They didn't.

"Do you want to talk about what happened?"

"No, Autumn. I don't want to talk about it. I'm too pissed off. I can't even think about it, much less discuss it yet."

Except that sweeping it all under the rug wouldn't work if we were both still upset. But maybe it was just as well we didn't hash it all out right now. I was still too raw and Zack was bound to make me angrier if he kept acting like a douche.

He replaced the nozzle and turned to face me. I watched him, scared to hear whatever he was about to say.

"I thought I was driving."

I let out the breath I hadn't realized was frozen in my lungs, then crawled over to the passenger side and he got behind the wheel.

"We've got more than four hours to go, according to the map." He glanced at me, eyeing my veggie burger as I adjusted its wrapper. "You look exhausted and it's not even five yet. We might be better off finding a hotel as soon as we arrive and getting a good night's sleep. We can get an early start tomorrow and still accomplish just as much but we won't be tired."

I *was* tired. "That seems sensible." I set my own food aside, unwrapped part of his burger and handed it to him.

He snatched it from my outstretched hand. "You made a hotel reservation, right?"

"No. Wasn't even sure you were coming or what I'd be doing." I bit into my veggie burger.

Zack concentrated on his food, lifting it to his mouth and steering with his thighs. He looked like he'd had lots of practice eating and driving. When he'd finished, he handed me his wrapper and started on his fries.

I glanced in the rearview mirror and saw a big rig slowly disappearing behind us. No sign of any other cars for miles. The awkward silence was weighing on me. "You think Charles is really dead?"

"I don't know." He stared ahead, a tic working in his jaw.

His brain was probably already considering all possibilities. When Daniel had become a clear threat, Zack had prepared for every scenario. He planned our next step in detail, always coaching me on what to do and what not to do.

"You must have a theory or two."

"Two," Zack said, waving his burger at me, the aroma of the meat wafting up my nose. Natural instinct told me to snatch it from his fingers, but good sense won over. I didn't want to take the time to stop for a replacement burger. "One theory is that Charles is dead. The other is that he's alive and healing somewhere."

I had hoped for something a little less obvious. Some insight that came from something I didn't know. "You read all of the books your dad left for you, right? Did you find anything that explained how to kill a werewolf?"

"No."

"For all we know, it could require a silver bullet," I said.

"Maybe."

Zack drove me batty. Was he keeping information to himself? Not that I could complain if he was, since I hadn't yet told him everything about Renzo.

I turned my attention to the scenery as we passed countless windmills, dry patches of desert with lonely far off buildings that looked like sheds, and the occasional clump of wooded areas filled with giant pine trees. But the scenery wasn't interesting enough to prevent my brain from racing from one obsession to the next.

If I couldn't prove my innocence to Mr. Collins, my parents would get called back to town. And then there was the stress over whether or not Charles could be waiting for us when we returned. I shuddered to think about him being alive and the revenge he'd want on me after I'd torn him apart.

I needed something to keep myself too occupied to dwell on any of that. "Do you mind if I read a book?"

"Not at all."

He acted a little too relieved for my taste. I wondered why he bothered coming along if hanging out with me was such a chore, especially when he could be making out with Gina. I tried not to growl as I dug my e-reader out of my purse.

After reading the same line over and over, I finally gave up actual reading. I couldn't concentrate on anything with Zack next to me and he wasn't exactly a chatterbox. So I pretended to be engrossed in the book while images of him and Gina played in my head over and over.

"Autumn?"

My heart leapt. Did he want to apologize? Beg my forgiveness? Promise to tell Gina off in front of the entire school? "Yes?"

He cast me a quick glance. "That dark sports car has been behind us since we stopped for food — always keeping the same distance."

My heart rate sped. "Why didn't you tell me sooner?"

"I didn't want to worry you unnecessarily unless I was sure."

The dark car stayed far enough behind and almost blended with the asphalt. I couldn't tell the make or model. Possibly blue, but definitely sporty.

"You think it's Renzo?" I asked.

"With him or Alura, we'd probably be fine. If they catch us, we could say we got back together and decided to celebrate by being tourists. At this point, I think they're only dangerous if they find out you're a shape-shifter or that we killed Charles."

Too late for the former. "What if Charles isn't dead and that's him following us?"

"Home or Yosemite, it wouldn't matter. Wherever he found us, we'd be in for the fight of our lives."

# CHAPTER TWENTY-SEVEN

"COULD YOU MAKE me any more nervous and paranoid?" I glanced back at the car again. Yep, still there. Zack was right — whichever city Charles attacked us in shouldn't matter to me. But it did. The idea of being ambushed seemed much scarier away from home where everything was unfamiliar.

"Sorry." Zack's eyes left the road long enough to give me an apologetic look. "But I just want to be honest and not keep things from you."

Like the way I was keeping things from him. Maybe it would be better if Zack and I didn't talk after all. I squinted at the screen, trying to make out the words, but I still couldn't get past the first paragraph. Whatever. Staring at words that I couldn't focus on sure beat trying to make conversation with Zack.

Now and then, I checked the car behind us. Zack kept his eye on it, too. The hours stretched on and I spent most of the drive looking out my side of the window.

Just after the sun set, the blue car veered into the right lane. Instead of taking the exit, it sped up and closed in. Just when I thought it might just ram right into the back of my Mustang, it switched lanes and roared ahead of us.

As the car passed, it was too dark to tell the color, but by the shape, I'd guess it was Renzo. "Looks like they're not following us."

"Or that's just what he wants us to think. If he pulls over and turns off his lights, we'll easily miss him as we pass and he can get behind us again."

Lovely. I slumped in my seat, not bothering to comment. All week I'd looked forward to our weekend getaway. But our break-up drama had followed us and, apparently, so had Renzo.

"We're almost there. Okay if we stop for food before we find a hotel and check in?"

"Yeah."

He stopped at the first drive-thru we came to, then hit the road again. As I ate, I checked the info I'd gathered the night before on the hotels.

The sign over the freeway rang a bell somewhere in my subconscious. "This is our exit. It's hard to tell by the pictures, but the rooms look pretty nice."

"That's the beauty of not making a reservation." Zack signaled, then swerved into the right lane. "If it ends up being a dump, we'll move on to the next one."

My boyfriend had been irritating, distant, angry — any number of things — the entire trip, but I loved the way he acted so calm when my nerves were on edge. Otherwise the trip would be miserable. I hated knowing that no matter what I might learn about my parents, I'd still be mad at them. If

I failed and didn't learn anything at all, I'd likely be even more pissed. Having Zack with me made either scenario a little less awful.

Up the narrow road, the trees gave way to a towering building, which reminded me of a French chateau, out of place in America and far from home. Lit windows glowed from the rooms, some of them partially hidden by trees. The tops of the windows arched, flanked by shutters and the stone exterior reached high up to a sharply pitched roof.

I wondered if the inside would be as charming as the outside.

We weren't officially in Yosemite, but the area still boasted plenty of vegetation. I opened the door the moment the car stopped moving. "It smells absolutely divine around here."

He closed his eyes, inhaling deeply. "I could get used to this."

I shot him a hopeful smile. "We could stay another day regardless what we find out tomorrow."

"It's probably not a good idea to stay any longer than we need to." He climbed out of the car and headed toward the hotel entrance.

I followed, not wanting to ask why we shouldn't stay. Knowing the reason wouldn't make him any less of an ass.

"I hope it's not too expensive," I muttered, although I wasn't sure why I was worried. My mom's credit card sang to me from a little compartment in my purse. It's not like my parents were strapped for cash. Still, I'd had too many years of living frugal to be too extravagant.

Zack continued, passing through the front door and stopping at the front desk, which was more like a long counter. Brochures sat at the end of the glossy, dark surface and framed certificates of excellence hung on the wall nearby.

A small woman looked up from a computer monitor and smiled. "Good evening."

I lowered my voice, hoping to seem more mature. "We'd like a room please."

"Do you have a reservation?"

"No," I replied.

"That's all right. One bed or two?" she asked, clicking a button on the keyboard.

"Two," I said, my eyes darting at Zack for his reaction.

His face remained blank.

The woman tapped keys again. "I'm sorry, we only have kings left. Will that be a problem?"

"It's fine," he said.

A tingle raced through my body, all the way to my toes. Okay, a king was huge. He could have his side and I'd have mine.

"I'll need to see your ID."

I fished in my purse and handed it over, my palms sweating. I'd never rented a room before.

*Relax. It'll be fine*, Zack said. *We're legal and we can pay. That's all they really care about.*

He was right. A few minutes later, we were all checked

in. We returned to the car, grabbed our bags and found our way to the room. Our very expensive room. I cringed to think how my parents would react when they saw the bill. No matter their reaction, it would be worth it.

The suite had ample space for a bedroom with a king sized bed and a sitting room with a chaise lounge. Both spaces had a giant flat screen TV. The bathroom was the size of my bedroom at home, marble everywhere. I eyed the jet tub, noting the little bottle of bubble bath waiting for me on the edge.

By the time I'd finished poking around, Zack was already comfortable and watching sports. I flicked a thumb to the glorious place of refuge I'd just left. "I'm going to take a bath."

"While you're doing that, I'll go for a quick run. I wouldn't leave you alone, but —"

"I know you have to morph, Zack." I paused, wondering if an invitation to join him would be coming.

"I'll be quick. If I'm back and asleep before you get out of the bath, you take the bedroom. We don't want it to go to waste." His eyes left me and got stuck to the television screen.

Not only did I not get invited to go with him, but he'd dismissed me for sports. Jerk. Why keep me as his girlfriend if he's going to be a douche bag?

I snatched up my pajamas and toothbrush, then stomped to the bathroom and slammed the door. Forty-five minutes later, I came out and found Zack on the couch. His eyes were closed, shadows and lights from the television alternating over his face. Dejected, I made my way to the room, crawled into bed and settled near the edge. I turned to lie on my side toward the nightstand and reached for my e-reader.

Seeing Zack in the doorway, I flinched. "Did I wake you?"

"I wasn't asleep." He ran his fingers through his already tousled hair. "The scent of the... whatever you're using. It called to me. Smells nice."

"Bubble bath," I said.

"Yeah." He tapped the inside of the doorway with the palm of his hand.

Was he going to just stand there and watch me or was he finally ready to talk about it? "Did you change your mind?"

"About what?" he asked.

If he didn't spit out whatever was on his mind and do it soon, I wouldn't need Charles or Renzo to kill me. Zack was going to drive me to do it myself. "About sleeping out there."

He looked up at the ceiling.

I tucked the covers up to my chest. "Sleep here if you want, but stay on your side."

He strode to the other side of the room out of my line of vision. I returned my attention to the e-reader screen, trying very hard not to be aware of his every move. As I struggled to focus on the words calling to me, I tried not to hear the rustle of fabric that told me he was undressing.

Before I could stop myself, I glanced over my shoulder to see him clad only in boxers. I looked away, making my motions fluid, so I didn't look jumpy.

The mattress dipped as it took his weight. "I'm sorry for being rude," he said quietly, dangerously close to my ear. "It's just that I'm still worked up over that whole thing."

"Yeah, but you won't talk about it."

"I can't just yet." His hand found my hip and warmth spread over my skin.

Making a conscious effort not to melt into him, I covered his hand with mine for a moment before releasing it and returning my attention to my book. As if taking the hand squeeze as encouragement, he scooted closer, burying his face in the back of my neck. No way would I allow it to go any further, considering what he'd done.

But I couldn't make myself push him away either. "Zack?"

"Yeah?" His breath tickled the back of my neck.

"Thanks for coming with me."

His arms tightened around me. "You're welcome."

"Good night," I whispered.

His hand moved a fraction of an inch and every nerve in my body stood at attention. Knowing he was awake only increased the tension in my limbs. I prayed he would hold very still and fall asleep soon. If not, it was going to be a very long night.

# CHAPTER TWENTY-EIGHT

WHEN I OPENED my eyes the next morning, the first thing I saw was Zack's chin. Slowly, I pinpointed each of our body parts. We faced each other on our sides, almost hip to hip. The palm of my hand was flattened against his chest and my knee was wedged between his legs. His arm was carelessly draped over my waist.

So far, not too bad.

Then I realized my other hand was cupping his face. It seemed like such an intimate gesture — practically equivalent to saying *I love you*. Not something I wanted him to know just yet, especially now that we were barely speaking.

I held my breath, fervently hoping I could detach myself without waking him. My heart beat wildly at the thought of Zack waking up and catching us this way. In this vulnerable position, I wouldn't be able to resist if he made a move.

With almost imperceptible motions, I slowly separated my hand from his cheek and tucked it close to myself. I breathed a sigh of relief, then removed my other hand from his chest. Now it was a matter of freeing my knee.

I slipped my hand into the small space near my knee and his legs, then lifted. Holding up his leg so his knees wouldn't slap together, I gingerly reclaimed my own. Free at last, I rolled over and slowly got off the bed.

Creeping into the other room, I turned on the television and listened to the news while I dressed, then darted into the bathroom to wash up.

I loved healing quickly. I never woke in the morning looking scary — no blood shot eyes from lack of sleep and no bags under my eyes. I didn't even want to imagine if I were human and what I could've looked like on the three hours sleep I'd gotten.

"Hey."

I jumped, turning from my reflection in the mirror and nearly jabbing my eye with the mascara brush. From the look of Zack, he didn't suffer from the myriad of human ailments either. He looked scrumptious, his hair disheveled, his boxers sitting a little too low on his hips.

"Good morning," I squeaked.

"It's early. Maybe we should get breakfast downstairs and if it's still too soon to knock on doors, we can go to the hospital."

"That sounds like a plan." He looked so yummy, I wanted to touch that cute little curve of muscle just above his waist, and run my thumbs over his six-pack. And if I could do all that with my mouth, even better.

I blinked, attempting to eject that image from my

head. Not going to happen. I dragged my eyes from all that bare skin and resumed fixing my face.

Since he hadn't moved, I wrapped it up and scurried past him with my head down. "Bathroom's all yours," I mumbled.

When he emerged a few minutes later, he smelled fantastic, the bare skin of his chest glistening with tiny beads of moisture and his wet hair exploding in every direction from towel drying. Since I couldn't bear the temptation of watching him get dressed — and, really, why did he have to do it right in front of me? — I distracted myself by organizing my suitcase.

When Zack was ready, we took the elevator down to the hotel restaurant. The hostess seated us at a booth and I played with my fork while we waited for our server. After a couple minutes, I couldn't take it anymore.

"Zack, I know you don't want to talk about it but... well, you know we can't go on like this indefinitely."

"I realize that, Autumn. But I just can't yet." He squeezed the butter knife, his knuckles turning white. "I can't."

"Whatever," I muttered, wondering what his problem was. Kissing Cameron had been an accident. He'd mauled Gina on purpose. The end.

Still, I loved him and if I could save our relationship, I wanted to try — preferably while we were still out of town, so we could make the most of this trip. If I got the information I needed soon, Zack and I might even be able to see some of Yosemite without worrying about Renzo. If he was following us, he already knew we were together. If he planned on acting on it, wouldn't he have already done so? I mean, if seeing us get a hotel room together last night didn't make him take action, then I could assume we were safe for now.

My cell phone rang and I fished in my purse for it. The screen lit up with "Mom." Oh, no. She rarely called. What if she had arrived home and wondered where I was?

"Aren't you going to answer that?" Zack asked.

"It's my mom." I stared at the phone like it was an F on a report card, then turned it so he could see the screen. As if he wouldn't believe me. Duh. "I can't tell her I'm out of town. What if I lie and she asks more questions and I slip up? It's too easy to get caught."

The ringing stopped.

Panic crept into my voice. "What should I tell her? I have to call her back or she'll worry. But if she's home and I say I'm at a friend's house, she'll wonder why I don't come home right away.

"Relax. We just need to think of a place you could be all day." He tapped the table with his fingertips. "Like Magic Mountain or Disneyland."

"That's perfect!" I pressed the send button and waited while it rang.

"Hi, sweetheart," she answered.

"Hey, mom. What's up?"

"I'm home. Thought we could spend some time together. Where are you?"

I took a deep breath, reminding myself to be calm. Knowing my mom, she wouldn't stick around long anyway and I wouldn't get caught. No need to panic. Unless she picked this trip to veer from her routine and stay the night, then it'd be the rottenest luck ever. "Magic Mountain. With some friends." Duh. It's not as if I'd go alone.

"Oh, that's nice. You're out early though. What time do they open?"

What time *did* they open? I wanted to weep. Or bang my head against the wall. "Oh, we're not actually there right this second. We stopped for breakfast."

Just then, a waitress arrived to take our order. If Mom heard the waitress, it added authenticity to my story.

*Garden omelet, hash browns, English muffins*, I told Zack silently.

"You sure you don't want to come back?" she asked. "I've got until this evening."

No! No! This can't be.

*Tell her you're carpooling and you're the one driving,* Zack told me telepathically, taking a pause to give the server our orders. *And that your friends will be really disappointed, because they've been planning it all week.*

Oh, hallelujah for Zack and his quick thinking. I repeated what he'd said and she seemed mollified, although disappointed. The waitress left and Zack's eyes met mine.

Why was my mom home anyway? Did she get the credit card statement and wonder about the new charges? No, she wouldn't get the bill so soon. But what if the credit card company had called to alert her of suspicious activity? Had she been in the safe and noticed the missing items?

Oh damn, I wished I'd used my own money.

"You think you might be back by eight?" my mom asked. "I'm leaving tonight."

Of course she was. Which was a good thing this time or I'd have to come home. "Everyone will want to stay until it closes. Then maybe stop for food. That's the plan anyway. I'm super bummed to miss you though. Next time, call first and let me know." Like a normal parent would. "Give Dad my love, would you?"

"Sure. He's wrapping up in Montana right now. We'll get settled in New Mexico, then come back here in a few days. We'll see you then, okay? Have fun at Magic Mountain, sweetie."

It was a narrow escape, yet I couldn't help feeling disappointed that she wasn't staying longer. Why wouldn't she spend the night? What was the hurry?

After we hung up, I stared at my phone. "You could hear her talking. You think she bought it?"

"Yes," he said confidently. "From what you've told me about them, if she suspected anything, she would've insisted you come home."

"I have this vision of her figuring out what I liar I am and staying until I get there."

"If that happens, then tell her the truth — that you were out of town with your boyfriend. What's the worst that can happen? She'll worry about you?" Zack laughed once. "Doesn't she excel at that already?"

I nodded, but my mind was reeling over the fact that he'd referred to himself as my boyfriend. Was he still mine? Did I want him to be? I loved him, yes, but... Images of him and Gina popped into my head and I inwardly flinched.

"By the time she catches on, we might have some information on your birth parents. Or your current parents if it was just a matter of a name change. If they get mad at you for lying, you can point out the whoppers they've been telling."

"True," I said.

† † †

We arrived at Oakhurst General Hospital and took the elevator to the maternity ward on the fifth floor. We approached the wide Formica counter and waited for the woman on the other side to finish her phone conversation and notice us.

Moments later, she set the phone down and smiled. "May I help you?"

"I really hope you can. My name is Autumn Rossi. I was born here eighteen years ago. How do I go about getting my medical records?"

"Honey, from that long ago, it'd be in archives."

"What floor?" Zack asked.

"From eighteen years ago?" She looked doubtful.

"Yes, it's really important." My stomach clenched and I fought to keep my voice even. "I found out I might have been adopted and want to confirm it. I couldn't be the only adopted child ever to search for her biological parents, right? They'd have to keep records somewhere."

Her brows flew up. "Adopted, huh? That kind of

information isn't necessarily released to the child."

"I'm eighteen and it's *my* medical record." My brow furrowed and I hoped I wouldn't have to spend the rest of the weekend researching my legal rights.

"Oh, in that case..." She waved a hand as if to wash away what she'd said. "Go down the hallway to the elevator." She grabbed a piece of paper, sketched a map of the building, and marked an X. "Go to the first floor, make a right then go to the end of the hall. You'll have to sign some forms, pay a fee. And they'll want to see your ID to prove who you are, of course."

"That won't be a problem. I have a copy of my birth certificate, too, but the last names are different."

"You'll have to talk to Records about all that. I don't know how it works, but I do know it's going to take a while to find those records," she said.

"We can do the paperwork, then come back at lunch or something," I said.

"Lunch?" She gave me a you-can't-be-serious look. "Oh, honey, it could take days, maybe weeks."

My heart sank. "That long?"

Her tone softened as she handed me the piece of paper with her notes on it. "They'll have to look through thousands of records, hon. It won't be instant like we have nowadays. Don't fret. Maybe Archives will be slow today and they'll get lucky locating it. You won't know until you check."

It was sweet of her to try to give me hope, but my guess was that she had it right with her first assumption. We'd have to find another way.

We filled out the forms anyway, then slogged back to the car. Zack didn't start it up, almost as if he sensed I needed to sit and not talk for a minute. I stared out the window at the blanket of asphalt and the street lamps interspersed between cars, trying to pull my emotions together.

With no information at all on my parents, not even a home address, where would we start?

"It's after nine now so we can start knocking on doors," Zack said.

I nodded. "Let's drive."

The Mustang purred to life. Once out of the lot, he looked both ways, but didn't choose either. To the right, a rural road stretched ahead. To the left, a gas station, a small convenience store and a handful of quaint shops scattered the street — which didn't seem much more promising than the trees to the right.

Zack finally made a decision and hung a left but after only few blocks, the buildings became scarcer. That's all there was of the town? I deflated, slumping in my seat.

The Mustang cruised along at a speed I was sure was well below the limit. He was probably making sure I had a chance to look around. But at what? We passed a stretch of farmland and beyond that, a sprinkling of houses.

Just ahead, I eyed what appeared to be an ancient convenience store. It looked like one of those family-run places where the owner worked it himself and knew everyone in town. "Pull over."

Before the car had totally stopped, I was already opening the door to jump out. I bolted for the barn-like store and leaped the two steps, landing on the wide wood porch. Chimes sounded as I swung open the door. A moment later, they were dinging again and I knew Zack had come in behind me. Even without jingles, I'd know he was close.

The smell of musty wood mingled with fresh brewed coffee. I scanned the crowded and well-stocked but tidy store, wondering what could possibly be lacking considering the shelves were packed with everything you could imagine. Bread, cereal, mayonnaise and mustard.

I strolled toward the cash register, noting the next aisle with miscellaneous first-aid products, toothpaste and various bathroom items. At the opposite end of the store, along the wall, milk and other dairy products sat behind a glass door, safe from the heat.

A thin man with deep lines etched into his weathered face stood behind the counter. "May I help you, miss?"

"I hope so." What should I say? The truth? Why hadn't I thought to bring a picture of my mom and dad? How could he possibly help me if he didn't know who I was talking about? "Um, this might sound a little crazy, but I'm looking for my birth parents. I was born at Oakhurst General, but I was adopted and grew up out of state. Were you, by any chance, living here eighteen years ago?"

He smiled proudly. "I've lived here all my life. I'm Earl."

I squeezed his outstretched hand. "I'm Autumn and my parents are Richard and Patricia Nicholson. Ever heard of them?"

"As her biological parents, they should resemble her a little," Zack said, stepping forward.

The old man eyed me. "Richard and Patricia Nicholson... does ring a bell."

Familiar wasn't good enough. Besides, the name wasn't exactly unusual. It would probably sound familiar to anyone.

"If I needed anything and didn't want to drive very far, wouldn't I have to shop here?" Zack asked.

"You got that right." The man grinned, obviously proud of his store. "Only two choices. Shop here or drive at least a half hour. That or folks nowadays order online and all that."

"So you'd pretty much know everyone who lives within, say, a five mile radius?" Zack asked.

"About that, yes."

"So, if her parents had lived here, you would've known them. No Internet back then." Zack didn't say it like it was a question. He stated it with finality, as if trying to jog the man's memory. "Young couple with a baby would've come in for diapers and that kind of thing."

The man stared off into space and I didn't want to distract him from pulling up the images he needed. "About eighteen years ago," I said softly.

"Patricia and Richard, yeah, I remember. Kept to themselves, which couldn't have been easy since they looked like they belonged in Hollywood or something.

People who stand out like that, you remember them."

My pulse jumped and I slowed my breathing in hopes of appearing calm. "I want to find them. Can you think of anything that would help me?"

The old man shrugged. "They weren't very chatty. They were here nearly a year. Once they came home with the baby, they moved away and I never saw them again."

Zack and I spent a few more minutes with the storekeeper, trying to squeeze more details from him, but we'd exhausted his memory. We thanked him and left.

"Not much to go on," I said, sliding into the passenger seat.

"We've confirmed they lived here. That's a start." He turned down a side road, then slowed the Mustang. "There're some houses up ahead. Let's knock on some doors and see what we can find out."

Just before the first house, he killed the engine and rotated in his seat to face me. "How did you know to stop at that store? You jumped out like your ass was on fire. Did you remember it or something?"

"Nothing like that. As soon as I saw it, I got this image of an old couple who've run the store for fifty years. Thought maybe they'd remember my parents."

"Good call." Zack glanced around. "Thought maybe you saw Renzo and got spooked. Haven't seen any sign of him, though."

"Hard to be sad about that."

I eyed a little blue Cape Cod style house with worn and chipped paint. Old bottles and paper littered the bottom of the chain link fence that barely contained the overgrown and yellowing grass. "What if we knock on the door and they think we're axe murderers or something?"

Zack laughed. It had been a while since I'd heard that sound. It was nice.

"Girls who look like you aren't axe murderers." He waved a hand at me as if that said it all. "Go on. I'll wait here."

My head snapped around, my eyes cut to his. "You're not coming with me?"

"You're the one who brought up the axe murderer scenario." He scratched his chin and shrugged. "They might be more willing to talk if it's just you. I can roll down the window and listen in. If I think of something that might help, I'll talk to you silently."

I nodded and reluctantly exited the Mustang. At the top of the steps, I rapped my knuckles on the door and waited. A moment later, a hairy, middle-aged man in a wife-beater opened it, a remote control in his hand. The stench of stale smoke and rancid alcohol wafted through the doorway. "Yeah?"

"Hi." I forced my lips to curve up. "My name's Autumn. I… I'm looking for my real parents, Richard and Patricia Nicholson. They lived around here about eighteen years ago. Would you by chance remember them?"

His eyes lowered to my chest and paused a moment before sweeping the length of my body and the heebie-jeebies got personal with me. "Name sounds familiar. Would you like to come in? I have more beer inside."

I heard the Mustang door slam and footsteps on concrete.

"Did you say beer?" Zack grinned. *Pervert*, he added silently.

The man gave a short, polite laugh. "Actually, uh, I've only lived here a couple years. I don't think I can help you."

"Well, thanks for your time," Zack called over his shoulder as he dragged me away from the house. Once at my car, he opened the door and practically shoved me inside, then slammed the door. "What a pig."

"I could've taken care of myself, Zack. It's not like a human can do much to hurt me."

"Right, while I sit here and watch? I don't think so. The dude was slime. More than twice your age and inviting you inside for beer? Creepy. I'm coming with you from now on."

"You don't have to."

"Yeah, I do." His voice was firm like his words were final.

"Okay." I averted my face and smiled.

I felt ridiculous driving the short distance from Pervert's house to the next one just a half block away, but we were already in the car and Zack was being way overprotective — which was actually kind of sweet.

Zack parked and we resumed our door-to-door search.

"Hi," I said to the kid who answered at the door. He looked about thirteen years old. "Are your parents home?"

"No."

"Will they be back soon?" I asked.

He shrugged, looking from me to Zack, but not volunteering anything else.

"Okay. Well, maybe we'll come back later," I said.

Without saying a word, the kid shut the door. Rude.

"Let's move on," Zack said.

Deflated, I followed him down the sidewalk to the next house. I knocked, then paused to listen. It sounded like muffled voices and scrambling over a blaring TV, followed by footsteps coming toward us.

The woman who answered looked disheveled as she tugged on the bottom of her shirt. I didn't even want to know what she'd been doing.

"Hi." I smiled. "My name's Autumn and I was hoping you could help me. I'm looking for someone."

Her brows raised, eyes darting to Zack. She looked him up and down appreciatively. "Aren't we all?"

I ignored her leer at my boyfriend, explained my situation and asked if she remembered my parents.

"Oh, honey, I would've been just a little girl back then."

Did she think I was blind? The woman had to close to be fifty years old, more than old enough to be my mom. I forced my eyes still so they wouldn't roll. "Well, thanks for your time."

Heading down the path back to the sidewalk, I plastered on a big, fake smile. "We've made so much progress already."

Zack turned and blocked me from walking, grasping my shoulders. "Each house with nothing is another house we can rule out. We're narrowing the field,

Autumn. We'll just get closer and closer. You found the guy at the store, right?"

"Yes. But if my parents kept to themselves, it's possible that even if we found someone else who remembers them, they may not be able to give us anything more than the guy at the store."

My stomach dipped. It was an awful thought, the possibility of never finding Richard and Patricia Nicholson, never knowing the truth.

# CHAPTER TWENTY-NINE

"I'M STARVING," I said.

The houses were spread over long distances — unlike the tract houses in southern California that were sometimes crammed so tight you practically lived with your neighbor. While we covered a lot of ground, there weren't many people to talk to. And those who were willing to speak with us hadn't coughed up any usable information.

"I'm hungry too. Let's take a break," Zack said.

Unless we wanted to drive back to the hotel, there were only a handful of places to eat — a drive-thru, a deli and a diner. After the long drive yesterday, I didn't want to drive any more than we had to. And I wanted to sit and relax while someone took my order, so we chose the diner — a decision I almost regretted the moment we sat. The seats at the table were covered in orange vinyl and the place smelled of old grease. But my growling stomach became less discerning by the second.

After we ordered, I contemplated any possible way we could speed up the search and end my suffering. Except, as soon as I got what I needed, Zack would want to leave and go back home. Then we'd have to go back to pretending.

"Anxious to get back?" I asked.

"Not really. But we should leave as soon as we can."

"What's the hurry?" He and I were better off here, away from outside influences — like Gina. Once we returned home, Zack might totally close up. "Maybe that wasn't Renzo behind us. I haven't sensed any werewolves since we got here, which means we're safe. Don't you think?"

When he only frowned, I barreled on. "At least here, I don't have to watch Gina making moves on you." I hoped bringing Gina up would trigger memories of Cameron hitting on me. I was pretty sure Cameron had accepted my rejection on Friday, but Zack didn't know that.

Zack stared out the big window of the diner. "With all these trees here, you'd think there'd be werewolves around."

Or maybe he didn't care about me anymore. Maybe he was just trying to rescue the damsel.

I sighed. "Maybe it's more about the people and less about the forests. With bigger cities, it's easier to get lost in a crowd. And doesn't the werewolf king keep tabs on his people? If a lone werewolf were on the loose, chances are, he doesn't want to be found, even by us."

Zack nodded. "But if I didn't want to be found, I might hide out in the woods."

I'd store that in the mental vault in case I ever had to look for Zack. Thinking about his inevitable departure made me wonder if I was being petty over the Gina thing. Maybe he really had been just trying to help me...

"We should consider seeing some sights before we leave. Seriously, when will we get another chance to come back here? Besides, it's tourist season and a weekend. I doubt we'd be alone, even in the woods. If we find the information we need today, we can be tourists tomorrow."

"It's your call." But he didn't seem thrilled.

"Zack, I know you're mad at me and, yes, I'm pretty pissed at you, too. But we don't have all the time in the world, so can you at least *try* to enjoy this trip?"

His jaw ticked and his shoulders tensed. "It's not *you* I'm mad at. Well, maybe a little bit. It's... everything."

"Like?"

His eyes darkened. "Not now, Autumn."

"When then?" I waited for him to answer, then reached across the table and covered his hand with my own. "So you're just going to be cranky? And ruin the entire weekend? Who knows when we'll be alone together again? Could be never."

The realization made my stomach drop.

He lifted his chin, his green eyes melting into mine. "Okay, let's go sightseeing, but only after we've covered more ground."

† † †

The next few houses were a bust, and disappointment smothered me as we parked in front of yet another house. As if weighted down, I slowly climbed out of the passenger side. "Zack, I can't leave here empty-handed. I can't continue in ignorance. I can't."

He rounded the hood, surveying the area.

I stayed put, waiting to see what was up. "What are you looking for?"

"We're getting farther away from the store with the old man," Zack said. "Where we are, right here, you'd have to drive four miles to his store." He flipped his thumb in the opposite direction. "Or you could go the other way and add a few minutes to your trip for a bigger store with a wider selection. We need to canvas the area where residents most likely went to *his* store. This isn't it."

"Makes sense. Let's bail and restart on the other side of his store." I hurried into the Mustang with renewed hope.

Zack pulled over several minutes later. We knocked at the first house and a bleached blonde with very big hair opened the door. I guessed her to be around my mom's age or a little older. She wasn't too bad looking and kept herself in shape. Especially her top half which screamed boob job and Botox.

"What can I do for you, honey?" She curled her full red lips.

I gave her my spiel and waited for her to tell me she'd just moved there or one of the other half dozen things we'd heard since breakfast.

"Richard and Patricia Nicholson..." She nodded thoughtfully.

"Somebody looking for the Nicholsons? From twenty years ago?" a deep voice boomed from behind the well-endowed blonde.

"Yeah." She dropped her arm and let the door swing open.

A man appeared at her side. He wasn't much taller than her, balding and wearing a handlebar mustache. "I remember them. Kind of hard to forget. That Patricia..." He whistled. "She was a knock-out."

The blonde raised one eyebrow. "My exact thoughts about Richard." She pretended to fan herself with her hand.

My heart raced. I'd found someone who actually knew my parents. I'd ignore the part about their hotness... Eew. "So what else do you know about them?" I bit my lip.

The man shrugged. "They didn't say much. Stayed inside most the time."

"Did they have a baby?" Zack asked.

"Yes, though Patricia's pregnancy was difficult," she answered. "Spent most of it on bed rest, so we didn't see much of her and Richard rarely left her side. They stayed a few weeks after the baby was born, then moved away. Kind of odd to just up and move with a newborn and all. Never said good-bye or anything."

"Do you know where they lived?" I asked.

"Sure, they were our neighbors." The man pointed directly behind us. "We had the best view of them."

"I'll say." The woman giggled. "They seemed very

much in love, if you know what I mean."

I bit my lip, not wanting a visual of that. But I kept my mouth shut not wanting to derail them from coughing up any new information.

"Being neighbors, you talked to them now and then, right? Maybe had them over for a barbeque?" Zack asked.

"They were good neighbors. Always waved, always friendly. But they never accepted party invitations."

"Before they moved, did they say where they were going?" Zack asked. "Or mention putting the baby up for adoption or anything like that?"

She looked to the man and they shook their heads. "No. But they talked about New York, I think."

No, no, no. Too far away. How would I ever find them among all those people?

Zack took my hand and gently squeezed. *They could've remembered wrong or maybe your parents were covering their tracks and lied about where they were going. We don't know yet.* He switched back to speaking aloud. "Can you think of anything else that would help us find them?"

The couple looked at each other, shaking their heads. "No," they said in unison. "Sorry. That's all we remember of the Nicholsons."

† † †

Over the next two hours, most of the people we interviewed had no idea who Richard and Patricia were. Anyone who remembered them didn't have any more information than we already had — which was where they lived, what they looked like and that they had a baby. I was hungry again and the sun was already disappearing behind the trees.

"We should do dinner and call it a night," I said, standing in front of a house that looked like so many others we'd stopped at. Or maybe we'd already been there. Had we gone around in a circle? "The houses are beginning to look the same. It's becoming a blur. You sure we weren't already here?"

"Positive."

"So far, the only thing we've learned is that my parents were here and they had a baby. I already knew all that. What an epic failure this trip has been."

Plus, Zack still wouldn't talk to me about us and that drove me nuts.

"Let's hit one more and we'll eat, okay? Then we'll do something fun tonight and start again tomorrow."

"And what if we don't find anything tomorrow?" I asked.

"Shh." He laced his fingers through mine and held my gaze. "Then we'll come back next weekend."

"Really?" My eyes burned in gratitude. Zack may have poor judgment on where to draw the line when trying to get info from skanks, but in the end he was always there for me.

"Really. C'mon."

We walked the stone path to the modern stucco covered house, carefully avoiding the rose bushes that reached out to snag our clothes. I knocked on the door.

It seemed like the door opened by itself until I

lowered my gaze to a tiny, older woman peeking out from between the narrow gap. I told her why I was there and asked her about my parents.

The crack widened and she stepped into the doorway. "Yes, I remember them. Lived just a few houses away. They were nice neighbors. The couple that lived across from them was noisy though, always throwing parties." She shook her head.

I smiled, remembering the mustached man and the busty blonde. I could totally see them loud and partying. "Yeah, we met them earlier today."

"Do you remember anything about Patricia or Richard that might help us find them?" Zack asked.

"Not really. My memory isn't as sharp as it used to be. Sometimes I think of something days later."

"How about I give you my cell phone number? Then you can call me if you remember anything." Reaching into my purse, I fished for a pen. After rummaging a few more seconds, I found a receipt to write on. As I pulled it out, my mom's ID clattered to the ground. I bent over, snatched it up and stuck it between my fingers while I wrote my cell number on the tiny piece of paper.

"That's her," the woman said.

I hadn't realized she'd stepped out of the house. She peered up at my hand — the ID actually. Stuffing the pen back in my purse, my gaze shifted from the plastic card between my fingers to the little old lady. "Excuse me?"

She thrust a finger at my mom's picture. "That's Patricia."

# CHAPTER THIRTY

I STARED AT my mom's picture, my pulse speeding. She *was* Patricia Nicholson, my birth mother — the same mother I had always known. Which meant she was a shape-shifter and I hadn't been given up for adoption. "Are you sure? Here, look again."

"I'm positive," she answered.

"There's no doubt in your mind that this is Patricia Nicholson?" Zack asked.

"None at all. Except when I knew her, she had dark hair. Strange..." She eyed the ID more closely. "That license hasn't expired yet so it's not that old. Funny, she looks *exactly* the same as she did eighteen years ago." She looked up at me as if somehow I'd be able to explain it. "Like she hasn't aged a day."

Chills ran through me, but I shrugged, knowing I couldn't tell this woman the truth — that my mom hadn't aged because she was a shape-shifter. "The picture's deceiving. She still looks young now, but I think —"

"She must have renewed by mail a couple times and they used her old picture," the woman explained, grinning as though proud of herself for figuring it out.

"That must be it." I beamed.

"Her name is different here. She changed it, did she?"

"Apparently." I had to get away before she learned something she shouldn't. "Which is why I'm here. I saw the birth certificate, which had different names so I automatically assumed they were different people."

"Didn't you ask them about it? You could've saved yourself a trip," she said.

"She didn't want to make them feel uncomfortable, like she didn't trust them," Zack said. "They went out of town so we seized the day." *I'm nervous about giving out too much information*, Zack slipped in silently. *We should get going.* He grabbed my hand and turned to go.

"Just one more thing." Jerking Zack to a stop, I pulled out my cell phone — something I should've done hours ago. Between finding that birth certificate and everything else I had going on back home, I must've gotten brain damage or I would've thought of the pictures I'd taken with my phone.

After locating one of my dad, I flashed the screen at the old woman. "Is this Richard Nicholson?"

"That's him." Her eyes narrowed at the picture, then shifted to me suspiciously. "He looks *exactly* the same, too."

Oh, God. My parents were so not human.

"It's a *really* old picture I scanned and e-mailed to myself." I put my phone away, so she couldn't examine it further. "Well, thank you so much for your help."

I could barely concentrate as Zack guided me to the

car. My ageless parents — both total liars. How could they not tell me what they were and that I was a shape-shifter too? It was a huge thing to leave out. I itched to tell them what I thought of their lying to me my whole life.

As soon as we were back in the car, I pressed the button to wake up my phone.

"What are you doing?" Zack asked. "Calling your mom?"

"Of course." My thumb moved to press the send button.

He snatched the phone away from me.

"Hey! Give it back."

"Autumn, how long have they been gone?"

"Three or four weeks, I guess. Why does it matter?"

"Think for a minute. They've been over-protective your whole life, then you blackmailed them into taking a vacation without you, now suddenly they're everywhere but here. They hardly even call. Why would they desert you like that when it's so unlike them?"

I froze as reality hit me. "They're probably on the run from werewolves."

"Exactly. Maybe the reason they stay away is because they're having a tough time shaking the guys who are tailing them."

I stared at my phone in Zack's hand, knowing I couldn't use it. "That's why their trips are so quick and probably spur of the moment."

"Because they have to be careful. The last thing they'd want to do is come back and lead anyone to you."

"Great. Thanks, Zack. Now when I should be angry, I'm afraid for them."

"I'm not suggesting you forgive them and I'm not saying you shouldn't be mad. I'd be pissed as hell. But it might be a good idea if you didn't unleash your fury just yet and add to their problems. We don't want to throw them off so they do something careless and put themselves in danger." He handed me my phone. "Also, keep in mind that once they know you've hit shape-shifter maturity, they'll want you to run with them."

My heart stopped at the thought of moving again — of moving constantly. "I won't go."

Zack's frown disappeared and he looked relieved. Did I dare hope he was glad I'd be around a while?

"They could be very insistent. And, let's face it, you'd be safer with them. They've been running for a while now and they're still alive. I'm thinking they know what they're doing."

Trying to get rid of me now? "For someone so convinced they were human, seems like you've given this a lot of thought."

"I like to be prepared for anything." He started the car. "After we eat, what do you want to do tonight? It'd be cool if it was something we can't do back home."

I laughed, glad that he was loosening up at last. It almost felt like old times. "That's easy since we pretty much can't do *anything* together at home."

He chuckled softly. "We have tonight and part of tomorrow to make up for it."

That sounded promising.

† † †

We drove into the next town where they had a mall and other normal things as well as an endless selection of restaurants of every kind. We picked Mexican food because Zack was in the mood for salsa.

"You think everything out so thoroughly," I said. "Have you thought about why my parents would keep a secret like this?"

He dipped a tortilla chip into the small bowl, filling the curve with salsa. "No. Sorry."

I broke a chip in half. "Maybe my dad is human and they weren't sure I'd be anything but human, just like him."

"According to their neighbor, he's not aging. My money's on shape-shifter."

"You were wrong about them last time," I teased. "It's possible my dad just looks young. And they might have thought I'd be human too."

"It doesn't work that way. I'm full werewolf even though my mom is human. It's the same with shape-shifters. They'd have to know that."

I stared down at the tortilla chip I'd just picked up. "I can't think of any other reason they'd need to keep it a secret."

"Maybe they didn't have a reason. Maybe they just couldn't figure out the right way to say that you were different. Then so much time passed and they decided to wait until you began maturing."

"That could be why they always hovered over

me — they were watching for signs." I moved the chips and salsa out of the way when I saw the food arriving. "But that's no excuse. They shouldn't have kept it from me for so long."

After spending the rest of dinner discussing our evening plans, we finally decided on a movie. We liked the idea of not having to drive far since we'd already done our share to get to Yosemite — with more ahead tomorrow.

Zack held my hand in the theater and it sent tingles up my arm. But that was as far as he went. God, we hadn't kissed since Thursday morning and I had the strong urge to throw myself at him. Then I remembered what had happened with Gina. I *was* still angry for what he'd done, wasn't I?

Back in our room, I grabbed my e-reader and wiggled around in bed until I was comfortable. Would he sleep next to me or in the other room? I didn't have to wonder for long.

"Is that a good book?" He sidled up to me.

"Yeah, it's great." Especially now that I could concentrate on the words. I kept reading, but I wanted to reach for Zack. It had been way too long since I'd felt his warm lips on mine. But I had no intention of indulging myself until he talked to me.

"Let me see." He snatched the e-reader out of my hands and set it on the nightstand near his side of the bed.

I flipped over and shot him a mock glare.

"No more reading this trip." He moved my hair off

my neck and lowered his lips to my skin. Tingles of heat spread through me and my body vibrated with anticipation.

Zack had that look on his face — the same one he had whenever he forgot what we were risking by being together. I wasn't exactly opposed to getting lost in a make-out session with him. Except a little hand holding at the movies didn't make up for the Gina fiasco and the last few days of him being cold to me.

"Well, I hope your entertainment substitute doesn't include making out because that's not going to happen until we've talked about what happened." Not wanting to sound mean, I softened my voice. "Don't forget, Zack, I have just as much to be angry about as you do, if not more."

He reached over to his nightstand and fetched my e-reader then thrust it at me, his expression blank. "It's probably for the best."

I took the book, my mouth gaping. "So... you still won't talk about it?"

"Nope." He shook his head and crossed his arms over his chest.

"I don't get it. We could've hashed it out already and be kissing right now." I knew that wasn't subtle but I *really* missed that part.

"The subject is off-limits." He shook his head. "I'll get too worked up. Give me a couple more days to get my head together, okay?"

At least he gave me a time frame. But two more days of denying myself? Blah. Maybe he was right about it being for the best, though. It had already seemed like forever since we'd kissed and the longer it went on, the more I craved him. If we got started... in a hotel room... all alone...

Not a good idea.

† † †

Zack had crawled into bed last night just as I'd nodded off. With no hope of working things out just yet, I'd let myself fall asleep. We checked out of the hotel the next morning and drove into Yosemite National Park. It was still early, but apparently the other visitors didn't think so. The place was buzzing.

Even though Zack was still a little broody, I vowed to enjoy him as much as I enjoyed the beautiful, majestic Sequoia trees. I told myself to forget everything going on and just take pleasure in being with him.

"These trees are enormous, unbelievable." I handed him my phone. "Take a picture of me next to this one."

Instead of following orders, he looked for a passerby to take a picture of us both. Brilliant idea. The only pictures I had with both of us were from prom. I wanted as many more as I could before he left.

Hours later, we trudged to our car, ready to head home. I made my way to the Mustang while Zack stopped at the gift shop for water.

I froze. About three cars from where I stood sat a midnight-blue Jaguar.

# CHAPTER THIRTY-ONE

I SCANNED THE area for Renzo or Alura, wondering how many Jaguars that exact color and model one should expect to see in the course of a week. Should I call for Zack and get the hell out before we found out who owned the car? My fingers twitched at my side while I contemplated what to do next. Moments later, Zack handed me a bottle of water.

"You think this is Renzo's?" he asked.

"Seems likely." If only I'd taken note of his license plate number.

*We could wait around and find out or we can move on.* He shrugged. *Or we could get a little closer and see if we smell werewolf.*

*This doesn't worry you?* I asked. Zack seemed barely rattled.

*Of course it does. I don't believe Renzo's our friend, but I also don't think he's a threat right now. Probably just keeping tabs on us.* He brushed a hand along my lower back. *So long as no one knows what you are, we're cool.*

Then we definitely weren't cool. The freaking werewolf was supposed to be on vacation. Why the hell was he following us? The breeze picked up and a few way-ward strands of my hair tickled my nose — along with the scent of werewolf. Zack and I glanced at each other.

"Fancy meeting you two here," I heard Renzo say from somewhere behind me.

Zack turned to face the familiar stranger. "Not really since you followed us," he said in a flat voice.

I swiveled toward Renzo and leaned against Zack, so I wouldn't miss anything spoken silently. I gave myself a quick reminder that as far as Zack knew, Renzo still thought I was human. Therefore, I had to act like I had no idea that werewolves existed.

"Hi. Oh, my gosh, what are the chances of seeing you all the way out here? Is Alura with you?" I asked.

"She's around," Renzo answered, still looking at Zack. *Get rid of Autumn so we can talk.*

Zack bumped my shoulder. "Mind waiting for me in the car for a minute?"

"I'm being banished?" I hated the thought of missing out on whatever was about to happen. Worse, I couldn't even talk to Zack silently or Renzo would sense the energy radiating from us. He'd know that Zack knew about me. I had no choice but to oblige.

"Just a couple minutes." He jerked his head toward the Mustang. "I won't be long."

"Fine." I stomped to my car, got in. Inserting the key, I rolled down all the windows and listened in as I watched them.

"It's been over a week since anyone's seen Charles. Nine days to be exact." Renzo's eyes stared into Zack's.

But the younger werewolf stood his ground, folding his arms over his chest. "Like I said before, I can't give you information that I don't have."

"I think you know more than you're saying," Renzo stated, then continued when Zack only stared at him. "I can't help you if I'm not properly informed."

"I'm not your responsibility," Zack said. "Why would you help me anyway?"

"You're young with your whole future ahead of you." Renzo kept his voice low and level. "I hate to see it cut short when you've only just begun."

"That doesn't change the fact that I have no idea what happened to Charles. I like to think that the king's people would be smart enough to realize I couldn't have killed him. If you're that worried, why haven't you called the authorities?"

Renzo studied Zack a beat. He stood very still and stayed quiet so long, I thought he might attack. Just in case, I kept my hand on the door, ready to jump out and help.

"You should know that there's been trouble in the woods near your house."

"What kind of trouble?" Zack asked.

"Nothing serious. But the forest rangers are finding animal parts like tails and antlers. They know something is killing them, but they can't figure out what. But I think *you* know.

Zack's head tilted. "You think it's Charles."

"Yes, and I think you killed him. Or you *thought* you did. But he's out there healing and when he's strong enough, he's going to come after whoever botched his murder."

Shaking his head, Zack tightened his lips. I wanted him to ask Renzo how to kill a werewolf for real, but the question might draw attention to the fact that we didn't know how to do it and therefore might've been the ones who killed Charles incorrectly the first time.

"I was badly injured years ago. These fine scars all over my skin? They'll go away eventually. The majority of my injuries healed, but it took weeks. I lived in the forest and fed off animals until I was strong enough and looked presentable again. Charles wouldn't care about impressing anyone. He only needs to be stronger than his murderer to exact his revenge. And if he's up to killing bigger animals now, he'll be able to handle a fledgling very soon."

All my breath left my body as terror consumed me. If Zack and I ran now, maybe Charles wouldn't find us. Maybe we could meet up with my parents... yeah, bringing a werewolf to them would go over well. Whatever happened, Zack running without me wasn't an option.

Zack nodded, his face appearing free of any emotion. "And you followed us all the way out here to tell us that? Though I appreciate the heads up, your speech is wasted on me. I didn't kill him. I have to get back to Autumn now."

"And once you're home, you'll pretend you two are broken up? Is this for my benefit or for Charles?" Renzo asked so quietly, I almost missed it.

"Autumn and I are trying to work things out. See

you around." Zack pivoted and walked away, his face a mask of fury.

Renzo stared after him with something akin to daggers in his eyes. *If he'd wanted us dead, he wouldn't have warned Zack about Charles. Better yet, he would've killed us himself. Could it be that he really did want to help, but was frustrated because we refused to cooperate? Or was he trying to trip us up? Was he trying to earn our trust so we'd confess?*

*Did you get all that?* Zack started up the engine and backed out, his hands gripping the steering wheel.

*Yeah.*

Once we were on the road and way out of Renzo's range of hearing, Zack let loose, his voice heated. "Charles is alive. He's out there and once he's healed, he's coming after us."

My stomach fluttered in fear. "But I ate his organs! In what kind of messed up world does someone live after that?"

He stared at me blankly.

Okay, maybe I was freaking. "It's two against one, Zack. We still have a chance," I said with much more confidence than I felt. "We handled him before and we have a better chance while he's not fully healed."

"He's not stupid enough to come after us unless he's strong enough to kill us. I'm not so sure the two of us can fight Charles off again. We took him by surprise before and that's the only reason we're not dead. No doubt though, if he finds either of us alone, we will be. You go nowhere without me, understand?

You're sleeping at my house tonight."

"No problem." I hoped he didn't notice my trembling voice. I mean, seriously, if I acted all panicked, Zack would become even more angry and protective. "We'll tell everyone we're back together and everything's back to normal."

"Our makeup needs to happen *at school*. It needs to be big and public."

"Why?"

"Because we need everyone to witness for themselves, especially Cameron."

"And Gina," I added narrowing my eyes.

"Right. Which means we're not back together yet as far as my family is concerned."

"Then what are we going to tell them? If we're not a couple, why am I spending the night?"

"I'll think of something." A moment later, he growled and slapped the dashboard. "All this time lying about being broken up and it's all been for nothing. We're screwed either way."

I didn't have a comforting reply, so I let it pass without comment. I waited a beat, then asked, "So how do you want us to get back together? Am I just supposed to forgive you for making out with my archenemy?"

"Not totally sure yet. When the time comes, just follow my lead." His eyes darkened. "This sucks on so many levels. Us being together at all times increases your chance of being discovered."

"No one will figure it out." No one who didn't already know anyway. It was pointless to tell Zack now that Renzo had known about our fake breakup since the beginning. And besides, that information might lead to me telling him that Renzo already knew I was a shape-shifter. That would send Zack into a protective frenzy.

As if he wasn't already there.

"But if they do, I can't protect you, Autumn. Not against older, stronger werewolves." He growled again, gripping the steering wheel. "Damn it."

"Maybe we can trust Renzo. If he really wants to help, maybe he can protect us."

He scoffed and stopped for a red light. "We don't know anything about him and he's still a werewolf. He lives under the king's rule. I don't care how nice he seems, you can't trust any of them."

"Okay." Apparently, Zack forgot too easily *he* was a werewolf too, and perfectly trustworthy. There had to be others like him. "Do you think Renzo followed us all the way out here or do you think he tracked us?"

"That had to be his car we saw on the highway." The Mustang began to move again and the freeway on-ramp came into view. "Or he could've gotten it out of Maya or Trevor..."

"You think either of them would give a virtual stranger that kind of information? I think she would've texted me if Renzo started asking questions."

"They wouldn't have told him *willingly.*"

"Oooookay..." I frowned, confused. "You think he threatened them or something?" A chill rushed up my spine.

"Did you read any of that old, thick book with

the gold writing? The one about werewolves?" Zack slowed, then turned onto the freeway and leaned his head against the seat.

"I just finished the SWAAST one." Shape-shifter Werewolf Alliance Against Slavery and Tyranny had been enlightening, giving theories about the werewolf king and the legend of Hannah and Eli. But it talked more about shape-shifters than werewolves. "Until yesterday, I haven't had much time to read."

Zack signaled to merge into the next lane. "You should definitely read the big werewolf book, but I'll give you a crash course now."

I turned to face him and settled in for the long ride. "I'm all ears."

"So werewolves and shape-shifters are all about changing shape, right? We're dealing with shapes and forms. The theory is that we can do it on humans, too."

"We can make a human morph?" That couldn't be right.

"No, not exactly. Since humans aren't genetically capable of being anything other than human, we can only reach them on a telepathic level. Like we shape an idea and put it in their head. The trick is that they still have their own free will, so we can't force them. But if they think it's their idea, they'll do what we want."

"Seriously?" Maybe I could *encourage* Gina and Natalie into confessing. But then, Zack would've already known that so why had he spent all that time with Gina unless he wanted to?

"Wouldn't work for us, though."

"What?" Disappointment sliced through me like a scalpel. "Why not?"

"Only the old werewolves can do it, when they're powerful enough. Never try it on one of them though. Even if it were possible to plant a thought into a werewolf, they'd sense what you were doing and you'd piss them off. The consequences would be deadly."

† † †

Zack grabbed our stuff from the car and ushered me ahead of him. Inside his house, the living room was empty but I heard distant noises. "Let's unload, then find everyone," he said.

He plopped the duffle bags on his bed and we followed the voices to the backyard. Maya and Trevor sat at the bottom of the steps and Mac stood with Cara at his side, an arm draped over her shoulders.

"Hey." I beamed down at Maya. "What are you guys doing out here?"

Maya smiled and nodded toward Cara.

"The little guys just went to bed so we thought we'd take advantage of the gorgeous evening," Cara said, giving me a welcoming smile.

I looked up at the stars. "Yeah, it's nice out."

Maya reached up to take my hand. "Did you have a good weekend? Find out anything about your parents?"

I gave a careless shrug, knowing what she really wanted was the juicy details. "We had a nice time."

"She's going to stay the night. I'm not comfortable leaving her alone in the house after it's been empty all weekend," Zack said.

"That's fine. We love having Autumn around. I'll have that extra bed set up," Aunt Cara said. "Are you guys hungry?"

"No, we're stuffed," Zack replied. "Mom asleep?"

"Yes, but she had a good day," Cara said. "I think she's out of the woods."

Maya slipped past Cara and dragged me inside with her. "Details," she demanded once she'd closed the door.

I chuckled. "There's nothing to tell. All we did was sleep and he didn't kiss me even once. We're still broken up. I'm sorry."

"That's so lame." Her eyes narrowed. "What's up with you two?"

"Nothing. Until I hear something profound from his lips, like he shouldn't look at other girls or he can't believe how stupid he was for thinking anyone but me could make him happy, I'm not budging."

Maya sighed. "You're doing the right thing. I just wish he'd hurry up with those magic words. You guys so belong together."

The door swung open. Zack and the rest of his family filed in, forcing Maya and me into the hallway.

"I have to go. We have school tomorrow," Maya said.

After she left, I grabbed some of my things from my bag and dashed into the bathroom to shower. As soon as I finished and turned off the water, footsteps sounded outside the door. They traveled down the hallway into Zack's room.

"Zack, what are you doing?" Cara whispered, but I could still hear her.

"I was about to change my clothes, but you're in my room," he answered lightly.

"No, I mean with Autumn." She waited a beat. "You two aren't back together, but you're acting as if you are."

Zack groaned. "It's no big deal. Just didn't want her over there all alone."

"Mm-hmm. You still care for her, don't you?"

Zack hesitated a moment, before answering. "Yes, I do."

"Then stop bringing other girls to the house and work it out," she ordered. "We miss her." The door closed and the sound of footfalls receded.

My eyes misted as I tiptoed into Zack's room.

He closed the dresser drawer and glanced over at me. *You can't sleep here. It's too easy to get caught. All we need is for anyone to see you're not in your bed.*

*We'll tell them we made up*, I said, even though we really hadn't. But after this weekend, I was heading in that direction...

*No. I want to do this right. Go.* He shooed me away.

I sighed and left. We really needed to come out of the closet soon. Then Zack needed to talk to me about our issues. Tomorrow would mark four days without a kiss from him.

And now I had to sleep alone.

Unacceptable.

† † †

Zack avoided me the first half of school on Monday. Probably to remind everyone we were still apart. When lunchtime rolled around, Zack still hadn't made any moves to reconcile. I slogged over to John's table and sat with him, Ashley and Janine.

"He's watching you a lot," John said, his eyes darting toward Zack. "I think he's regretting the breakup."

I took a bite of my grilled cheese sandwich and shrugged, but my stomach dipped in excitement at getting back together — if we ever really talked it out, that is.

"You look better today. Alive, instead of one of the undead." He snickered.

"Friday wasn't my best day ever," I said, tearing off another chunk from my sandwich.

"So, you want him back?" John eyed me as he sipped from his soda can.

"Honestly? Yes and no." I dabbed the napkin at my mouth and pushed my tray away. If Zack was going to fix this, now was the time since lunch was just about over.

"Better decide fast 'cause he's on his way over." John looked up as a shadow fell over me.

Finally. And he'd brought Trevor and Maya with him. Okay...

# CHAPTER THIRTY-TWO

"AUTUMN," ZACK SAID as my eyes met his.

"What are you doing?" Maya asked him. She and Trevor flanked Zack, looking puzzled.

An eerie silence had settled over the room, as if everyone in the cafeteria were dying to see what would happen next.

"Sshh, Maya. Just listen." Zack returned his attention to me. "I was thinking about the things you said before and you're right. I'm sorry for being such an ass. You deserve better than that."

My stomach spun again. I almost grinned, but then decided I shouldn't give in too easily. "Oh, yeah?" I drew my brows together to appear skeptical.

"Checking out other girls wasn't right and I can't believe I was that stupid. I know I have no right to even ask you this, but... if you can forgive me, I promise I'll work hard to try to be the guy you deserve."

Wow. My eyes blurred immediately.

"Well..." I'd somehow lost perspective. I should forgive him now, right? Even though we hadn't even talked? Wait, he was apologizing for what everyone *thought* he'd done, not for making out with Gina. But with the entire cafeteria watching, I had to say something. Rising, I set my drink on the table and spoke from my heart. "I've missed you."

Carefully taking my face in his hands, Zack kissed me in front of everyone. It was slow and deep and my brain began to simmer. I contemplated skipping school and dragging him to my house where we could be alone. But that was out of the question. Instead of twining my arms around his neck and pulling him closer like I really wanted to do, I rested my hands on his hips, looping my thumbs in the waist of his jeans. A moment later, he released me and looked into my eyes.

I was breathless.

Zack kept his hands around my face, thumbs stroking my temple as he turned to John. "Do you mind if I steal her?"

"Please do." John motioned us away, flashing a mischievous smile. "She's been miserable company for days."

Zack tugged on my hand and led me through the rows of packed lunch tables toward the back exit. Just before we reached the doorway to outside, we neared Cameron's table. I glanced at Zack to see his gaze fixed on Cameron. Zack's look said it all — *She's mine.*

I almost told him that his territorial display of testosterone was unnecessary and that Cameron already knew, but then I glanced over at Gina and everything slipped my mind as a gust of hate blew my way.

Stopping outside in a long passageway between two buildings, Zack boxed me in with his arms on either side, his palms flattened against the wall.

"That was nice," I breathed. "Perfect."

"I've got my moments." His eyes smoldered and he edged closer.

"Wait," I said, holding my hands up so they met his chest. "You did an impressive job convincing everyone and that kiss was dreamy, but we still have to talk. You promised."

The warning bell rang and he straightened. "After school, I need to go to work, but we'll talk tonight, okay?"

The talk — finally.

† † †

Knowing my parents were shape-shifters, and most likely in danger, inspired me to work hard on sorting out the cheating situation, so the principal wouldn't call them. Especially, since they'd worry over something I hadn't done in the first place. The entire situation was wrong on so many levels.

Natalie wasn't at last period, the scene of the crime. How was I supposed to trick her into confessing if she never showed up? I hated the idea of going to her house and luring her into a confession while I recorded it. But if I had to, then so be it. Time was running out.

After school, Zack waited for me outside, falling into step with me as I headed to my car. "You're okay with driving me to work?"

I shook my head. "Just drop me off at your house, so you don't have to worry about getting a ride home."

He nodded, looking relieved. "I like that even better."

Of course he would. If he had my car, I couldn't go anywhere and get into trouble. Not that he'd have to worry about that. The thought of Charles hunting me down and catching me alone made my insides quake.

† † †

After dinner at Zack's, he and I attacked the kitchen as usual. As I was finishing up the counters, I froze with the sponge in my hand. "Zack, I only have three outfits and they're all dirty. Even if I do laundry here, I'll still need more clothes. Whether we go to my house or go shopping and buy all new stuff, we're still exposing ourselves to Charles."

The silence stretched. Finally, he wiped his hand on the dish towel and turned to face me. "Right now, your house is the very worst place to be. We're better off buying you all new stuff."

"I don't know." I shook my head, thoughtful. "To me, the idea of walking into a store is just as terrifying. If Charles is old enough and can control someone's thoughts, he could kill us publicly and there would be no one able to testify. He could get us in the parking lot or jump me in the dressing room." I shuddered. "And it may not even be just him anymore. For all we know, he's called in reinforcements."

"You're not helping." A low growl began in Zack's throat. "How about we don't do any of the above?"

"Nothing's going to get better until Charles is really dead." I leaned on the counter, just inches from Zack. "In the meantime, the only way to avoid him is to stay here, not even go to school. How long can I keep that up? We have to go to my house sooner or later. I choose now, while we still have a chance he's still too weak to hurt us."

Zack shook his head. "No way."

I wasn't deterred. "If we go in through the front door where the neighbors might see, we'll be able to sense him before we ever step inside. Once we know it's safe, we lock the doors. Okay, it's not one hundred percent safe, but then no place is safe. Not for us."

I waited a beat. "If Charles is lurking, by the time he breaks down the door, the neighbors will probably call the cops. And it's not like we won't hear him or have some warning when he's busting up the place to get to us. Wouldn't we be out the back door by the time he's inside?"

"I can tell you really want your stuff." Zack pinched the bridge of his nose and sighed. "Fine. We'll check for his scent before we step foot inside. We'll go through the front, like you said. Keep in mind that if he really is alive and he wants us dead, he'll be pissed off enough that he might not care about breaking werewolf law. Or any law."

No matter how big I talked, terror practically immobilized me. And now that I'd worn down Zack's resistance, I was rethinking my strategy. "Maybe I should call my parents for help," I suggested halfheartedly.

"Might not be a bad idea." He eyed me. "Except, if Charles attacked, they'd probably be willing to sacrifice themselves for you. Parents are like that."

"But it'll be four against one. Except if they knew

I was in danger, no way would they let me stay." I shook my head. "We should go to my house tonight, while there's still a chance that Charles might not be strong enough to hurt us."

Zack reached a hand behind my neck and pulled me close, his other hand fixing my hip against his. "Maybe you should fly to New Mexico and be with your parents. They've been running at least eighteen years, right? We know they're good at it. You'd be safer with them."

His words were telling me to go, but his hands were telling me to stay. I knew he was right and I belonged with my parents so long as Charles was around. But sadness washed over me at the thought of leaving Zack. And if I left, who would help and protect him? If I stayed, two were better than one, even if we were both newbies.

He yanked me up against him, his lips at my ear. "Call them. Find out where they are and then go. It's the smart thing to do."

My lungs felt heavy, maybe because Zack was all over me and I wanted him *never* to stop touching me. Or maybe it was the thought of never seeing him again.

I lifted my face to his. "I'm not going to leave you to deal with Charles on your own. I'd rather be *right* than smart." Zack and I had never talked about the future other than the very real knowledge that he would run soon. Alone. We'd never made a commitment or voiced our desire to be together beyond graduation. "I want to be with you. As long as the ride lasts, I'll be on it."

He studied me, scanning every inch of my face. "Is

there anything I can say to talk you out of staying?"

I brought up a hand to touch his cheek. "No."

He turned his lips into my hand, closed his eyes and kissed my palm.

It didn't matter that Zack never put his feelings into words. I knew he cared. I still wanted to talk about what happened with Gina and Cameron, so it would never come back to haunt us. But I wasn't mad anymore. Zack didn't like Gina — it was me he wanted.

I leaned into him and stretched up on my toes, watching as his soft full lips whispered my name.

"All right, you two." Favianne stood in the kitchen doorway, hands on her hips. "As reluctant as I am to interrupt, I need some company."

Zack released me and chuckled. "We have to go to Autumn's for a few minutes and pick up some things, since she's staying a while. You wanted to watch that movie later, right?"

"Yes. Unless you two want to be alone."

"We have all night for that," I said.

"Autumn, this is my *mom* you're talking to." He groaned. "Geez."

My face heated up. "No! I just meant that she goes to bed early, so you and I can hang out later."

She smiled and wagged a finger at Zack. "And now we know what's on *your* mind, *tesoro*."

Trying not to laugh, I steered him out of the kitchen and to the front door. "We'll be back later."

I hoped...

† † †

We ambled down the sidewalk, holding hands in silence, while I tried not to think about what might be waiting for us. I wanted to think about something else. "Tomorrow, I'll figure out a way to make that whole cheating thing go away. It'll be one less thing to worry about."

Except I still had no idea how to prove my innocence. If I was still alive after tonight.

"I can't think about that now." He tugged on my arm and coaxed me to a stop, lowering his voice to a whisper. "Once you open the door, turn on the lights first thing, then go in slowly and open all the curtains. If he's around, he'll be less likely to do much if anyone can see from outside." He released a breath ripe with frustration. "Maybe we should wait until dark."

"And that would help how?" I just wanted to get it over with.

"I don't know." He took my hand again and we continued walking.

At the top of the front steps to my house, we stopped. Two seconds passed as we stared at the door, neither of us in a hurry to go inside.

"I meant to give you something before we left, but my mom distracted me." He wrapped an arm around my shoulder and turned me toward the door. With his free hand, he reached into his waistband and brandished a knife, keeping it low so our bodies blocked anyone from seeing it. "I snagged one for each of us. But Aunt Cara will kill me if she doesn't get these back. They're her best ones. Very sharp."

I stared at the knife, not wanting anything to do with it. "I wouldn't even know how to use it."

"You never know what you're capable of. Survival instinct kicks in and you figure something out." His lip curled up. "Just like last time."

"I morphed into a bear. If I do that again, I can't hold a knife." I inhaled, trying to find Charles's scent.

"I don't pick up a thing. If he was around recently, we'd smell it." His eyes cut to mine. "You ready?"

I nodded, my palms folding over the handle. My adrenaline spiked and my limbs trembled, my instinct screaming at me to run and find the safety of my parents' protective bubble. But I squelched it. I wouldn't leave Zack to battle Charles alone.

He reached for the doorknob and my hand gripped the handle of the knife. The light switch was just inches from the door that we left wide open. Careful to keep my back to the wall so I could see any movement in the house, I flipped the switch and parted the living room curtains.

"I still don't smell anything," I told Zack.

"Me neither."

Setting my cell phone on the dining room table a few feet away, I freed my hands and returned to stand beside Zack. Together, we crept farther into the house. My lungs worked overtime to detect anything unusual.

Zack and I ascended the stairs together, on alert for the merest flicker of movement. Once inside my room, we paused and held perfectly still.

*Do you feel that?* Zack asked.

*I'm not sure.* As I scanned my room, I sensed an energy. But it wasn't obvious like when we'd encountered Renzo or Alura. Faint, like a memory. Maybe Charles had been in my house days ago, before I'd left him for dead, and I just hadn't noticed. *If he was here, we'd know, right?*

*We should smell him.* Zack nodded, his muscles taut as he surveyed the room. *Let's just do what we came here to do and get the hell out.*

I found a suitcase on the top shelf of my closet and worked at breakneck speed to gather everything I could think of that I'd need. Moments later, Zack grabbed the overstuffed suitcase and we raced down the stairs. I flew out the door so fast that I almost forgot to lock it.

When we reached Zack's front porch, luggage rolling behind us, my nerves were raw and my throat ached. As soon as I saw Zack's mom waiting for us on the living room sofa with a ready smile, the tension in my muscles waned.

Favianne muted the TV. "Anything in particular you want to watch?"

After the stress of the last few minutes, I was dying to melt into the couch and think about absolutely nothing. Especially not Charles. "Whatever you want to watch is fine."

"We'll be right back." Zack dragged my suitcase to my new room, which seemed smaller with him in it. The lack of space didn't stop him from shutting the door and closing us inside. He wrapped me in a hug and my body melted against his. *Let's never go to your house again*, he said.

Eventually, I'd have to go back, but not while Charles was on the loose. I nodded against Zack's chest. He'd promised to talk about what was bothering him, but getting into a deep conversation was the last thing I wanted to do at that moment. If he didn't plan to let me out of his sight for a while, there would be other opportunities.

† † †

When we arrived on campus the next morning, I spotted Natalie getting out of Gina's car. Good, they were both there today. I vowed not to let sixth period pass without getting what I wanted. I just needed to figure out how to accomplish that.

Lunchtime rolled around and I sat next to Zack, slumping in my chair. If only I was an ancient werewolf and could plant an urge to confess in their heads. I glanced at Gina and Natalie for the hundredth time that day, trying to figure a way out of my mess.

What if my parents were ancient and that's why I could keep up with Zack? But was being stronger than your average newbie shape-shifter enough? Couldn't hurt to try. If either of them would be susceptible to mind-shifting, it was Natalie. I'd start with her.

As she lifted a wrap sandwich to her mouth, I sent her a silent message. *You have a burning desire to tell the truth. Speak up, Natalie. Tell everyone what you've done.*

She stopped mid-chewing, waited a beat, then resumed. Had she paused as a result of my interference or had that been a coincidence? Wait... if I were going to put a thought in her head, shouldn't it be in first person?

*I can't live with the lies. I must tell everyone the truth, starting with what I did to Autumn.*

Natalie set her sandwich down and stared at her tray as she fidgeted with a napkin.

*I think you're actually getting to her*, Zack said, gazing at me in awe. *Amazing.*

I hadn't realized he was touching me and listening in.

My gaze went back to Natalie. As I mentally closed in on her, the people around me faded to the background. I focused on her, hard, until I could see the flecks of brown in her eyes and I could smell her sweet, floral perfume and the fruity scent of her dark, curly hair.

*The entire student body should know what I did to Autumn*, I pushed into her head. *The whole truth. Right now, here in the lunchroom. The truth must be told.*

Natalie flattened her palms on the table and moved to get up, her gaze flicking to me.

"Where are you going?" Gina asked.

"I'm going to talk to Autumn and tell her the truth." Natalie stepped away and headed toward me.

A warm glow spread through my limbs. It was working! But would she really go through with it?

"What?" Gina shrieked, attracting the attention of most everyone in the lunchroom. She scrambled off her seat and groped for Natalie's hand. "You can't do that!"

Natalie sidestepped Gina and strode away, as if on a mission. Midway, she halted and frowned.

Were the affects fading? *No more lies and scheming. I want to be a good person,* I fed her again. *Gina's a liar. I won't listen to her.* I added for good measure.

Gina caught up to Natalie, snaked around and blocked Natalie's path. As if oblivious to the obstacle, Natalie brushed past her friend and marched forward until she stood in front of me.

"Girl fight! Girl fight!" Greg, Jeff and a few other guys chanted.

"Quiet," Zack growled to himself.

*Tell the truth, so everyone can hear,* I told her. *Do it! Now!*

"I have something I need to say." She clapped her hands above her head until all eyes were upon her. "I don't know if you all heard, but Autumn got caught cheating. Mr. Collins is threatening to call her parents and put it on her permanent record."

What the hell? Was Natalie trying to humiliate me by making it public knowledge? Maybe it was only my imagination that I'd gotten through to her. *Autumn must be vindicated,* I told her.

Glancing over at Gina, I saw her approaching, terror in her eyes. I could hear her erratic heartbeat and could smell the bitter scent of sweat and fear.

I couldn't help myself as I sent Gina thoughts. *I'm tired of all the lies, tired of feeling dirty all the time.*

"We framed Autumn," Gina said.

*Say it again, but louder, so everyone can hear. Mean it,*

I commanded. Activity at the entrance of the room drew my attention. Mr. Collins. Perfect! I wondered how much he'd already heard. It probably didn't matter since Natalie looked like she was on a roll. But just to make sure...

*Keep going. Tell the whole truth. Get it all out,* I ordered both of them.

"We set Autumn up so it looked like she cheated on her Social Science test," Gina repeated, speaking loud enough to reach the four corners of the hushed cafeteria. "It was my idea."

*I can't stop yet,* I told Gina.

"We had it all planned ahead of time," Gina continued. "Autumn was distracted that day which made it even easier to make her look bad. After class, she bolted. Natalie stayed after and asked Mr. Collins for help. He was only too happy to help a student in need, someone who seemed to be taking such an interest in his class."

"We sat down at his desk," Natalie said. "The stack of answer sheets was right there and as soon as he looked away, I searched the pile for Autumn's test, then Peter's. Once I'd stuffed them under my shirt, I told him I had to use the restroom."

"And I was waiting for her there," Gina said. "Inside a stall, we changed all Autumn's answers to match Peter's, then Natalie ran back to the classroom."

"As soon as Mr. Collins looked away long enough, I put the papers back, then told him I had to get going." Natalie turned and walked back to her seat as if in a daze.

"But that's not all," Gina said, still rooted to the floor. "I lied to everyone about something else."

# CHAPTER THIRTY-THREE

"DANIEL DIDN'T WANT me," Gina said. "He wanted Autumn and it made me crazy. At first, I was pissed that she'd gotten herself grounded and couldn't go to his party, because then I'd have to go alone. Or I'd have to get someone to go with me who wasn't as popular. Then I got to thinking and realized the party gave me the perfect opportunity to steal Daniel. Of course, I could've tried with Zack, you know, since we'd already gone out a couple times. But he always seemed to be holding back, like something was on his mind. Or some*one*."

*Go on*, I urged her.

She glanced at Zack. "Zack's way out of my league anyway. I knew my best chance was with Daniel, so I helped him get really drunk at the party and came on to him. We were in his room and his shirt was off and all he talked about was how much he loved Autumn. Eventually, I wore him down. After cheating on her once, getting him to do it again when he was sober was easy."

I closed my mouth, my eyes darting around the

room. There wasn't a person anywhere who didn't look completely stunned and engrossed in her confession, even Natalie.

As if coming out of a trance, Gina shook her head and scanned the room. She covered her mouth and made an odd, strangled noise, then ran away sobbing.

Guilt overwhelmed me for humiliating her so thoroughly.

*Don't feel bad for her, Autumn*, Zack shot into my head. *After all she's done to you, she doesn't deserve it.*

The warning bell rang and the audience came alive, low murmurs escalating into a dull roar. Zack draped an arm around my waist to escort me to class, but I hesitated knowing Maya wouldn't leave it at that. My eyes shot to her.

She rose and sprinted to us, Trevor at her side. "Autumn, that was amazing! It was weird though, like they were hypnotized or something."

"Maybe they were," Trevor said. "Maybe someone slipped them drugs or truth serum or something."

"It doesn't matter," Zack said. "Mr. Collins and several other teachers heard the confession. Even if Gina and Natalia retract everything or blame it on hypnotism, their entire speech enters enough doubt to absolve Autumn."

"This is so great," Maya squealed.

"We'll talk later." I laughed at her enthusiasm. "We'd better get to class or we'll be late."

† † †

When I walked into my last class, Mr. Collins asked me to stay after. A tiny part of me wondered if he was so mean and hard-core that he'd consider their confession not enough proof. At the end, the classroom emptied and I approached his desk.

He steepled his fingers, his eyes solemn. "I'd like to apologize," he said once the room had cleared out.

"You would?" I asked.

"You were right the other day. Everyone is innocent until proven guilty. I shouldn't have assumed, especially with your clean record. I want you to know I'll make sure this is all cleared up and that it never comes up again."

"Thank you, Mr. Collins."

"And I can assure you that Natalie and Gina will be penalized for their conduct."

Ouch. "I don't know... Confessing in front of everyone took a lot of courage. Couldn't have been easy. And now that everyone knows all the gory details, I think they'll be suffering enough."

Mr. Collins' brows shot up. "You don't want them expelled?"

I shrugged. "Not really. They took responsibility at great risk to their reputations. But you should do whatever you think is right. Just don't do anything because you think I need revenge. I'm fine."

He gave a curt nod. "See you tomorrow."

I took off to the restroom to freshen up. As soon as the door closed, it opened again. Gina barged in, glaring at me, her jaw clenched. "*You* did this. How?

Did you drug me? Do you know how humiliating that was?" she shrieked.

"Almost as humiliating as having your boyfriend cheat on you with your best friend? But slightly more humiliating than being accused of cheating?" I asked, rocking back on my heels, arms folded.

"Don't be cute!" She took a menacing step closer.

I didn't want to have to beat her up. I didn't think her psyche could handle any more embarrassment.

"You drugged us, didn't you? Some sort of truth serum."

I shook my head. "Nothing so diabolical."

"Then how?" she demanded.

"I willed it. I commanded you telepathically to tell the truth. Then you did." I smiled, knowing it was the exact truth, but fully aware that she'd never believe it in a million years.

"This isn't funny," she hissed. "God, you're such a bitch. That's why Zack has to take breaks from you and get some action with me."

She stormed out, leaving me alone to freshen up. I tried not to gloat. Really, I did. As I brushed new gloss over my lips, I couldn't stop the grin. I didn't try to hold back as I exited the restroom and strolled down the corridor.

Maya, Trevor, John and Janine were among the crowd outside, their eyes bright with excitement. I spied Zack beyond them.

*You're a celebrity now. Too good for the likes of me.* Zack gave me a crooked smile, looking way too sexy.

*I'll be right over here, patiently waiting for my turn with you.*

I rolled my eyes but wanted to laugh. And gloat. I really wanted to gloat as the congratulations poured in. After a while, my friends were satisfied and gradually dispersed.

"I'll see you later, right? At Bill's?" Maya asked.

"Yeah," I said.

"Text me when you're on your way." She waved and left.

Zack put his arm around me and guided me to my car.

"Do you have to work today?" I asked.

"No. I asked Tim to cut my hours." His mouth thinned. "This way, there's less time that you're alone and vulnerable to Charles."

"I think I can handle extra time with you. But, you know, someday, we're going to have to talk about it."

"Yeah, I know. This Charles situation has me so amped up, I can't deal with one more thing. I promise we'll talk though. I swear. Soon."

"Sure. Speaking of Charles…"

"What?" His brows furrowed.

I stopped in front of the passenger side of the Mustang. "I really want to get my laptop from my house. I wished I'd remembered it yesterday."

"You can use mine. I don't want to go back there unless it's absolutely necessary," he said. "It's riskier each time we go."

"You're right." I sighed and plunged a hand into my purse, looking for my cell phone to text Maya. Where was it? I rifled through the bag again, but my phone wasn't anywhere. I squeezed my eyes shut in frustration as I remembered setting it on the table of my house the night before. We'd been so anxious to get the hell out of there that we'd rushed off without it.

"What's on your mind?" he asked, reaching for the car door handle to open it for me.

"My cell's at my house." I did a whine-moan combo. "What if my parents call and can't reach me? What if they think something happened? They're probably already freaking out. What if they come back and run into Charles?" The pitch of my words had risen to dangerous heights.

Zack grabbed my shoulders. "Calm down. We'll go back to your house. It'll be fine."

"No. We can't. Like you said, it's too risky." Panic crept into my voice. "We could stop and buy another phone, but I keep getting visions of Charles showing up at the store. We could be safer in a public place or he might be pissed enough to kill everyone there. That's unthinkable. But I *need* a phone."

"It's dangerous not to talk to your parents too. You know how they are and we can't have them worried about you. They could slip up and get caught."

I nodded, knowing we had to go back to my house at some point. Even if my parents returned and Charles didn't attack, how would they find me if I was at Zack's and they couldn't reach me?

"Get in. We'll be fast. We'll get your laptop while we're there."

We parked in front of my house and I sat still, a sinking feeling in my stomach. Would today be the day or would we escape unscathed again?

"What did you do with Cara's knives?"

He reached over and opened the glove box, took one out and handed it to me. "Let's get this over with."

I climbed out of the car and slipped the knife up my sleeve, thankful I'd dressed for the overcast day and worn a long-sleeved shirt. Just like the day before, we opened the door in silence and entered, little by little, our eyes darting around and looking for anything suspicious. The sun shone through the open curtain and everything looked exactly like we'd left it — as far as I could tell.

"I don't smell anything," I said.

"That doesn't mean he hasn't been here. This morning, I was going over last night in my head. If Charles came in earlier today and went directly upstairs without touching anything, his scent might be too light down here to detect."

"Right." I tried not to panic, but the only thing I wanted to do was run screaming and call my parents for help. But putting them in more danger wasn't an option. "Zack?" I swallowed the mass of fear crawling up my throat. "If he's here, then he heard us come in."

Zack stood at the bottom of the stairs, looking up. After a moment, he motioned for me to follow then started up the stairs. At the landing, I stopped but he continued on. I didn't smell Charles or sense him, so why were my knees weak and my hands trembling? It had to be my imagination. I mean, there was no trace of Charles anywhere.

By the time I resumed my climb up the stairs, Zack was already several feet ahead of me. He paused at the top which gave me a chance to catch up to him.

"Something isn't right." Zack locked into place, his body alert and ready. He ventured into the hallway, but I stayed near the top of the staircase.

Yeah, something was definitely off. I couldn't smell Charles or detect him at all, not physically anyway. But my heart knew he was close. I just knew it. Something was different... I stared at the wall next to the doorway of my dad's office. What wasn't right?

After I'd ransacked it the other day looking for clues about my parents, I'd left the door open and rushed off to get ready for school. When I'd gone into my room last night, I had looked into my dad's office and noticed everything was exactly as I'd left it. I was absolutely positive the door had been open when we'd left last night. Now it was shut. And if Charles was in that room, maybe we couldn't sense his energy past the wall.

"Zack, get back here!"

I rushed to him, but before he could get out of the way, the wall thundered in an explosion of drywall and dust as a massive human form burst through. Zack crashed to the ground, but sprang to his feet an instant later. By then steel arms had already imprisoned me, a sword pressed against my neck.

"Oh, you can try," Charles told Zack. "But her head will be gone long before you get to me."

Zack froze mid-lunge and scowled.

"Kill me and let him go," I said.

Charles laughed and the cold steel pinched my skin. "Why do that when I can kill you both? I'll cut off your pretty little head and have his too before he gets away."

"So now what?" I asked, feeling foolish for trying to bargain with him. He'd kill us both, no matter what deals we struck. Why? Because he *could*. I craned my neck to risk a glance at him and shuddered. His face wasn't just scarred like Renzo's — he looked like he'd been put through a wood chipper.

"Let her go and I'll come with you willingly. We can leave now, tonight," said the guy who'd made me swear not to bargain my life for his.

"Oh, that's rich!" Charles growled. "As if either of you could make any deals. No, this is the end. I'll cut off your heads for your parents to find. How would they like that, little one?" he whispered into my ear, making the hairs on my neck stand up.

"So that's it, huh? You cut off our heads and that kills us?" Zack asked.

I wondered if Charles noticed Zack inching closer.

"Yes, you completely detach the nerves and any-thing that feeds the brain. Then you separate the parts and make sure it can't repair itself. Don't you wish you'd known that when you thought you killed me?" A low rumble built in his chest. "Stupid fledglings."

I couldn't see Charles's face since my back was against his chest and I'd been watching Zack. But I could smell Charles. He reeked of dead animal and rotting clothes. But his stench was quickly forgotten as I remembered the knife I'd slipped into my sleeve just moments ago.

"Please don't kill me," I whined, just to distract him as I let my arm drop, nudging my wrist against my thigh to loosen the blade. It inched down my arm until the handle connected with my thumb.

"If you return to the king and tell him how you failed, you'll look like a wuss. But if I go with you now, no one ever has to know."

Slowly, my other hand slid across my stomach toward the knife in the sleeve of my other arm.

Charles snorted. "Nice try, but I'd rather be a fugitive than let you two live after what you did to me."

How could I use the knife most effectively so Charles got maximum damage? And could I apply enough force with him behind me? I twisted slowly to meet his gaze, hoping he wouldn't tighten his grip and press the sharp blade harder to my skin. He didn't.

As if Charles knew he had my attention, he leered down at me. "You would've been fun to keep around for a while, sweetheart."

My stomach lurched and I gripped the handle of the knife, turning toward him just a little more. "Your loss."

"Renzo will kill you for hurting us." Zack's face looked pained, helpless, as he shifted his weight to his other leg, which somehow brought him closer. He now stood about three feet away.

"Renzo?" Charles's voice became dangerously low.

"Midnight-blue late-model Jag, dark hair, little fine scars all over his face. Yeah, *that* Renzo." Zack was bluffing. Renzo claimed he wanted to help, but would he actually kill a scout for us? Unlikely, but Charles didn't know that.

"I haven't seen the Jag in days. Of course, I've been living in the forest and eating rats for a while so what would I know?" Charles snickered and the blade eased off my neck a fraction. "Time's up. Say good-bye to your girlfriend, Zack."

With all my strength, I thrust the knife deep into his gut. Charles grunted and dropped the knife, then growled as his hand shot out to close around my throat. Breathing wasn't necessary, and even if he broke my neck, I now knew that wouldn't kill me.

But I couldn't afford to be out of commission in any way at all. Incapacitation would lead to decapitation. I thought about morphing into a small animal and slipping through his fingers, but I'd be so much easier to kill if he caught me. I needed every ounce of ferociousness the shape could provide. I needed to be the biggest, baddest animal around.

My body quaked as I once again morphed into a bear. The increase in my size sent my body exploding outward and Charles's grip around my midsection slipped. He didn't lose much time though. His sword thrust into my side and pain sliced through me.

I staggered back against the wall. My insides felt like they were being ripped apart and I let myself slide down the wall until my furry rump hit the floor. Zack morphed and leapt. Charles sidestepped and lunged for me.

Rolling on my side to avoid Charles, I saw my knife crimson with Charles's blood just inches from me. In one swift movement, I grabbed for it. Damn paws! I roared and flipped over on my back, but Charles was already charging, eyes wild with rage and the long blade aimed at me.

Zack hurled himself into Charles, knocking him down the hallway. They tumbled further away, white drywall dust clinging to them as they struggled for the sword. Weak as I was from loss of blood, I couldn't allow Charles to hurt Zack. If only he and I could continue to keep Charles off each other and stall death. But how long could we keep that up?

I fought through the blood loss and weak limbs to fling myself at Charles, my giant paws slashing at his flesh. He struck out at Zack, flinging him against the far wall, then whipped around, sword in hand.

Screw this.

I shoved forward, opened my jaws as wide as I could and covered his head with my mouth. His arm flailed and the sword cut into me. He couldn't see, but he didn't need to. Fire burned my neck. I increased the pressure, using the full force of my jaws and his skull cracked. As my paws held him down, I tugged. Bone snapped and flesh ripped. Just as I prepared to give his head one final yank to separate it from his shoulders, Charles wielded his sword and more pain shot through my neck. A moment later, his body pitched forward. His head slipped from my mouth, fell with a *thunk* and rolled in the opposite direction.

But he'd already done his damage. Like an old building being detonated, my knees buckled and I crumpled in a heap. The floor-boards thundered when they met my rump and the room spun around me.

I morphed into my human form.

Zack was calling my name, but his voice was faint. I raised a weak hand to touch the fleshy chasm the blade had made at my throat. My fingers slipped on something gooey. So much liquid...

My eyes closed.

Numbness set in and I vaguely wondered how bad it was. Had Charles severed my head? My hand flopped to the floor with a thud. I was cold, so cold, and I was floating. A tremor began in my fingers and spread to my knees until my legs and arms were quivering, too. Then frigid cold settled over me like a dry ice mist.

Somewhere far away, voices raged, but I couldn't follow the words. I drifted off, succumbing to the white light beckoning me. I thought of emerald green eyes and how I'd never look into them again.

# CHAPTER THIRTY-FOUR

I OPENED MY eyes and scanned the dimly lit room. *My* room, *my* house. The mattress creaked as someone sat next to me, but it wasn't Zack. I turned my aching neck to see Renzo.

Renzo? My spine stiffened.

"I won't hurt you," he said in a soothing voice. "Relax."

If he was going to kill me, wouldn't he have already done it? Instead, he was by my bedside. My shaky limbs wilted. "Where is he?"

"Zack? He went to check on his mother."

Zack was alive. I let my lids shut and took a moment to breathe in the relief.

"He'll be disappointed he wasn't here when you woke."

My head felt fuzzy as I faced Renzo and blinked. "What are you doing here?"

"Tending to you, obviously. How are you feeling?"

"But why are you h—?" I coughed and pain sliced through my neck. "I feel like I died," I whispered.

"Almost. You've healed quickly, though, considering the damage. I'm impressed."

A fire worked its way through my throat as I gulped. I needed water desperately. "Thirsty."

"Here." He handed me a cup with a straw.

I sucked up every last drop, the cool water soothing the burn. "Who are you?"

"Renzo. Did you lose your memory like you almost lost your head?" He touched my forehead with his index finger.

"I mean who *are* you? What's your real name?" I studied him. Zack clearly favored his mom with his dark hair, but in my foggy haze, I couldn't help noticing Zack's eyes and brows were eerily similar to the man sitting beside me.

"Renzo." His eyes narrowed.

"Ever gone by the name Lucio Gavino De Luca?" I whispered, wanting to be discreet so Alura wouldn't hear from wherever she was. Plus, Zack could make an appearance any moment.

"Your questions never stop." Renzo made a quick grunt. "Wouldn't Zack know his own dad if he saw him?"

"All the pictures of his father disappeared and Zack was very young when his father died," I said. "You didn't answer my question."

"Rest now. You're weak, hallucinating from the pain meds I gave you."

I groaned and rubbed the skin at my throat, feeling a scar running from one side of my neck to the other, just above my collar bone. Having expended too much energy with that little movement, I left my hand there. "I'm not going to give up."

"So I've seen." He breathed deeply and grated out four words. "My name is Renzo."

That was his name today, but what about when Zack was a boy?

Oh, man, I was really reaching to think Renzo was Zack's dad. I didn't even like Renzo, did I? Of course not. Still, there was something about him... However flawed he might be and whatever demons haunted him, he'd be loyal. Maybe even die for ones he loved.

But was he *our* friend? If not, why was he there? Why hadn't he already killed us? Because I wasn't buying the whole vacation thing anymore. Not after he followed us to Yosemite. He had a secret agenda — keep us safe, then take credit for delivering a new recruit and a slave to the king in one fell swoop? Charles was too dead to tell anyone what really happened. Or was he?

"Charles... where is he?"

The door opened and my heart thumped faster, expecting to see Zack.

"How's our patient?" Alura asked, her voice musical and soothing.

"More water," I said. "Please."

She beamed. "That's a good sign. I'll be right back."

"Charles is dead." Renzo patted my hand comfortingly. "For real this time."

"Are you sure?" I asked.

"Positive. This time, you killed him properly." A corner of his mouth curled up. "Unlike last time."

I nodded, but even that motion hurt. "Why?"

"Why what?"

"Why haven't you turned us in?"

"I've known Charles a couple hundred years. He's a lowlife. You're both young and I don't think it would be fair to cut your lives short when his life was worth so little."

"That's nice of you." I didn't totally believe him, but it was obvious he wasn't going to give up any more information. "So why are you here?"

Alura returned with a cup and straw. I was so grateful, I could have kissed her. She gently propped my head up and I took a sip of glorious, cool water.

"We weren't sure if you'd make it," Alura said. "It was a clean cut except for a small section holding you together. If you'd fallen differently..." She shook her head, her expression grave. "But you're very strong and you healed well."

So I'd been *that* close to death. I shuddered at the thought.

"Autumn!" Zack raced through the doorway, setting a tray of food on my nightstand. Alura got out of the way as Zack shoved past Renzo. He leaned over, his arms wrapping tightly around me, his face against my cheek. "I didn't think you'd wake so soon or I never would've left. I've been so worried about you," he rasped into my ear.

"I'm okay." I brought my arm up to touch him, then let it drop to my chest. That was when I noticed that my arm was covered in white cotton — not what I'd worn that day. "Who dressed me?"

Alura raised a hand. "Me. You needed a bath too. You were a bloody mess. Literally."

"Thank you," I said, wishing she wasn't so likable. Could she and Renzo be trusted? I turned to Renzo who'd stepped aside so Zack could claim his spot on the chair beside me. Zack gently squeezed my hand. I raised my brows, first at Renzo, then Alura. "How did you two end up here?"

"The longer Charles was missing, the more suspicious we became that something was off." Renzo gave Zack and me a scolding look. "We decided to keep tabs on you. When we realized Autumn was a shapeshifter and there was a chance that the two of you overpowered him —"

"Wait." Zack held out his palm to stop Renzo. "You knew about Autumn?"

I prayed that neither of them would let on that I'd been fully aware that they both knew I was a shapeshifter. I'd confess to Zack later, when I had more strength to deal his anger.

"Yes. That's when I suspected that Charles had figured it out too and you both had probably felt threatened and defended yourself. But, being rookies, you didn't know how to kill him."

"So you were stalking Zack and me to protect us?" I asked, shooting him a look full of suspicion.

"Just keeping an eye on you both, in case Charles showed." Renzo glanced at Alura, then continued. "We were here last night and followed you when you left. We think he slipped inside as soon as we were all gone. We figured that might happen, but we assumed you'd be smart enough not to return."

"Apparently not." I sighed.

"Since you live here, that's not a surprise," Alura said in a soothing voice. "Maybe it's for the best that you returned so soon. He would've been even stronger tomorrow."

"You've been keeping an eye on us, but for what purpose?" I tilted my head, trying to figure Renzo out. "To protect us? Epic fail. Because I'd already ripped his head off by the time you arrived."

Renzo leaned back in his chair and eyed me. "Very impressive how you two handled yourselves."

"Thanks." I eyed Renzo, wondering why he never answered my questions. What was he up to? "So what took you so long to get here?"

He shrugged. "We were down the block where you wouldn't sense us. Too far away for us to hear, but when you didn't come back out, we figured something was wrong and went inside."

"You should rest your throat." Zack squeezed my hand, then turned to Renzo. "You said you weren't going to turn us in and Charles is dead. So what's next?"

"You finish school," Renzo said, his tone firm. "And we'll take it from there. Your mom is unwell, correct?"

"Yeah, she's doing better at the moment, but with her condition we never really know from week to week what to expect."

"You'll stay after graduation and spend as much time with her as you need."

"Are you my supervisor now?" Zack asked.

"No. I told you I'm not a scout," Renzo answered. "I'll be around for a while though. I trust you'll let me know if any other werewolves make an appearance."

"Yes," Zack and I said in unison.

"The blood is cleaned up and a contractor will be here tomorrow after school to look at the wall," Renzo said. "You'll want that fixed before your parents come home. It'd be difficult explaining to a human how a werewolf took out a wall."

Since I still didn't trust Renzo completely, I let him continue to believe my parents were human. "He took out the whole thing," I said. "Both sides of the wall at once. I guess he healed pretty quickly to have that kind of strength."

"He probably removed the other side of the wall ahead of time, leaving just enough to appear normal from the hallway," Renzo explained. "Then he only had one side of the wall to go through to get to you."

"Don't worry," Alura said, "we'll make sure it gets fixed quickly so you don't get in trouble."

My parents would understand, but Alura and Renzo didn't need to know they weren't human. "Thank you so much for arranging it."

Alura straightened. "I think it's time for us to give you some privacy. We're glad you're awake and healing. Make sure you have a good meal, then get some rest. You should be in pretty good shape by morning."

"Thanks." I smiled weakly, half hoping they'd stay. I didn't know much about them, but they obviously cared enough to help us. Zack would probably say I was too trusting. Maybe he was right. Maybe not. "You guys should stay here. It's probably more comfortable than your hotel room."

"That's a kind offer." Renzo narrowed his eyes. "But we'll stick to room service."

Alura leaned over and kissed me on the forehead. "Be well. And try to stay out of trouble."

Zack walked them to the door and returned moments later. He crawled in bed with me, slipping an arm under the cover and splaying his hand over my stomach.

"Hungry?" He nodded toward the plate of pasta on the nightstand.

"Starving." In only a matter of minutes, the swelling in my throat had decreased. "I'm feeling better by the second. I could probably even feed myself."

"I'll do it." He leaned over for the plate. "Save your energy for healing."

I opened for a forkful of what looked like cheese tortellini smothered in a wine cream sauce. I chewed and swallowed. "Lord, that's good. Cara made this?"

"Yes."

"God, I love her." I opened for more. Energy surged through me and I scooted up on my pillow.

"Look at you," he said, his mouth curving up. "You're moving much better."

"I can feed myself, not that I'm not enjoying this." I grinned.

"Now that you're eating, you'll heal even faster. You might even be up for school tomorrow. You'll probably still have a scar on your neck though. That might take longer to heal," he said, offering up another forkful. "And it'll be hard to explain."

"Then I'll wear a cute scarf and everyone will assume I'm covering up hickies. Since we just got back together, it's almost expected." I opened for the next bite.

"I want to give you a hicky." Zack's gaze went to the blanket covering my stomach. His index finger touched just above my belly button, then he leaned over and pressed his lips to the same spot on the blanket. "Right here."

Damn it. As good as Cara's cooking was, I'd just lost interest in it. I was far hungrier for Zack than the pasta.

"Sorry. I distracted you." He moved to the end of the bed. "You need to eat. I'm staying over here until you finish."

I wanted to wolf it down so I'd have Zack sooner, but my body needed all the nutrients the food had to offer, so I took my time chewing.

"I hope Maya and Trevor weren't too disappointed that we flaked on them today," I said between forkfuls. "What excuse did you give them?"

"I said you weren't feeling well. Cramps. It was all I could think of that wouldn't make them worry you were coming down with something."

"Good thinking."

When I'd scarfed the last bite, Zack took the bowl and set it on the nightstand. "How are you feeling?"

"Pretty damn good. My throat doesn't hurt anymore and I'm tingling all over. It's like my nerve endings and everything are coming to life." But I had a feeling the tingling might be because of the way he was looking at me.

"Well, you should get some rest." Zack moved off the bed.

"What? I thought you were going to give me a hicky." Wow, did I really just say that?

Zack chuckled softly. "I said I *wanted* to, not that I *would*. You can't spend your energy on me when you need to heal. And I don't want to accidentally hurt you."

A part of me knew he was right. "I'll probably be almost like new in a few minutes."

"It might *seem* that way to you. Renzo said the major stuff heals quickly, but sometimes the smaller things, like tiny blood vessels, take longer so you shouldn't do anything strenuous and risk re-injuring yourself."

"Speaking of Renzo, he knows I'm a shape-shifter now and that we're dating. Since we're both still alive and he didn't report us to the king, he couldn't be all that bad," I said.

"Charles got William and Daniel out of the way for us and he was more dangerous than them. For some reason, Renzo is protecting us and I'm grateful for that. But he still has secrets and until he opens up, I can't trust him completely."

"I suppose you're right." But I wanted Zack to be wrong. "You're staying the night, right?"

He shook his head. "I'm afraid you'll tempt me into doing something I shouldn't, and you'll end up straining yourself."

"I promise to be a perfect angel." I grinned.

Instead of coming to bed, Zack came around to my side and gently lifted my covers. He moved my shirt and lowered his mouth to my exposed stomach, his lips landing just above my belly button.

One Mississippi... two Mississippi... three Mississippi...

"Mmm." I touched the nape of his neck with my fingertips, prickles of heat spreading toward my toes. One thing was certain — Zack was good for my circulation.

He abandoned my stomach and gave me a searing kiss. I wound my fingers through his hair and pulled him closer.

He straightened suddenly. "This couldn't be conducive to healing. I'll be over there." He pointed to a chair. "You go to sleep."

Despite the disappointment weighing in my gut, my eyelids drooped. He tucked the comforter under my chin and an instant later, I succumbed to the will of my lids.

† † †

"Good morning." Zack rested on his side, his free hand removing a wayward tress from my forehead.

"Morning," I returned.

"Stay here and I'll get breakfast ready."

Zack cooking breakfast? I grimaced.

"Relax." He grinned. "We can do cereal."

"I'm fine to cook." I tested my legs by swinging

them off the bed and onto the floor, then rose to my full height. "I feel..."

He rushed to my side, his hands shooting to my hips to steady me. "Are you okay?"

"I feel... exactly like a normal shape-shifter. Good as new."

"Okay, you *feel* that way but it doesn't mean you are. I want you to take it easy today."

I touched his face. "Thank you for worrying about me, but I don't think making an omelet will be too strenuous."

He helped me cook breakfast, even though I didn't need it. I'd never liked my parents' hovering, but from Zack, it was nice.

† † †

Zack parked and walked around the car to my side, but instead of walking me to class, he hesitated. "Autumn."

"Yes?" My fingers automatically reached for my scarf to make sure it lay securely around my neck to conceal my scar.

"It's been stressful, worrying about Charles and Renzo. Between them and dealing with the fake break-up and guys trying to hook up with you, I've been going crazy. But that's over now and the urge to pulverize Cameron has passed." He took a deep breath. "My head is clear again. I'm ready to talk about it."

"Right here? Now?"

"Yeah. We're a little early." He glanced around the

school lot before focusing on me again. "The reason I got so upset was because we were supposed to be broken up. See, in the eyes of everyone else, you were no longer my girlfriend. So that left you open to creeps like Greg and also decent guys like Cameron. A guy who'd be better for you than a werewolf."

"Cameron is *not* better for me. How can you say that?" I cupped his face and waited for him to meet my gaze. "I don't feel the same way about him. It's *you* I want."

"But that's not what I was thinking at the time. The only thing going through my head was that you were on the market and a big free-for-all for every guy looking for action. I'd watch these guys leer like you had a big bull's-eye painted on you. And the whole time, I wanted to tell them you belonged to me. *Me*. Instead, I had to watch them slobber over you. And when you told me Cameron kissed you, I almost lost my mind. Because there wasn't a damn thing I could do about it."

"I'm sorry." I brushed my lips against his, secretly taking pleasure in knowing that he'd been just as miserable as me during our pretend break-up.

"After you told me that he'd kissed you, I kept wondering if you liked it. I obsessed on it."

Uh-oh. Zack wasn't actually asking me to respond, but I could tell he expected me to. I didn't want to tell him that it wasn't awful. But I needed to tell the truth. I didn't want any more lies mucking up my life. I licked my lips, nervous at the myriad of possible reactions Zack might have. "Well, kissing Cameron... could never compare to kissing you."

Zack's scowl softened.

"How was it making out with Gina?" I asked.

He grimaced. "Weird. The whole time, all I could think about was you. I didn't throw her out, because I didn't want to let you down and I'd gone too far to give up. It never occurred to me you'd be upset since you knew it was fake. Autumn, you need to believe me that I didn't want to be with her — for the same reason I stopped seeing her before you and I ever double-dated with Trevor and Maya."

"And what reason was that?"

"I didn't feel right about being with one girl when I was thinking of another," Zack said.

I assumed that *I* was the girl *now*, but who was it before he really knew me? "Thinking of who?"

He gave me a lopsided smile, a dimple appearing on his left cheek. "Since that first day you bumped into me, you're the only girl spending time in my head."

I felt my eyebrows scrunch together. "But you couldn't stand me."

"True. So imagine how frustrating that was for me when you were the only thing on my mind."

I blinked. What a confession.

He frowned. "Should I not have shared that?"

In answer, I flung my arms around his neck, pushing him against the car. He bounced off the fender laughing.

"I wish I'd known all that," I said. "It would have saved me so much angst. And I'm sorry about letting Cameron kiss me. I wasn't thinking. I should've expected it. Yet when it happened I was so completely stunned, I couldn't react properly during or after."

"Which is why from now on, you'll never speak to another guy ever again." A corner of his mouth twitched. He grabbed me by my hips and lifted me to the hood of the car.

"Just like you'll never speak to any other girl ever again." I raised one brow.

"None that count anyway." He grinned, tucked my calves behind his thighs and brought his palms down so they lay against the hood on either side of me. "I have to make sure you can't get away."

"Hmm. This from the guy who can't even say out loud how he feels about me."

"Actions speak louder than words." He dropped a kiss on my shoulder. "Besides, saying that would be like lying."

"What?" I tried to squirm away.

"If I put my feelings for you into words." His lips curved up as he held my hips, which kept my butt firmly planted on the hood. "It's just... it'd be an understatement."

I stopped struggling. "Because you *more* than like me?"

"Maybe." Zack's mouth curved up on one side.

Oh, why wouldn't he just say it? But did it really matter? I knew how he felt. And he knew I knew. Verbalizing it was just a formality.

Finally, we were free to be together, at least for now, and I wanted to enjoy it — out in the open, for all the world to see.

"Shut up and kiss me," I said.

"I can do that." Gripping my hips, he scooted me closer and wedged himself between my thighs. His lips touched mine and heat pooled in my belly. Then he whispered against my lips, "This is where I want to be. Right here. With you."

He closed the distance again and kissed me long and slow, as though I belonged to him.

And I did.

# THE END

If you enjoyed this book, please recommend it to friends, reader's groups and discussion boards or tell others how much you enjoyed it by reviewing it on Amazon, GoodReads or your own site.
Thank you and happy reading!

)

BOOKS IN THE SHAPES OF AUTUMN SERIES:

*Thrown to the Wolves: The Legend of Hannah & Eli* (Shapes of Autumn, prequel)

*My Wolf's Bane* (Shapes of Autumn, book one)

*Wolves at the Door* (Shapes of Autumn, book two)

*Dead Wolf Walking* (Shapes of Autumn, book three)

*The Dark Wolf* (Shapes of Autumn, book four)

*Lord of the Wolves* (Shapes of Autumn, book five)

† † †

For updates on releases, please visit
www.VERONICABLADE.com

# ACKNOWLEDGMENTS

I ALWAYS SAY it takes a village to write a book. When telling a story, I visualize everything so clearly and the story unfolds beautifully in my head. But getting it down on paper? That's another matter entirely. So I depend heavily on feedback from multiple readers, which is pivotal to making my story the best it can be. I'm forever grateful to my virtual team, whether they are trudging through the worst of the mistakes or cheering me on at the end because it's all coming together.

I don't know what I'd do without my very talented writer pals PR Mason, Laura Sheehan and Felice Fox. And of course, there is the awesome Susan Hatler — not putting my work through her before publishing it would be unthinkable. Susan, I love you more than ever! I'm grateful to those who beta read Wolves at the Door, like Megan Durrance, Shelby Ray, Kimmie Easley, April Schiff Pohren, Emily Mansfield McNew — and the list goes on. You know who you are — thank you all so much!!

I'd like to thank my sister-in-law Allie who inspired me to write the Shapes of Autumn series; a warm and fuzzy thank you to Sara E who is ALWAYS there for me; my earlier beta readers Sausha, Jen B, Karie, Hayly, Athena, Lee, and many others whose enthusiasm for my stories keeps me believing in my writing. And a very special hell-yeah to Rose Nomura for her gorgeous cover design!

Last, but not least, big kisses to my amazing husband who tolerates gross acts of negligence on my part when I get sucked into a story and who never stops believing in me. Baby, you're the best husband in all the land!

*Thrown to the Wolves:
The Legend of Hannah & Eli
(prequel)*

*My Wolf's Bane (book one)*

*Wolves at the Door
(book two)*

*Dead Wolf Walking
(book three)*

*The Dark Wolf (book four)*

*Lord of the Wolves (book five)*

Different species. Mortal enemies. It'll never work, but they'll die trying.

# FREE E-BOOK OFFER

For a limited time, *Thrown To The Wolves: The Legend of Hannah & Eli (Shapes of Autumn Prequel)* is available for free from my website.

Find out more at VeronicaBlade.com

# More Titles by Veronica Blade

A newbie witch enlists help from the scrumptious school bad-boy to make her life and death choice between two battling covens.

A Cinderella who spends her nights as a wolf. A prince with a taste for blood.

Sofia lays her hard-won anonymity on the line by saving the most popular boy in school. Worse, she's been exposed to the vampire hunters who attacked him.

The witch queen must make the impossible choice between abandoning the throne and her people, or spending eternity with the man she loves.

# More Titles by Veronica Blade

Should a woman who's unable to forget her first love give "happily ever after" one more try?

When good-girl Maddie switches places with her famous bad-girl twin Jackie, she has some pretty high stilettos to fill.

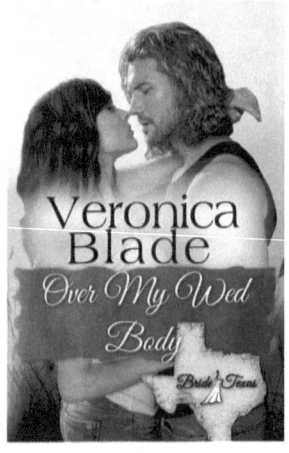

When Hunter realizes he botched the annulment of his marriage to his longtime friend, he must decide if she and their marriage are worth fighting for.

A micro trilogy including Single-Handed, Singled Out (book two) & Single-minded (book three).

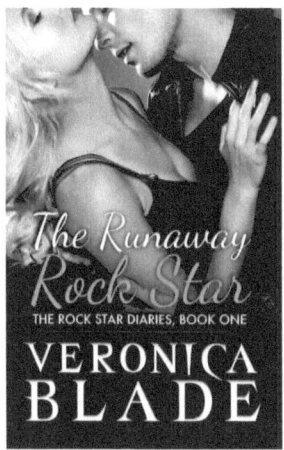

# ABOUT VERONICA BLADE

VERONICA BLADE LIVES near Carson City, Nevada with her husband and furbabies but also spends a lot of time in southern California. She writes sweet romances to live vicariously through her characters. Except her heroes and heroines lead far more interesting lives—and they are always way hotter.

)

*You can visit Veronica Blade on Facebook, check out her website at VeronicaBlade.com or follow her on Twitter @VeronicaBlade. You can even e-mail her at veronica@ veronicablade.com. She loves hearing from readers!*